SOMEWHERE IN CRIME

Dave McVeigh
Jim Bolone

AUTHOR'S NOTE

During the summer of 1979, Mackinac Island became the backdrop for the filming of the movie *Somewhere in Time*, starring Christopher Reeve, Jane Seymour, and Christopher Plummer. This historical event is well-documented. All other elements presented in this story are purely fictional. Our story invents interactions with the movie's cast and crew and descriptions of the crew members themselves, but these portrayals are the fictionalized product of our imagination. All incidents, dialogue, and character names (with the exception of some well-known historical figures), are products of the authors' imagination and are not to be taken as accurate. Where real-life historical figures appear—namely the actors from the film—the situations, interactions, and dialogue are entirely fictional. In all other respects, any resemblance to actual persons, living or dead, is entirely coincidental.

The short version? *Somewhere in Crime* is all made up.

Also, note that the book has some mild profanity (but zero F-bombs). If it were a movie, it would be rated PG-13.

Enjoy!
-Dave and Jim

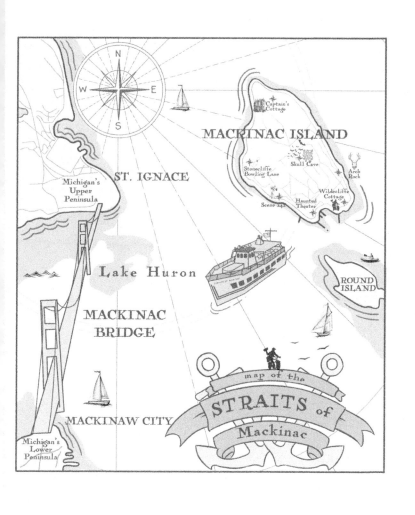

PROLOGUE

2009

Sunlight illuminated Main Street on Mackinac Island. Kitchen exhausts emitted enticing aromas of breakfast, drawing flocks of hungry gulls eager for scraps. The scent of horse manure blended with brewing coffee and freshly-stirred chocolate fudge. Rocked by the wake of a ferry, a buoy clanged in the choppy waters of the Straits of Mackinac, the narrow passage that separates Michigan's Upper and Lower Peninsula.

Jack and Erin McGuinn, and their two children, John, nine, and Sara, six, wandered down Windermere Pointe, a stretch of rocky beach near the aqua shallows of Lake Huron. Across the harbor, a seaplane descended, skipping across the calm surface of the lake before drifting to the edge of Round Island. Shielding his eyes against the bright sun, Jack watched as the plane slowed and then surfed its own wake for a few moments. The pilot cut the engine the plane floated silently.

"See how it barely touched the surface of the water?

That's the exact same concept as stone-skipping," said Jack, calling to John and Sara. He picked up a flat stone and displayed it to them. "Nice and smooth."

Though forty-one, Jack looked younger, with longish, dishwater blonde hair and a sunburned nose. He wore a pair of scuffed hiking boots, worn and softened by years of use. With his hand, he made a skimming motion to demonstrate the concept of stone-skipping, complete with sound effects, a repetitious "pa-chow" somewhere between a rock skipping and a laser blast.

He handed the stone to Sara, guiding her index finger around the edge and showing her how to bring her arm back and release. "Make sure you get some spin. Use the index finger. It's all in the wrist. Show your big brother how all the ladies in da house do it."

Sara smiled, thrilled with her dad's undivided attention. She pulled her jet-black hair from her eyes and squinted flinty-eyed towards the water, then wound up and tossed the rock. It whirled through the air, lighted on the surface, and skipped, not once, but four times. Her eyes widened, and she turned and beamed at her father triumphantly.

"Boom." A spin move and a theatrical bow.

"Wow," said Jack.

"She held it wrong," said John, looking over with a skeptical shake of the head. "Her index finger wasn't over the point of the rock; hardly any spin."

"Hardly any spin?" Jack said. "Come on! Celebrate your sister. Don't be a jerk. Nobody likes jerks. You know why?"

John tried to remain aloof, but his dad had his number. "Because they're jerks?" he asked, fighting a grin.

"I don't care what all the guys on your baseball team say about you behind your back, you're not nearly as dumb as you look. Besides, you own a solid personal record: twelve skips. That's not half-bad. Granted, it's nowhere near my personal best of twenty-three, but I'd never hold you to that standard. It would be a form of child abuse."

Jack shifted his tone, suddenly professorial. "Studies show the offspring of great stone-skippers–such as myself– are often miserable failures in life. They just can't live up to the legacy of their father's fame and talent. I won't let that happen to you, Johnny-boy."

"Yeah, yeah. You won't need to, old man," John shot back. "Someday, I'll crush that record."

Erin's voice called over, her Irish brogue as distinct as the day they met. She'd been unusually quiet, walking a few steps ahead. "It's only stone-skipping, Jack. It's not flossing and brushing, which they both skipped this morning when you insisted we get out before the water got choppy."

The kids turned in unison to Jack, awaiting a response. He chose to mine the comic vein, feigning shock and indignation.

"Only stone-skipping? *Only stone-skipping!* Was Barry Sanders *only* a running back?"

"I have no idea who Barry Sanders is," Erin said.

"He's only one of the best running backs in the history of the Detroit Lions! He's the Yo-Yo Ma of … what is that thing you play again? I always forget." Jack looked off, finger on his chin, faux straining to recall. "The big fiddly thing."

The kids chuckled, enjoying their father's impromptu performance.

"A cello!" yelled Sara. "Mom's the principal 'big-fiddly' player in the Detroit Symphony Orchestra," she stated.

"Right. A *cello*. Anyway. I'd take twenty-three skips over

a lousy flossing session any day. Teeth come and go. But stone-skipping on calm water? That's forever!"

"You know, guys, I think I'm gonna take a nice long bike ride," Erin said, glancing at her parked bike near the road.

Not just a ride, Jack thought. A *nice long* ride. He could almost smell the pungent aroma of a doghouse, all moldy Alpo and rotting dog turds.

Sara tugged on his shirt. "Can I go with Mom?"

Arms on Sara's shoulders, he whispered. "I think she needs a little time to herself." He watched as Erin walked towards her bike, an old green Schwinn one-speed parked near the shore road. He'd restored it twenty years ago, during the chaotic summer of 1989, and maintained it lovingly ever since. Erin kicked the stand with the toe of her tennis shoe and straddled the old bike.

Jack approached. "I'm sorry, baby," he said. "I know I get a little worked up when I'm on the island. I revert to my primordial, immature, irresponsible self." Although intended as a joke, it didn't ease the situation.

She looked towards the road. "I remember that immature, irresponsible self, Jack." She eyed the kids. "And that immature, irresponsible self is about to raise two kids with cavities and no breakfast in their tummies."

She recognized her bratty tone and didn't like the sound of it. "Listen, I'll see you guys a little later," she sighed. "I want to take a ride. Let you take charge for a while. Who knows, I might even swing by Horn's for a Bloody Mary, like the old days." She pedaled off on the squeaky Schwinn, her raven-black hair and sundress blowing in the breeze. She called back over her shoulder. "Maybe meet a handsome sailor with a big yacht and sail away." She coasted for a stroke, then pedaled hard.

"Mommy's just kidding!"

With that, she was gone. The children watched her disappear from view. Sara turned to Jack without hesitation. "Are you guys gonna get a divorce?"

"She's right for once," John added. "This is how it starts. My friend at school said his parents started arguing about stupid little things at first, and then they couldn't stop. Then the mom threw a toaster at the dad's head, with toast still in it, and he had to go to the hospital. Then they got divorced."

He guided them along the beach, a gentle hand on each of their shoulders. Jack always spoke to his kids like they were fully grown adults. He couldn't stand the patronizing tone that some parents took when talking to their kids, as if they were addressing cute but dim-witted poodles.

"We're not arguing. Arguing is when I say something stupid back to her. And I know better. Besides, our room doesn't even have a toaster."

Sara's eyes thinned. "She could throw a bar of soap."

"Come on! You guys are overreacting. Besides, I think I can dodge a bar of soap." He crouched down to Sara's eye level. "Mom's just reminding me, in her unique, Irish way, that I'm having all the fun while she's stuck with boring 'mom duties.' And it's not fair. But she might not fully understand that being the most interesting dad on Mackinac Island is actually pretty hard work." He stood up and struck a few ridiculous muscleman poses. "You think all this energy grows on trees?"

John shook his head, not buying it. "I don't think she's very happy with you, Dad."

Sara, emulating her older brother, joined in. "We just don't want you and Mom to get a divorce."

"*Divorce?* Where do you guys get these crazy ideas?"

"Desperate Housewives," said John, tossing a rock towards the lake.

Jack looked out into the straits as the rock splashed. His eyes fell upon the iconic red and white Round Island lighthouse across the bay, and a rush of memories consumed him like a floodtide. He staggered back a few steps, his boots crunching into the rocks. Jane and Chris. A bowler hat. A pocket watch. The summer of 1979. He steadied himself and looked toward his kids as if in a dream.

His kids.

"Okay, you annoying little worry-warts. Let's go for a walk. I want to share a crazy tale about the summer of 1979, twenty years ago, when I was so freaked out that my parents might split up that I—drum roll please—solved a murder."

From their shocked faces, Jack knew they were instantly hooked.

"... or did I?"

"They let out a synchronized gasp.

"Murder?" breathed John, eyes wide. "Seriously?"

"Yup. Murder. Movie stars. A cannibal. I mean, this is one helluva yarn. It's got everything."

"Dad, you said …" Sara suddenly looked concerned, lowered her voice, and whispered. "You know. H-E— double hockey sticks."

"You're a hundred percent correct. I should never swear, and I promise to toss a ton of cash in the swear jar when we get back to the house. But the truth is …" He turned to her and shook his head helplessly as if he had no choice but to swear. "... this *is* a helluva story. There's just no other way to say it." Jack stopped and dug into his beat-up Jansport backpack, tossing them each a bag of Doritos. "Here. This is a long story. You'll need extra nourishment."

Jack suddenly felt a flash of guilt as he watched his kids tear open the bags like vultures. Erin had a point. He wouldn't be winning any Parent of the Year trophies this morning. Doritos for breakfast? Disgraceful.

Oh well.

He launched into the story.

More or less, it went like this ...

CHAPTER ONE

The Paperboy

I n the summer of 1979, I didn't know that adults—
even seemingly shiny happy people like my parents—
fought. And sometimes, silently and without an
ounce of malice, they tore each other apart like wolves. I
also didn't know that a young, beautiful worker in the
prime of her life could die a violent death on an island
most famous for taffy, fudge, and horse-drawn carriages. I
also didn't know anything about making movies. But I'd
learn a little about that too.

I know what you're thinking, and it's true. There was a
lot going on that summer.

Superman is coming!

It was a constant refrain early in the season, echoing
frantically off the whitewashed Fort Mackinac walls and
jagged limestone formations that lined Manitou trail on the

island's east side. It was a bona fide mania, living rent-free in the brains of anyone who'd ever choked down popcorn in a darkened theater. Hollywood was coming to our tiny island in Northern Michigan to film a movie starring Christopher Reeve, the hottest young star on the planet.

Look up in the sky!

It's a bird!

It's a plane!

Who gives a steaming pile of draft-horse crap? I had more important things on my mind that morning: roughly forty-seven newspapers to fold, and the town needed me far more than some pretty boy in a red cape. This giddy obsession with the Hollywood production was already getting crusty, and they hadn't even arrived yet.

Besides, I was a Batman guy.

It was the first boat of the day. I was on the Arnold Line ferry dock, straddling my orange Schwinn Sting-Ray. The bike was fitted with a wire basket in front and two panniers on each side of the back wheel. I'd nicknamed the rig "Sluggo" in honor of the dishwasher at the Chippewa Hotel who occasionally slid me a pilfered cinnamon roll from the hotel kitchen in exchange for a copy of the *Detroit Free Press.*

Folding newspapers, when done right, was art, and I had it down like Picasso. Classically trained but suffused with modern, unpredictable lines. Like the great artist himself, I had destroyed all the rules. My streamlined origami jets sliced through the air and slid to a perfect stop every morning on the lawns and porches of the island.

Today's load of deliveries was a tasty blend of the *Island Gazette,* the *Wall Street Journal,* and the *Detroit Free Press.* The folding was proceeding nicely. A radio strapped to the bow of a sailboat in the marina was blasting *Heart of Glass* from some New Wave band called Blondie. The dreamy beat echoed across the harbor, harmonizing with the idling diesel of the *Straits of Mackinac II*, one of the many ferries delivering tourists to the island every half hour. The groove energized me, and the newspapers practically folded themselves. I folded left-to-right, one-fifth of the way across, tucking the remainder back into the tube, and then dropped the sleek projectiles into a growing pile in Sluggo's basket.

I was a machine.

"Quite the technique there, boy."

I glanced up to see Cap Riley smiling down, his sturdy arms planted on the upper-deck railing of the ferry. Riley must have been in his late forties, yet ageless, in wire-framed sunglasses, a khaki uniform, and a worn captain's hat.

"Thanks, Cap. My dad taught me the basics, and I modified it. He was the island paperboy too. With my folding method, the papers are more aerodynamic. Speeds everything up. I can finish my route in forty-three minutes, fifty-two seconds."

Riley removed his sunglasses and wiped one of the lenses with a handkerchief. "Well, you know, as a captain, I love a tight schedule. But you're eleven. What's the rush?" What *was* the rush? I decided to let the question go unanswered with a little verbal judo.

"Actually, I'm almost twelve."

"Right. You're eleven."

"Anyway," I gestured to the stack of papers in my basket, changing the subject. "I've never *once* shredded the peacock."

Riley squinted, baffled. "Shredded the peacock?"

"Shredding the peacock is what happens if you don't

roll a paper right and the wind catches it. The paper comes apart, and the sheets fly everywhere. I heard it can be a real mess."

"Fascinating," smiled Riley. "So, what's next on your impressive career journey, boy?"

Riley had always taken a keen interest in my life. My parents, who were friends with him from their frequent ferry rides, would sometimes take me down to the dock to spend the day on the boat with him. Riley would relax and catch up on the latest news or peruse a John D. MacDonald paperback. I'd sit perched on his captain's barstool and take the helm, the Great Lakes' shortest First Mate. We'd stayed close ever since.

I looked towards the end of the dock. "I think I want to be like those guys. A dockporter."

Riley followed my gaze to a gathering of sunburned dockporters in worn khaki shorts and hotel golf shirts hovering near a luggage cart, trading jokes and cackling like pirates. He nodded approvingly. "It's the next logical step in your career progression. Kid with your attention to detail and personal charm? You'll clean up."

Riley checked his watch. "You got it all figured out. A cottage on the East Bluff, an intact family unit, and a rock-solid plan for your future." He turned to the pilot house but paused and looked over his shoulder. "A little advice from an old captain."

"What's that?" I called up.

"Keep it to yourself. You know what they say: if you wanna hear God laugh, tell him your plans."

With that, he headed into the pilot house and shut the metal door behind him. A moment later, the ferry's diesel engine revved, churning lake water.

I stared dumbly for a moment. *Wanna hear God laugh, tell him your plans?* What was *that* supposed to mean?

I returned to folding, already behind schedule, when one of the folds went rogue and began to blossom. Quickly, I creased the wayward paper back into shape, clicked the stopwatch mounted in my basket, and hit the road.

The Haunted Theater on Main Street was one of the island's most incongruous tourist attractions. The worn, red-carpeted steps and stately Greek pillars gave the place a disconnected, almost arrogant appearance, as if it had no interest in taking part in the quaintness that defined downtown Mackinac Island.

At one point, the Haunted Theater had been a working movie house. I saw *Chitty Chitty Bang Bang* there when I was about three. But now, tourists paid four bucks to wander through the winding halls as wax figures of ghouls and monsters lurked in the corners, and a "phantom of the cinema" chased them around, with haunting organ music blaring.

Piercing shrieks of exhilaration and terror would spill out onto Main Street and blend with the clomping of horse hooves, squeaky bikes, and the occasional ferry boat horn, adding to the unique cacophony.

Since the theater had been converted, I'd never been inside. But I was intrigued with the ticket-taker who lingered on the steps, recruiting "fudgies,"—the semi-affectionate term we used to describe day tourists—to enter. A cigarette constantly dangled from his lip, and he sported long, blood-red hair that contrasted with his zombie-pale skin. As always, he wore a black concert T-shirt and jeans. He was leaning against a pillar as I passed and glanced up, catching my eye as I stole a curious sideways look. He exhaled a stream of smoke from his nostrils, watching me intently with his striking, lizard-green eyes. He nodded and slowly grinned, revealing a row of nicotine-stained teeth.

He didn't scare me. At that moment, it felt like we were both privy to some dark secret.

Pedal-pedal-*fling*. Pedal-pedal-*fling*.

That was the process.

My delivery routine was automatic as I effortlessly extracted papers from all three baskets and delivered them with precision perfected over the last three summers. I passed the Spata's residence and tossed their paper with a practiced flick of the wrist. It landed perfectly on the front porch, slid a few feet, and tapped against the screen door like a hungry poodle begging to be let in. *Boom*. Perfect. In the news business, we called this "porching."

I reached back and grabbed a *Wall Street Journal* out of the right rear pannier and tossed it toward the Medical Center. Even on Mackinac Island, those doctors loved their financial news. A quick double-toss and the medical staff was supplied with everything they needed to invest the cash they pulled in daily like so much whitefish.

Another perfect landing.

I approached a row of quaint cottages, each one painted in a different, vibrant hue. I pulled out a notebook from my front basket to double-check the order. Three copies of the *Detroit Free Press,* and one *Gazette* were scribbled on the list. With swift precision, I launched each paper with barely a glance. Pedal-pedal-*fling*.

For some inexplicable reason, my thoughts returned to Cap Riley. I had known the man for years and yet I'd never heard him utter a meaningless word.

Except for today.

"Wanna hear God laugh? Tell him your plans."

What the heck does that even mean?

I shook it off. *Focus, Jack.* Stick the landing on this last paper, and I'd be free as a bird for the rest of the day. Maybe meet up with my pals Smitty and Gordo at the Stonecliffe bowling alley, or skip some stones at the cove across from the Mackinac Hotel, where the water was always smooth as glass.

I approached a yellow cottage on the left side of the road and prepped my toss. Eyeing the porch with the squint of a major league pitcher in late innings, I launched the *Gazette*. The folded paper rocketed into the sky, arced, and began its end-over-end descent. I was invigorated by a sudden rush of energy, knowing that the workday was almost over and it wasn't even 9 am.

But it wasn't energy I was feeling.

It was wind.

A rogue gust burst through a row of lilac trees and quickly dismantled the sloppy folds, sending the once-neat newspaper scattering into the air, page by page like feathers. Helpless, I watched, finally understanding the origin of my own weird phrase.

The peacock had shredded.

I dropped Sluggo on the sidewalk with a metallic clatter and sprinted after the first page, lunging for it mid-flight. Once in my hands, I crumpled it with a quick yank, ending its zany journey.

The other pages would be more of a challenge. A mini typhoon had whirled across the street, its whipping cross-winds sending pages flying in all directions, a dusty, shrieking ghost party of newsprint.

In the midst of the storm, the unmistakable sound of horse hooves echoed down the street, as if on cue. My heart sank. It could only mean one thing: a carriage tour was approaching, and the fluttering newspapers could easily spook the horses into a frenzy. Now I wasn't just the lousy paperboy who shredded the peacock. I was the irresponsible fool about to cause a runaway.

I pranced like a ballet dancer, leaping, lunging, and snatching airborne pages of island news. Percussive hooves and jingling bridles were closing in. I caught a quick glimpse of a news article about a Mackinac Island teen doing charity work in Costa Rica.

Good for her.

An ad for Uncle Grizzly's Old Tyme Photos.

How fun.

An obituary for an old-timer.

RIP. Sucks for him.

I sprang and snared the fluttering lifestyle page out of the branches of a tree, just as a photo essay about the summer's Lilac Pageant soared past. I grabbed that too.

Winded, I checked up and down the street. If nobody witnessed this fiasco, I might get away with it. No harm, no foul. The carriage clopped closer. The final page of the paper appeared as if summoned from the realm of spirits. The wind caught it, and it flew toward the street, directly toward the team of horses. The brown one, drenched in sweat, reared back with a loud bray as the passengers let out a collective shriek. I lunged for the paper, but it sailed just out of reach. The horses bolted down the street, the driver yanking hard on the reins. I watched in disbelief as the rig disappeared from view, the sound of galloping hooves and terrified screams bouncing off quaint cottage walls and windows.

The damage was done. Now it was all about pride. I continued to chase the paper, hurdling over a white picket fence and into the well-tended yard of a row cottage. The last sheet of the *Gazette* was in my sights. It drifted downward and then caught another gust carrying it to the cottage's front porch. I bounded up the stairs two at a time. Just as it was about to blow off the veranda, I dove, both arms outstretched like Pete Rose stealing second base. Another hand suddenly ripped the elusive leaf of newsprint out of my reach.

A small hand.

A small *female* hand.

I hit the porch floor with a thud, the side of my face grinding into the sandpaper-soft outdoor carpeting.

A girl's voice. "Finally. I've been waiting for the latest edition of the island paper for an hour. I guess this will have to do. What's this about an unsolved murder?"

The voice began reading.

"Twenty years ago this summer, Mackinac Island experienced its only murder. The death shocked the community and remains unsolved to this day. The twenty-five-thousand dollar reward for information remains unclaimed.' Whoa! Creepy!"

I gazed up to find a girl standing over me, completely absorbed in the article in her hand. She wore a pink Devo T-shirt and a plaid skirt over tight, black biking shorts. Her hair was kissed by the sun, her nose was slightly sunburned, and her eyes shone with intense curiosity.

I hopped to my feet. My head struck a flowerpot in a low-hanging crocheted hanger, almost sending the plant to the floor. I steadied it with one hand and brushed gardening soil out of my hair with the other.

"Hi," she smiled. "I assume you're the paperboy?"

"Yes."

She held up the ravaged remnant of the paper. "So, where's the rest of it?"

"It sort of … got away."

A smile lit up her face. "I know. I saw you through the

window. It was wildly entertaining. You should take up ballet."

I could feel a hot flush of shame warm my lower neck and begin its slow march upward.

"That's a shame," she continued. "I was looking forward to reading about what goes on here. Boat races and softball games. You know. Fluffy Island stuff. All I got was death. Although watching you chase the paper down like a maniac made it *totally* worth it."

The way she stressed *totally* was intriguing.

She handed me the page. "Can you deliver another later? Like, you know, the whole thing?"

I nodded, took the page, folded it up, and stuffed it in the back pocket of my cargo pants.

"Where are you from?" I asked.

"Los Angeles. We're here for the summer. My dad is the production designer for the movie. He's scouting."

"Cool." I had no idea what 'scouting' was.

She fixed me with a look. "How old are you?"

A beat. *Should I?* "Almost twelve."

"Got it. So you're eleven. I'm thirteen." She grinned. "An older woman."

"I kinda have to go," I said. "But if you ever want to hang out with my friends and me …"

"Give me your hand." She produced a black Sharpie and wrote a phone number on my palm.

I looked down at the fat digits, then back up. "I'm Jack."

"I'm Jill," she said. "Maybe we can go up a hill and, you know, fetch a pail of water." She smiled at me with an expectant grin, eyebrows raised like a comic waiting for a laugh. "You know. Jack and Jill went up the … ah, forget it."

"No, I get it. Cute." *Cute? Did I just say cute?* I turned and tromped down the porch steps.

She called out to me. "By the way, Superman is coming in a few days. It's going to be an epic summer!"

"Yeah. I know all about it," I called back. "But I'm more of a Batman guy."

CHAPTER TWO

Wildcliffe Cottage

I propped Sluggo against the weathered side of Wildcliffe, my family's summer cottage at the far end of the East Bluff. Wildcliffe Cottage was the ultimate victory lap for my dad's father, who we uncreatively called "Gramps." He was a simple man with a keen eye for finding deals. In the post-World War Two era, Mackinac Island was still a diamond in the rough, and he bought the four-bedroom Victorian-era cottage for a song. Since the front porch parties got wild and the cottage perched near a cliff, he named it Wildcliffe.

Again, a simple man.

The bathtubs had feet, and the light switches push buttons rather than switches. The oak floor, sloping gently like the back of a slumbering cat, had borne the weight of nearly a hundred summers. More than a cottage, Wildcliffe was the heart of our universe. Harsh Mackinac winters had left their mark, the paint was faded, and the walls cracked at the seams, but each summer, it flourished as a living scrapbook, pages filled with memories, growing thicker with each passing year. I stomped up the front porch steps when the first whiff hit my nostrils.

Bacon.

It meant only one thing. Big Jack, my dad, was on the rock. No one else cooked it. My big sister Beth wouldn't come near the stuff, claiming to be a vegetarian, although more than once, I'd stumbled upon a pile of beef jerky wrappers in the kitchen garbage can, which led me to believe her militant anti-meat stance had more to do with leftover hippie-dippy 70's fashion than any real commitment to the animal kingdom. And my mom, Ana, nearly burned down our downstate home in Brighton, Michigan with a bacon-induced grease fire a few years earlier. After that, she promised she'd never cook swine again.

Big Jack's eyes lit up when I strolled into the kitchen. "There he is!" he said. "Paperboy, scholar, and fudge connoisseur. You're just in time."

Mom sat at the kitchen table with Beth. She looked up with a smile, her eyes sparkling. "How were the deliveries today, Jack? Any unexpected run-ins with rabid dogs or exotic, dangerous women?" She had a gift for injecting a hint of adventure into the most mundane of motherly questions.

I absently touched my rug-burned left cheek and inhaled the sizzling pork grease. For a moment, I almost told her the truth: *I shredded the peacock, which caused a runaway on Market Street, but then I met a California girl in a Devo T-shirt, all because Cap Riley suggested I should avoid making God laugh. Oh yeah, twenty years ago, there was a murder.*

I chose the boring route. "Nope. Nothing special."

Armed with salad tongs, Big Jack transferred hot, dripping bacon slices onto a paper towel-lined platter, placing it in the center of the small kitchen table where Mom and Beth divvied up the newspaper.

"How was the drive, Dad?" I asked. During the summer, he'd make the four-hour drive from his downstate Oldsmobile dealership on Friday afternoon, racing up I-75 to catch the last ferry to the island.

"Fantastic. Ernie from the parts department lent me his Fuzzbuster, so I flew like a goddamn eagle. Eighty-five the whole way up."

"Language," Mom murmured without looking up.

"Fuzzbuster?" I asked.

"Yup. It beeps whenever it detects a police radar, so you know to ease off the pedal. Amazing technology." Dad was a true gadget freak, an early adopter before the term existed.

"It's also illegal," Beth piped in, not looking up from a crossword puzzle. "The 55-mile-per-hour speed limit reduces gas consumption. There's an energy crisis, or haven't you heard?"

Big Jack shrugged, unfazed, as he poked a row of sizzling meat with a spatula.

"I sell cars, darlin.' I try to ignore terms like 'energy crisis.' And not for nothing, when exactly did my little girl become such a raging tree-hugger?" He shook his head and looked at Mom. "Where did we go wrong with this little girl, Ana?"

Mom ignored him, and crunched down on a slice of bacon. My head pivoted to Big Jack. He sighed and raised a brow.

"Your mother wants to be in the movies. We were just discussing it."

Beth turned a newspaper page and murmured under her breath. "And it's not going well."

Mom shook her head. "I don't want to be *in* the

movies. You make it all sound so sordid. I want to apply for the assistant wardrobe position. They're hiring locals, and I think it would be interesting."

Big Jack sighed. "You don't need those Hollywood phonies." He loved the word *phony* and wove it into his sentences whenever possible. He leaned in to kiss her neck, but she pulled away.

He straightened and continued. "This summer's got big potential. Frank Overton, a big-wig veep at General Motors, is spending a month on the West Bluff. I want to get to know him. Talk about ideas for the dealership. We'll go to parties, and play some tennis. I'm no fan of that schmoozy crap, but with my bride by my side? Biscuit City!" He snapped both fingers and flashed a cheesy smile, awaiting a reaction.

"We don't play tennis," said Mom. Chilly.

"Well, time to learn!" he countered, still fighting to keep it light.

"Sounds like what you need is a trophy wife, Jack." She pulled a section of the paper toward her. She never called him Jack. It was always *honey, dear* or *baby.*

"Well, if you could explain why this is so important, I'd understand. But Frank Overton is a very big—"

"—Dad! *Superman* is coming to Mackinac Island. She doesn't want to play freaking *doubles* with some lame business freak named *Frank.*"

Beth looked away from the crossword puzzle and scanned the front page for something to quench her eighteen-year-old curiosity. Gossip. Disco. Death. But this morning, it was Jimmy Carter's meeting with Russia about something called SALT II. I still didn't understand why the newspapers gave so much coverage to SALT or why Russia was involved. Sugar, I could understand. But SALT? Made no sense.

I waited for Beth's follow-up. "And, like any middle-aged woman, she's interested in sewing Superman's tights." She turned the page with a flutter and looked up at him with a shit-eating grin. "It's not wildly complicated."

Mom burst out in laughter. "What can I say? I *needle* the help I can get." She smacked Beth's shoulder. "Get it? *Need*-le?"

Beth nodded in mock agreement. "*Seams* reasonable. Get it? *Seams*?"

"I get it! They're sewing jokes!" shot back Mom.

Now they were both in hysterics, laid low by a potent mix of morning caffeine and bad puns. I looked at Big Jack. With a plastered-on grin, he was gamely attempting to appear amused, and failing miserably.

Mom, wiping away a tear of laughter, noticed his fake grin and softened. "I'm sorry. We're just having fun."

Beth also wiped her eyes with her shirt sleeve and respectfully gathered her wits with a deep, steadying breath.

Mom continued. "It's no big deal. They need a local seamstress who they don't have to pay very much to … I don't know what."

"… sew buttons on Superman's red underwear?" said Beth, resuming her hysterics. I joined in, nearly spewing my Minute Maid orange juice all over the kitchen table.

"Beth! Now that's obscene!" said Mom, but still with a smile. "Besides, I heard it's a period piece. 1912. A romance. He won't be wearing tights." She slipped into contemplation, and her eyes fixed on a faraway scene. "More like fitted waistcoats. Heavier fabrics. Like flannel."

Beth turned a curious smile toward Mom and let her continue.

"If it's an urban setting, there's probably some interesting ideas with hats. Men's bowlers were very in style then, so we could …" Mom stopped, suddenly aware she was dreaming aloud.

"Fitted waistcoats?" said Beth. "Bowler hats? Looks like someone's been doing their homework." She turned back to the crossword. "Oh, I know this word! Kryptonite!" She chuckled at her dry little joke, but all conversation had stopped, and silence descended on the kitchen like a gray morning fog.

Big Jack sat down at the table. The old chair creaked. "Ana, what do you say—play us a song on the piano like you used to? I'm thinking "To Sir, With Love," since we all know you can play that one blindfolded." He paused. "Literally." And it was true. My mom knew the song so well she could play it blindfolded.

"No. Not today."

She picked up her plate and headed toward the sink to start on the dishes. Big Jack plucked a slice of bacon from the platter, regarded it blankly, and then crunched down on it. He stared at the opposite wall as if a connoisseur of vintage wallpaper patterns. Then he nodded to himself as if amused. In the distance, I heard the clip-clopping of a carriage passing by. The cannon at Fort Mackinac boomed, causing seagulls to shriek and the window pane to quiver.

My thoughts drifted back to my ride past the Haunted Theater early that morning. To the long-haired ticket-taker, grinning at me.

————————

I wasn't sure why I felt the need to connect with my friend and future rival Gordon Whittaker, but I continued pounding on the back door of his family's palatial cottage on the West Bluff until my knuckles hurt. Usually my instinct would be to seek out Smitty. Smitty was ideal for moments like this. A ride around the island with him was like chugging down a cold can of Mountain Dew. Sweet and pure. No bullshit.

But Gordon had something specific to offer: experience. His father, a real estate developer from nearby Traverse City, had recently announced to the family over dinner that he and Gordon's mother were divorcing. Soon after, he was flaunting his much younger, much blonder girlfriend around town, relishing his mid-life crisis like a college student on Spring Break. Gordon, his mom, older sister, and younger brother, humiliated beyond words, carried on grimly as if it was just another Mackinac Island summer.

Was I about to join Gordon in Splitsville, swapping dark stories and cynically milking the side benefits of two screwed-up adults competing in Who's the Better Parent Olympics? I could already see the effects on Gordo. His once happy-go-lucky attitude was hardening.

This is crazy, I thought. *I'm overreacting.* I quit knocking and left, rubbing my reddened knuckles.

I stopped at British Landing, the halfway point of the eight-mile ride around the island, planting myself on a green picnic table at the Cannonball Drive-in. I ordered a fried pickle, and for the next half-hour listened to the unsteady clamor of tourists tooling past on their rental bikes.

If forced to choose, I was with Big Jack on this one. My mom was never like the other mothers I knew. Quiet, graceful ladies who served perfect bacon strips to their families, enjoyed soft radio hits like "Sailing" or "Summer Breeze," and checked up on their children's progress by attending PTA meetings scheduled on a calendar stuck to the refrigerator by a magnet.

Mom's spirit veered toward the gypsy end of the spectrum, at least as gypsy as a Midwest auto dealer's wife was allowed to get in the seventies. We all reveled in it. She was a fantastic mother and wife. But around her fringes lingered a hint of risk, some dangerous secret that might provoke an escape. After all, isn't wandering part of the gypsy way?

A job in the movies was just too close to the fire.

The only thing I knew about Hollywood was that if you went there, you were likely to become a drug addict, an alcoholic, or, even worse, get divorced like the talk show host Johnny Carson, and then you had something called *alimony*, which I suspected was a medical condition similar to a hernia.

I loved movies as much as the next kid, but movie stars were just not like ordinary human beings, and the mysterious Oompa-Loompas with cameras that filmed them frightened me for reasons I couldn't pinpoint. I pulled my windbreaker collar against a cool blast of Lake Huron wind and hiked back to Sluggo for the long ride home.

Best to monitor this rapidly-developing situation first-hand.

Mom and Beth were in the den, giggling through a new show called *Mork and Mindy*, a weird spin-off of *Happy Days* that made no logical sense. *Happy Days* took place in the 50s, and *Mork and Mindy* was set in the present day. This unforgivable gap in logic kept me from becoming a fan.

I peeked in and barely got the 'good' of 'goodnight' out before being shushed by Beth and waved off. She leaned toward the TV set, trying to catch a critical snatch of dialogue from the bemused actor who played Mork.

"Goodnight," I repeated, but neither of them heard me.

I wandered off to track down my dad. He sat on the porch swing looking out at the harbor below, blowing slow smoke from a fat cigar. Occasional gusts off the straits pushed the Wildcliffe sign in short, creaky sways.

"Goodnight, Dad."

I startled him out of a reverie. "Good night, hotshot." He waved his cigar in front of his face. "Just finishing off the last of the Montes."

I'd learned *Monte* was short for *Montecristo*, his favorite cigar. Big Jack had very few vices, but he loved his stogies, often smoking them in the car, even in winter, directing his exhalation through the cracked-open driver's side window. His method was mostly ineffective, and eventually, the backseat of the spanking-new, straight-off-the-showroom-floor Oldsmobile would be enveloped in a putrid, choking cigar fog.

"Stinks," I said, waving away the smoke, yet grateful to be on the Wildcliffe porch rather than suffocating in an Oldsmobile rolling down the Lodge Freeway.

"Keep thinking that. It'll save you a fortune when you're old."

"Yep. Well, anyway ..." I started to leave.

"Kid."

I stopped short. "Yeah?"

"What do you think?"

"About?"

"Mom. The movie thing. Joining the circus. Am I …"
He trailed off.

I finished his sentence. "Overreacting?"

He looked straight ahead, observing a line of lights from a colossal ore freighter passing through the dark, narrow straits. A deep hum reverberated from the ship's engines, half a mile away.

"Yeah. Am I overreacting?"

I wanted to machine-gun him with a violent burst of truth.

No! You're right! This whole movie thing SUCKS. She might get funny ideas. She might change. And how are we supposed to compete with the Man of Steel in a turn-of-the-century waistcoat! You couldn't diagram a bigger threat to the McGuinn family in a LAB! You have to do something!

But for the second time in a day, I lied. "I guess it's okay."

Big Jack took another deep pull off the Monte and blew out the smoke with a sigh. *"You guess it's okay."* He pondered my response, then smiled at some secret adult observation. "I can see you'll be absolutely no help to me whatsoever."

I waited for more.

Nothing.

I shrugged. "What do you want me to say? It's grown-up shit."

"Hey! Where did you pick up that language?"

I took his question at face value. "Beth. Mom. Gramps. *You.*"

"Well, don't let me hear it again. You've got your whole life to be a foul-mouthed little jerk. Enjoy your innocent phase." This time, he blew a smoke ring that hung magically in the air before dissipating.

"Sorry, Dad."

"It's okay. Night, kid."

I turned away and headed to bed, leaving him in his contemplative Cuban haze.

After an hour of fiddling with an old Brownie camera I found hidden in a drawer on the back porch and reading the latest issue of Mad Magazine, the one with the *Animal House* parody, I fell into a light, restless sleep, still in my clothes.

I eased into a bizarre, cinematic dream starring the actor John Belushi dressed in Socrates-style white robes. He was teaching me how to play a musical instrument he called a "sax-o-fart." To my surprise, I was getting pretty good.

Muffled shouting interrupted my jam session. I rubbed the sleep from my eyes, trying to shake off the disorientation and focus on the source of the noise.

I pushed myself up and shuffled down the hall to my parent's bedroom door like a zombie and leaned in, pressing my ear against the heavy oak door. Their voices were calmer now, sounding more like mature adults. *Discussing things.*

Mom spoke softly. "It's Mackinac Island. We have the best neighbors in the universe. Do you think someone will run off with the front porch swing? The kids are self-sufficient, and I'll be on the island. Hell, I'll bring Jack with me if you want."

"To a movie set?" Big Jack asked.

"Why not? It's an adventure."

"For who, exactly?"

"For *me*, Jack. You've got the business to keep you involved and alive. I need something too. Why do you think I keep bringing up the Cairo trip? And if you think I don't notice you've been putting it off for five years, you're wrong."

Cairo trip, I thought. What the hell was the *Cairo trip?* She had bracketed the words as if it was a term, some concept all adults understood, like *saving for retirement* or *life insurance.*

"Here we go again. I'm never here, never home, never buying plane tickets. Does it occur to you that I'm trying to keep the business running?"

"Yes. It occurs to me," Mom shot back. "And it also occurs to me that what you see as a burden, I see as a gift. You *do* something."

"Wait a minute! Do you think being a mother and wife is, what? … *nothing?*"

He voice rose again. "Jesus, Jack! Of course not! But, like you, I can do both. What are you so afraid of?"

"I'm hardly afraid, Ana. It's just that we have opportunities! Frank Overton is a—"

"—very important man, I know. You told me."

Silence followed by a sigh. "You were a dreamer when we met and always have been," Big Jack said. "I guess I shouldn't be surprised that working with movie stars would be more important than helping me with—"

"—wait just a minute! A *dreamer?*" Mom's voice was a venomous hiss. I had to press my ear closer to the door to hear her. "Now it's a *dream* to get a job?"

Silence hung in the air briefly before Big Jack finally spoke up. "Ana, regardless of what I say, you're going to do exactly what you want, the way you have since day one."

Her reply was cold. "Now see, that's where you're wrong, Jack. This is the *first* time."

Footsteps approached the door.

I turned on my socks, half-sprinted down the hallway,

and slipped into my bed. Moments later, their door slammed shut, echoing through the hall like a musket shot.

Beth's bedroom door was ajar, and the light was on. I pushed it open slowly and peered in. She sat on her bed, legs crossed. She almost looked like she'd been expecting me.

"Did you hear all that?" I kept my voice to a high whisper and gestured toward the hall.

"You mean the world's loudest door slam? No. Pray-tell, kind stranger. Whatever do you speak of?"

"C'mon, Beth. Don't be a smartass. Not now. What's happening?"

She made room on her bed and patted it. "Sit, dog." I sat down beside her.

"They're fighting. That's what married people do, apparently. They pretend to have it all together for a while, but eventually, some random wire gets crossed, and the grownup bullshit machine just shorts out."

She quietly sang a verse from Cheap Trick's *Surrender*, playing a little air guitar to bring home the point. *"Mama's alright, Daddy's alright, they just seem a little weird ... surrender, surrender ...."*

She chuckled at some silent inside joke and stowed her air guitar. "Buckle up, hotshot. Things are about to get weird."

Then she did something she'd never done. She put her arm around my shoulder and pulled me close. "Okay," she said, releasing me. "That's all you're getting. Vanish. I can't be seen with you."

I nodded in understanding.

But I didn't leave.

CHAPTER THREE

McGutterbutt

I porched the last *Detroit Free Press* of the day, glancing back to admire the rolled-up paper as it settled to a halt inches from the screen door of Bayview Cottage. I coasted down a slight grade. The day's plan was set. Finish my paper route, connect with Smitty and Gordon, ride up to Stonecliffe, and bowl my ass off. It was the only way to clear the dark dust bunnies clogging my mental filter. My "family issues," as I'd heard the TV psychologists call them.

The McGuinns weren't perfect. But in my mind, we were damn close. Gramps was a genuine World War II hero and now the ceremonial mayor of Mackinac Island, whatever *that* meant. Dad was a successful businessman who wore ties and aftershave and had a shoe-shine machine in his office that vibrated like an electric hummingbird. Mom was beautiful, creative, and, as Big Jack had said, could play "To Sir, With Love" flawlessly on the piano. Blindfolded. And despite Beth's tendency to act like the world's foremost expert on all subjects, she was, in fact, very, very smart.

Families like the McGuinn's didn't have *issues*.

Bowling was the obvious antidote to my anxiety. My overheated brain could cool down if my pals Smitty and Gordon kept the conversation light and stupid. I'd bet the house on my skills, and the universe would magically reset like a rack of pins.

I was a solid bowler back then. Brighton League high average in the 12-and-under division. Decent hook for a kid and a better-than-average backspin.

We were meeting in front of Doud's Mercantile to load up on Now and Laters and Bubble-Yum for the long ride up the hill. Stonecliffe was a turn-of-the-century English Tudor hotel set deep in the woods. Back then, it attracted an elderly clientele looking for a slice of Victorian luxury, complete with four-poster canopy beds and long afternoons sipping gin fizzies and playing euchre on the sprawling back lawn. But what most guests didn't know was that Stonecliffe concealed a marvelous secret hidden deep within its winding halls: a bowling alley.

One single lane.

But one single lane was all we needed.

Energized by the plan, I pedaled past the Murray Hotel on Main Street, where a thin man with soulful eyes and a discolored Detroit Tigers cap plinked out a melody on a beat-up dulcimer, his mallet bouncing off the strings with exquisite skill. He sported a long mid-1970s beard that placed him somewhere on the spectrum between hippie and Mennonite. He was part of the Main Street aural tapestry, his music no more noticeable to me than the clip-clop of horse's hooves or the blasting of a ferry horn. But today, the music drenched me with wave after wave of sadness. I watched him play as I passed, craning my neck until he was obscured by the Main Street traffic.

Was it possible to feel nostalgic if you weren't quite twelve?

I waited outside Douds, propped against a lamppost, relishing a grape Tootsie Pop, determined to reach the soft tootsie roll center, contemplating just how many licks it might take to get there. My gaze swept the corner, vigilant as a sentry.

Smitty approached on his beat-up old Sears-model bike, weaving through the traffic, black Chippewa hair flying in the wind like a pirate flag. My eyes drifted to his face, and my sucker slipped from my fingers. It hit the curb and splintered into a hundred purple crystals. Something was *very* wrong with Smitty.

What looked like a bloody, gruesome flesh wound partially obscured his left cheek. I leaned forward, horrified, and shielded my eyes from the morning sun to get a better look. Oddly, he displayed his signature toothy grin, unfazed by his gash. He proudly raised a half-eaten slice of toast in his right hand in salute. I wasn't seeing blood, but a three-inch swath of strawberry jam smeared across his left cheek. He skidded to a stop, oblivious to his sullied mug.

"What's up, paperboy?" he called over. "Ready to lose a little do-ray-me at Stoner-cliffe?"

I pointed to his cheek, nearly touching the long glob of jam with my finger.

"You've got some jelly on your—"

Gordon interrupted me, riding up on his yellow Schwinn five-speed, looking blonde and preppy in a green Izod shirt and crisp khaki shorts.

"Hey, look. Two turds, just standing on the corner." He hit Smitty with a shocked doubletake. "Hey Pigpen, you know you got half your breakfast smeared across your cheek?"

Without missing a beat, Smitty wiped the jam off his face with the backside of his hand and inspected it curiously.

"Rule one," he said. "Always leave some extra for dessert. Rule two? Avoid bumps in the road if possible. I screwed up rule two." With a single motion, he wiped the jam from the back of his hand onto the toast and stuffed it into his maw.

"*Mmm.* Delicious. Admit it, Gordo. You're jealous right now." He smacked his lips loudly. "You *wish* you had my toast. Want some?" Smitty opened his mouth wide, exposing a mush of jam, toast, and saliva.

My eyes moved off Smitty's disgusting display and landed on an intriguing detail. "Gordo. Your belt is MIA. What's up with that?"

He looked down and shrugged. "Guess I forgot. I was in a rush to get out of the house this morning. Place sucks."

Smitty and I exchanged a glance.

"Forget it, ya dweebs," said Gordon, annoyed. "It's no big deal."

But it *was* a big deal. At the beginning of every summer, the three of us would hit the Big Store, a massive souvenir shop on Main Street, and select new belts for the season. At two bucks a pop, they were paper-thin, a crudely constructed blend of imitation leather and wonky buckles, and spelled out *Mackinac Island* in colorful, fake Indian beads. It wasn't exactly high fashion, but to us, they were as close to gang jackets as we'd ever get. Forgetting to strap it on in the morning was an unforgivable lapse in brotherhood. We'd let it go.

This time.

The ride from Main Street to Stonecliffe was a journey back in time. Downtown traffic dissipated, and the clip-clop of passing carriages faded. We'd push our bikes up Grand Avenue, then take a hard left onto Hoban Road, where the ride leveled off and the leg-burn cooled. Another mile and a half would put us at Stonecliffe's entrance. We rode past summer cottages enveloped by aged pines, wrangled oaks, and towering elms. Eventually, the houses became fewer and farther between, giving way to dense woods crisscrossed by manure-glazed horse trails.

The sky was darkening, and a faint rumble of thunder echoed across the bay behind us. Our banter tapered off, replaced by bike pedals scraping against chain guards and bike tires humming over pavement.

"Looks like Wendigo weather," Smitty said, glancing toward the sky.

Gordon stood on his pedals to pull up his shorts with one free hand. "What does that even mean?"

"*Wendigo,*" Smitty said. "You guys never heard of it?"

"Nope," I responded, huffing as we struggled up an incline.

"I tell ya. You suburban kids. You call yourselves educated, but you don't know nothin' about anything. It's the *Wendigo!*"

"Smitty," I said. "No matter how many times you say the word *Wendigo,* we still don't know what it means."

Smitty slowed a bit. "It's an Indian legend. It's part

undead spirit and part, like, creepy, murderous … freak? I don't know how to describe it. It's like a monster. I guess."

Gordon nodded gamely. "Sorta like Michael Myers from *Halloween?*"

"Sorta." Smitty responded. "Actually, no. Not really. More like the alien from … you know … *Alien.* But instead of killing people in outer space, this thing kills people in the north woods." He looked back at us, perplexed. "Seriously?" he said. "You guys really don't know about the Wendigo?"

"Still don't," I shot back. "So you can stop asking."

"Geez. I'm just sayin'. It's … you know … the *Wendigo.*"

"Let it go, Smitty," I said. But the sound of the word lingered.

Wendigo.

A wind rustled pine branches, and we fell silent again, unconsciously picking up the tempo. As daylight dimmed into a soupy grey, bowling at Stonecliffe was sounding better by the second.

Gordon broke the silence. "But it's cool you guys have your own monsters. I mean, we stole your land. We turned your hunting grounds into golf courses and K-Marts." He turned to me. "What else did we do, Jack?"

I thought for a few seconds. "Okay, here's one: we made you Catholics. Well. Not me. But … someone."

"Yup," replied Gordon. "Good one."

"I mean, you had your own thing going," I continued. "Your own gods. Your own legends. Then some dude in a black dress from France shows up in a canoe holding a cross. Next thing you know, you're spending football Sundays eating sugarless wafers and apologizing for shit you didn't even do."

"Right, said Gordon. "But you held on to your monsters. *Respect*."

"This *Wendigo*," I asked. "What does it look like?"

"Oh man," Smitty said, relishing the spotlight. "It's crazy. It has antlers like a deer, but it's super skinny, like it hasn't eaten in years. But it's also covered in muscle, and its teeth are sharp as razors, and all bloody," he said.

"Damn," I said, glancing toward the dense, darkening forest, noticing the sharp, antler-shaped tree branches for the first time.

"And get this," said Smitty. "It's a cannibal. It eats human hearts while they're still beating. Nona used to tell me stories about it. 'Behave, little boy, or the Wendigo will suck your eyeballs out, eat your heart, and leave what's left of your bloody little corpse in a cave for the rats.'"

We let the gruesome anecdote land in silence. I wiped sweat off my forehead.

Gordon spit. "Wow," he said. "Nona sounds pretty cool."

"She's *very* cool. Her farts smell like a combo of burnt Fritos and dirty feet, but mostly, she's top-notch. She lets me eat Reese's Peanut Butter Cups by the dozens. The last time I was there, I puked on her couch 'cause I ate so many." He grinned. "It was awesome."

"Let's pick up the pace, ladies," I said. "I got money to win. The last one to Stonecliffe buys the first round of Pepsis." We shut up and pedaled hard. The truth is, I was no longer enjoying the ride.

I felt a sinking feeling as soon as the ball hit the gutter on my very first frame. Usually, I dominated these amateurs with ease, but today my body felt like it was made of gelatinous goo. It was as if I'd caught epilepsy on the ride up. To make matters worse, we were betting a buck a game.

It was well into the third frame when I had to accept the cold, hard fact I no longer knew how to bowl. My skills —finely tuned during long winters at Brighton Lanes—had evaporated like horse pee on the pavement on a hot summer day. The lane at Stonecliffe had no pin reset machine, so after each frame, the bowler had to jog down the lane and reset the pins by hand.

But today, resetting pins would not be an issue. Instead of focusing on the ten pins in front of me, I could only see the blank look in Big Jack's eyes as he puffed his Monte and gazed over reflections in the harbor.

Thunk. Ball two dropped into the gutter and rumbled away, stopped dead by the worn pad that lined the back of the century-old lane.

Smitty called over. "Look on the bright side, Jacky. Keep it up, and you'll never have to reset any pins. We'll be home by dinner!" He and Gordon burst out laughing and high-fived each other. *Such wit.*

Gordon, never one to miss an opportunity to kick a friend when they're down, chimed in. "What's wrong with you? You're bowling like you got a load in your pants." I slunk back as Smitty plucked what looked like an ancient cannonball from the rack and strode toward the line.

Gordon fixed me with a sideways smile. "Seriously. Tell your shrink, Dr. Gordo, all about your problems. Enjoying wearing Beth's sundresses a little too much? I warned you not to try those things on. It can only lead to confusion."

"Beth doesn't wear sundresses," I muttered. "She wears T-shirts with dumb sayings."

Smitty called back. "That's because she can't find 'em. They're all hanging in your closet!"

The guys exploded in another wave of hysterics, and

Smitty tossed a strike. I slumped into a wooden chair and stared out a small, grimy window. Rain was pelting the glass, and a depressed, soaked sparrow perched on the ledge outside, flinching at every drop. I could relate.

I watched Gordon take a long pull off a Pepsi with one hand while holding up his beltless khakis with the other. His home life was undoubtedly worse than mine, but somehow he could still pick up a spare and chug a soda simultaneously. I leaned my head back against the wall and let out an audible sigh, the sound muffled by the crash of pins.

To say the bowling outing wasn't serving its purpose was the understatement of the summer. Not only was I a nervous wreck about my parents, but I also lost about three days' worth of wages.

———

We stepped out into the light of the late afternoon sun. Smitty spoke up, "Pay up, McGutterbutt. You owe me six smackers."

Gordon, eager to pile on, added, "Four for me, Sir Sucks-a-lot."

I fished around in the side pocket of my cargo shorts, searching for stray bills to settle my debts. As I pulled out the cash, a scrap of folded newsprint fell out and fluttered to the lawn. I settled up with the guys and picked up the folded paper. It was the elusive, flying newspaper page from the *Island Gazette* I'd absently stuffed in my pocket the morning I'd met California Jill.

The headline screamed:

Who Killed Marjorie Kitmore?
$25,000 Reward Remains Open for Island's Only Murder

Gordon and Smitty strolled off toward the bike rack. I slowed, absorbed, and read. It was a story of a gruesome murder that occurred in 1959. The article appeared on page 8, nearly lost amidst more palatable summer anecdotes like ice cream socials and retirement parties. I sat on a weather-worn bench near the driveway, devouring the details. Before Marjorie, according to the article, the most noteworthy crimes to hit the island were drunken bar fights. A petty theft ring operating out of a local saltwater taffy shop. A few minor drug busts. But not one murder. On Mackinac Island, most bucket-kicking was chalked up to the traditional ravages of old age, the occasional accident, or the requisite war dead. People didn't generally die from having their beautiful faces bashed in and their desecrated bodies stuffed into Skull Cave.

But that's what happened to Marjorie Kitmore.

The Kitmore family had posted the reward in the fall of 1959 after it became apparent the police and FBI were striking out. The main suspect was an islander from the village, Eddie St. Germain, but there wasn't enough evidence to charge him. The article also included a picture of Marjorie. Twenty-one years old when she was killed. Caught in mid-smile, her soulful eyes looking directly into the camera with an alluring innocence.

My eyes ping-ponged between the photo and the $25,000 reward. Thoughts formed slowly like clouds merging and dissolving continuously against a blue sky. The ideas morphed, transformed, elusive and intangible.

A plan?

It was close enough to reach out and grab, but not yet

—

"It's the Wendigo!"

I flinched like I was avoiding a wild pitch. Smitty was lurking behind me, breathing Skittles and Pepsi all over my neck. I hid the article like I'd been caught doing something dirty.

"What you got there, McSpaz? A little light reading about our local island murder?"

I looked up at him. "You know about that?"

"Sure," shrugged Smitty. "Everyone in the Village knows about the Kitmore murder. A lot of folks are still mad about how it all went down. You know, Old Luke was close to that guy Eddie."

"Who's Old Luke?" I asked.

"He's just … Old Luke." He cocked his head like it was the most ridiculous question he'd heard all week. "But seriously, you have this weird look on your face. You okay?"

I hopped up. "Yup. Let's roll," I said. I wasn't ready to share my cloudy, unformed notions with Smitty or anyone else.

He draped his arm over my shoulder as we walked to the bike rack. "Listen, man. I'm really, really sorry," he said, his tone shifting. "I know it's gotta be tough. One day you have it, and one day it's just … gone. Can't imagine."

Did he know what was going on at home?

"Sorry about what?"

"I'm sorry you forgot how to bowl."

CHAPTER FOUR

Hollywood on a Dock

Later that week, the three of us rode on a luggage rack mounted on the back of an island taxi, a creaking carriage painted yellow and red, pulled by two massive draft horses. Island taxis occasionally left their rear luggage racks folded down, and, like nimble ninjas; we'd *occasionally* hop onto the back for a quick, illegal ride around town. The driver—I think this time it was Taxi Chad—was usually too busy navigating his horses away from wayward tourists to shoo us away.

We hung our legs off the rack and passed around a tub of leftover popcorn scored from the 4-H horse show at the island school. Smitty's standard joke was that 4-H stood for "Head, Heart, Hands, Help … *yourself to the leftovers.*" A few crafty seagulls drifted behind, dead eyes darting, scheming for an angle.

We looked out toward the harbor as the carriage rolled past the marina. A small armada of ferries and barges circled the break wall and pivoted toward the Arnold Line dock. Gordon broke the silence as I shoveled another handful of popcorn into my mouth.

"Do you guys even know what 'Mackinac' means?"

More silence.

"Didn't think so. It's short for *Michili*-mackinac."

"Hm. Interesting," said Smitty, visibly uninterested.

"And that means the land of the sleeping turtle," he continued. "Think about it. *A sleeping turtle.* As if a turtle isn't already slow enough, this turtle is *asleep.*" He waited for a response and got nothing.

"So what?" I asked.

"This island is boring. Nothing ever happens. It's a sleeping friggin' turtle."

The carriage veered right off Main Street, and the traffic thinned. Gordon was irritable lately, snapping for no apparent reason. Things were getting worse at Casa Whittaker. There was talk of something called a *custody battle.* I didn't quite understand what it meant, but the word "battle" didn't sound hopeful.

My mind hopscotched with rapid-fire connections. *Were the McGuinns next?* Mom had applied for the seamstress job with the movie and had her interview in a few days. Big Jack seemed to have shut down completely, spending his island weekends smoking cigars on the front porch by himself instead of frying bacon and cracking dumb jokes.

My mind hopscotched to the Marjorie Kitmore article. I'd reread it every night for the last week, fixating on her photograph before reluctantly turning off my lamp and falling into an uneasy sleep.

"You guys ever see that dude selling tickets outside the Haunted Theater?" I abruptly asked the guys.

Smitty looked over. "The burn-out with long red hair?"

"That's the guy."

"Yep. Get this: They call him Blaze.*"

"Who does?" I asked, genuinely curious.

Smitty shrugged. "I dunno. They do."

"Blaze," scoffed Gordon, as if it were the most idiotic nickname since *Shortcake.* "Figures. It's probably because he's always *blazing* doobies.

"I heard he did time in juvie," said Smitty. Back then, there was nothing more terrifying to a kid than "juvie," shorthand for *juvenile detention center.* You could almost smell it.

"I heard his old man is a big city detective, " Gordon added.

This caught my attention."What city?"

"I dunno. A big one. I heard he got busted trying to swipe a couple of bags of returnable cans from a Kroger's."

"I heard he tried to rob a Bennigan's restaurant with a toy pistol," said Smitty. "So his cop dad pulled some strings and shipped him up here. Now he's layin' low. Flying under the radar." Smitty gave a knowing nod. Our man with the inside scoop.

Gordon spoke up. "Can you imagine being a big city detective and having a dirtbag like that as your offspring? It's like a sick joke."

"How do you know he's a dirtbag?" I asked.

"He looks like one," said Gordon. "Besides. Why do you care about some frybrain ticket-taker all of a sudden?"

I fell silent as the horses continued clopping along, pondering Gordon's legitimate question. *Why indeed?* I wasn't sure myself. But that elusive formation in the clouds —my plan—was slowly taking shape. What captured my imagination was a single word. Not *dirtbag, burnout,* or *frybrain,* but a different word, the one used to describe Blaze's father. It appeared flashing and flickering like a red neon sign at night.

The word was *detective*.

———————

As we turned toward the Grand Hotel hill, three tan
college girls in cut-off jeans skip-jogged past in the opposite direction, clutching cameras. We could hear their
giddy chatter as they passed us.

"How do you know Christopher Reeve is on the ferry?"

"Sara told me! She said it was the 3:30 Arnold Line
from St. Ignace! She's got all the inside scoop on the Hollywood stuff! She's been hooking up with a grip who came in
early for the shoot!"

"What's a grip?"

"He's, like, a crew guy that, like … does stuff. I don't
know! Who cares? Hurry up! We'll miss the boat!"

A third girl, heavier than the other two, piped in as she
struggled to catch up.

"Christopher Reeve is just so super *fine!* I'm going to
buy him drinks at Horn's Bar and see if he really is the
Man of Steel!"

"Betty! Yuck! You're so crude!"

"Got that right, sister!"

They disappeared, cackling like benign witches, into
the distance. Smitty nudged Gordon with the popcorn tub.
"Hey, Gordo'" he said, mouth full, and gestured. "Something's *happening.*" The three of us shared a nod, hopped
off the luggage rack, and sprinted toward the Arnold Line
dock to join the fray.

———————

The Arnold Line dock was a madhouse as a well-oiled Los
Angeles film crew crashed headlong into a stark reality:

they were filming a movie on an island where "faster" meant adding another horse. Regardless, it was a D-Day-esque invasion, minus guns and bombs. Efficient and mechanical. Carts of moviemaking gear rolled down the landing ramps of freight barges with a roar of metallic wheels on corrugated steel. I caught glimpses of crates neatly hand-labeled as *props, extra bulbs, power cables,* and, more ominously, *wardrobe.* A growing crowd on the dock murmured in anticipation. The gear was here. Movie stars couldn't be far behind.

Half the island was on the dock that day. Many clutched bright red notebooks and pens purchased minutes earlier at Alfred's Drugstore, where they sold Bic pens bundled with red spiral notebooks slapped with a sticker that read 'Official *Somewhere in Time* Autograph Kit.' They flew off the shelves.

An important-looking man with salt and pepper hair and a scowl oversaw the madness. He wore a khaki safari vest with oddly shaped pockets, which gave him the look of an irritable lion tamer. Nothing was going according to plan in his world. He charged up to a dray idling next to the freight building, the horses twitching off flies and snorting in the sun.

"For god's sake, man! Are you the only driver taking the camera packages to the Mackinac Hotel?" He spoke in a distinctly English accent. "Because this rig won't cut it. We need to clear this dock and reconvene for a production meeting at the soundstage in ninety minutes!"

Halfway through a Mars candy bar, the hefty driver stared back blankly, not the least bit rattled by the Brit or his Monty Python accent. One of the horses whinnied and farted. The Very Important Brit steamed off in a huff.

My pulse quickened.

It was very exciting.

No! It was nothing special. Just a bunch of workers getting off a boat.

… *To make a movie.*

… *With my mom!*

Two thin, middle-aged men with matching leather shoulder bags stepped down the boat ramp, deep in a heated conversation. I wandered away from Smitty and Gordon to eavesdrop on their conversation.

"Listen, it doesn't matter what Jane says," said the Harried One, pushing thick black rims up his nose and nervously running a hand through thinning hair. "She's just wrong! The line works perfectly the way it's written."

"Read it to me again," said the calmer of the two.

The Harried One flipped through a few pages of what I assumed was a movie script, stopped, and began reading aloud.

"Close up, Richard, smitten by this woman whose photograph he fell in love with at another time. His point of view as she speaks. 'Are you the man I've dreamed about all these years? The man I've had visions of my entire life?'"

He looked up from the script, radiating like Jesus after delivering the Sermon on the Mount. "I think it's perfect! It sums up her conflict. We can't change a single word."

The Calm One shook his head. "But it doesn't matter what *you* think. It matters what *she* thinks. She's the star. And she thinks it's—and I quote—*a bit wordy*."

"Wordy? I worked on that line for a week! We even workshopped it with a focus group!"

The Calm One waved him off. "What about this: *Why are you here now?* Would that work?"

"No. That's horrible."

"I agree. But it's also not *wordy*."

They continued their harried brainstorming as I

scanned the crowd. Through the throngs, I spotted California Jill holding the hand of a silver-haired man in his 40s, who I assumed was her father.

What did she call him again? A production designer?

She wore red checked slip-on shoes and a yellow T-shirt emblazoned with *the B-52's*. I was pretty sure it was the name of a band. She was, objectively speaking, adorable. She smiled at me, broke from her father, and bounded over. I felt my breathing quicken.

"Hey!" she asked, pointing at me. "Is it you?"

"What?"

"Is it you?" she repeated, this time louder.

I looked around. "Is *what* me?"

"You're the paperboy, right? Jack? You were chasing the *Island Gazette* around my yard the other day. Then you freaked out the horses, and they ran away. Remember?"

"Oh yeah. That, um, might've been me."

Suddenly, behind us, I heard an exclamation of pure joy from the Calm One and turned to look. He was snapping his fingers frantically with one hand and pointing at us with the other.

"That's it! *Is it you?* That's the line!"

The Harried One stopped to process the idea, then broke out in a slowly widening smile.

"Is it you? You're right! *Is … it … you?* It's so simple. It'll work!" He scribbled it down in the margin of his script, and the two of them broke out in an impromptu—and very awkward—high-five dance, heading down the dock with a new spring in their steps. I had no clue what it meant and turned back to Jill, who was equally baffled.

She shrugged and gestured toward the unloading crew and equipment. "Exciting, right?"

"I guess," I shrugged, feigning nonchalance.

Gordon and Smitty sauntered over, no doubt

wondering when I had time to make a new friend. A new *female* friend.

"So. Where's Superman?" asked Smitty, his eyes darting around the dock.

"And the Bond girl? Jane Whatshername" asked Gordon. "That's who I wanna see. She's *hot.*"

"Seymour," said Jill. "They're not on this boat. They fly in tonight on a private plane."

"I see how it is. Big shots," Smitty said.

"Nah. My dad says they're cool. He says most actors are nuts, but Christopher Plummer, Christopher Reeve, and Jane Seymour are really normal."

Smitty glanced at the blue, cloudless sky. "I was kinda hoping he'd fly in wearing blue tights carrying Jane under his arm like a sack of oats."

Gordon squinted at Jill. "How do you know so much about all this movie stuff?"

"My dad's on the crew. Production design. He brings me with him whenever he shoots in the summer. We're from California."

"*Swimming pools, movie stars,*" added Smitty.

"Not quite," she said. "We live in the Valley."

Gordon pointed at her shoes. "I figured you weren't from the Upper Peninsula wearing checked sneakers."

She looked down. "Vans. The surfers wear them." She smiled approvingly like she and her shoes were old pals. "I think they're rad."

I turned to Jill. "This is Smitty and Gordon. This is Jill. She's renting a place off Market Street. I delivered her paper."

"Sort of," said Jill with a wink toward me.

"How cute. Jack and Jill," said Gordon. "You two gonna fetch a pail of water?"

"I see you've learned your nursery rhymes," Jill shot back.

Gordon nodded at her sassy retort. *Approved.*

I craned my neck, hoping for a clearer view of the ferry. More carts lumbered down the ramp, pushed by dockporters, and the crowd surged forward, instant cameras at the ready, clamoring for a shot.

"Where's Chris!"

"Where's Jane!"

"Where's Captain Von Trappe!"

Suddenly, the Very Important Brit hopped up on an empty luggage cart and raised a bullhorn. The small crowd shushed itself over a squeak of feedback.

"Hello, good people of Mackinac Island!" There was good-natured cheer. "Clearly you're all excited to meet our esteemed thespians, Mr. Christopher Reeve, the stunning Jane Seymour, and of course, the legendary Christopher Plummer—Captain Von Trappe himself." The prickly film field general had magically transformed himself into a charming English gentleman. The crowd loved it.

"And there may be a moment when you *will* take pictures with our stars, as we will intrude on your lovely island for at least two months." More cheers.

"But I regret to inform you that our actors are not on this particular vessel."

The crowd booed, albeit good-naturedly.

"We want Superman!" one of the giggly waitresses screamed.

The Very Important Brit smiled, white teeth gleaming in the sun. "I understand perfectly! And you will get your chance. But in the meantime, I am more than happy to sign autographs. Why, I'll even sign their names. A stand-in, if you will." He lowered the bullhorn and hopped off the cart.

He was kidding, but the crowd instantly pushed forward, extending pens and snapping photos. The Very Important Brit broke out in a big, honest laugh and gamely began signing autographs.

"Jeez. Guy's a complete nobody, and even *he's* getting mobbed," I said.

Smitty nodded, observing the chaos. "I know, man. What a bunch of *losers*." He quickly turned to Gordon. "You gotta pen? I wanna get that Brit's autograph. He seems very important!"

Gordon flashed a pen. "Way ahead of ya, Mary." The two locked arms and disappeared into the crowd, leaving me behind with Jill as carts unloaded, and the crew organized themselves into small battalions.

Grip department! … Stack gear over by the soda machine! … cameras go on the green dray! … the production assistants have all the hotel assignments! … call sheets, get your call sheets!

I watched it unfold impassively. If the world could endure the threat of nuclear war, the demise of disco, and the loss of Elvis, surely I could survive a summer of filming a Hollywood movie. What's the big deal?

And then it hit me. This was my island. Okay, maybe not entirely mine. I was just a summer kid, way down low on the totem pole compared to the year-round Islanders who truly ran the show. But my family owned a cottage, my parents contributed to the Round Island Lighthouse fund, and Gramps was the ceremonial mayor—whatever that meant.

And me? I was the paperboy! Let's face it; the town would be clueless without my skills. *Pedal-pedal-fling!* But Hollywood had swooped in and seized control of the dock as if their ancestors paddled to the island three hundred years ago! It was a disruption of the natural order of things. On Mackinac Island, you had to earn your place.

Work your way up. Put in the miles. Yet, here we were, allowing them to cut to the front of the line while we clamored for autographs like giddy schoolgirls as they did it.

Or was I just jealous?

Regardless, the idea of Mom joining the ranks of this mesmerizing, organized, creative brigade made me feel vaguely ill.

"Not joining your buddies?" Jill asked, snapping me back to the moment.

"Nah. It's no big deal."

"Oh, right," she said, a knowing glimmer in her gaze. "You're more of a Batman guy."

CHAPTER FIVE

Interview with a Cult

I don't know what I expected to see when I walked into the *Somewhere in Time* production offices that day. But my guard was up.

Mom and I hiked down Mission Hill from the East Bluff, lugging two black Hefty bags full of old clothes. We were heading to the Mackinac Hotel, where the crew was headquartered. Mom wore an orange sleeveless shirt, navy culottes, and brown sandals. She had a new bounce to her step and I struggled to keep up.

"Why are we bringing all this old stuff?" I asked.

She looked over her shoulder. "When I called about the interview, the woman from the wardrobe department said they needed to see samples. I don't know exactly what that means, so I just grabbed this stuff to show that at least I know how to sew." She looked over at me and smiled as I caught up. "By the way, it's rather chivalrous of you to accompany your mom to her big interview."

"Thanks. What's shovel ... rist?"

"*Chivalrous.* Polite. Like how the Knights of the Round Table behaved around their mothers. Or their wives. Or their girlfriends. Or all three." She smiled at her slightly naughty joke, but it flew straight over my head at the time.

I wasn't about to spill the real reason I had volunteered to accompany my mom to the interview. Big Jack was still downstate, and I'd be damned if she'd breeze onto a movie set unaccompanied. As the acting Man of the House, it fell to me to keep a skeptical eye on these Hollywood characters and their charming shenanigans.

We approached the terrace leading to the soundstage, where hammers pounded and voices echoed in the corridor. My heartbeat quickened. Was it the adrenaline of seeing the curtain lift on filmmaking magic? Maybe a little. But I also felt something else as we pushed through the heavy wood door to the production office. I didn't have a word for it then, but I do now.

Dread.

The hallway of the production offices was a madhouse as a wildly focused crew crisscrossed and collided, hauling racks of clothes, crates, and light stands, all running in different directions, barking orders. *Bobby needs a double CTO for the key light! The stand-in is wearing the wrong necklace! Craftie's out of blueberry muffins!*

Throughout the madness, Mom never slowed down. That morning she appeared nuclear-powered, and her ponytail bounced as she maneuvered balletically around the chaos.

"So, who are we meeting?" I called ahead.

"Her name's Cynthia Moorhouse. She said to follow the signs toward the wardrobe department. Oh, there it is!"

A sign reading WARDROBE led to a long flight of

stairs. We paused at the bottom of the steps, catching our breath.

"Come on up!"

At the top of the steps loomed a large, dark-haired woman in a tie-dye T-shirt and white overalls. An earth-mother type? I was immediately suspicious. It was almost 1980. Why was she dressed like that? What if she was some hippie freak who lived in the California canyons and hung out with the remaining Manson family members? I'd swiped Beth's copy of *Helter Skelter* during my winter break and devoured it. I felt I had a good handle on how these California types operated. It wasn't all surfboards, palm trees, and *Fun, Fun, Fun*. There was some freaky stuff going down out West.

We trudged up the stairs with our Hefty bags. Earth Mother checked her clipboard when we got to the top. "Ana McGuinn?"

Mom smiled. "Cynthia Moorehouse?"

Cynthia pointed. "Orange top, just like you said."

Mom pointed back. "White overalls, just like you said."

"You passed the first test of any worthy wardrobe assistant," Cynthia smiled. "You can identify overalls."

As they shook hands, Mom introduced me. "And this handsome young squire is my son Jack."

I barely gave her a head nod. Cynthia smiled, unfazed by my icy greeting. "Great to meet you. Jack. Follow me!"

She guided us through a door. We emerged and instantly froze in awe, practically bumping into each other. The space overflowed with vintage attire. Racks and shelves stacked with neatly arranged fabrics. The walls were covered with draped textiles, and rows of mannequins showcased an assortment of 1912-era hats, dresses, canes, and eyeglasses, each meticulously labeled. It was like discovering a colossal attic in a tiny old house. Impossibly vast. The lingering fragrance of incense added a distinct bohemian vibe.

I knew it. Hippies.

Mom fumbled her words as she absorbed the expanse.

"Good God" was all she could manage. Her eyes danced around the display like an overwhelmed little girl on Christmas morning. She cleared her throat. "I brought a few samples of ..." she hesitated as we plopped the bags on a large work table. "Samples of my work." She smiled, flustered. "I'm sorry. I've just never described it that way. *Work*. Sounds pretentious compared to what you do. It's more of a hobby."

"All good, Ana," said Cynthia, approaching the pile. "Whatcha got here?"

Ana? I thought to myself. *How did they get chummy so fast?*

Mom plucked a blazer from the bag. She held it up by the shoulders and displayed it for Cynthia. "I made this for Jack a few years back. It's a sort of mini-Savile Row idea." She hesitated, then charged ahead. "I got the idea from a Life magazine ad." She turned it, displaying the cut. "Extra wide notch flat lapels, large pocket flaps."

I swiveled to face her, my eyebrows raised in surprise. She spoke with such authority.

Mom continued. "I couldn't find anything close to what I wanted at JC Penney, so I picked up the fabric and ..." she pantomimed, pushing a button. "... fired up the ol' Singer Slant-O-Matic 500 and got busy!"

"Good!" replied Cynthia. "That's exactly what we use here." She gestured to a line of four glimmering sewing machines, then looked closer at the blazer. "You nailed the seams. Beautiful work."

Beautiful work? This was not going well.

"It didn't fit!" I blurted out. They both turned to me with matching puzzled looks.

"What do you mean *it didn't fit?*" asked Mom.

"It was super tight in the shoulders. I didn't want to make you feel bad, but I didn't like wearing it all that much."

She shot me a doubtful look. "That's interesting. This is the first time you've ever mentioned that, and you wore it about ten times. In fact, I remember you getting quite a few compliments on how handsome you looked."

I shrugged and looked away. "Just sayin'.'"

She was right. I *did* look handsome in it. I loved that blazer so much that I sometimes wore it around the house when nobody was home, holding a toy pistol and re-enacting the opening credit sequences from James Bond movies.

Mom shrugged it off, returning to her garbage bag show-and-tell. She removed a few faded, mothball-smelling dresses from the Hefty bag.

"I also designed the costumes for my daughter Beth's high school play. They did *Guys and Dolls.*"

Cynthia inspected the dresses, dragging her fingertips over the hems, nodding. "Lovely work, even for a high school play."

"A *public* high school play. Not exactly a big budget," added Mom.

I coughed conspicuously. "That play was boring."

Again, their gazes swung toward me. "I'm not saying you didn't do a good job. It's just that the show was a little underwhelming, you know? A bunch of guys singing. Some dolls. It was … kinda … I dunno … blah." I smiled as if we were old friend just keeping it real.

"How old are you, Jack?" asked Cynthia.

"I'm … almost twelve."

Cynthia turned to Mom and smiled. Some secret female code flashed between them. I didn't like it. Not one bit.

"How about your mom and I chat, and you can check out the soundstage. They're filming the portrait scene. It's really neat." She gestured toward the door. "Just follow the signs to the red light. If anyone asks, say you're working with Cynthia in the wardrobe department. It's dark, and there are a lot of lights and cables, so watch your step."

Mom nodded a bit too vigorously for my taste.

"Wow, Jack. Yeah. Go! I'll track you down after. Have fun!"

And just like that, I was banished from the interview. It looked like 'ol Earth Mother Cynthia had her darning needles deep into Mom already, and she didn't even have the job.

Neat.

There is no more condescending blow-off to a kid than the word *neat*. Winding through the halls, I silently kicked myself. I had clearly overplayed the blazer-not-fitting comment. A bad tactical move. And what was that *Guys and Dolls* review nobody asked for? Stupid! Mom was now alone with Cynthia, while I wandered in the cinematic wilderness.

I spotted a red spinning light at the end of the hall and headed toward it. A hushed group waited at the giant stage door, staring at the light as if expecting a revelation. It blinked off, a loud bell rang, and they piled through the door like Tokyo subway riders. I didn't enter with them as much as picked up my feet and allowed myself to be swept into the darkened soundstage by a riptide of Hollywood humanity.

I immediately stumbled over a cable that appeared out of nowhere, snaking along the cement floor. Across the massive stage, workers in black T-shirts put the finishing touches on an old-time photography studio set. The contrast between the exquisite turn-of-the-century details and the ragged craftspeople who created it was almost comical. In the distance, the crew adjusted large lights and tweaked the positioning of props. The director, an animated man who sounded vaguely European, gestured toward an armchair and spoke to an assistant.

An involuntary smile crept across my face.

It was pure magic.

The din of construction lowered, and the boisterous chatter quieted to professional murmurs. Jane Seymour, stunning in a sheer white gown and holding a matching white feathered fan, carefully stepped over lighting cables and onto the set. She paused momentarily, admiring her surroundings, and seemed to drink in the lighting. With a smile to the crew, she took her seat. Every sweaty, dust-covered man on the stage—and probably a few women— unconsciously sucked in their guts, flexed their shoulder muscles, and raised their heads to reduce the appearance of double chins. I say this with confidence, as I was among them. Fresh out of sixth grade, she made me feel old and out of shape.

She whispered something to an assistant cameraman holding a tape measure *(an off-color joke?)*, and they both laughed. I inched closer, now just ten feet away from the camera.

The director spoke. "Okay, Jane. As you know, this is the backstage photo shoot. Your character Elise is sitting for a publicity shot, and Tim here, playing the photographer, is coaxing you into a happy thought. We'll shoot Chris's reaction after lunch, so you'll have to fake it."

She smiled. "You mean, like … *act?*"

Her English accent, cut with a sweet sarcasm, made my knees tingle. I stumbled back a few steps.

"You got it," responded the director with a grin. "Act! Everyone's tired. We need a little life on the set. Give it to us!"

"Okay, positions and last looks!" boomed a voice. Was it the Very Important Brit? I couldn't tell in the darkness. "Very quiet! We're rolling on this one!"

"And … *action!*" shouted the director.

Seymour began working her fan as the actor playing the photographer delivered his line. "A little smile," he said, standing behind the old-time camera. "Perhaps you could think of something happy or bright?"

She looked toward the camera with a Mona Lisa smile. The tingly numbness in my knees was now inching north-ward, overtaking what could politely be called my "swim-suit region."

I stumbled back a few steps and felt the frigid clunk of metal against the back of my skull. I pivoted and watched, in dumb fascination, as a light on a ten-foot stand tottered, then collapsed into another light with a thunderous crash.

Sparks. Shattering glass.

Then another one went down.

"Ah, shit!" yelled an electrician.

Then another one went down.

"Heads up!" screamed a grip.

"Who the *ffffff* … !" yelled someone else.

After four mini explosions of glass, the most expensive domino display I'd ever seen was over. There was a beat of silence. It felt like every head turned to me on a swivel as I stood, petrified, amid the chaos. One remaining light cast an eerie glow on my face. My hands covered my ears. The moment went on and on.

"Who … are … *you!*" yelled a voice. It was definitely the Very Important Brit.

I cautiously lowered my hands from my ears. *Should I lie?*

"I'm … Jack." Meek. Pathetic. I grasped for something else to say and settled on my original directive. It came out like a question, and halfway through, my voice cracked.

"I'm with Cynthia? In wardrobe?"

I didn't dare move a muscle for fear of being tackled and handcuffed. Slowly, laughter broke out, then spread across the set. Soon, even Jane joined in.

She squinted into the darkness and shot a double thumbs up in my direction. "Nice job, Jack! Things were getting a tad dull around here!" She settled comfortably back into her antique chair and prepared for another take.

A Bond Girl just gave me a double thumbs-up!

"Reset quickly, boys!" called the director. "We got energy happening! Let's shoot one right away!"

I watched in amazement as the crew replaced bulbs and repositioned lights like a pit crew at the Indy 500. The scene was reset before another wave of shame could crest and crash over me.

The director called out. "Jane, this time, I want you to think of our clumsy little friend lurking in the darkness. Jack-Be-Not-So-Nimble. Give me a real smile. Still subtle, but real."

"Got it, boss," she called back as she resumed fanning herself.

"This take's for you, Jack-Be-Not-So-Nimble," she called out. "It's a keeper! I can feel it!"

"And … *action!*" the director yelled.

A cryptic, beautiful smile spread across her face,

hinting at secrets untold. This time, no lights collapsed. This time, the only sparks shot from Jane Seymour's eyes. She held her radiant smile for what felt like an eternity. Finally, a voice.

"Cut! Beautiful! Unforgettable!" called the director from the dark. "You just stole their American hearts. And if you didn't, well ... they don't have hearts. Let's move on!"

I've never been a big romance guy, but to this day, the portrait scene affects me. The power of new love is beautifully captured as Seymour's character Elise, steals a glance at her newfound love, Richard, portrayed by Christopher Reeve. It happens in a mere instant, conveyed through a simple smile.

But that's not why I love it. I love it because I know she wasn't smiling at Richard. She was smiling at me.

"How was the interview?" I asked.

Mom was practically race-walking as we navigated our way out of the production offices and toward the shore road, again lugging our Hefty bags.

"You go first," Mom said. "How was the shoot?"

"It was ... pretty neat."

Neat? That word again. But what was I supposed to say? *I destroyed four movie lights, humiliated myself, and shared a semi-intimate moment with Jane Seymour, who, incidentally, puts all three Charlie's Angels to shame.*

It was bad enough that my mission had failed so spectacularly. I was there to shield her from this traveling circus. Instead, I got seduced like a Michigan rube playing three-card Monte in New York City.

"*Neat?* I don't think I've ever heard you use that word, Jack McGuinn."

"They filmed a scene with Jane. She's pretty … pretty."

"Pretty … pretty. There's an understatement. Ms. Seymour's going to be the cause of a lot of cold showers this summer."

"Why cold showers?" We took a sharp right towards Mission Hill.

"Dumb joke. So, ask me about *my* thing." She waited for about a millisecond. "Never mind. I'll just tell you." She stopped, turned, and raised clenched fists into the air.

"I got it!"

"Got it?" I faltered, my words muffled by a gleeful embrace.

"Wardrobe assistant! Mostly basics. Clean up. Prep work. Boring stuff like that. But Cynthia said depending on how I do, I might get to work with *the talent.* I think that means the actors." She broke away with a victory spin.

"Can you believe it?" She tousled my hair. "I'm working in the movies!"

"Congrats, Mom. That's … great." I took a deep breath and continued. "Make sure to call Dad and let him know." It was Friday, and I knew Big Jack would soon be leaving the dealership for the drive north. He'd want to know about this new development.

Mom nibbled on her index finger as she walked. "Your father won't be up this weekend."

"Why not?" Big Jack never missed a weekend on the island.

Mom's eyes drifted toward the Round Island lighthouse in the distance. "It's something to do with one of his suppliers, I think," her was voice vague and distant. "He has to deal with it personally, but it wasn't clear. I'm sure it'll be fine."

She grew quiet. We walked the rest of the way up the hill to Wildcliffe in silence, the air now strangely heavy.

It would be over a month before we saw Big Jack again.

As we trudged up the hill, my eyes lifted toward a cluster of clouds. They initially formed the silhouette of an elongated George Washington, then mutated into Scooby-Doo sporting a top hat.

As we trudged up the gravel Wildcliffe driveway, I couldn't help but glance skyward again. I stopped. My heart skipped three beats, and a surge of tachycardia gripped me.

In mid-flight, a hulking cloud-demon lunged. From its elongated, slender head protruded puffs of antlers. Its arms bore three menacing claws, and a face materialized against the vibrant blue backdrop, eyes gleaming with a sickening intensity, mouth widening in a silent, atmospheric shriek. A cold tingle raced through my ears and scalp, and my throat constricted.

I whispered. *"The Wendigo."*

Mom's voice carried over from the porch, interrupting my horrific vision. "Come on in, Jack! I'll whip up a PB and J for you."

I tore my gaze away from the demonic image and looked toward the house. Mom was waving me in. I smiled wanly, waved back, then looked skyward again. The clouds were already transforming into something else. Wispy, long cloud-hair. A smaller puff slowly emerged from its face. Like smoke.

A new vision, this one of the red-haired figure outside the Haunted Theater, grinning and blowing smoke. The ticket-taker. *Blaze.* Son of a big-city detective.

"You deserve it, Jack!" Mom called. "You're my lucky charm!"

And the cloud shapeshifted again, the visage falling apart and reassembling into something unrecognizable. I took a deep breath, forced my frozen limbs to move again, and made my way toward Wildcliffe for one of Mom's sandwiches.

I now knew exactly what I had to do.

CHAPTER SIX

Meeting Blaze

Reflecting on the summer of 1979, some things are clear. A Hollywood film crew did descend upon the island. Superman did arrive—although sans red cape. I did stumble upon the Marjorie Kitmore murder. But how I found myself shifting nervously from foot to foot in front of the Haunted Theater at 8:30 AM on that misty mid-June morning remains a mystery. I want to think it was more than random cumulus cloud formations that brought me there, but I'll never be sure.

Tentatively, I climbed the matted and frayed red-carpeted steps and approached the glassed-in ticket booth. Campy organ music piped through a single speaker mounted on a pillar pointed toward the street. Creepy, whimsical melodies clashed with the muffled intensity of heavy metal blasting from an 8-track tape player inside the booth.

As I approached, a prone figure came into focus, feet

up, clad in black jeans and a black T-shirt. His long, red hair was clean but stringy. A cigarette protruded from behind his left ear, and he wore black Converse sneakers, the white rubber parts darkened with a black marker, lending a weird homemade touch. His left foot tapped against the register to the beat of the music.

He held a magazine featuring a big-bosomed woman in a pink T-shirt. She looked exquisitely happy about being that month's cover girl. The magazine was called *Gent*. Below the title, in smaller letters, was printed *Home of the D-cups*. I was no genius, but I surmised the need for a D-cup was related to her ample breasts.

I was frozen, unsure of my next move, then stepped forward and tapped the smudged glass with a knuckle. Without looking up, the figure in the booth reached over and turned down the music.

"Are you … Blaze?" I asked. It occurred to me I had no proof this was actually what he called himself.

A curt voice. No eye contact. "We open in thirty."

"I don't need a ticket. I wanted to ask you about …" I trailed off. What *did* I want to ask him about?

"About what?" he said without looking up.

"Just some ideas I wanted to discuss … um … if … could we … like …"

He lowered the magazine quickly, eyes narrowing, and stared daggers. "Listen, kid. I ain't Socrates, and even if I were, I wouldn't waste *ideas* on you." He resumed leering at the pictures in the magazine, then flipped the page.

"How much is it? I mean, the tour."

"Since we're not open yet, I'll give you a special price —*double*. Four bucks." Still not looking up.

"Wait. Why do I have to pay double?"

"Like I said, we're not open. And obviously …" he thwacked the girlie mag with his middle finger, "I'm busy."

He looked up. "Plus, my Spidey sense says you want to talk to me about thirty times more than I want to talk to you. And that, Thelma, costs money."

Thelma?

His lips thinned as if he'd smelled something horrible. "Wait. Seriously? You're wearing a *KISS* T-shirt?"

I looked down at the bold orange and yellow KISS logo ironed on my white Haynes T-shirt. Beth worked at a Main Street T-shirt shop and gave it to me the summer before as a birthday gift. "Yes," I said. "This is a KISS T-shirt."

He snorted. "Price just went up again. Now it's four-*fifty*. KISS is a bunch of clowns. The Monkees of metal. You should be ashamed to wear that rag in public." I noticed his T-shirt said Black Sabbath.

"I really don't want to take the tour," I said. "I'm here to talk to you."

Blaze sighed, set the magazine down, and leaned in closer. He spoke so quietly that I had to press my ear to the glass.

"I get that. But if you want a backstage pass, VIP meet-and-greet with me," he hooked his thumbs toward his chest. "You take the tour." He pointed towards the entrance. I noticed his fingernails were also painted black. "And if you waste one more millisecond of my precious reading hour, the price goes up to *five* bucks."

I was frozen solid.

"Tick-tock, little man. Make your move."

I glanced uneasily toward the entrance. A misaligned sign nailed to a door read *Prepare Yourself* in dripping, blood-spattered letters. He fixed me with a waiting gaze, eyebrows arched. I reached into my pocket and fished out money.

Blaze grinned ear to ear and half-whispered what

sounded like a poem. "Pay your ticket, take the ride. The journey goes on, but your soul just died."

He cackled as he took my cash. "Don't worry, paperboy; there's a vending machine near the exit where you can purchase fresh undies, because you're about to crap clean through the ones you got on." I stopped short.

"Joke. All harmless fun. You know …" A Cheshire cat grin spread across his face. "… kid's stuff."

As I stepped away from the booth and towards the entrance, I couldn't help but wonder: *How did he know I was the paperboy?*

Moments later, I pushed the clicking turnstile and took a final, furtive glance toward the ticket booth. "Excuse me, how do I …"

He was gone.

The door slammed loudly, and I was in total darkness.

The sound of ghoulish laughter oozed through crackling speakers above. I relaxed a bit. I knew this routine all too well. The typical *bwa-ha-ha-ha* type of stuff. Stock in trade for every two-bit spook house along the trick-or-treat route. My heart rate barely ticked up.

But with a deafening blast, loud heavy metal kicked in, blending perfectly with the sinister wails of laughter in a distinctly unsettling way. I didn't know it then, but the song was "Electric Funeral" by Black Sabbath. The pounding drums shook the foundation of the building as the strobe lights flickered in an eerie red, blue, and green dance overhead. The piercing screeches grew in volume and then slowed down to a quarter pitch like a wobbly player with a dying battery. Heavy footsteps closed in, accompanied by a blood-curdling, high-pitched wail.

I took off running down the strobe-lit corridor. Looking over my shoulder, I saw a figure shrouded in a tattered black cloak gliding toward me like a wraith. I smashed headlong into a black plywood wall. The barrier gave a bit, and I was hurled back, stumbling and struggling to stay on my feet. The strobe lights flashed faster, blinding me. A freakish shriek ripped through the air from my left as I struggled to get my bearings. I spun around, trying to locate the source of the sound, but the disorienting lights made it impossible.

Three battered, dirt-covered coffins ascended from beneath the floorboards. The rickety lids creaked open, revealing the putrid remains of bodies clad in tattered red colonial military coats, with decaying teeth and empty eye sockets. Above me, a neon sign flickered on, its letters spelling out the words: *Forget the Redcoats! Remember the DEADCOATS!* It should have elicited a mocking laugh, it was so off-the-charts corny. But on that particular morning in 1979, I screamed like a baby.

My breathing was ragged, and I could hear myself whimpering. The strobe lights flashed faster, and the music got louder. As I staggered through the darkness, I couldn't shake the thought: *Could an almost twelve-year-old kid die of a heart attack?*

For what felt like hours, I sprinted through the winding halls. Crude wax monsters howled and moaned as if they knew exactly what was happening to my jackhammering heart and were determined to cause it to burst like a water balloon.

Funny thing is, the wax monsters were as familiar to me as the Ryba's Fudge Shop sign on Main Street. Pictures of them were displayed on a poster hanging near the entrance. For years, I'd laugh scornfully at tourists fleeing from the place, faces contorted with fear, shrieks reverberating down Main Street. But now I understood. Either I was a spectacular coward, or the Haunted Theater was spectacularly underrated.

I skidded to a halt under a barely lit emergency exit sign and pounded on a wooden door, convinced nobody would hear me over the steady shrieks, strobes, and grinding guitars.

"Let me out! Let me out! Let me—"

The music cut out without warning, and overhead fluorescent lights flashed on. I squinted, blinking in the harsh light, and looked around. There was laughter, but now it was more human and tinged with apprehension.

"Calm down! It's over! It's all just wax and lighting."

Blaze strolled up the hall wearing a grin and a cape. Heavy work boots had replaced his Converse. I turned to face him, fighting back tears. It all came out like a gust, my voice high-pitched and wavering.

"You went too far, you, you … *dirtbag!* I should report you! Get you fired! That's child endangerment or some-thing! I don't know what it's called, but it's *PROBABLY ILLEGAL!*"

Blaze's arms stretched open in supplication. His earlier swagger had given way to genuine worry.

"Okay, okay! You're right. I may have gone a little overboard. But there's no need to report me."

I hunched over, hands on my knees, stifling sobs. He placed a hand gently on my back. "Breathe, dude. It's over. Let's get you a Coke and a smile."

I straightened, still gasping, and eyed him warily.

"It's okay, man," he said. "You passed the test. You get to behold the inner sanctum." He gestured for me to follow. I hesitated for a moment. My breathing returned to normal, and my heart regained its proper functionality. And, truthfully, *beholding the inner sanctum* did sound pretty damn cool.

I followed him through the emergency exit door.

———

We entered his emporium-like inner sanctum. The smell hit me hard. Slightly pissy. Cigarettes and dirty socks. Empty tuna cans. Rotting fast food. I breathed out of my mouth. Two of the four walls were covered from floor to ceiling with aluminum foil, shiny side out. A small wooden desk sat against the wall upholstered with posters of MC5, Deep Purple, Alice Cooper, and Led Zeppelin. Dark bands. The heavy stuff. A shelf held a stack of girlie mags and paperback books. Nietzsche. Balzac. Kerouac. Whitman. I didn't recognize the authors' names, but they sounded smart. A rusted, decaying mechanical torso, crowned with a ghoul's head stared at us with dead eyes.

Blaze removed a Coke from a small refrigerator, cracked it open, and handed it to me.

"The real bands are the ones you see in these posters. Not four circus freaks in make-up, breathing fake fire, and puking fake blood."

"Yeah, well, I still like 'em."

"Yeah, well, you're still wrong. I bet you have a KISS lunchbox. Don't tell me. You and three of your fruity little buddies dressed up like KISS for Halloween. Won first prize at the 5th-grade costume contest."

How the hell did he know that?

"You did! Oh my God! Don't tell me you went as Paul Stanley, the Star Child."

How did he know that too?

"I knew it. Anyway." He gestured to the lair. " So this is

it. Aluminum foil was my touch. Creates better black light."

I nodded. "Cool."

"Damn right, it's cool."

He took a drag. He tapped the end of the smoke into the ashtray, pinched the tip with his fingers, then smelled and licked them before placing the used smoke into his pocket.

Very weird.

He pointed at me. "Speak, midget. My earlier sympathy is wearing off. Why are you here?"

I took a breath. "Is it true your dad is a detective in a big city?"

A fleeting flicker in his eyes, quickly concealed, as if the question caught him off guard. "That … is confidential."

"Okay. But if he is, you must know something about police work, right?"

"I *am* police work. Why do you think the old man shipped me off to Mackitraz Island? To learn how to make peanut brittle?"

I had to know. "Why did he?"

"Thank you for asking, counselor. I got two DUIs. Then I 'accidentally' ran over the chemistry teacher's mailbox with my Camaro." He bracketed the word *accidentally* with air quotes.

"Wow," I responded. I had no idea what a "DUI" was, but at least he didn't rob a Bennigan's.

"Yeah. Dear old Dad figured this was the only place I couldn't crack up a car. And damn, is he right about that. Because there aren't any cars! I don't even leave the lair unless it's to buy Camels or an egg salad sandwich at the Pickle Barrel."

He wandered to a Black Sabbath poster and settled with his back to me. "So my dad may or may not be a cop.

I don't trust you well enough to say for sure. But if he is? Trust me. My DNA does *not* match." He turned back to me. "So I ask again. Why are you here?"

I took another long breath. It was time. "Mainly because of my mom and dad. I think their marriage is in the shitter. They never talk anymore. The house is really weird now."

In the shitter? Who was I trying to impress?

Blaze sucked in what sounded like a giant phlegm dumpling and swallowed.

"Well, first off, you need a shrink, not a delinquent like yours truly. But I will say this: Your parents' problems are likely your fault. Being stuck with the same partner your whole life is torture enough, but having some brat ask you for blueberry pancakes every morning? I'd bash myself in the temple with a ball-peen hammer. Where does one even get blueberries?" A snorting laugh escaped through his nostrils. He shook his head as if pondering one of Life's Great Mysteries.

I didn't laugh. *My fault?* He'd hit on my own worst fear. Were my parents not sick of each other but sick of me? I let the concept dissipate like a fart, but it lingered.

"Regardless, your pathetic little yarn makes less sense by the second."

I continued. "Well, I figured you might know about investigating and stuff. Maybe you could help me."

I reached into my pocket, removed the crumpled article, unfolded it, and handed it to Blaze. "I want to solve this cold case. The Marjorie Kitmore murder. It happened twenty years ago."

Blaze took the article and scanned it. A hint of a smile played at the corners of his lips.

I continued. "There's a reward."

Blaze's eyes never left the page. "A reward?"

"For solving the murder. Twenty-five thousand dollars."

He looked up. "See, you should have led off with that tasty little morsel. It could've saved us both a lot of wasted time. So, what's solving this murder gotta do with your folks being all screwy?"

"It's kinda complicated."

"Yeah, well, I'm kinda bored. Amuse me."

"First off, my mom—Ana is her name—got a job in the wardrobe department on the movie. And my dad—we call him Big Jack—is jealous. Or something. Now they're fighting about it. He thinks she'll like it too much and, I dunno, maybe … leave us?"

"Okay." Blaze stroked his chin like a doctor pondering a diagnosis. "Marginally interesting. He thinks that, or *you* think that?"

"I dunno. Both of us? Anyway, I have this theory: If I can get the reward money, I can buy them an all-expenses paid cruise to Cairo, which I heard is in Egypt. Mom always wanted to go there, but my dad's always super busy with work."

No matter how ridiculous my explanation sounded, a huge weight had lifted. I would never have guessed that the metalhead ticket-taker at the Haunted Theater would become my confessor, but that's how far gone I was in the summer of 1979. And it was only June.

I continued. "So I'm thinking if they can get away from it all and go to Cairo, just have an adventure together, maybe they can—"

"—wait, stop, stop, stop!" Blaze waved his hand in front of my face. "Sorry. I misspoke earlier. Totally my fault. As it turns out, I actually don't give a rat's ass about your family issues." He nodded thoughtfully, placing his finger on the side of his nose.

"But I do like money."

A weird grin spread across his narrow face like one of the crudely crafted wax devils he tended. A peculiar pause descended, stretching out until it became awkward. He was somewhere else.

Then he spoke. "Okay. I thought it over. *I'm in.* I'll go 50-50 on the reward. This'll be our base of operations." He headed to a wall and carefully untaped a frayed Farrah Fawcett poster, rolling it up gingerly as if it were a Dead Sea Scroll.

"Now." He gestured to the empty space. "What's missing here?"

"Um ..." I stammered.

"Um? *Evidence,* dipshit! Go get some! No stone unturned. Or, as I like to say, no turn unstoned. Tomorrow at five pm, we get started for real."

It was all happening much faster than I expected. "For the fifty percent. Does that ... mean you'll come with me ... when I, I dunno, like ... investigate stuff?"

"Jesus! Negatory!" He edged closer, the pungent scent of his smoke assaulting my nostrils, and jabbed a finger into my chest. "I'm the mastermind, see? I stay right here. If you need someone to get their hands dirty in the field, find yourself a sidekick. And your loudmouth little buddies are *not* an option. Loose lips sink ships."

"How do you know about them?"

"I'm on the street every day. And I got two eyes and two ears. Just remember, this island is tiny, and everyone talks. Keep this scheme on the down-friggin-low, got it?"

"Got it," I nodded solemnly.

He checked his watch. "Now get out of here. I gotta reset the spring loader in the banshee cave, then hose down that pile of wet turds you dropped near the decapitated fur trader display."

"What? I didn't leave any turds!"

"Sure you didn't." He grabbed the handle of a rusty toolbox by his bed. "Leave through the back exit. Stealth mode. Nobody can know about this unholy little alliance. I don't need 'corrupting minors' on my rap sheet."

He let out a thundering cackle. "Buckle up, Encyclopedia Brown Underwear. Shit's about to get real."

CHAPTER SEVEN

Night at Skull Cave

I turned onto Market Street with a rush of optimism I hadn't felt since before the bad-bacon breakfast. Blaze wasn't the obvious choice to play Gandalf to my bumbling Bilbo in this Lord-of-the-Rings of a summer, but I'd take it.

At least I had a plan.

The old door to the *Island Gazette* offices on Market Street creaked open, and I was immediately assaulted with the familiar scent of ink and newsprint. My time as the paperboy had made me a regular in the busy office, and I strode in with the confidence of someone who belonged.

For additional insurance purposes, I whistled an off-key rendition of the *Andy Griffith Show* theme. It was an obvious choice and way before my time, but I was willing to take the risk. Exuding a vibe that shouted "well-behaved, well-adjusted kid" to everyone in earshot was vital.

Patrice, the plump-and-always-smiling assistant editor,

scribbled away on a small pink notepad, a phone receiver pressed against her ear. I waited patiently until she hung up, looked up, and smiled. Without hesitation, I asked her about back issues from 1959 with the aw-shucks innocence of a kid with nothing to hide.

"1959, huh? Interesting," she said, fixing me with a curious look. "Wasn't that the Marjorie Kitmore murder summer?" Blaze's words echoed, blasting from an imaginary, Haunted Theater speaker mounted inside my brain, full of distortion and reverb: *loose lips sink ships*.

Yet here I was, strutting into the *Gazette* office like Columbo with a lit cigar and a rumpled raincoat, asking questions about a murder.

A silver crucifix hanging from Patrice's neck caught an overhead light and projected a blinding ray of purity into my iris. I took a steadying breath, then lied through my teeth. I calmly explained I was doing an "extra credit school project" about reporters. An essay, no less. I needed back copies to learn how reporters covered big stories. And wasn't this the biggest story ever to hit the island? She considered my explanation like a food critic pondering a souffle. I waited anxiously for judgment but never broke eye contact.

"Wow. Just … *wow*," she said.

Wow, I thought. It could mean so many things. The silence continued until her gaze became uncomfortable.

She shook her head slowly, put both hands on her wooden armrests, and pushed herself to a standing position.

"Yes. *Wow*." She pointed at me, then broke out in a wide smile. "Paperboy, essay writer, and an all-around nice kid. Jack McGuinn, I'd be over the moon if either of my twin boys had half your gumption. Instead, those two losers sit on their butts and play Atari all day, even when it's sunny out."

I slid a winning smile into the cylinder and pulled the trigger. "Well, Patrice. I figure it's never too early to get those extra credits for college." *What a load of crap. I was eleven. Well, almost twelve.*

"Let me get those papers for you. 1959, comin' right up!"

She padded off to the records room. Now it was Patrice's turn to whistle the theme from the *Andy Griffith Show*, absolutely thrilled to be assisting such an upstanding young citizen.

I made my way to the end of the Arnold Line dock with the back issues of the *Gazette* in my basket and took up a spot on a bench behind the freight building. I'd purchased three *Somewhere in Time* autograph kits from Alfred's Drugs, which I intended to use as detective notebooks. I flipped to a pristine page and meticulously penned a bold header in red ink. I held the page at arm's length and scrutinized it. It was right about then that I should have tossed the half-baked plan overboard like a spoiled fish.

The heading read:

FIELD NOTE: Skull Cave. Marjorie's last night alive.

I tiptoed through the Wildcliffe kitchen, my senses alert for any signs of life. I was in no mood for casual chit-chat with

Mom, Beth, or Gramps. Big Jack was still downstate, apparently preoccupied with his vague "supplier" issues.

I didn't buy it. He was avoiding the island.

The Wildcliffe kitchen had the vibe of a rustic, small-town diner. In better times, it was the nerve center of McGuinn, Inc., with friends and family swapping stories and blabbing loudly about sports, politics, and island gossip. An open-all-night hotspot for Toll House cookie dough experiments and a launching pad for impromptu midnight bike rides to Fort Holmes, the island's highest point.

But tonight, the kitchen was as silent as a mausoleum, the quiet occasionally punctuated by an odd, revving hum. After rummaging through the cupboard, I found a red plastic flashlight and extra batteries.

I grabbed my canvas courier bag off the kitchen table with the *Island Gazette* logo, threw in my notebook, a few pens, the flashlight, and the Brownie camera, and slung it over my shoulder. I made my way up the stairs, eager to trace the source of the intermittent hum, and approached my parent's bedroom. The sound was from Mom's sewing machine, but it wasn't coming from the master bedroom. It came from across the hall.

Mom was now bringing her work home.

And she'd moved into the guest bedroom.

I tip-toed closer, pressing my ear against the cool oak door. She revved the sewing machine in short bursts, like an lead-footed street racer at a stoplight, itching for the green light and the open road. She was also singing. I recognized the tune from the *Camelot* soundtrack, one of her favorites.

"It's May, It's May. The lusty month of May!"

—RRRR! went the sewing machine.

"That lovely month when everyone goes …"

—RRRR!

"… blissfully astray."

"Blissfully astray?" I whispered to myself. I removed my notebook from the courier bag and scribbled furiously.

FIELD NOTE: AM (Ana McGuinn) singing. Has moved rooms. Sounds happy. This is bad.

"Why, if it isn't Creepy Jack: Boy Stalker," a familiar voice whispered. I turned around to my left. Busted. Beth was grinning at me from the top of the staircase, gripping a coffee cup full of Cheese Tid-Bits. She wore a blue T-shirt with iron-on letters that said I'M NOT A FUDGIE. I LIVE HERE, AND I DON'T ANSWER QUESTIONS. Beth had a side hustle printing T-shirts with smart-ass phrases and selling them around town.

I backed away from the door. "She's singing," I whispered, gesturing to the door as if Beth had asked me what Mom was up to. She eyed my courier bag.

"Little late for deliveries, isn't it?"

"I forgot to hit the Keough's place. I owe 'em a *Wall Street Journal.*"

"Nope." She shook her head. "Not buying it. It's yesterday's news, sport." She checked her watch. "Almost literally." She squinted, pointing at my notebook. "You've been acting weirder than normal lately. What are you up to? You know I won't rat you out, so spill it."

I stopped and slumped against the hallway wall. "Don't you think it's weird what's going on around here?"

Beth raised an eyebrow. "I'm choosing to reserve judgment. But continue."

"Well. First of all, she's not even in her room. Dad hasn't been here in weeks. And she's *sewing*. It's almost eleven at night. This whole thing is … it's … *indecent*."

"*Indecent*. That's funny." Beth softened. "Come here."

I approached, and she put her hand on my shoulder and led me down the hall, out of earshot of the guest room.

"Of course, it's weird," she said. "Marriage is weird. Kids are weird. And parents? *Super* weird. Think about it. Two random strangers, probably wasted, hook up at some college party in 1950-something. Twenty years later, I'm talking a paranoid paperboy off the ledge. Who also happens to be my *brother*. Weird, weird, weird."

"Yeah, yeah, yeah," I said. "Everything's weird to you. But don't you think Mom's changed since she took the job? It's like the movie is all she cares about."

Beth shrugged. "Sure. Maybe she's changed." She gestured toward the guest room. "Or maybe, just maybe, this is who she really is. Maybe she changed way back when. *For us*. And now she's changing back to her original self, which, technically, doesn't qualify as change."

She nodded, seemingly impressed with herself. "Damn. That's actually a pretty good theory." She looked at me. "Come here."

I did. She hugged me, then stepped back.

"Alright. Go on with your dopey little mystery mission," she said. "But do me a favor: don't die. I don't want to be the last person who saw you alive. I'll end up getting blamed." She pivoted on her heels and marched toward her room. Before disappearing inside, she cast one final glance at me.

"Hotshot."

A fingernail moon hung against a splash of stars. In the distance, the straits roiled with choppy waters as an old boat plowed through the lake, its engine sputtering, struggling to maintain a rhythm.

Legs burning, I navigated Garrison Road's uphill twists and turns, wheeling northward. There wasn't much time to snap any decent photos of Skull Cave before Mom discovered the slumbering form under my comforter consisted of four moldy pillows and a deflated basketball. Although, at this point, I doubted she'd even check. After all, there were corsets to be hemmed.

Not that I was bitter.

As I passed through alternating warm and cool thermoclines, my thoughts drifted to the night's destination. Old history books about the island were scattered around Wildcliffe, and I'd scanned them all. One ragged paperback sat on a dusty shelf, an arm's reach from my go-to toilet. It was called *Attack at Michilimackinac, 1763*.

According to the book, Alexander Henry, an English fur trader, had narrowly avoided death during a violent Native American uprising called Pontiac's Rebellion by hiding out in a tiny cave in the middle of the island. He woke up the following day, relieved to find his scalp still firmly attached to his head. He also discovered, with dawning horror, he'd been dozing on a heap of human skulls and bones. It turned out his cozy little hideaway also happened to be an ancient burial ground.

Hence the uncreative—yet highly accurate—name of one of the island's favorite tourist attractions: Skull

Cave. This was the exact spot where Marjorie Kitmore's body turned up one grim morning in August of 1959.

And what exactly did I expect to find? No idea. I'd pored over every article in the *Island Gazette* and *Detroit Free Press*, looking for something amiss. The police and the FBI had scoured the area for a month in 1959 and returned with zilch. But somehow, the island paperboy, armed with a barely functioning Brownie camera and an autograph kit, would smash the case wide open. Doubtful. Yet I felt compelled to see if I could capture something that might bring new light to the shadows of Skull Cave. A "new perspective," as the detective novels called it.

I leaned Sluggo against a tall pine and walked toward the cave. The truth was, calling it a "cave" was a colossal exaggeration. In reality, it was nothing more than a crack in a limestone boulder. I'd been to Carlsbad Caverns once on a family vacation and knew what a real cave looked like; miles of twisting, illuminated rock passageways sliced with stalactites and stalagmites.

Skull Cave was nothing like that.

From this distance, it reminded me of a demented Jim Henson puppet. Agonized eyes stared toward the stars. A long twisted mouth in mid-groan peeked out of the pine trees. I moved the flashlight slowly to the left and then to the right. The multiple, lifeless sockets seemed to follow me.

Calm down, Jack. Just snap a few photos, take a few notes, and be in bed before midnight—nothing to get worked up about.

I pondered the gruesome details of Marjorie's death. She'd been "dismembered," which I assumed meant "cut up." Was it the work of an ax, a saw, or perhaps something more surgically precise? The police couldn't say. And what kind of twisted human—a human who possibly still walked the face of the earth at that very moment—could do something so horrible?

I reached into my bag, retrieved the Brownie, and raised it. The camera's absurdly large flash illuminated the rock outcroppings as sweat dripped into my eyes. I couldn't see a thing but continued as if the act of simply *doing* might help slow my heartbeat. I walked a few steps closer.

As I approached the cave's gaping maw, my veins filled with ice. It occurred to me: had they ever removed the skulls rumored to be inside? *Stupid*. Of course. It was hundreds of years ago. I stepped deeper into the darkness.

Sshhrr. Snap.

Frantic, I spun around. Snapping twigs cut through a low drone of wind. Was something else with me? I aimed my quivering flashlight beam at the inky blackness of the trees. I heard it again.

Sshhrr. Snap.

I pointed the beam in a new direction.

Was something shambling toward me? Something inhuman that didn't dig pain-in-the-ass kids equipped with old, crappy cameras, poking around where they didn't belong? I swallowed the metallic puke of rising terror. *Focus*. I turned back and moved toward the cave. Another gust of wind blew through the trees, accompanied by what now sounded like running footsteps.

Sshhrr. Snap!

Not two steps but four. Like an animal.

Sshhrr. Snap! Faster.

I bolted toward the mouth of the cave. Like a marine under heavy fire, I hit the ground and scrambled across the rugged terrain, determined to reach the cave's narrow opening. With my bare elbows digging into the gravel, I pulled myself forward, driven by a mixture of desperation and curiosity.

The space was cramped, but I managed to squeeze myself in, moving deep within the fissure—*where bones lay stacked?*

I looked around.

My flashlight!

I rifled through the courier bag, but it wasn't there. I must've dropped it as I ran. I glanced outside to where I'd just been standing. The flashlight sat in the dirt, the beam catching the red reflector of Sluggo, creating a menacing, unblinking red eye that cut into the darkness, illuminating the cave walls.

Some detective.

I raised the camera, advanced the film, and snapped. The strobe effect created a display of flickering light and shifting shadows, blinding me with an otherworldly halo.

Advancing the film again with a mechanical grind, I sensed a shadow strafing the rock to my right, barely visible in the red light of Sluggo's reflector. It twitched. I lurched back, banging my head against a limestone outcropping. I squinted and looked closer. A tiny bat dangled from the rock, its leathery wings spread wide, casting a freakish Bella Legosi shadow. It squeaked and took flight. Another one followed, and then another. It quickly became a steady stream, an endless wing-filled screeching thundercloud rising into the night, blocking out what was left of the moon. Sealing me in.

My heart jackhammered.

So much for being a Batman guy.

In horrified fascination, I watched as more bats streamed out of the shadows, wings beating in a deafening rhythm. They moved with fluid grace, almost choreographed, like a demonic ballet. My mind flashed to stories I'd read of vampire bats and the blood they chugged down like so much Gatorade. I jammed my head deeper into the dirt of Skull Cave and waited.

They would devour me, bit by bit.

I didn't want to cry. But I can say it now, thirty years later, I did. It came out as a gasping sob, but I stifled it because whatever was out there was much worse than bats, and I couldn't be discovered. It knew where I was hiding, and I was confident that, in due time, it would approach, loping, staggering through the swirling swarm of bats. With a swift swing, its sharp, three-pronged limb would slice through my soft neck like a Ballpark Frank hotdog.

My entire system shut down, overwhelmed with tension and fear.

I must've fallen asleep.

Because I dreamed.

I dreamed of a beast with antlers, lit by the red glow of my bike's reflector. Emaciated. Decayed. But alive. Each rib protruded through its malnourished but somehow muscular flesh. Its sunken eyes held an insatiable hunger. Tears of rage and blood. Antlers, twisted and sharp, ringed its skull like a sick crown.

I dreamed of the Wendigo.

A young girl's voice read slowly as if reciting an essay for her second-grade class. "According to tradition, this is the cave where the English fur trader, Alexander Henry, hid during the Native American uprising of 1763. He claimed the cave floor was covered with human bones." She gasped. "Human bones? Ew. Yuck!"

Opening my eyes, I recognized the words from the green Michigan Historical Marker plaque placed strategically at the opening of Skull Cave.

Morning sunlight. I was still alive.

With slow, painful movements, I grunted and rolled onto my back to survey my surroundings. No skulls, bones, or bats in sight. Sitting up, I brushed dirt clumps from my hair, wincing at the electric currents of pain shooting through my own skull and down my neck. Layers of gray dirt coated my T-shirt and cargo shorts.

I pulled myself out of the cave, my backside sliding through the gravel, and emerged into the blinding sunlight, squinting like a newborn. A family of four sauntered around the green plaque, looking clean and civilized. The young girl's eyes widened when she noticed me—a prone figure encased in a second skin of grime, pulling itself through the dirt like an ancient sea crab.

Her gasp transformed into an ear-piercing shriek.

"Daddy! Look!" she exclaimed, her voice tinged with terror. "It's Alexander Henry from the sign! He's alive!"

"Oh, for God's sake, Tara," her bored dad responded as he snapped an artsy, low-angle photo of a random pine tree. "That's just a story. Probably made up for tourists to sell more ..." He trailed off, following her gaze toward the cave. I struggled to my feet.

"Oh, dear God, you're right! *Everybody run!*" he shouted.

In a synchronized frenzy, the family erupted into a chorus of screams, stumbling over one another as they rushed toward their rental bikes.

"Go! Go!" the dad bellowed.

"Don't look back!" cried the mom.

And just like that, they vanished, fading into the distance, leaving only the rhythmic tapping of an early-rising woodpecker and the whining of distant seagulls. Readjusting my courier bag, I retrieved my now-dead flashlight and shambled toward Sluggo. My head hurt. I'd missed my paper route. I'd been traumatized to tears, likely by an oversized wolverine with insomnia. It was time to head home and find out whether Mom had discovered her sleeping, chivalrous son's head was an old basketball.

Despite everything, I smiled as I passed the green Michigan Historical Marker.

Alexander Henry ain't got nothin' on me.

CHAPTER EIGHT

On the Set

FIELD NOTE:

Surveying AM on the movie set for suspicious inter-actions with Superman. BJ (Big Jack) downstate for 16 days and 7 hours. AM is now fully moved into guest room. No break in the MKC (Marjorie Kitmore case). Skull Cave recon mission a complete failure.

I t was 8 am. I sat on the Haunted Theater's red-carpeted steps, casually observing the *Somewhere in Time* crew as they set up a scene for the camera in front of the Shepler ferry boat docks.

Okay, that's not entirely accurate.

I wasn't sitting. And I wasn't casual.

I was peeking around the corner, scanning the set with a pair of Big Jack's Bushnell binoculars. Only my head was visible in a Detroit Tigers baseball cap pulled low. Blaze lingered behind me, taking a deep drag on his second lung dart of the morning, listening to me mutter.

"They rolled in here with their semi-trucks full of equipment and just drove down the street this morning like they own the place! They brought *cars and trucks* onto Mackinac Island! I mean, that's against the law!" I said.

Blaze seemed amused by my self-righteous indignation. "That's showbiz, baby. They do what they want. You know, you sound like a grumpy old man." He broke into an impressive old man's voice, wagging his long, skinny finger at nobody in particular. "Get offa my lawn, you rotten kids and take them damn cameras and lights with ya!"

I adjusted the viewfinder, zooming in tighter. Lights rolled into place, illuminating a horse-drawn carriage. Panning left, I spotted two yellow director's chairs with the names Christopher Reeve and Jane Seymour printed on the back. I panned right and spotted her. Mom chatted with Cynthia near a rack of Victorian-era costumes. Her fingers moved, emphasizing words, while Cynthia listened intently.

Thick as thieves.

The Very Important Brit, decked out in his standard khaki vest, barked out orders on a megaphone. "Last looks, everyone! This next one is for a picture!"

Mom retrieved a brown wool blazer from a rolling clothes rack, meticulously dusting off any lingering lint. My eyes followed her movements through the binoculars. Momentarily hidden by the carriage, she reappeared, assisting Christopher Reeve into the blazer. With an actor's practiced ease, he slipped one arm in, then the other, obediently turning to face her. He stood ramrod straight as Mom reached up to adjust his lapels and tweak the knot of his bow tie.

My own knot formed. I had witnessed this ritual countless times between Mom and Big Jack before they embarked on their evenings out. Mom adjusting Big Jack's tie. Reeve shared a private joke, and Mom chuckled, absentmindedly tucking a strand of blondish hair behind her ear. She effortlessly smoothed the back of his jacket.

The binoculars now felt slippery in my clammy hands.

Reeve settled into the carriage, and soon after, Seymour leaped up, signaling the arrival of the camera. I panned away. My viewfinder randomly landed on Jill, standing near an immense snack table. She weighed her culinary options, wearing a Dodgers baseball cap, white-and-red-striped leggings, and a T-shirt with a logo reading XTC in a neon pattern. She grabbed two Oreos from the table, then—almost slyly—a third. I jerked a notebook out of my courier bag.

FIELD NOTE: CJ (California Jill) is on the set. Research XTC. Another cool New Wave Band?

I raised the binoculars and panned back to Mom, who presented two, vintage bowler hat options to the director. With a pointed finger, he indicated his choice, and she handed it to Reeve in the carriage, who slid it on his perfectly-shaped head. I bit my tongue and whipped the binocs back to Jill. She scrutinized one of the Oreos as if it held some enigmatic secret, inspecting it from various angles. Then, with a powerful chomp, she ate the whole thing. Suddenly, as if detecting my presence, she looked up, her gaze locking on me like a homing beacon.

Rather than scurrying off like a normal peeping tom, I froze. Would she recognize me from this distance? In pristine, Bushnell-quality, 6x magnification, she smiled sweetly and waved.

Yep.

"Ah, rats," I said, lowering the binocs quickly. Blaze squinted toward the set. Jill waved and gestured for me to join her.

Blaze broke into a hissing laugh. "Oh my God. I am truly screwed. You gotta be the worst detective I've ever seen in my life!" Shame crept up my neck like a swarm of fire ants. Jill continued to wave me over.

"You're in luck," said Blaze, watching her. "Looks like your girlfriend's got a soft spot for the lurking, creepy type. What are you waiting for? Go chat her up, Norman Bates." I didn't know who Norman Bates was, but coming from Blaze, I assumed it wasn't meant as a compliment. I methodically folded up the Bushnells and placed them in the courier bag at my feet. My earlobes glowed hot, like coals on a barbeque.

He was right.

I was the worst detective ever.

———

I stood beside Jill, observing take three of the scene. Or was it take four? Each appeared indistinguishable from the last. Christopher Reeve and Jane Seymour guided a horse-drawn carriage down the street, while extras in period costumes dutifully followed their scripted paths in the background.

But I was more interested in Jill. She smelled like Hawaiian Tropic on a California beach. It was intoxicating. "You seem unhappy, Jack," she said, her eyes never leaving the scene.

"What do you mean?" I asked, turning to her.

"You're a paperboy on one of the coolest islands ever. I'm not bragging, but I've seen quite a few islands.

Santorini. Maui. Corfu. All on shoots with my dad. I would think you'd be happy. But this is your face." She drew an upside-down half-circle with her index finger. "Worried. Maybe even sad. What's wrong?" Her directness knocked me back a few steps.

"What? No way. I'm great," I sputtered.

What could I say? That every time I glanced toward Mom, cheerfully tweaking some stranger's waistcoat, I felt a vague, deep fear? That I was beginning to detest this magical circus? That I was wondering if I should also detest Jill on principle, if only for her genetic association with this mafia of make-believe?

I pointed at the street. "The pavement isn't accurate. I saw pictures of the island in the olden days, and the streets didn't look like this. Back then, they were just gravel and dirt."

She followed my gaze toward Main Street and shrugged. "No biggie. They'll make it work. My dad said the cameraman is a genius. Besides, it's just a quick shot in the script."

"You read the script?"

"Yup. It's how my dad taught me to read after my mom took off," she said.

"Where did your mom go?" I asked.

She gave a casual, *who knows?* shrug, but a tinge of sadness crossed her face as she turned away. "Anyway, I help my dad in organizing his photos and drawings. We pin them up on a wall back home and make sure everything is labeled. He's great at his job, but a little sloppy with the details," she remarked. "You know how those creative types can be."

I nodded. "Yeah. Totally." I had no idea how creative types could be.

We watched the next few takes in silence. I wondered

what it would be like to have an organized person like Jill helping me with the investigation. I had to accept that despite Blaze's obvious intelligence, he scared the crap out of me on a daily basis. Just that morning, he asked me if I wanted a "Hertz donut." I'd said sure. Who doesn't want a donut? Then he hauled off and punched me in the solar plexus hard enough to induce a coughing fit. *"Hurts, don't it!?"* he yelled, following it with a high-pitched, sinister giggle.

I barely knew Jill, but it was hard to picture her doing something like that.

"So," she said. "When were you planning on explaining why you were spying on me? Pretty freaky. Don't you think?"

"Sorry about that. I didn't mean to … see you. It was an accident."

"You're lucky I don't tell my dad. He once took a karate class with Bruce Lee. He can probably break your clavicle."

"I wasn't spying on you. I was spying on … well … my mom." *My mom?* God, I no longer sounded eleven. I sounded three. Shame crested again like a Pacific wave, but I desperately paddled ahead of it. "That's her over there." I pointed to Mom, who was busy fussing with an extra's bonnet.

"Oh, yeah. I've seen her around," Jill said. She turned, looking at me sharply. "But honestly, Jack. I can't decide which is weirder. Spying on me with binoculars, or spying on your *mom* with binoculars."

"It's her first day on the set. She's in the wardrobe department. She was working in the office, but she just got promoted." I eased comfortably into a white lie. "I told her I'd stop by, but didn't want to distract her. She gets a little …" I trailed off.

"Motherly?"

"Yeah. That's it. *Motherly.*"

"Motherly," Jill echoed. She pulled the brim of her ball cap down a few inches. "That must be nice. *Motherly.*"

"It used to be nice. Now she's always working on the movie. I don't see her all that much."

"Don't worry. This'll end," she said. "It always ends."

The scent of Jill's Hawaiian Tropic, the exchange of family mysteries, and the bustle of a movie set were making it hard to maintain my sanctimonious pose. It felt good standing with Jill, chatting about life. Maybe it was time to ditch all this cold-case madness and settle into the warm embrace of Hollywood. Enjoy the summer. Go with the flow.

"Hey, Jack!" Gordon's voice called from behind me. "Guess who helped me get dressed this morning?" I spun around and saw Smitty and Gordon walking toward me, outfitted in 1912 suits and flat-brimmed straw hats. "Your mom!"

They both froze and struck poses like models in a JC Penney catalog.

"Your mom is the bomb, Jack," Smitty declared. "Wait. Did you hear that? *Mom? Bomb?* I made a rhyme!"

"Everyone loves her!" continued Gordon. "She hooked us up with this killer wardrobe. It even fits."

Smitty snapped his suspenders. "We're in the movie, dude! Extras!"

Gordon nudged Smitty. "We're not extras, man. We're *background talent,*" he said, apparently now an expert on Hollywood lingo. "*Extras* is an outdated term. I learned that in the tent."

Smitty adjusted his hat, giving it the perfect tilt. "By the way, no bowling today. We'll be on set until dark."

"We're supposed to remain *on call*," added Gordon. More lingo.

The Very Important Brit suddenly bellowed through his megaphone. "Everyone, take your position for the wide shot!"

The boys nudged each other. "That's us! See ya, Jack! See ya, Jill!" said Smitty.

"Have fun fetching a pail of water!" called Gordon. They sprinted off, joining a coterie of costumed extras to prepare for the next shot.

And just like that, the Marjorie Kitmore case was back on. The Hollywood cult not only had a grip on my mother, but now they had picked off my two closest friends. It was time to even the playing field. I turned to Jill. "Would you help me with a project?"

"What project?" she asked.

"It's a school paper," I lied. "I'm doing an extra credit project this summer. I could use your organizational skills."

"A school project? Look at you. Mister Smartypants. What's it about?"

"A murr—" I caught myself, realizing I was about to say *murder*, and lingered on *"rrrr,"* desperately trying to think of something logical to replace *murder*. She stared at me, waiting.

"Mermaids! It's a project on mermaids!" I blurted out.

"Wait. You're doing a project on *mermaids?* What kinda freaky school do you go to?"

"Did I say *mermaids?* I meant to say merrr-*chants.* Merchants! You know. People that sell things. My project is about the town's history."

She looked at me as if weighing my story for some hidden meaning. "Then why did you say, *mermaids?*" It was a perfectly legitimate question.

"I have no idea," A nervous chuckle. "It just kinda

came out that way. Merchant. Mermaid." I shrugged with a cockeyed smile as if to say *these things sometimes happen.*

"You're very weird, Jack," she said. "But why not. I need something to do this summer. I can't hang out all day on the set eating Oreos. I'll turn into a blimp."

And just like that, I had a sidekick for my "extra credit school project," also known as the Marjorie Kitmore case.

The lies were starting to stack up.

CHAPTER NINE

Milton's Meltdown

Another meeting in the lair.

What a waste of a night, I thought to myself as I tacked another photograph on Blaze's wall. The result of my excursion to Skull Cave the week before was a major disappointment. Why I even bothered to shell out the cash at Benjamin's Photo Shop to develop the blurry images was probably the biggest mystery of all.

Blaze hovered behind me, shaking his head and snorting in derision every ten seconds. "What are these exactly?"

"The photos I took at Skull Cave."

"I know *that*. Let me rephrase. What are they … *of?*" Blaze leaned in, studying one of the prints. He squinted, then took a few steps back. "Like this one here?" he asked, indicating a particularly esoteric print, a formless mush of light and dark.

"That's the one … I think … I'm … I dunno," I stammered.

"Reminds me of the deepest recesses of my anus after a Mexican dinner. These are horrible. You got nothing."

I didn't have the energy to disagree. When lined up, the photos looked like Rorschach Tests. Formless blobs that yielded nothing of value other than to prove I had no idea how to take quality photographs.

"You gotta get your ass in gear, Peanut. This is my payday, too, and at the rate we're going, we'll *owe* the Kitmore family money just for being so worthless."

I walked away from the wall and plopped down on the couch with a sulky sigh.

Blaze eyed me sourly. "What's your problem, man?" he asked.

"All you do is pick on me! *You* try sleeping in Skull Cave surrounded by bats! "

He responded calmly, like a patient teacher. "Well, I pick on you because ..." he paused, then yelled, "... *YOU'RE USELESS!*"

He towered over me and gestured toward Main Street. "As we speak, your dear old mommy is measuring Christopher Reeve's *inseam*. Do you even know what an *inseam* is?"

"No! And I don't wanna!"

"It's the distance between the bottom of the leg and the crotch." He cupped his own crotch through his jeans to make the point crystal clear. "She probably knows all his … *measurements.* "

I wanted to punch him in the neck, the leering creep, but instead, I sulked even harder.

He pressed on. "Why do you think these creative types come to small towns? To make their movies more *historically accurate?* No way, dude! It's not about quaint Main Street or the sprawling Grand Hotel porch. They can build that in Los Angeles and be home in time to catch *Three's Company*." He raised a finger. "They make movies on locations to meet local hotties. To swim around like big fish in small ponds for a few months. And I've seen your mom. She's a looker, for an older broad."

He walked over to the nightstand and pushed play on his 8-track.

"Lesson time," he said. Deep Purple's *Highway Star* kicked in. He held out his right palm. "In this hand: a car dealer in a charcoal grey suit who spends his days explaining the benefits of catalytic converters to housewives from Ferndale. And in this hand …." He held out his left hand and stared at it in wonder. "*Superman!* Nobody can compete with that."

He hit a few chugging power chords on an air guitar as he spoke. "Listen. When I first heard about your dilemma, I thought you were delusional. I was like, *Cairo?* I only joined your weird little quest out of greed and sheer boredom." He hit another invisible chord with a Pete Townsend windmill move, then began air-drumming near my head with astonishing precision. "But now I get it. Your instincts are spot-on. Mom's getting a taste of Hollywood life. Dad's gone AWOL. Your perfect little familial unit is headed straight for an iceberg! Crash. Sink. Drown."

"I know all that! I came to you, remember? So what do I do?"

He leaned in. Menacing now. "I can tell you what you *don't* do. You don't waste our time snapping dog-crap pictures of Skull Cave twenty years after the murder. You don't stalk random movie brats with daddy's binoculars. And you *don't* sit on your ass whining! We need a *suspect.* Someone the cops missed. So convince me to stay on this crazy train, or I'm out." He stuck a finger in my face. "Impress me. What do we know?"

I sighed, pulled myself to my feet, and walked to our anemic wall of crime. "Fine. Here's what I know: In the summer of 1959, Marjorie Kitmore—the daughter of a rich doctor in Scarsdale, New York—worked as a waitress on the island. She was in some love triangle with an islander, Eddie St. Germain, and a bartender, Lance Rossellini. Rossellini was the son of some rich guy in Grosse Pointe. Lance and Marjorie started dating right after she arrived on the island in May. She liked him, but it wasn't deep. Pretty soon, she started seeing Eddie. He was creative. Interesting. He told her stories about Native American lore, like the Wendigo."

"Okay," Blaze nodded calmly. "Go on."

"Then she … you know …" I trailed off. " … died."

Blaze waited for more. "That's *it?*"

"Um. Yes."

"You just recited what was in the newspapers. The same worthless information any idiot with a second-grade reading comprehension could dig up." He shook his head in disgust. "I really need to rethink this whole relationship."

He turned his back and walked to one of the tinfoil walls and froze, as still as a Buckingham Palace guard. A full minute passed as *Highway Star* continued to grind away. It was very strange. Then he broke out of his stillness and turned towards me.

"I thought it over. I'll stay on the case. But not because of the geyser of obviousness you just spewed all over my lair. I'll stay on the case because you're so desperate. It's borderline funny."

I sighed in relief. "Thank you." I meant it. He was all I had. "So what do we do now?" I asked.

"Dig up a fossil."

"Like, a dinosaur fossil?"

"Yeah. A dinosaur fossil. No, dipshit! Do you know any

old people on this godforsaken rock? Someone who was around when this all went down in '59?"

I returned to the wall. It was a jumbled mess, more like the refrigerator door of a busy suburban family than the work of a qualified detective. But one yellowed scrap of paper caught my eye. I'd sliced it out of an old *Gazette* and stuck it on the wall earlier in the week. It was a tiny advertisement for piano man Milton Baxter from an August 1959 issue.

I plucked it off the wall, scotch tape and all, and scanned it.

Enjoy piano styling, comedy, and a night of vaudeville fun at the Governor's Lounge. Special guest singer Marjorie Kitmore.

I couldn't locate the town of Vaudeville on a map, but I was pretty sure it was south of Alpena and, to the best of my knowledge, was populated mainly with comedians and piano players from the good old days. Regardless, Milton Baxter was from there.

"My Gramps is friends with this piano player, Milton. He's old."

"Good. Now you're investigating. Go talk to him."

I hesitated. "Right now?"

"Yes!" He clapped his hands and pointed toward the door. *"Right now!"*

———

Gramps handed me two Macanudo cigars he'd removed from his blue blazer's inner pocket. The dimly lit pool hall above Horn's Bar was thick with smoke and the sound of pool balls clacking. Gramps was well-known in the joint, and his rough-and-tumble construction worker pals regarded me with mild amusement. An eleven-year-old paperboy scoring stogies in the beer-soaked pool hall was not an everyday sight.

"Come with a couple of good cigars, or the old SOB won't even make eye contact, much less waste time helping you on some school project," Gramps said.

"Thanks, Gramps." I slipped the cigars into my courier bag. "Gotta run!" I hugged him awkwardly and headed toward the door.

Gramps called to me. "Jacky! Remember to ask him about Minneapolis flappers!"

"Ask Milton about flappers," I mumbled as I dug out my notebook from the courier bag and began scribbling.

I walked through the creaking door, out into the light, and exhaled heavily. Now I'd lied to my grandfather. There was no extra credit school project. One of Big Jack's mantras was, "A lie may take care of the present, but it has no future." I tromped down the stairs of the pool hall, feeling guiltier with each step. At least I'd learn something about "Minneapolis flappers."

I liked birds.

"You two married?" asked Milton Baxter. He was approaching eighty but regarded Jill and me with a young man's sparkle. Sharply dressed in a gray, double-breasted suit and a green bow tie, he hit a few ominous notes on a scuffed piano, emulating the *Jaws* theme. *Dum-dum, dum-dum, dum-dum.* I flushed with embarrassment, but Jill just smiled. He winked. Not leeringly, but endearingly. For a "fossil," as Blaze had crudely put it, the old piano man was magnetic.

He puffed on the cigar I had given him, exhaling the smoke slowly as if testing the quality of my gift and finding it acceptable. "So my wife said to me the other day, 'Our new neighbor always kisses his wife when he leaves for work. Why don't you do that?' And I said to her, 'How can I? I don't even know her!'"

He played a ragtime rim shot. "I know. It's a corny bit, but it always gets a laugh."

The late afternoon sun cast a dust-speckled, golden glow over the empty Governor's Lounge, the piano bar of the Island House hotel. In 1979, raunchy rock and roll like *My Sharona* and saccharine disco like *Hot Stuff* dominated FM radio, yet old Milton Baxter managed to pull in a crowd four nights a week and a matinee on Sundays. His gravelly voice, bawdy jokes, and legitimate piano chops were a welcome retro respite from the chaotic Real World just across the Straits.

Milton took a sip from a glass of red wine and set it back on a coaster atop his piano. "Merlot from St. Julian winery in Paw Paw, Michigan. Ever been to Paw Paw, young lady?"

"No," Jill answered. "I'm from Los Angeles. My dad works on the movie."

"Well, well! Guess we got a Hollywood type here. Anyway, Paw Paw makes a decent Merlot, if you're into that flavor. But I'd wait a few years before you take up boozin'."

We didn't have a clue what he was talking about, but we smiled indulgently. I had brought Jill along to help me gather information, but the trip to the lounge had been a bust so far. An entertaining bust, but a bust all the same. Jill was still under the impression that she was helping me with my "extra credit school project" and, thankfully, hadn't asked too many questions.

"Anyway, kids, where were we? Oh yes, you asked about certain historical events here on the island. Mainly

Marjorie Kitmore." He looked at me, suddenly serious. "Remind me how Marjorie Kitmore fits into your ... *school project?*"

I was momentarily thrown. "Well, Mr. Baxter, she—"

"—Milton," he interrupted with a raised hand. "Call me Milton."

"Milton. Yes, sir." I immediately regretted not preparing better for a question I knew was coming. "The project is about Mackinac Island. I'm writing about different kinds of events. And ... because, like, history is good and bad, right?" *Rambling.* "And since we're talking about how ... like, the good things that happened with the businesses and whatnot, like the ... *merchants.*"

My words came out in stilted blasts of verbal diarrhea. Twisted syntax. Barely stitched-together phrases. It was a slog. Still, I had to slip in the word *merchant* just for Jill, who probably wondered why I asked him about a murder. I became acutely aware of the sound of my own stammering as I plowed ahead.

"Yeah, because, like, a murder would be something that would, you know, affect the ... *merchants.*"

A hook! A connection! *Merchants and murder.* Time to wrap it up.

Milton's doubtful gaze lingered, but he nodded slowly, apparently placated by my gibberish stew.

"Okay. Fine. Marjorie was a very creative gal. But she grew up protected. Rich family. She'd probably never left Scarsdale, New York, and here she was, on a little island in northern Michigan. Meeting new people. Living the wild life." His entertainer's smile vanished. "I remember her telling me these vivid stories about the Wendigo, of all things. They got more detailed as her relationship with that local boy bloomed."

The old man shook his head slowly. "And then, one day, they told me she was dead."

"*Wendigo?*" asked Jill. "What's that?"

"Well, if you don't know, I won't be the fella to tell you. I can't have your nightmares on my conscience."

He shook his head and knocked off a quick boogie-woogie riff, then stopped abruptly, as if an idea had just hit him. "That little ditty reminds me of Minneapolis flappers. I had a week of gigs in the Twin Cities in '29, and I could barely walk to the train station after they were through with me. Peeled me and squeezed me like a Florida orange. Jesus. Those were the days." He looked off, deep in some amorous reverie. "Gettin' old ain't kid's stuff."

I didn't care about flappers and had no idea what Florida oranges had to do with anything. I was too busy scribbling down the scant new information on Marjorie. I looked over. Jill produced her own pen and a sleek pocket notebook that made mine look as bulky as the yellow pages.

"Wen … what again?" she asked, clicking her pen and preparing to start jotting.

"Wendigo. But I didn't tell you that. My corrupting days are long past. Now I'm just an old piano man desperate for stogies." He held up his smoldering cigar to prove his point.

"What else did she tell you?" I asked.

"Well, I didn't know her all that well. She sang with me now and again. She loved Billie Holiday and Sara Vaughan. Such a soulful voice for such a young woman. He began to play a haunting version of "Stormy Weather."

"She had fallen hard for an islander, Eddie St. Germaine. He was a garbage dray driver for the State. Hauled trash from downtown to the dump on the back side of the island. He was a tough kid. Not exactly the type she could bring home to meet the parents. Handsome as hell. He looked like a painting of a Chippewa warrior—if that warrior was dressed in green government-issue coveralls stained with old ketchup."

Milton's fingers traced a tune. "Eddie had an unusual talent. He designed jewelry. Carved scrimshaw. A tough guy like that with such a delicate touch was unique. And she fell hard."

"What's scrim–shhh …," I asked.

The music paused as he shifted his focus to me. *"Scrimshaw,"* he said. "It's engraving, usually done on bone or ivory. It takes a special talent to do it well." He mimicked the carving motion with his hands as if sculpting a piece of ivory in the air. "There was an artist from Boston who passed through here one summer and taught Eddie how to carve. Eddie blew all his paychecks on ivory from New England. He could never afford to take her on a proper dinner date, so he engraved this pocket watch to make up for it. Eddie replaced the pewter cover with one he made completely from ivory. Amazing piece. I remember it had some sort of turtle design. It must've taken him weeks to engrave."

Milton shook his head. "She loved it. Never took it off." He slowly rolled his fingers over the keys and grew pensive.

"What else?" I blurted out. It wasn't brilliant, but it got Milton talking again.

"One night, she came in to sing. Maybe a week or so before they found her body up there at Skull Cave. She looked different. Pale and sad. Thin. I told her she didn't have to perform if she wasn't feeling well. I'd been doing the same stale act since the depression and would be just fine. But she insisted. Said she wanted to sing. *Needed to sing* was actually how she put it."

Milton looked at the ceiling, straining to recall the night. "I think she asked me to play "Crazy He Calls Me" by Billie Holiday. I barely knew it, but I muddled through." He began to play the song. "When she opened her mouth, the audience was instantly mesmerized. You could've heard a pin drop. She was *pitch-perfect.* But every time she turned to the side—and I was probably the only one who noticed —the red stage light lit up tears streaming down her face." Milton's expression changed. "Now, I know it's a morbid thing to share with a couple of kids, but it reminded me of blood."

Milton stopped playing and looked up. "After the show, I pleaded with her to tell me what was wrong. But eventually, I just gave up. She headed out into the night, and I packed up and went home. That was the last time I ever saw her." Suddenly, his gnarled hands pounded on the keys, producing a loud, dissonant chord, and Jill and I flinched in unison.

"Jesus, Mary, and Joseph, I failed that poor girl!" he cried. His sob echoed through the lounge, and a tear dropped onto the keys. Jill placed a gentle hand on his back, and after a moment of deep, wheezing breaths, he composed himself.

My question started as an itch and then grew. A sneeze in a library. Unable to stifle. Destined to blow.

"Milton."

"Yes?"

"Did … the *police* ask you about this?"

I knew I had made a grave tactical error as soon as it slipped out. Jill shot me a withering look, shaking her head, and Milton looked up quickly, wet eyes narrowing. His charming aura vanished.

He spoke slowly in a new, hissing voice. "When an old man shares a story that haunts him. When he sheds tears, you show respect. You don't dump a load of salt on his open wound by asking about the *goddamn police!*"

But I couldn't stop. "The police were investigating the murder. Seems like that might've been … I dunno … *useful* … information?"

"What are you implying? That I had something to do with it?"His eyes hardened. "Why don't you tell me again why you're here, boy? Only this time, say it slowly, and tell the truth."

I stammered. "Like I said, I'm doing an extra credit school project."

He hopped up quickly from the piano bench. It crashed to the floor. Jill and I jumped back, shocked at his cat-like speed.

"*An extra credit school project?*" he spat with contempt. "What kind of sick school project has you harassing an old man? Digging up a tragedy that happened twenty years ago?" He advanced slowly toward us, his face now twisted in fury. "You're lucky your grandfather is an old drinking buddy, you little punk, or you'd be seeing stars. And not the Hollywood kind!"

With a forceful jab, he pointed toward the batwing doors. "Now get the hell outta my lounge!"

"But I—"

"—*But* my ass! GO!" he roared.

We both pivoted and bolted through the doors, barreling into the hotel lobby. Milton's thunderous cries followed us.

"Didn't that poor girl suffer enough?!"

CHAPTER TEN

Beauty, Meet Beast

I raced down the front walk of the Island House, trying to catch up with Jill, who was marching away in long steps, head down, arms folded.

"You better start telling me the truth, Buck-o! I don't appreciate being chased out of bars by pissed-off octogenarian piano players on my summer vacation." She stared straight ahead without making eye contact.

"What's an oxygen—arian?" I asked, struggling to keep up.

"Octogenarian. An old person."

"Why not just say *old person*?"

"Why not just answer my question?"

Jill turned and glared but didn't slow her pace. "First, you made that sweet man cry. Then you turned it into some interrogation. Asking about *murder* and *police?* You're lucky he didn't kick you in the nuts!"

"Slow down. I'll explain everything."

She stopped in the street and fixed me with an expectant look.

"Fine. Explain this *extra credit school project* because it's not adding up. I think you lied to me."

Swarms of tourists on bikes passed by.

"Spill it!"

"Right here in the middle of the street?"

She gestured in exasperation. "Anywhere you want!"

"I know a better place. We can talk in private."

The Turtle Wizard Arcade next to the Shepler ferry line dock wasn't exactly private, but it was loud enough to mask our conversation. We strode straight into a cacophony of bells, beeps, boings, and click-clacks and made a beeline for the Elton John *Captain Fantastic* machine—my personal favorite.

Jill slowed to observe a SweeTart-buzzed crowd of kids gathered around a new game called *Space Invaders.* "You don't wanna play that one?"

I glanced over at the crowd, "Pinball's my game." I dropped a quarter in the machine and pushed the fat, red start button. The machine *ding-ding-dinged* to life.

The arrival of the *Somewhere in Time* crew may have been the big story of 1979, but for the under-15 crowd, the bigger story was the arrival of *Space Invaders.* I personally found the cloying computer graphics cheap and boring. No bells. No style. No risk of a tilt from an overzealous hip check. Nothing *real.*

A traditionalist, even at eleven.

Okay, there were other factors.

Mainly sex.

By age eleven, everything I'd learned about the idealized, objectified female form came from the artwork on pinball machines. How they snuck that much smut into games designed for kids was one of life's wondrous mysteries. Breasts. Midriffs. Legs. All illustrated in a sexed-up style intended to fry a kid's brain like a water-damaged transistor. The *Evel Knievel* game featured two naughty sidekicks in Daisy Dukes near the flippers. The *Happy Days* machine had a big-busted woman in a snug plaid shirt tied under her ample cleavage, lustfully sizing up a pool-shooting Fonzie. One day, a *Playboy* pinball machine was rolled into the arcade, complete with a pipe-smoking Hugh Hefner sandwiched between two scantily-clad bunnies. Playboy bunnies! How was this even legal?

Despite the tantalizing distractions surrounding me, I concluded my semi-private confession to Jill. As my fingers worked the flippers, I apologized and admitted that my interest in Milton went beyond an extra-credit school project. I intended to solve a murder that had eluded police for twenty years.

Jill's eyes widened. "Wow. Okay, that's … *wild*," she nodded. "So, what's your plan for the reward money if you actually, you know, crack the case?"

I avoided answering, pretending to focus on the game. Admittedly, I'd omitted a few details, slanting the backstory to make myself sound like a noble crime fighter. How could I explain that my real motive for solving the case was to finance a cruise to Cairo for my screwed-up parents? I mean, things were going so well between us. Why inject family dysfunction into the story?

"Hello?" she called out, waving a hand in front of my face. I snapped back to reality. "Seriously," she asked again. "What will you do with the reward money."

It all came out in a tail-raising blast of horseshit. "Charity. I'm donating all the money to charity."

My latest lie had the intended effect. Jill stepped back, stunned.

"Cool! I wouldn't have pegged you as a do-gooder type. Which charity are you donating to?

I paused, studying her intently for any trace of skepticism, but her blue eyes revealed something new: admiration. I liked it.

"Why? You got an idea?"

"Definitely!" Jill said. "Save the Narwhals Foundation!"

I nodded thoughtfully, feigning contemplation, then solemnly rendered my verdict like a benevolent benefactor.

"Okay. Save the Narwhals it is." *What on earth was a Narwhal?*

"No way! I'm so impressed, Jack. Seriously, the Narwhals need our help. They're one of the rarest species in the world."

"I know. Narwhals are exquisite creatures," I replied, my attention fixated on the blinking bumpers of the pinball machine. I silently pleaded that she wouldn't quiz me on the details of Narwhals and shift the conversation to other topics. As *Captain Fantastic,* the illustrated Elton John peered over his shoulder with a cold stare. He knew what I had just done. *More lies.* The steel ball rolled directly between my haplessly flapping flippers. Four bells counted down, and that was that.

"Aw," said Jill. "Game over." Her eyes scanned the arcade. "Hey, look! It's a Superman game! How perfect for this summer! Let's play it next!"

I looked over. The game's display boasted a chiseled rendering of Christopher Reeve as the Man of Steel effortlessly lifting Lois Lane in his arms, whisking her away to the Fortress of Solitude, likely for some Supermanly hanky panky. Her blue skirt wafted in the breeze, exposing her perfect legs.

My mom owned a blue skirt just like that.

"Look up in the sky!" Jill called out playfully. "It's a bird. It's a plane. It's—"

"—hey." I had to make it stop. "Wanna meet my friend Blaze? He's super weird. His dad's a big-city detective. He's sort of my partner."

"Blaze," she repeated. A faint smile. "Cool name. Okay. Let's meet Blaze."

And with that, we headed out of the Turtle Wizard Arcade, leaving behind Captain Fantastic, Space Invaders, and a steaming pile of horseshit about Saving Narwhals.

"This is seriously weird," Jill whispered as she wandered around Blaze's tinfoil lair, taking in the details, stopping at the wall adorned with pinned and taped-up information on the case.

"Toldja," I said.

Since my last visit, Blaze had added hand-scrawled letters that read *WALL OF DEATH*. Over the previous week, it had gotten complicated, a collage that had outgrown its boundaries like weeds in an unkempt yard. Blaze had also added naked lady pictures—likely ripped from Gent magazine—to the board. Mortified, I quickly ripped them off the wall and crumpled them up.

Jill was unfazed. "Too late," she said, her voice tinged with amusement. "Already saw them. Your friend's a real class act." She sniffed in the odor of old socks and stale cigarette smoke and held her nose for comic effect.

"She-*ew.* Stanks."

Bringing Jill to the Haunted Theater was risky but calculated. Blaze had a talent for thinking outside the box, and his dad was a detective. His hidden lair also provided a base of operations. Jill, on the other hand, was level-headed and organized, despite her funky New Wave outfits. It might just work.

Suddenly, terrified screams echoed through the plywood walls, and Jill looked at me.

"Don't worry," I said, playing the Manly Insider. "You get used to it. Just some scared fudgies."

She nodded and resumed her examination of the wall, leaning down to untack a series of articles with yellow highlighted paragraphs, rearranging them in a neat, diagonal pattern. She took a few steps back to admire her work.

"Way better. My dad worked on *McMillan and Wife* for a while. It's a detective show."

"My family watches it," I said. "Sunday Night Mysteries, along with Columbo and McCloud." My stomach tightened. I remembered Sunday nights in Brighton, all of us bathed in a cathode TV screen glow on the couch, Mom's head nestled in Big Jack's lap. We'd pass around a bowl of buttered popcorn, trading far-fetched theories on the true identity of the killer.

Better days.

"My dad made a wall like this," she continued. "I can't remember the episode, but Rock Hudson's character connected the clues of the murder with different color strings." She nodded. "I'll steal some colored string from the set later, and we can make this look way better."

Blaze barged in through the door, fully attired in a long black cape with a black stocking pulled over his face. His aquiline nose was smushed flat, and he was out of breath. He approached Jill, wagging a finger. "No, no, no! Who gave you permission to approach the Wall of Death?"

She didn't flinch. "Are you aware you've got pantihose on your face?"

Blaze pulled off the stocking with a flourish, his hair springing like a dandelion blooming in time-lapse. He reached into the pocket of his black jeans, removed a pack of Camels, and pulled out a cigarette. The act seemed to calm him.

"Who is this smart-ass female, and what's she doing poking around my lair?"

I took a deep breath. "Blaze, meet Jill. She's ... helping."

"Helping?" He looked at her closely. A slow grin creased his face. "Wait! I know you. You're the pop-tart on the set who Jack was stalking with binoculars last week. Am I right?"

I dropped my head.

Jill was unperturbed. "Total coincidence. I happened to wander into his line of sight. The truth is, he was stalking his mother." My chin dropped even further, grinding into my sternum.

"You ask me, that's even weirder," said Blaze, lighting up his smoke with a skull-engraved zippo.

"That's *exactly* what I said!" said Jill.

Blaze regarded me with a raised red eyebrow. "Can I trust her?"

"Yes!" I immediately recognized I sounded too eager but couldn't stop. "She's smart and organized, and she works on movies, so she knows how to—"

"—Jesus! Save the sales pitch, Romeo. She can stay. But keep this caper strictly need-to-know. No jabbering to those Hollywood types, or you're out." He stopped short. "And this ain't coming out of my share. Got that, Nancy Drew?"

"Don't call me that," she said through gritted teeth.

"Don't flatter yourself." He jerked a thumb in my direction. "I was talking to him."

Jill's hand shot up to stifle a giggle.

"But I do have a name for you. With those stupid, checked shoes? *Hollyweird.*"

The dreaded gathering of beauty and the beast was not the bloodbath I'd expected.

Blaze looked at me, all business. "So whatcha got, Sherlock Homo? Did you dig up fossils per my instructions? Give me an update."

Jill and I obediently planted ourselves on the couch, and Blaze pulled up a rusty folding chair.

I removed a notebook from my courier bag, and we ran down the details of our interview with Milton. Blaze was uncharacteristically silent as he blew elaborate smoke rings and nodded thoughtfully. At one point, he raised a hand and stopped me. "Okay. I think I get the basics. So, what are your gut reactions to this Milton character?"

"Well," I said. I glanced at my notes. "I think he's hiding something. The old guy has a serious temper. He practically chased us out of the bar."

"What do you think, Hollyweird?" asked Blaze.

Jill shook her head. "I think he's just lonely and wants to live his life. Jack set him off with all these questions about Marjorie. Then he brought up the police, and the poor old guy snapped. He does not strike me as the murderous type."

Blaze nodded. "You guys think it was a professional relationship, or was there something more *salacious* at play?"

We stared at him dumbly. *Salacious?*

"You know. Some hanky-panky. Shakin' sheets. Doing the devil's dance." Blaze rubbed his hands together lewdly.

"Gross!" said Jill. "He was sixty. She was twenty."

"Oh, come on! You know how showbiz works. Age doesn't matter to these creative freaks. The younger, the better. So what else do we have on the old guy? Any history of mental illness? Dirty secrets? Police record?" Blaze snapped his fingers and pointed at me. "This ivory pocket watch. Sounds like he remembered it pretty well."

"Yeah," I said. "It was almost like he, I dunno … he—"

"—*Has it?* Fondles it like a rosary before he showers? He probably does. Killers always take a souvenir. And since I doubt he kept her bloody heart in his fridge for twenty years, he probably snatched Eddie's little love token. The stopwatch or whatever you called it."

Jill's face twisted with concern. "Wait. Who said he's the killer?

"Nobody. *Yet.* Table that." Blaze leaned in, his voice dropping to a sinister whisper. "Didn't you also say Marjorie was obsessed with the Wendigo before she was killed? That's some supernatural shit."

Jill's eyes widened. "*The Wendigo.* That word again. What is it?"

Blaze's eyes shined as he hopped out of his chair. "Follow me, children. It's story time."

———

"Cuddly lil' bitch, ain't he?"

My eyes landed on a wax rendering illuminated by gelled red and blue stage lights. It was a seven-foot-tall, skinny but muscle-bound monster with long, spiking antlers, fangs, and a deformed crown. Fake blood dripped down its ravaged chin, and he gripped a severed, bloody frontiersman's head like it was a bowling ball. I walked behind Jill and passed it slowly, taking in the yellow eyes.

Blaze stopped to admire the rotting figure.

"We mothballed this freak at the beginning of the

summer. Some upright citizens felt it was too scary for the youngsters, so the owner relented, which pissed me off royally. The truth is, it's the creepiest thing we got." he sighed. "It ships out next week to a funhouse in North Carolina called Joyland." He looked up at the demon as if it were an old comrade he'd sorely miss.

"What is it," asked Jill.

"The Wendigo. It's an Injun thing," he said to Jill.

"Engine? Like, in a car?" she asked.

"Not engine. *Injun.* Like peace pipes and tee-pees, like *heya - heya - heya - hoya."* He danced around and chanted in a grotesque parody.

"It's 1979, you heathen," snapped Jill. "It's not *Injun.* It's *Native American."*

"Noted, Sugar. But I'm telling a story. We got Franken-stein, Dracula, and the Werewolf. Injuns have the Wendigo. And let me tell you, their psychotic demon is *way* scarier. Cop a squat. I'll tell you all about it."

We looked around. There were no chairs.

Blaze pointed at the dirty floor. We sat down as he pushed play on the 8-track. There was a pause, a tape *thunked,* and a dirge pulsed through the speakers.

"Careful With That Axe, Eugene. Pink Floyd. In case you're wondering. A real melon-twister," said Blaze. He flicked his lighter, fired up another cigarette, and exhaled from his nostrils and mouth. The smoke caught the colored lights and drifted upward.

As it turned out, the burnout taking tickets at the Haunted Theater was also a master storyteller. He had done his homework, and his story was consistent with what Smitty had told us that overcast day before my bowling fiasco. But it was much creepier from this skinny, black-clad, highly intelligent dirtbag.

The short version? A north woods hunter, trapped in a

blizzard, kills and eats his companions and then transforms into a demon with a never-ending hunger for human flesh. The Wendigo can assume different forms and lurks in the forest, always searching for its next victim.

Blaze continued, prowling the storage room like a caged animal. "Unclean and reeking of death, it stalks the north woods, never satisfied." His eyes shone with intensity as he spoke of the Wendigo's insatiable hunger, weakness, and greed.

A creeping sense of dread enveloped me. There was an eerie connection I couldn't ignore, as if the insatiable hunger of the demon mirrored my relentless pursuit to reclaim what I had lost. *Selfish.*

The cash reward was a glimmering beacon of hope I had fixated on as the solution to all my problems. *Greed.*

And there was my ever-expanding comfort with bending the truth, even as recently as an hour ago, with my pledge to Save the Narwhals. *Lies and more lies.*

A piercing scream erupted from the speaker, shattering the dank storage room air around us. I twitched and stole a sideways glance at Jill.

She was perfectly still.

Later, the three of us stared at the Wall of Death, pondering three new notes stuck into the drywall with tacks. MILTON'S MELTDOWN, WAS EDDIE POSSESSED? and FIND THE WATCH.

Blaze broke the silence. "Eliminating suspects is like a good fart. You gotta let 'em rip one by one until you find the silent but deadly culprit."

"Did Daddy Detective teach you that little gem?" asked Jill with a grin.

"He's a pig, not a poet." He plucked the scrap that said MILTON'S MELTDOWN off the wall. "Lean on the piano man. Learn more."

"That might not be so easy," I said. "We pissed him off. I doubt he'll talk to us again."

"*We?* I remember it being *you*," said Jill. "I was the one with a hand on his back while he was crying, remember?"

Blaze rolled his eyes. "We're all very moved, Mother Teresa. But it's time to drink concrete and harden up." He scratched his chin. "Maybe a little field trip to the old guy's bachelor pad. Gather some clues. Hunt for pocket watches."

"Wait a minute," Jill said, raising a cautious finger. "You're seriously suggesting we break into his home?"

"Look who woke up. Of course."

"It's against the law," said Jill.

Blaze threw up his hands. "Know what else is against the law? *MURDER!*"

Murmurs emanated from outside, followed by knocking.

"Excuse me? Hello? Is this place still open?"

Blaze checked his watch. "I gotta roll, Jack and Jill." He grabbed his cape off the floor, pulled it over his shoulders, and fished in his pocket for his pantyhose. "Doodie calls!" He followed with a fart sound. "Get it? Doodie?" And just like that, he was gone.

Jill fixed an unwavering gaze on me. "I know what you're thinking, but let me be clear: If you break into Milton's place, I will never speak to you again. I'm okay with solving old crimes but not committing new ones."

I winced at the resolute tone in her voice.

"Give me your word," she pressed.

My brain was like a front-loading dryer full of old

boots, schemes and lies thumping against each other in an endless spin cycle.

"I promise," I said, hoping to avoid her stare. I turned away, faking a loud cough, and silently mouthed, *"... that I'll think about it."*

Jill nodded, oblivious. "Good. Let's beat it. I've had enough darkness for one day. Maybe even one lifetime."

We weaved through the corridors and emerged into the alley behind the Haunted Theater, our eyes narrowing against the afternoon sunlight like waking moles crawling out of a burrow.

CHAPTER ELEVEN

Where's the Penny?

FIELD NOTE: Subject AM already on set when I left for the paper route at 7:30 am. Six days without home-cooked breakfast. "Let's Get it On," playing in the living room stereo. Investigate the meaning of the song. Execute Operation Excavate Fossil. Recruit S&G as a backup.

"Where are the damn pennies?!"

"What pennies?"

To my right, two men with beards and thick glasses, one large and one skinny, huddled around a rolling cart, hand-labeled as PROPS with tape and a magic marker.

"I had sixteen pennies arranged on this cart! Where are they?"

"Umm. The production assistant—I think his name is Stan?—took them. He thought it was some loose change lying around." He paused, then continued. "Truthfully, so did I."

"*Loose change?* No!" hissed the heavy one. "Those are *picture* pennies! Go find—what's his name again?"

"Stan."

"Stan! Find him!"

"No-can-do, boss. He's off for the rest of the day. He took the noon ferry to the mainland to buy canned chili. Said he doesn't like the kind they sell on the island."

"Chili?" said the heavy one, as if it was the most baffling word in the English language. "*Chili?* We need those pennies! They're for … the penny scene!"

The lobby of the Grand Hotel was an electrified warzone, awash in lights, cables, cameras, and crew. I'd been loitering like a common lookie-loo for ten minutes, trying in vain to catch the attention of Smitty and Gordon and rope them into my latest scheme. They'd been preoccupied, decked out in period costumes, and herded into various positions by a cute, serious young woman in a T-shirt, headset, and clipboard. They listened as she explained the scene, gesturing emphatically. Gordon nodded, while Smitty peppered her with questions.

Mom was across the lobby. She smiled and waved while she measured the hemline of an evening dress, too busy to break away for a hug. I'd survive just fine, thanks. I had pressing action items on my list, and small talk with my mom wasn't one of them.

Still. Would it kill her to swing by and ruffle my hair?

The props duo resumed their anxious exchange.

"So, who's going to inform our director we don't have his polished 1979 pennies? Because it sure isn't me," said the big one. His gaze fixated on the empty space where his cherished coin collection had been, as if staring might somehow summon them back into existence.

"I had them laid out right here! They were labeled, clear as day, as *picture pennies.*" The thin one gave his best beyond-my-pay-grade shrug as his eyes darted, searching for another task to remove him from the ass-chewing he knew was coming.

"Take ten, everyone, while we reset the camera!" announced the Very Important Brit over his megaphone.

The boys finally noticed me and strolled over. I felt instantly grubby with my courier bag and sweat-ringed *Spirit of '76* T-shirt, a little snug in the shoulders, three summers after the bicentennial.

"If it isn't Hansel and his loyal sidekick Gretel," I said. "You two look cute." *Did I sound jealous?*

Smitty gave his hat a spirited tilt. "Thank your mom."

Gordon, in a tweed jacket and a gold watch chain, joined in. "Ana decked us out special for this scene, so we'll make the final cut. Pretty slick, right?"

Ana? I bristled. Big Jack could call her *Ana.* But not my buddies. This whole "production family" vibe made me vaguely ill, and the ever-present knot in my stomach tightened a bit more.

"So what did that woman in the headset say to you?" I asked, only mildly curious. It was a calculated warm-up talk before the recruitment effort started in earnest.

Smitty shrugged. "She kept saying I had to *mime* speaking to Gordon. I was like, 'What? I don't know how to *mime.*'" He pretended to be trapped in a box. "Plus, it doesn't make sense for the character. A *mime* in the background? What kinda weird movie is this?"

"She didn't mean to act like a mime, genius. She just meant you don't talk. You just *pretend* to talk." Gordon said, shaking his head. "Two weeks as background talent, and this guy still doesn't get it."

"Then she shouldn't say 'mime.' Mime's pull on invisible ropes and stuff."

If I didn't introduce *Operation Excavate Fossil* now, we'd be discussing miming techniques at sunset. "Listen up. I got a mission," I said. "You know that piano player? Milton Baxter? My Gramps is planning a surprise eightieth birthday party for him." This part was true. His 80th birthday was next week, and Gramps *was* planning a party for him.

"He needs me to get a few things from his apartment for the surprise. Mostly it's taking pictures and some other stuff."

Like Marjorie's ivory pocket watch from 1959.

Gordon leaned in, eyes flickering with suspicion. "Does the old-timer know about it?"

"Nope," I replied. "And he can't know about it. And neither can anyone else."

Smitty's eyebrows shot up. "So it's a break-in?"

"In a manner of speaking," I said.

"But the break-in is approved? By an actual adult?" asked Smitty. I nodded with as little vigor as humanly possible. It was for the greater good of society, right? I was trying to avenge a murder victim.

—For a trip to Cairo! Oh, the lies. They stacked up like cordwood. Narwhals. School projects. Surprise birthday party missions.

"So when is this little mission?" asked Smitty.

"Tomorrow. Milton's off the island for one night."

Smitty shook his head. "Can't do it. I promised to help Nona remove old bikes from the barn before the city assessor comes over. I need you guys."

"So we do it the next day," I said.

"She's got stomach issues. It's called Irresistible Bowel Syndrome." He looked away for a moment. "Is that what it's called? Irresistible? Anyway, she gets confused when plans change. She's liable to crap herself."

"That's nasty," said Gordon.

"You don't need to tell me it's nasty. It's happened before."

"We have to do Milton's tomorrow," I said.

"Fine, Jack. I'll send Nona to Wildcliffe, and you can clean up after her. I'm tellin' you. It's deadly."

"Flip on it," said Gordon.

"Props department!" A burly camera assistant in a green windbreaker caught our attention as he approached the props cart. He was holding a camera lens in his right hand. "We need to shoot a test with the penny for the next scene. Is it camera-ready?"

The props guys shared a sheepish look.

"Not exactly. No. The penny is not quite camera-ready. It's … well, it's … missing," said the heavy one.

"*Missing?* Please tell me you have backups," said the frowning camera assistant.

"We *had* backups. Fifteen, to be exact." He exhaled. "But they're gone too."

"We think someone spent them," stammered the thin one.

"What? What the hell can you buy on this island for fifteen cents?"

"It's sixteen cents."

"Whatever! Chris and Jane are both in this scene, *and the penny is the entire point!* They're over there in the room waiting. This is a disaster!"

The crew gathered around, murmuring worriedly, some checking their pockets like New York City subway riders approaching the turnstile. The camera assistant left to report the bad news to the Very Important Brit. A multimillion dollar Hollywood production was about to grind to a halt over one cent.

"Heads, we go to Milton's tomorrow. Tails, we go to Nona's," said Smitty. I nodded and flipped the coin I'd just yanked from my pocket into the air, caught it, and slapped it on my left arm. I pulled away my hand, looked down, and smiled.

"Boom! Milton's tomorrow! Nona will have to shit and bear it."

A grumpy Smitty leaned in, checking my work. His eyes slowly widened. "Dude." He pointed at the shining coin on the top of my wrist. "Check the date." I brought the penny to my eyes.

Impossible. Glistening with a radiant copper glow, were four numbers—1979.

Without hesitation, Smitty hopped up on a wooden box and called out to anyone who would listen. "Hey, everybody! My best friend Jack here has a 1979 penny!"

A loud cheer rippled the lobby. Like Charlie Bucket gripping the final golden ticket, I was surrounded. Smitty and Gordon lifted me on their shoulders in a spontaneous moment of pure absurdity. All the energy in the Grand Hotel lobby suddenly focused on a sweaty paperboy with a courier bag, triumphantly holding a single penny aloft. From my elevated vantage point, I caught a glimpse of Mom, her laughter mingling with bewilderment. I reached down and handed the precious penny to the propmaster, who spirited the coin away to be polished to a gleaming copper sheen and get "picture-ready."

Through the crackling megaphone the Very Important Brit spoke, his Very English voice spiked with relief. "I am pleased to announce that we have located a proper 1979 coin!" More cheers.

"Due to the literal penny-pinching of the young chap currently being paraded around the lobby, we will make our shooting day. The Great Movie Gods have smiled on us yet again!"

More crew laughter. Some off-megaphone conversation I couldn't hear, then he was back. "I would also like to add that this young savior happens to be the son of Ana McGuinn, our local assistant seamstress!" An even bigger cheer echoed through the Grand Hotel lobby. "Thank you Ana, for spawning such thrifty progeny!"

For those few minutes, I was a hero. I basked in the adulation as the entire production began chanting my new nickname, including a beaming Jane Seymour and Christopher Reeve. *"One-cent McGuinn … One-cent McGuinn … One-cent McGuinn … "*

I won't lie.

It was fantastic.

Wait! It can't be fantastic! A chilling notion swept through my mind: could this be their insidious indoctrination? My gaze darted across the sea of faces surrounding me, each Hollywood smile radiating a mix of amusement and adoration. Yes! This must be their ploy! They ensnare unsuspecting souls by imbuing them with a false sense of heroism, a delusion of being the Chosen One, or in my case, The Kid With the Penny.

Run!

"One-cent McGuinn … One-cent McGuinn … " The chant began to morph into something else I remembered from the *Ghoul Show*, a Detroit late-night program that showed old horror movies. The film was called *Freaks*. In one scene, circus performers begin chanting, almost like an incantation …

Gooble gobble
Gooble gobble,
We accept her
We accept her.
One of us
One of us!

The lobby was melting into a blur, a symphony of distorted sounds. Each syllable slowed down and twisted, oozing with an unsettling dread.

One-cent McGuinn ...
one of us ...
One-cent McGuinn ...
one of us ...

Wait! *One of us?* Did they really say that? I wasn't sure, but there was no reason to risk it. "Sorry! Gotta go!" I hopped off the guys' shoulders, ducked around light stands and tripped over carts full of gear. Bounding down the steps of the hotel two at a time, I sprinted to Sluggo without looking back.

A narrow escape.

CHAPTER TWELVE

Break-in #1

I sat with the boys at the very end of the Arnold Line dock late in the afternoon, feet hanging over the water. *Operation Excavate Fossil* was on. It was a vulgar code name, but Blaze came up with it, and I didn't protest.

A gentle breeze swept across the dock, causing the paper diagrams to rustle as the guys studied them with furrowed brows. Meanwhile, deckhands rolled a cart loaded with beer kegs toward a waiting dray. I'd meticulously sketched out everything, using red and blue arrows, with timelines down to the minute. The plan was mostly borrowed from the *Blaze Field Manual*, a twenty-five-page binder with a red plastic cover Blaze gave me earlier in the week. He claimed it was all "official detective procedures" swiped from his cop dad's files. The binder contained information on surveillance techniques, fingerprinting, and tailing leads. Despite blacked-out sections ("redactions," Blaze called them), the writing style was oddly familiar and easy to read. I studied it nightly, absorbing every word.

"Yeesh. A lot of detail here for an *approved break-in.*" Gordon looked up from scanning his sheet and fixed me with an odd look.

"I guess," I shrugged. "But I figured we should have all bases covered." I was talking fast, and my voice sounded pinched and nervous. "You can never be too careful."

Smitty turned his sheet sideways, upside-down, and sideways again, straining to comprehend what he was looking at. "You're giving this to us now? We don't even have time to memorize it. Plus, I'm terrible at math."

"It's not math, Smitty. It's a diagram of Milton's place, plus our entrance and exit route."

"Yeah, well, it looks like math." He pointed to some scribbled figures. "These are numbers. Numbers are math."

"Don't worry about memorizing it. You can hold it. Just stand post on the balcony with binoculars."

"Okay. I guess," said Smitty, then began reading from his sheet. "Three taps on the window followed by three more." He looked skyward. "What if I had a code word instead?"

"No," I was getting anxious. "Three taps, pause, three taps. That's the plan."

He raised a hand. "Just hear me out, buddy. I'm thinking. What if I whisper 'road apple fudge,' then pause, then say 'road apple fudge' again? Because tapping on the glass could be anything. A bat. A tree branch. But I bet nobody will say 'road apple fudge.' Twice."

"Fine," I said. Smitty's logic, as usual, was irresistible.

Satisfied with his input, he nodded, folded his sheet, and jammed it in his back pocket.

"Alright then. Let's do us some breakin' and enterin'!"

"We have twenty minutes to get in and get out." I rechecked my Omega stopwatch for the fifteenth time since we had ditched our bikes in the bushes behind the Yacht Club. The fog was so thick it nearly swallowed up the porch of the Waterview Inn and Boarding House, locally known as the "WibHo." The only light came from a flickering street lamp overhead. Armed with plastic flashlights, we made our way around back and up the rear fire escape to Milton's apartment balcony.

"Don't leave home without it," I said as I pulled out the expired American Express credit card I'd swiped from Big Jack's cigar box. I stuck it into the window jamb, and jiggled it like I'd read about in the *Blaze Field Manual*. It didn't budge. I jockeyed the card, trying not to rattle the window and wake the other tenants or the fussy, vigilant owner, Kitty LaFromme. The window sill was painted shut. Sweat flowed down my back and into my ass crack as I struggled. The lighthouse in the distance emitted a long, gloomy tone. I'd heard it a thousand times and never cared, but that night, it sounded like a warning. We could still scrap this scheme. We hadn't done anything illegal.

Yet.

"Or we could just walk in," Smitty said. He turned the knob of Milton's back door and gently pushed it. It swung open. Like a magician, he gestured with his right hand and whispered, "Presto!"

I clicked the stopwatch and steeled my back as we flicked on our flashlights, walked in, and closed the door quietly behind us. Smitty remained on the balcony, keeping watch. Whether I found the evidence I needed or not, there would be no calling this little drop-in anything other than what it was: a break-in.

Our beams strafed the living room, illuminating details. A soft quilt here. Stacks of books on a shelf. A few odd figurines. A rickety wood rack loaded with bottles of red wine. Merlot from Paw Paw? Worn Persian rugs masked dust and scuffed hardwood. Photos and posters on the walls; maybe a hundred, many of Milton posing with various famous ghosts from the past. I recognized a few: Frank Sinatra. Abbott and Costello. Was that John Wayne? The place smelled like stale cigar smoke and Glade air freshener. Small trinkets and statues crowded the end tables. It was overstuffed and made me think of New York City. I'd never been to New York City, but I imagined it populated with semi-retired artists who wore hats and had steamer crates full of memories and were always photographed in grainy black and white film.

"Remind me again why we're here," asked Gordon, with a tinge of impatience.

I felt a slight surge of panic. "It's Milton's 80th birthday party, remember?" I said. "Gramps needs some … stuff. Take some pictures of those celebrity shots over on that wall. Avoid reflections with the flash."

Gordon rolled his eyes but took the Brownie from my outstretched hand. "Sure thing, bossman."

I silently repeated to myself, *the greater good, the greater good, the greater good* like some sort of demented activist.

"And what's your mission again?" he asked.

"I'm looking for newspaper clippings and a few, what's it called—*mementos*—that Gramps wants me to grab."

"Mementos," repeated Gordon. "Right."

I wandered down a hallway as Gordon headed off, passing a row of unevenly-hung black and white photos. I peeked through the open door to Milton's bedroom, where the scent of cigars lingered in the air. It was intense but not altogether unpleasant. Gramps and Big Jack were both cigar smokers, and even though I whined about the stench, it was reassuring.

My flashlight scanned a small table and spotted a chair with a mirror ringed by lightbulbs, just like I'd seen in Miss Piggy's dressing room on *The Muppet Show*. Taped on the mirror were more photographs and mementos. I looked closer for something to connect Milton to the murder.

Nothing.

Of course, there was nothing.

I glanced down at the stopwatch. *Seven minutes.* I broke my gaze, dropped to all fours, and shined the light under the bed. There were three dusty cardboard boxes visible. I reached under and pulled them out, one by one. The first contained moth-eaten sweaters, all neatly folded. The second had cracked dishes; the third was a *National Geographic* magazine collection from the 1950s.

I shoved the boxes back under the bed and looked up, aiming my light towards a rack of neatly hung suits, all gray. A hat rack. A bow tie rack. The notion I would somehow stumble upon a bloodstained scrimshaw necklace was the fever dream of a fool. I hopped to my feet and scanned another room corner, passing an identical rack loaded with more red wine.

A wine rack in the bedroom? Apparently, Milton was a bit of a boozer.

As I approached the far wall, a framed, black-and-white photograph caught my eye. It was an elegant woman from the '30s or '40s, her smile radiant. The photo was a shrine of sorts, adorned with multiple newspaper clippings encased in ornate frames. Intrigued, I leaned in to read.

Corrine Schaffer debuted last night as part of a duo of Baxter and Schaffer. The young woman's singing ability and magnificent comic timing impressed everyone. The pairing of this dynamic team shows significant promise.

And another framed clipping:

Corrine Schaffer, the singing comedienne, was a crowd-pleaser with her songs and impersonations. Her vocal stylings, accompanied by the always entertaining Milton Baxter, were the night's highlight.

Adjusting my flashlight, I aimed it straight at the portrait, and that's when it became clear. It was in the curve of her lips, the twinkle in her eye, the hint of mischief that lurked beneath the surface.

She was a dead ringer for Marjorie Kitmore.

The same almond-shaped eyes, hair styled in a similar, casual, *I don't give a damn* fashion I'd seen in the photo from the *Island Gazette*. The flashlight slipped from my grip, and I staggered backward. I noticed a row of red, half-melted candles surrounding the display.

"What are we doing here, McGuinn?" hissed Gordon, breaking me out of my trance. He'd wandered into the bedroom and seen me staring at the photograph, slack-jawed.

I pointed at the portrait. "She looks just like Marjorie."

Gordon followed my gaze. "Who's Marjorie?"

"It's impossible, but it's her."

"What do you mean it's impossible?" Gordon's voice rose. "I thought we were here for some, whatchamacallit, knick-knacks for some stupid party!" He shined his light directly in my eyes and I squinted. "What aren't you telling us, McGuinn?"

"Give me the camera!" I hissed, lunging toward him. I had to get a shot before time ran out. He pulled it out of my reach.

"Not until you tell us why we're really here!"

I lurched towards him again and careened into the

rack. It toppled, and a loud crash reverberated through the room when it hit the floor. Bottles and broken wine glasses lay scattered in a crimson lake of Merlot that expanded across the hardwood. I staggered back a few steps, my tennis shoes slipping on the wine-soaked floor, and I slammed into a shelf of souvenir shot glasses, which also toppled with a crash. My right sneaker skittered from under me like Bambi on an ice pond, and I fell down hard into the glass shards and wine with a crunch.

"Holy crap!" Gordon whispered, eyes now flashing with genuine fear. Things had lurched out of control.

"Ow! My butt!" I cried, as he jerked me to my feet. A sleepy, grumpy shout echoed from the room below. Lights flashed on outside, followed by a cacophony of barking dogs. Smitty burst into the room moments later, almost yelling. "Road apple fudge! Road apple fudge! Road apple fu—"

"—Shut up! We get it!" I hissed. "Let's bail!"

We burst out the door and thundered down the stairs, our eyes fixed ahead. Broken glass clung to the seat of my black jeans like peanut brittle, but I wouldn't dare slow down. Voices echoed behind us through the thick fog, growing louder by the second.

Thank God for the fog.

Lungs burning, we sprinted the half-mile to our bikes, panting like dogs. No time for idle chit-chat.

"This never happened!" I whispered, mounting my bike.

Gordon pulled his hidden five-speed from behind a bush. He was livid. "Yeah, but it did!"

Smitty, on the other hand, looked exhilarated. To him, it was just another late-night island escapade to add to our list. "I'm out, dudes," said Smitty. "That was fun!"

And just like that, the three of us went our separate

ways, leaving Milton's apartment in wine-soaked shambles.

It would be a week until we saw each other again.

As I rode toward Mission Hill, the orange glow of the street lamps flickered through thick mist, which had swallowed everything in its path, leaving me with nothing but the sound of my panicked breath and the faint clicking of my bike chain. In the distance, a horse carriage full of rowdy drunks echoed laughter and shouts, piercing the night, gradually fading into the distance.

The moan of the lighthouse signal cut through the fog with its high-pitched wail. It lasted ten seconds before tapering off, leaving behind a faint hum as if taking a deep breath before letting out another.

I scaled the creaking back stairs of Wildcliffe. My clothes were ripped and soaked in wine. I stripped down and stuffed them in a garbage bag, making a mental note to drop them in a dumpster before Wildcliffe started to reek like rotting grapes. I washed up, inspected myself for flesh wounds, found nothing worth whining about, and crawled into bed wearing only tighty-whities and socks.

My eyelids instantly drooped. Sails on a windless ocean. My breathing came in hot, rushing gusts. Sleep crested and pulled me under. But I fought.

Wait! Something important. The moan of the lighthouse again. Soothing. Eyes closing.

What did I forget?

I fought sleep, grasping the image of the shrine with the woman's photograph. *She looked just like Marjorie.* But it slipped away like sand through fingers, deconstructing into something else. Maybe Jill? Yes, Jill. She was surfing a giant wave in the distance as I thrashed in the salty ocean, fighting the undertow. Failing to get her attention.

What did I forget?

With a final desperate effort, I struggled to wake up. To swim. But the undertow pulled me even deeper. Jill surfed by. Her board was translucent. Checkered Vans and a Devo T-shirt. She was scowling and flipped me the finger as she passed over. *You're a liar!*

The ocean was red.

What—

Like Merlot from Paw Paw.

—did I forget?

I was drowning. Jill was gone. But the Red Sea parted, and I caught a glimpse of Blue Sky. *Look! Up in the sky. It's a bird. It's a plane.* It's Mom in a revealing, blue skirt, tucked under Superman's bulging left bicep like a bag of oats.

On a pinball machine.

What did—

I forg—

Sleep won.

CHAPTER THIRTEEN

Party at Wildcliffe!

FIELD NOTE: hosting a party for Suspect A. Practice acting normal. Visit to his apartment still undetected. Investigate singing partner. Looks exactly like Marjorie - coincidence? I think not.

The days leading up to Milton's 80th birthday were some of the longest of my life. I lingered near the Wildcliffe phone for the first two days, waiting for the call. Jack McGuinn, the island paperboy, was under arrest. But there was nothing.

Was my heart-pounding paranoia the night after the caper just that: paranoia? My pulse finally settled into its familiar rhythms of an average kid who would likely never spend even one night in "juvie," surrounded by feral punks who'd revel in beating me senseless with bars of soap wrapped in towels. The walls were not closing in. The feeling I had forgotten something at Milton's apartment during our break-in was fading, replaced with the guilty, giddy rush of getting away with it.

Besides, *it was for the greater good of society.* That mantra was like the spackle I'd seen house painters use to cover cracks in the aging island cottages, a way to smooth over and justify bad decisions. I hadn't seen the boys since we split up that night, but Blaze was impressed by my discovery of the shrine in Milton's bedroom, and that felt good.

The more important news was that Big Jack was back on the rock for Milton's party. With very little fanfare—or explanation—he'd reappeared on the last boat the night before.

Mom, Big Jack, Beth, and I stood on the porch, looking toward the harbor at the descending sun as Gordon Light-foot's "Summertime Dream" played on the stereo. Behind us, Gramps mixed a cocktail and set a few bowls of potato salad on a folding table. A large banner behind him read *Happy 80th, Milton.* Big Jack put his arm tentatively around Mom's shoulder. She moved into him and smiled. I shot a hopeful look at Beth, who returned it with a baffled shrug.

My mind drifted to a few summers earlier, the night after the bicentennial celebrations. I was still buzzing with adrenaline from the fireworks display and unable to drift off to sleep. I tiptoed to the kitchen for a cheese sandwich and a glass of cold milk spiked with two scoops of Nestle's Quik from a steel can.

I padded past the living room and slowed. The fire-place cast an orange glow, which bounced off the aged wood walls. Big Jack and Mom were dancing cheek-to-cheek. A bottle of red wine and two glasses sat on a small table. I stopped to watch, fascinated.

Big Jack spotted me. A big-eyed boy in Detroit Lions pajamas. He spun Mom around and nodded in my direction. "Ana, we seem to have a budding spy in our midst." He winked at me. "Your mom has been trying to teach me to dance like Gene Kelly since college, Sport. I'm almost there."

Mom smiled. "Why are you still up, Jacky? Is everything okay?"

"I couldn't sleep, so I was gonna make a snack."

"Hogwash," said Big Jack, dipping Mom awkwardly. "You're here to steal all my moves, then use 'em to impress the cuties in your class. Isn't that right?"

I grimaced. "No way. I'm only in third grade. I don't dance with girls."

Mom laughed. "Neither does your father."

Big Jack staggered backward, hands on his heart, mock wounded. "Oof! My heart ... it's ... *breaking!*"

Mom smacked him playfully on the shoulder.

"Okay, Ana. Let's teach Jack that stupid disco dance you had us all doing at the French Outpost last week. What was it called again?"

"*The Hustle!*" Mom skipped to the stereo. "Yes, let's do that!"

She shuffled through a few 8-track tapes, found what she was looking for, and shoved the tape in the stereo. After a quiet moment, the shimmering rhythms of disco music filled the living room. Mom grabbed my left hand, my dad grabbed my right. For the next hour, they taught me the intricate steps of "The Hustle." I pretended to hate every minute of it, but I didn't.

I loved it.

I snapped out of my reverie and stole glances at my parents.

That morning, Big Jack cooked his signature bacon, even donning Mom's pink apron for theatrical effect. I munched on it at the kitchen table with Beth until the excess grease had my heart pounding like a dulcimer hammer. Mom was on set, but Big Jack quizzed me on all the island happenings, and Gramps told a few dirty jokes. It had almost felt normal.

And now, as Mom and Dad repositioned a few wicker chairs on the porch, there seemed to be a tentative cease-fire in the Great McGuinn Silent Summer Civil War.

"What time are the Hollywood bigshots expected?" asked Gramps.

"I have no idea if they are coming," said Mom, adjusting a lilac-patterned tablecloth. "When I left the set today, they still had three more set-ups. But Chris and Jane said they'd do their best to stop by."

"Hear that, Dad?" Big Jack said, loading up the mini-fridge with Stroh's beer. "Now she calls 'em 'Chris and Jane' like old pals." He smiled a bit too broadly, as if it was the world's wittiest observation. Mom darkened. She shook her head and headed inside without a word.

Eight o'clock and the party was cooking. Business owners, islanders, and cottagers mingled on the porch and front lawn, lured by juicy steaks on the grill and ice-cold brews from the fridge. The sizzle and pop of grease hitting the coals complemented the clinks of forks against plates. The Commodores cranked from the front porch speakers, electrifying the night air with unspoken expectation. *Would movie stars show up?*

I'd almost finished my second Ballpark Frank when I heard a voice behind me.

"Come with us!" Arms grabbed me from both sides, and I dropped my hotdog to the porch floor. Ketchup splattered my shinbone with gruesome, abstract art.

"Leave it." Gordon was on my right, Smitty on my left. They whisked me away to an inconspicuous corner like two Secret Service agents and turned to face me.

"Talk to us," Gordon demanded.

"About what?"

"About what? You know what!" he hissed, jamming his finger into my chest. "What did you get us into? And where are the 'mementos' for Milton's birthday? Wasn't that why we broke in?"

"Yeah," added Smitty indignantly, although I sensed he wasn't quite as keyed up as Gordon. "Explain yourself. You recruited us under false pre ..." He broke out his pissed-off guy act for a moment and scratched his head. "What is it again?"

"Pretext?" Gordon answered. "... I think. Wait. No. It's pre-*tense.*"

"Right," Smitty nodded. "What he said."

"Guys," I whispered, jerking my head toward Mom and Big Jack, who were chatting with Rick the shit-sweeper on the landing. "Not the right time to talk about this. My parents are right over there."

"You lied to us. Just admit it," said Gordon.

"Okay. I did. But it's ... " I couldn't help myself. "It's for the greater good of society."

Gordon looked suitably baffled. "Huh?"

Smitty brightened and motioned behind us. "Check it out! Famous people!"

Gordon and I turned. A carriage had pulled to a stop in front of Wildcliffe. Christopher Reeve hopped nimbly off the rig, dressed in faded blue jeans and a clean white polo, and took in the Wildcliffe front porch scene with a wide smile, like a man returning home. Jane Seymour followed him, effortlessly stunning in khaki shorts and a light blue sweater.

"What the—? What are they doing here?" Gordon asked.

"I guess my mom invited them."

Gordon blinked, then returned to his diatribe. "Listen. I got enough going on at home right now, what with all this custody crap. I don't need to get busted for breaking and entering, especially when I didn't know I was breaking *or* entering!"

"Actually, Gordo, technically, you knew you were entering," said Smitty. "Maybe not *breaking*, but you knew you were *entering*. Because you just, you know … entered."

Gordon shot Smitty a cold stare.

"What? Just sayin','" he shrugged, then took in the movie people unloading from the carriage. "Hey, we should get some autographs. I keep forgetting to bring a pen to the set." *On to the next thing.*

Gordon produced a Bic pen. "Way ahead of ya, turdbreath."

The two of them bounded off, but Gordon glanced over his shoulder and shot me a *this isn't over, pal* scowl.

I looked back to the carriage. Jill and her father hopped out. She wore cutoff jeans, a faded T-shirt printed with *The Clash*, and her signature Vans sneakers. Her father, in his mid-40s, wore a stylish red sweater and had the sun-kissed tan of a Californian.

The Clash, I thought. We didn't get much of The Clash in Michigan. Generally, Michigan radio oscillated wildly between Bob Segar's "Rock and Roll Never Forgets" and Captain and Tanille's "Muskrat Love." To this day, Jill's T-shirts introduced me to more new bands than a lifetime subscription to Rolling Stone magazine ever could.

The party surged a notch as the guests crowded around Reeve and Seymour. My gaze flicked anxiously. How would I steer Jill clear of Gordon and Smitty's path? The last thing I needed was those three comparing notes. And what would Milton say about my disastrous interview? Did Gramps have a clue about my probing into the Marjorie Kitmore case? And how would Big Jack take to Mom's fabulous new work friends? He was gulping Stroh's beer like water and was not much of a drinker. I'd be spinning plates while riding a unicycle on a tight wire. One wrong flinch and it would all come crashing down.

Mom caught my eye and gestured. "Jack! I want you to meet some friends."

I dutifully headed over. Mom smiled, and Big Jack put his hand on my shoulder.

"Jack, this is Christopher Reeve and Jane Seymour!"

Reeve, who was very tall and very good-looking, smiled and gave me a Superman-ly handshake. My right hand vanished into his massive mitt.

"Call me Chris." *As if.*

"Nice to meet you … Chris."

"Your mom is one in a million, Jack," said Reeve with genuine admiration. "She really looks after all us creative gypsies."

—*Gypsies always leave.*

Blaze's voice suddenly blasted through my skull like a flaming Black Sabbath power chord.

—And I love it when she measures my inseam! Do you know what the inseam is? It's the distance from the bottom of the leg to my — STOP!

I shook it off and stammered out a weak response. "Thanks, *Chris*. She's ... you know ... great." *Deep stuff.*

Seymour regarded me with a curious smile. Her finger extended in my direction.

"I feel like I've seen you somewhere before. Have we met?" Her aura radiated outward like the sun in one of those classroom posters of the solar system, dwarfing me like I was Mercury. Once again, I found myself staggering backward.

"Ummm ... I don't think so," I stammered.

She'd melted my brain, and my tongue was warm Silly Putty. Besides, what could I say? *Met?* Not exactly. I'm the clumsy idiot who knocked over the lights during your all-important close-up.

"Give me time. I'll figure it out," she said. "Nice to meet you, Jack."

I nodded and backed away from the group. I heard a voice. "Is it just me, or is this whole party situation totally bizarre?"

I turned around. It was Jill. "What do you mean?" I asked.

"Oh, I don't know," she said with a note of sarcasm. "Maybe that your family is throwing an 80th birthday party for a man you suspect of murdering someone twenty years ago. I think that's totally bizarre. And for the record, I still don't think he did it." She grabbed a chip from a bowl and crunched down on it loudly, scanning the porch.

If she only knew the extent of the bizarreness, her California head would explode like a pumpkin rigged with twenty-five M-80 firecrackers.

"Yeah, well, nobody here knows anything about that. This party was already planned."

"So. What's the latest on Project Narwhal? I haven't heard from you in a week."

"Project Narwhal?"

"That's what I'm calling the investigation," she said.

Wonderful. She named my lie like a cute new pet.

"Nothing new to report," I said. "Just doing some research."

"I see. Don't need my help anymore, I guess," she sniffed.

"No, it's not that. I'm just collating and evaluating some … ummm …" I trailed off.

"*Collating?* Do you even know what that word means?"

"Of course! It's when you, sort of …"

She was right. I had no idea what that word meant.

From across the porch, a familiar voice cut through our conversation. "Twenty-two years I've been living on this island. I guess it'll teach me to leave the door unlocked, old fool that I am."

It was Milton. He stood engrossed in conversation with Gramps, and a knot tightened in my stomach. This was not good. My eyes remained fixed on Jill, but I couldn't help but eavesdrop on their conversation, desperate to catch any fragment of information.

She continued, oblivious. "I guess I'm just surprised you never called after that day at the Haunted Theater with Blaze, because I thought we were—"

"—I'll be right back." I left her standing there, dumbfounded, and made a beeline for Gramps and Milton. The moment I approached, their conversation ceased, and a jolt of nerves surged.

"There's the intrepid reporter," said Milton.

I couldn't read his mood. He wore one of the sharp

gray suits and maroon bow ties I'd noticed in his bedroom during my break-in. It reminded me, as if I needed it, that I was slowly becoming a delinquent. "How's the extra-credit school project coming?"

I eyed him for a tell. Nothing. "It's, you know, getting there," I said, blindly playing along. "Thanks again for the interview."

Milton pulled out a cigar from the inside pocket of his blazer. "My pleasure. Make sure to include that Sinatra story I told you. Makes me look like a shooter. Just clean it up a little." He lit the smoke and took a pull.

There was no Sinatra story.

"And listen, I'm sorry about my little tantrum. Guess you played the wrong piano key. I'm getting a touch grouchy in my old age."

Gramps' brow furrowed. "Wait just a minute. What happened, Jacky?"

Milton waved him off. "Forget it, Gramps. The kid gave me the third degree about the old days. Lemme light that cigar." With a wink in my direction, he leaned forward with his lighter, making it clear that he was just fine keeping the episode confidential.

"I was telling your gramps," said Milton. "Some scoundrel broke into my place when I was in Cheboygan getting my choppers polished. I come back the next day, and my apartment is trashed."

"It's unbelievable," said Gramps. "They take anything?"

"Not a thing. That's the strangest part. Knocked over my wine rack full of St. Julian Merlot. Smashed up at least ten of my favorite bottles. Broke a rack of fancy wine glasses I picked up in Monte Carlo. The apartment still smells like a vineyard after a drought."

"Do they have any … any …" I trailed off. They both looked at me.

I took a deep breath and tried again. "Do they … have any … any …."

"Spit it, boy," said Gramps.

"Suspects?" finished Milton.

"Yes," I said, exhaling. "Suspects."

"Not yet. But Chief Richter mentioned they had a lead."

A lead! My pulse rate shot up.

"Probably some drunk college kid who stumbled in with a girl," said Gramps, his eyes twinkling with delight. "Thought it was his room. Musta had quite a fright when they got a gander at your false teeth floating in a glass of swamp water on the dresser!"

"Not to mention the fresh pack of adult diapers by the sink! Christ, that'll kill the mood *real* quick!"

I wheeled away, leaving them to their old man giggles. Milton called after me in between guffaws. "Stay young, paperboy!"

But the only thing I heard resonated and echoed like the voice in a low-budget movie trailer: *they have a lead … a lead … a lead.*

Plates wobbled. Walls closed in.

CHAPTER FOURTEEN

Cracked Like an Egg

I found myself alone in a dim living room corner, nervously stuffing a third burnt s'more into my mouth, racking my memory. *A lead!* That night had been shrouded in a thick blanket of fog. The drunk passengers in the cab? Highly unlikely. Another guest at the Waterview? No chance. We were in and out in twelve minutes, all dressed in black. Aside from demolishing Milton's apartment, it was a flawless mission. Searching for answers, I shifted my gaze to a framed souvenir map of the island that adorned the wall. My eyes scanned the familiar landmarks—Arch Rock, Sugarloaf, British Landing, Skull Cave.

Skull Cave. Home of the cursed.

I turned away, nearly choking on a saliva-soaked chunk of marshmallow.

Stay calm, Jack. Breathe.

From across the room, I caught a flash of a blue uniform draped on a beefy slab of a back. A glimmer of a silver shield. Unmistakable. Chief of Police Richter. What was *he* doing here?

Was I overreacting again? My dad always invited him to our barbecues. The chief turned toward me as if he could feel my gaze, eyes meeting mine with uncanny precision. Our gazes locked. Slowly, he raised a can of Coke, a silent gesture of acknowledgment. His expression betrayed nothing—no approval or disapproval—just a cop in a cop hat acknowledging the presence of the hosts' son.

Is he toying with me?

In a different corner, Reeve broke into a tune on our scuffed piano. Seymour sat comfortably beside him on the bench. The tune sounded like the opening bars of "Come Sail Away" by Styx. His fingers danced across the keys, and he sang along with a hammy, hilarious voice. Seymour giggled and hit a few high keys with a sloppy flourish. The party crowd gathered around, drawn in by the pair's undeniably radiant—yet approachable—movie star charisma.

Mom moved through the group with a jug of Carlo Rossi Blush, happily refilling drinks.

Reeve called out. "Ana! Play something for us!" Mom waved him off as she poured wine into a cup for Vic Stone, the burly head chef at the Lakeview Hotel.

Beth called across the room. "Yeah, Mom! Play that one you always did with the blindfold on!"

"Blindfold? Now *that* sounds intriguing!" laughed Reeve, as the room cheered and fingers tapped glasses and cans in anticipation. "Get over here. Let's see what you got!"

Sporting a sly grin, Seymour produced a red bandana from her purse, hopped up, and tied it around Mom's eyes. She guided her toward the piano, where she slid onto the bench. Mom wasn't a skilled musician, but she had mastered one song so well that she could play it blind-folded. It was a McGuinn family tradition.

That song was called "To Sir, With Love." Though I never quite grasped its meaning, the word "love" in the title made me believe it had something to do with my parents. Mom took a deep, nervous breath and began to play, her fingers gliding across the keys in a gentle cadence. As the party's chatter quieted, all eyes and ears turned towards her. She sang tentatively at first.

"Those schoolgirl days of telling tales
and biting nails are gone ..."

Her voice grew in strength. The blindfold wrapped around her head added a dose of absurdity, but the performance was magical. It hinted at memories made and the bitter-sweet reality of letting go. I'd seen her perform this parlor trick many times, but this time was different. Mom's singing grew increasingly confident, her fingers moving effortlessly across the keys. I couldn't help but wonder if she was trying to tell us something.

"If you wanted the moon
I would try to make a start
But I would rather you let me give my heart
To sir, with love ..."

As the final notes echoed through the living room, a collective sigh exploded into applause.

Mom pulled the blindfold from her eyes and smiled in

embarrassment and appreciation. Gramps whistled through his fingers, and Cynthia, Mom's boss, hooted like a crazed Lynyrd Skynyrd fan after an encore of "Free Bird."

Reeve stepped forward and tapped a wine glass, and the party crowd hushed. "First off, how great was that?" he laughed, gesturing to the piano. "I've seen some amazing things, but that was near the top of the list."

"And you would know amazing," added Seymour. "After all, you can leap tall buildings in a single bound."

"I also happen to be faster than a speeding bullet," he joked. But seriously, we wanted to thank the McGuinns— Ana and Jack and their lovely family—for inviting us all here tonight. What a beautiful evening." He looked directly at Mom, raising his glass a bit higher. "And to Ana, you've been a welcome, charming, beautiful addition to our film-making family. Your role on the crew may have started as a seamstress, but you've become so much more. Through your enthusiasm and deep love of this island, you have shown us the real beauty that lies beyond the camera lens. And that's the people. Here's to you."

The crowd erupted again, cheering and calling out *hear-hear.* As the din died down, one steady, sustained golf clap continued. I followed the sound. It was Big Jack. He picked up his beer from a table and walked unsteadily toward the piano. The room quieted.

"Well, as Mr. Kent—er, Superman—I mean to say, *Chris*—so aptly pointed out, that was some performance by our own Ana." He stared directly at Mom and blinked away what looked like a tear. "Although I'm not sure if it was the performance or that you just sang our song for total strangers when I haven't been able to get you to play that for me in months." He took another sip of beer. Mom had a frozen smile plastered on her face and daggers shooting from her eyes. There were awkward glances all around.

"In all seriousness. We welcome Hollywood to Wildcliffe. You've made quite an impression on the island, and while our family misses our beloved Ana as she toils away on, what is it, *fitted waistcoats? Bowler hats?*—I admit, it's beyond my limited creative abilities to explain what she actually does." He chuckled without a trace of joy. "But, regardless, we are honored to have you here."

More scattered, uncomfortable applause.

"Now, on to the *actual* point of the evening." It was a pointed dig, impossible to miss. He pivoted away from Mom and the Hollywood crowd gathered around the piano. "I want to introduce our man of the evening, a friend, to us all. A man with immense talent and a heart of twenty-four-carat gold who has made the island more melodic with his music and more comedic with his jokes."

He raised his can of beer. "I speak for Mackinac when I say Happy Birthday, Milton."

A loud cheer cut short the awkward toast. Without hesitation, Milton waltzed to the piano, sat, and kicked into upbeat ragtime. He may have been a suspect in a murder, but the old guy knew how to rescue a party. Big Jack wandered morosely out of the spotlight while Mom conspicuously headed off in the opposite direction.

I squeezed my eyes shut and envisioned an amusement park like Boblo Island or Cedar Point. Mom and Dad occupied opposite cars on a colossal, emotional Ferris wheel. As Mom ascended towards the night sky, surrounded by her fascinating new friends, Big Jack descended towards earth, clad in a gray suit and charcoal tie, selling Oldsmobiles. I secretly yearned for these two beautiful people to share the same car as they once did.

Feigning sudden interest in my Keds, I glanced downward, discreetly wiping away a tear of my own.

I needed to talk to my dad. I started towards him but abruptly halted when I saw him engrossed in a serious conversation with Chief Richter. Big Jack's piercing blue eyes broke away and scanned the room, then landed on me. A sickening wave washed over. I pivoted quickly on my heels and racewalked straight for the porch door without hesitation.

"Jack! Stop!"

I froze. I'd never heard Big Jack yell.

I leaned against the wall in the kitchen with Big Jack and the chief. The door was latched shut from the revelers, and the mood was miles from fun.

"Anything you'd like to tell us about the break-in at Milton Baxter's apartment?" Chief Richter asked.

Was I shaking? "Well. I heard about it. I mean, just tonight. I heard my grandfather talking about it with Mr. Baxter."

"That's it? *You heard about it?*" He shook his large head. "Anything else more useful you might want to add?"

I looked toward my dad. Stoic as a Roman. No lifeline there.

"Nope. I think that pretty much covers it," I said. My lips began to twitch as if an invisible fishing line was yanking them from five different directions. Would they notice? I would not—could not—cry in front of a Wild-cliffe party, so I breathed deeply and fought the urge by seeking out a distraction, focusing on a shelf lined with boxes of cereal: Count Chocula, Boo-Berry, and Franken Berry.

It did the trick, and my mind drifted away from the interrogation. Of course, I'd become a small-time criminal! My parents introduced me to sugary breakfast cereals with cartoon monsters on the boxes before I turned six. It probably made me hyperactive and more prone to bad choices.

Yeah! It was their fault!

This was just one of the many deranged rationalizations flashing through my mind as I focused on keeping my lip convulsions from spreading to the rest of my body.

"So you were nowhere near Milton's place on the night of the break-in?" asked Chief Richter.

"Ummmweeeeellll …" My weak response dissolved into a strange groan without any finish. I gathered my wits and blurted out, "No, sir."

There it was. I was fully committed to my lie. There was no turning back now.

"Interesting," said Chief Richter. "Then I guess maybe your dad was doing a little shopping at Milton's that night."

"Shopping? I don't understand."

That part wasn't a lie. I *didn't* understand.

The chief reached into a small leather case strapped to his leather belt and pulled out a Ziploc bag. He held it close to my face. I squinted to see through the cloudy plastic baggie.

There it was. Dad's old credit card, with his name printed in big, black, embossed letters. The very same credit card I had swiped from his cigar box and used to jimmy the window. The very credit card I had apparently left on the window sill that night when we bolted from Milton's in a panic.

Dumbstruck, I stared at the card like a not-so-bright golden retriever.

"I think we better take this outside," said Chief Richter.

With Big Jack on one side and the chief on the other, I was perp-walked through the living room and out the front door, past Milton, now wearing a paper mache birthday crown, as he played a rousing standard to the delight of the party crowd. Mom, busy chatting with Reeve and Seymour, was oblivious. But to my left, I could feel Jill watching. Me, Dad, and a giant cop.

It didn't take Nancy Drew to figure that one out.

I may have been a subpar detective, but apparently, I was an even worse criminal. I'll skip the details, but they took me to the backyard, cracked me like an egg, and scrambled me like the breakfast special at Jessie's Chuck Wagon. I took the rap, never mentioning my oblivious sidekicks. I told the chief I went to Milton's apartment to follow up on the extra credit school paper, decided to wander in when I found the door open, and accidentally knocked over the wine rack.

A quick look confirmed Chief Richter wasn't buying any of it. But after the requisite amount of whimpering, it was agreed I was a low flight risk. I could come into the police station for an "official interview" the next day. In classic Mackinac Island fashion, Milton's birthday party would continue without interruption.

Big Jack stumbled off to bed. He was exhausted, sad, pissed, and probably a little drunk. He told me he'd share the bad news with Mom the following day, not wanting to ruin her fun. I was left alone, sitting on the picnic table with the crickets, shoulders still hitching with lingering sobs. So many times during my confession, I wanted to scream at Big Jack, *I'm doing this all for you!* But it was all too complicated to explain, and I had dug too deep.

After about twenty minutes, I was able to breathe normally again. Listening to the grownups inside roaring at Milton Baxter's ancient routine, I heard Mom's infectious laugh keeping a comforting rhythm. Little did she know, her husband was passed out, and her chivalrous son had one foot in juvie.

I was frozen, unable to pull myself to my feet to head upstairs. All I wanted was to bury my screaming brain in the pillow. To awaken in the sweet sunlight of a new day to learn it was all just another horrible nightmare, like the *Drowning in Merlot* dream.

Only much, much worse.

"Is it you?"

I flinched. A female voice. British. I looked over my shoulder. In the distance, leaning casually against our dilapidated wooden fence, was Jane Seymour. There was no denying that perfect form and insanely recognizable accent.

She spoke again. "Is it ... *you?*"

This time, a new emphasis.

I looked around. There was nobody else in the backyard but me.

"Umm. Hello Miss Seymour." *Stupid, weak, and obvious!* "I mean. I'm ... we've met; I'm Jack. My parents own the cottage."

Even worse. It made me sound like some little boy with a mommy and a daddy. Far from it. I was into some heavy shit.

"I mean ..."

"Is it you?" This time, she was more emphatic. Almost demanding. What could she mean? And why did she keep asking me the same question?

Then it hit me. She finally remembered me from the day on the set. Well, I may as well cop to it. Hopefully, she'd had enough beer to laugh about it now.

"Yeah. That *was* me. I'm sorry about that. It was dark, and I didn't see the light behind me, and I stumbled back a little and—yeah, sorta knocked down some of the ..." I trailed off. "... lights."

"No—is it you?"

Maybe she'd heard about my terrible night. She saw me led out of Wildcliffe with Johnny Law and wanted to know if I was ... what? *Dangerous?* Maybe she secretly liked bad boys. Working all day with Clark Kent wasn't exactly sexy. Sure, he was handsome and tall and charming. And cool.

But me? I was *wanted*.

I might as well let it rip.

"Yup. It's me. It's a long story, but it involves a murder investigation. See, I'm zeroing in on a suspect and broke into his place to find evidence." No response, so I continued. "Truth is, he's right here at the party."

Nothing. I barreled ahead. "Yeah, I understand. Speechless. But when the truth finally comes out, they'll see I was right and—"

"Is it you?"

She took a few steps toward me. I could now make out her lush, auburn hair in the moonlight. I was still in the shadows, but she knew I was there. Why else would she continue to ask this intriguing and, let's face it, downright sexy question over and over?

"Is it you?"

I elongated myself, desperately trying to appear at least as tall as the shortest Hollywood actor she'd ever worked with. I couldn't believe this was happening. My mind raced with the mathematical implications. If she were twenty-

five, she'd be thirty-one when I was eighteen. The relationship could work if we stayed quiet about it all. Hollywood
was full of similar stories.

She stepped closer to me and passed into a pool of
light from the upstairs window. My heart raced.

"Is it —*ahh!*"

The second she saw me, she let out a piercing shriek
and stumbled back a few steps. Her hand moved to her
heart.

"Good God! I didn't see you there!"

She was wearing a small set of headphones and
holding what looked like a tape recorder in her right hand.
She pulled off the headphones and let them drop around
her neck. "I'm sorry. Were you speaking to me this whole
time?" she asked.

"I … ummm. I mean—"

"I had on headphones. I was rehearsing a new scene
they dropped on me and thought I'd duck out for a minute.
See, I often record my lines on tape." She indicated the
tiny headset. "My agent just sent me this little tape player
from Japan. It's called a *Walkman*. They tell me it's the next
big thing." She inspected it, turning it over. "Handy little
contraption."

She looked up. "You're Jack, right?"

"Yes," I stammered.

She took a seat next to me at the picnic table. "Would
you like some gum?" She pulled out a green pack of
Doublemint from her khaki shorts.

"Sure," I said, tentatively plucking a stick. We both
unwrapped our gum and, in unison, began chewing.

"Do you mind if I keep going?" she asked, gesturing
towards the Walkman.

"No, go ahead."

She slipped on her headphones and resumed repeating

her line in countless styles, embodying every mood, emotion, and intonation from her actor's repertoire. I sat and listened.

After about five minutes, she rose to depart, clicking off the Walkman. "Well, time to head back in. Mr. Baxter said he wrote me a naughty song. I'd quite like to hear it. Enjoy your evening, Jack." She smiled. "Or should I call you Jack-be-not-so Nimble?" She winked. "I told you I'd remember where I'd seen you before. Thanks for the inspiration during the portrait shot. It was just what I needed."

I resisted the temptation to inform her I was also the *Kid with the Penny*. And with that, she headed off, leaving me to the crickets, my delusions, and my gum.

CHAPTER FIFTEEN

The Chief

Chief Richter stared out the small window of his cramped second-floor office overlooking Market Street. Below, a horse-drawn carriage clopped past, harness jangling. The wood office chair creaked as I shifted nervously. "I understand I broke the law, and I know that what I did was really, really—"

"—*wait.*" He held up a finger and cocked his head to one side. "Let this carriage tour pass. I can't hear myself think."

"On your right is the Beaumont Memorial ..."

The tour driver below launched into a spiel about Alexis St. Martin, a fur trader shot through the gut in a barroom brawl in 1822. The soon-to-be-famous Dr. Beaumont, the resident at Fort Mackinac, nursed St. Martin back to health. While he was at it, he discovered that the golf ball-sized hole in St. Martin's abdomen was a perfect portal to observe the digestive system's gooey inner workings.

For the next decade, Beaumont transformed this ordinary fur trader into America's first human medical experiment. Everybody won, it seemed. The bulletproof St. Martin survived and thrived, fathering a gazillion kids along the way. Dr. Beaumont got hospitals named after him. And Mackinac Island tour drivers got another juicy story to tell sightseers as they clopped down Market Street.

The chief and I shared the moment and listened together through the open window as the guide spun the nauseating yarn about digestive fluids and musket wounds that never healed.

Finally, the chief shook his head and spoke to nobody in particular. "I musta heard that story over a thousand times by now, and it's still friggin' gross."

Then he was back to the matter at hand: terrifying me. "You're in a lotta trouble, Mr. McGuinn."

Chief Richter was a big man with a deep voice that reverberated like a soft roll on a kettle drum. Under his hat, he had a fair, freckled face, contrasting with dark, rough stubble. The pleasant scent of aftershave vapored around him, but there was always an undercurrent of unease. A teapot ready to boil.

"*Lotta* trouble," he repeated, in case it hadn't sunk in the first time. "Lucky for you, Milton isn't pressing charges. He believes that ridiculous story you told about some extra credit project for school. You stopped by his apartment to *follow up* and just *wandered in* to see if he was home." He emphasized the key phrases to drive home just how flimsy my story really was. I nodded along, terrified to disturb even a molecule lest it send him into some TV cop rage.

He continued. "He believes, as you told me, you knocked over his wine rack and hightailed it out of there. All just some ... " His hands fluttered in the air like birds to demonstrate just how ridiculous he found the explanation *"... accident."*

Leaning across his desk, his robust frame pressing against a worn typewriter, he jabbed a finger in my direction. "I did you a big favor by keeping quiet about that credit card you used to tinker with Milton's window lock. Your *Innocent Little Jack* tale doesn't hold water. It's clear as day you went there intending to break in. And we both damn well know it."

His voice began to rise. "I don't care how many free burgers I've eaten at Wildcliffe over the last decade or how kind your folks have always been to me. I'm an officer of the law. If you don't come clean with me right now, I'll see that the State of Michigan processes you like an ordinary juvenile delinquent. *On the mainland.*"

The way he said *on the mainland,* almost like he was saying *in Jackson State Prison,* made me shiver. The image of being pummeled by fellow reprobates with soap bars wrapped in towels returned.

"Am I getting through to you?"

"Yes, sir!" I sat perfectly still, eyes wide.

"Good." He slammed the return lever on the typewriter, and the carriage bell dinged. "I need one of those damned electric ones. This thing's stone age." With two sausage-sized index fingers, he pecked out something on a form, opened a manila file folder, and leafed through sheets of paper. I couldn't decide if he was done with me.

"By the way, what is there to steal in Milton Baxter's place?" he asked without looking up. "Expired prune juice? It was the wine, wasn't it? You were going to glink a few bottles of that Paw Paw stuff he drinks. And tell me straight. I'll find out anyway. I'll just be grumpier." He slammed the typewriter carriage back again. "If that's even possible today."

I cleared my throat. "I'm trying to solve a cold case."

His forehead creased, but he still didn't look up from his painfully slow typing. "Cold case?"

"Yes, sir. Marjorie Kitmore. 1959. She was murdered on the island. Her body was found in Skull Cave."

His fingers froze in mid-type. He looked up from the typewriter keys as if it was the first time he'd noticed me sitting there.

"Continue."

I took a breath and spilled it all. The backstory of the reward, my suspicions about Milton, and even my parents' rocky marriage. Leaving out Jill, Blaze, Gordon, and Smitty, I wove together the chaotic tapestry of the summer of 1979. It was the closest to *not lying* I'd been since June. The story took about eight minutes to tell.

When I was done, the chief pushed his chair back a few feet and looked out the window. He removed a tooth-pick from his chest pocket and started working on his back left molar. I listened to wood scraping against enamel and the low hum of a metallic fan sitting atop a filing cabinet. The muskets fired at Fort Mackinac with a *CRACK*, and I nearly fell out of my chair. My flinch must've amused him because I thought I saw a hint of a smile. After inspecting the thrashed toothpick curiously, he tossed it into the government-issue can beside his desk.

His voice assumed a faraway quality, dropping his tough-as-nails pose. "I told Marjorie's mother to drop that reward. That it was over. The police department failed her. We never found the killer, and it was time we all accepted it and moved on."

"You were around back then?"

"Yup. Rookie summer."

I leaned in, trying to appear calm but hanging on to

every word. He continued. "I told the mother no good would come from publicizing that poor girl's death. It would encourage every two-bit treasure hunter in search of money. But she couldn't let it go. Now, that reward story pops up every summer in the *Gazette* like a turd that won't flush. But I never thought it would be the paperboy chasing it."

"Who do you think killed her?" I blurted out. His gaze locked onto mine as if weighing whether to indulge me or throw me in jail.

"You got some sack, kid. I'll give you that. But you don't ask the questions. *I* ask the questions. Clear?"

"Yes, sir. Clear."

The chief shifted his weight and planted his heavy boots on the desk with a resounding thud, displaying soles etched with old gum and chunks of horse manure. He repositioned his hat, tilting it back a nudge.

"Summer of '59. Mostly they had me sweeping floors and keeping an eye on the drunk tank during the midnight to eight shift." He now spoke as if we were two old pals sharing a pint at the pub and catching up on old times.

"I always suspected that fancy prick—err, I mean that fancy *kid*, Lance Rossellini. The rich bartender Marjorie worked with. There was something off about him. Some say he and Marjorie were an item, at least for a little while in the Spring. He was this clean-cut, frat-boy type. He was always grinning with those perfectly white teeth. I thought he was an absolute creep. But the Feds? They had it in for Eddie, the dray driver. Once rumors got around that Marjorie had been hanging out with Eddie in the Village, learning about all that Indian stuff, they assumed something weird was happening. Maybe Eddie got jealous." He hooked his fingers in air quotes. "*Went Wendigo* on Marjorie.

Maybe he was possessed by evil spirits. Ripped her to shreds and stuffed her in Skull Cave."

In the overhead fluorescent light, the chief looked a thousand years old. "Granted, it did look ritualistic. It was just *awful.*"

He leaned forward, looking me straight in the eyes. But I sensed he was focusing on some horrible memory far in the distance, and I just happened to be in the way.

"I remember the night they brought Eddie in for questioning. The FBI sent a couple of ice-cold G-Men in black suits from Detroit, and they just skinned that poor kid raw. The lack of proof almost didn't matter. Eddie never confessed, and they had to let him go. But he was never the same." He shook his head. "He was dead a few years later."

He removed his hat and ran his hand through his short-cropped hair, releasing the scent of Brylcreem in the small office. "Lance split the island a couple of weeks later and never returned. After that, we only heard from his dad's hoity-toity Grosse Pointe attorneys." He paused, lost in thought. "But here's the kicker. They found fibers on Marjorie's body that matched a '54 Oldsmobile Super 88. It made no sense."

"Why?"

"We checked the records, and she hadn't left the island for months. And just in case she had, we searched the mainland. No cars matched. Not in St. Ignace or Mac City. Not Cheboygan. Nowhere in northern Michigan could we find a record of an Olds Super 88."

A moment of silence hung like a shirt on a clothesline after the chief said, "Olds Super 88." He suddenly leaped from his chair as if electrocuted, sending a cascade of files tumbling to the floor. "Jesus! Why am I talking to the world's dumbest detective? Can't even break into an 80-

year-old man's house without getting caught, and the door was unlocked."

"Milton was 79 at the time."

"Shut up." His eyes narrowed. "So ..." He looked over his shoulder as if someone might be listening, his voice dropping to a whisper. "You find anything in there?"

"Find anything?"

"In Milton's place. We never thought to talk to him in '59. It's actually not a bad lead."

"Thank you, sir." I seized on his compliment as an invitation to do a little minor-league bragging. "I found an old clipping in the paper that said Marjorie sang with—"

"Stop bragging!" He walked slowly around his desk and sat on the edge, looking down at me balefully, clearly playing an intense, mental game of *Should I or Shouldn't I* with himself.

"So, did you find anything?"

"Yes. In his room, I found—"

"Shut up! Nevermind! I don't want to know!"

"Sorry, sir. You asked, so—"

"Shut up! I know I asked," he replied, his voice raising a bit. "You got me all worked up!" He took a stabilizing breath, then said, "Fine. Tell me what you found."

"It was weird. Old photographs and newspaper clippings hung on his wall. All arranged like ..." I didn't know the word 'shrine' back then but if I had, I would've used it. "From the 1930s. A woman named Corrine. I guess she was a singer or something."

"An old timer's allowed to have pictures of women on his wall."

I paused, milking the moment, then continued. "But this woman? She looked *exactly* like Marjorie Kitmore. It could be her twin, only thirty years apart. I mean *identical.*"

The chief's eyes ignited, erasing two decades from his

weary face. In an instant, he transformed into a wide-eyed rookie.

I had Chief Richter.

He leaned in. "Did you take pictures?"

My shoulders slumped. "Well …" I launched into a convoluted story about why I hadn't. It was a slow-moving retelling of smashing the wine racks and slipping on Merlot. Keeping Gordon and Smitty out of the story made the telling even trickier, and I soon found myself twisted in logic pretzels. Thankfully, he cut me off with a dismissive wave.

"Nevermind. A simple *no* will do." He considered me and flexed his broad shoulders as if preparing for a boxing match.

"Let's you and me take a little ride to Milton's place."

We stood before Milton's apartment at the WibHo as Chief Richter's bristly knuckles rapped on the old oak front door. He jiggled the doorknob, but it was locked.

He sighed. "Well, at least the old fool finally learned to lock his front door," he mumbled. He thought momentarily, then reached into his utility belt and produced something.

"Look what I found," he deadpanned. "Fancy that."

I looked closer. It was Big Jack's expired credit card in a baggie. He removed it and shoved it in the door jamb. He shot me a sideways glance—*not a word, boy*—before jiggling the card in the lock. He grunted like a bear with a slippery fish, his big fingers fumbling.

"Mind if I give it a shot, sir?" I asked.

He gave me a cold stare and handed me the card. I slid

it into the door jamb. Within 20 seconds, the latch slid open with a soft click. I avoided eye contact with Chief Richter and handed it back.

"Keep it," he said. "It's your dad's."

"Isn't it evidence?"

"Don't be a wiseass."

My gut twisted with an immediate sense of unease. Milton's messy museum from a week earlier had been transformed. Even the air smelled different. More lilac than Glade. Less oppressive, devoid of wine and cigars. Only the piano and the brown-stained throw rugs looked familiar. The messy, bohemian allure of the place was gone. The photos and posters on the wall were pruned and neatly hung. Almost generic. Books and papers scattered like so much debris after a tornado were cleaned up. It was no longer the cluttered lair of an eccentric entertainer but the spartan home of a tidy, boring-ass old man.

Who would never kill anyone.

"Okay." Chief Richter's gruff voice echoed through the apartment as he scanned the room. "Show me the shrine."

I led Chief Richter down the dim hallway, unease settling upon us like a fog. I stood before the bedroom door, my hand shaking as I pushed it open with a creak. We stepped in. My worst fears were confirmed. Organized. Clean. Furniture, tastefully arranged. Understated elegance. A huge wine stain on the hardwood floor was the only evidence of my clumsy panic during the last visit.

"The pictures of the woman," Chief Richter demanded, his skeptical gaze scanning the bare walls. "Where the hell are they?"

Panic set in, and my heart raced. "They were right here!" I stammered, eyes darting around the room in desperation. "Six or seven of them, along with these red candles, lined up on the table. The place was a mess. But now, it's all cleaned up."

Chief Richter's eyes narrowed as he ran his hand along the smooth walls. "No signs of anything ever hanging here," he remarked, his tone heavy with suspicion.

My ears buzzed and my palms grew clammy.

"There are smarter ways to lie," he continued, his voice laced with anger. "Admit it, you broke in here, panicked, and made up the rest."

"I swear, they were right there on that wall!" I protested, my voice quivering with frustration and disbelief.

He stepped closer. "You know what I think? I think you watched too much Columbo and saw what you wanted to see. But you're not a detective. You're just a paperboy with a hyperactive imagination and family issues." He turned away. "I must've been out of my mind coming here." He checked his watch. "Let's go before Milton returns, and I have to arrest myself. Come on!"

We hustled out the door. Glancing over my shoulder, I caught sight of Chief Richter. His face was drained of color. He'd foolishly allowed himself to feel the one emotion he'd packed away twenty years ago with the efficiency of a military man, which I heard he'd once been. It was hope. The hope that he might finally be able to crack the Marjorie Kitmore case all these years later.

I slumped back into the chair in the chief's office. The overhead fluorescent lights shrouded his eyes with a distrusting shadow. Any camaraderie we may have built was replaced by a cold silence. As he started to speak, the radio on his desk crackled, and a garbled voice broke in.

"Chief. The movie people are asking about the landing craft for the Round Island shot. Is it ready?"

He snatched the radio mic from his desk. *"Now?"*

"Yep. Plus, they want to know if we can block off Main Street for some pickup shots on Wednesday."

"What the hell is a *pickup shot?*"

"I dunno. That's what they said. A pickup shot. I guess it's a Hollywood thing."

He looked at me, gesturing to the radio as if to say *you see what I'm dealing with? I don't need any more bullshit this summer.*

"Get out of here."

I got up to leave.

"Stop," he said, raising his finger. "One more thing. You owe the city twenty hours of community service shoveling shit." He waited for a moment, daring me to protest. "I did you a favor. It could be a lot worse." *Some favor,* I thought, but I didn't say a word.

"And I considered doubling it for that useless little field trip we just took to Milton's." He flipped a switch on the radio and fiddled with the dial.

"Report to Rick, the shit-sweeper at 12:30 the day after tomorrow. Grand Hotel Hill." He looked up. "Screw up again, and you won't be sweeping horse crap. You'll be hosing down *human* crap in the lavatory in the Mackinaw County Juvie." He turned his back to me. *"Now* you can leave."

I sat for a moment, unsure if the dismissal was official.

"Go!" he almost yelled.

As I shuffled out of the door of his office, I swore I heard him say, *"And check Kaplan College."* I turned back as the door slammed shut in my face. *Kaplan College?* I knew

Mackinac College was on the island, but it had closed years ago. I'd never heard of Kaplan College.

A small voice told me it was random chatter as Chief Richter returned to his police radio. But another voice—this one whispering in my ear so softly it almost tickled—wasn't so sure.

CHAPTER SIXTEEN

The Pep Talk

I stumbled out of the police station and stopped at the curb, letting my eyes adjust to the harsh light of an island afternoon. The world felt strange, and I couldn't shake the feeling of being watched.

"Watch the bike!" a dockporter warned as he whipped past, his basket piled high with a load of luggage, wavering but strong. A family of four wandered down Market Street in a fudge-induced stupor. Their young daughter stopped and stared at a team of draft horses twitching away flies. Her dad reached for her hand and pulled her close. As she walked off, her eyes trained on the horses until the Market Street crowd absorbed her.

I watched it all unfold with the detached gaze of a recently freed convict.

Okay, so that's a wild exaggeration. Scooping horse crap for twenty hours wasn't exactly hard time. But still, I was learning what we all discover eventually: the world keeps on going, unfazed by our embarrassing failures.

Indifferent. Unfeeling. The world didn't have an ounce of sympathy for me. The world wondered where to grab an affordable club sandwich and a draft beer, preferably someplace with a kiddie menu.

Exhausted, I yanked Sluggo from the rack and strained to raise my leg over the bar.

"Congratulations, McDork," I heard a voice say and looked up. Blaze emerged from the crowd, his spindly talons clutching a six-pack of Mountain Dew. Under his long hair, a grin radiated. I'd never seen him this far away from the Haunted Theater. He wore his usual: black jeans and black Converse, this time accented by a Scorpions concert T-shirt. He stood out among the summer resort-wear crowd like a Klingon at an Opera.

"Congratulations for what?" I asked.

He approached, his eyes flicking toward the police station. "It seems you got yourself into a toilet bowl of human fecal matter with the boys in blue. *Respect.*"

"Fecal matter?" It was a new one.

"Crap. Shit. Poo. So, did the sentence fit the crime?"

"They gave me twenty hours of shoveling … well, fecal matter. So I guess it did."

A snort that sounded like a laugh.

I squinted at him. "Have you ever heard of a place called Kaplan College?"

He doubletaked and gestured to his stringy red hair. "Do I strike you as somebody that would've heard of a place with the word *college* in it? Anyway, I'm grabbing a tuna salad sandwich at Ty's Restaurant. Meet me in thirty at the War Pig Room. I need a recap." He jabbed a finger at me and did his best Ricky Ricardo accent. "You got some esplainin' to do, Lucy. Maybe if you sufficiently entertain me, you'll receive your very own refreshing, sugary beverage." He raised the six-pack of Mountain Dew.

The corruptor.

As often as I'd visited Blaze's lair, which he'd rechristened the War Pig Room after some Black Sabbath song, I still loved it. The tin-foiled walls and the broken, discarded wax figures from the storage room gave the place the dangerous vibe of a low-budget horror film set. It was exciting in that room.

Gross and smelly, but exciting.

"Cop a squat, Agnes. I need details." I plopped down on the permastained couch and inhaled a mixture of French's Mustard and old socks. Blaze remained standing, holding a yellow legal pad and a red Sharpie. We looked at each other for far too long.

"You need an engraved invitation from the Pope? Spill it!"

For the next fifteen minutes, I recounted the twists and turns of the past week, starting with the mortifying credit card screw-up. Next, I delved into the Hollywood party bust, my interrogation with Chief Richter, and our visit to Milton's sanitized apartment. Blaze paced restlessly, occasionally interjecting to seek clarifications he'd jot down in his pad.

Finally, it was over. I looked up to see if he was still paying attention. He leaned against the far wall expectantly.

"And …?"

"And that's all," I said, "My pals are avoiding me. Jill's mad because I promised her I wouldn't break into Milton's.

My parents are worse than ever, especially now that they have a screw-up for a son. Chief Richter thinks I'm either nuts or a liar. And maybe I could deal with it if we were any closer to solving the murder, but we're not. And that's why ..." I trailed off, my breath escaping in a sigh. "... that's why I quit."

Blaze's clipboard clattered to the ground. *"Quit?"* he repeated, almost softly.

"I'm no good at this. It was a stupid idea from the start. I mean, *Cairo?* Like that's gonna make a difference?"

Blaze's jaded facade cracked briefly, revealing a quick glimpse of something I'd never seen: vulnerability. His gaze drifted off as if grappling with mild shock.

"I'm sorry, man," I continued, glumly picking up my courier bag and turning towards the tinfoil-covered door. "But thanks for your help, Blaze. I still think Milton is hiding something. You should run with it. Keep the money yourself."

"Quit!?" he bellowed, clearly recovering from his brief attack of feelings. He pointed at the couch. "Sit!"

I trudged back to the couch and plopped down. He grabbed a Mountain Dew off the scarred coffee table, ferociously yanked the tab off with a metallic scrape, and threw the ring on the floor.

"You see this?" he demanded, gesturing with a jab at the WALL OF DEATH. "What does it look like to you?" he pressed, his tone sharp with impatience.

The wall was a chaotic collage of names, places, newspaper clippings, a fragment of an island map from Orr-Kids Bike Rentals, and Blaze's hand-scrawled, smartass phrases: GOOD TIMES AT SKULL CAVE, UNCLE MILTY DID IT, and my least favorite: SUPERMAN + ANA = NEW BABY BROTHER. Thumbtacks with red and blue yarn connected elements, forming a tangled web that stretched from one end of the wall to the other.

Without Jill's design skills, it was a jumble of ideas, clues, and conjectures.

"A bad kindergarten art project?"

Blaze shot another glance at the wall. His facade dropped a notch, and he chuckled. "That's funny. Kinda does look like that." Then he turned serious. "Get up! Look *closer*."

He must have jotted down some new scraps of information and pinned them to the board while I was talking. RICHTER'S NEWS, connected by a red line of yarn to 1954 OLDS SUPER 88, and then a new line connected to a note that said FIND EDDIE'S LOVE-WATCH. Another new scrap said MILTON'S BODY DOUBLE with a blue string connecting to the picture of Marjorie I had sliced from the newspaper.

"Wait. Did you just add that stuff?" I asked, gesturing to the new information.

"Yeah. I organized it while you were boo-hooing about your week like Baby Huey." Now he grinned. "And buddy, it's pure gold."

My ears began to tingle. I didn't know what he meant by *pure gold*, but I wanted more.

"See? It's all connected. If you never chatted with the fossil—*my* idea for the record, but whatever—you would've never broken into his bachelor pad, right?" He traced his finger along the yarn.

"Yeah, but—"

"Zip it! I'm doing the talking. You'da never gotten busted. You'da missed out on your little heart-to-heart with the chief." Blaze traced another line of yarn. "Then it's no *Olds Super 88*, which might connect us to Eddie's Scrimshaw love watch. You'da never discovered that sweet Uncle Milton swept his pad clean of any creepy clues of a certain Marjorie lookalike."

Suddenly he unleashed a forceful blow to the wall, causing a handful of brass thumbtacks to dislodge and hit the floor with a clatter.

"This is your work! And the chief knows it. Don't you see it?" He said the next part slowly as if speaking to a dense child. *"He's trying to help you."*

I stepped back a few feet, taking it all in. "Why would he—"

"—confide to a certifiable simpleton like you? A fair question," he paused, gazing at the board, pondering an answer.

"Maybe it's because back then, when he had the chance, he blew it. Now, twenty years later, he sees you, this delusional kid. You don't know about gravity, so you think you can fly. He *wants* to be angry at you, but he sees you're making progress. You see things they didn't see. And, even more importantly, you care." He nodded, proud of his theory.

"But he told me to let it go, or he'd toss me in juvie."

"He probably means it. If you screw up again, he'll have to nail you." Blaze shook his head in wonder. "But deep down, he's winkin' at ya. Deep down, he's impressed."

I shifted my attention back to the wall, my eyes narrowing and my head tilting slightly. Something clicked, and it all began to make sense. Big Jack once told me that the definition of success is if you're even a tiny bit better than the day before. He was referring to my croquet ball juggling phase, but it was the same principle. I took in the wall with fresh eyes. It was a chaotic symphony. And every day, it got a tiny bit better.

"So Fart-y Boy. You still quit?"

I shook my head slowly. "Nope."

He smiled. "Good man. Then you get a little Scooby

snack."

He crossed to a shelf and retrieved an 8-track cassette from a battered case. He displayed the plastic tape in his hand for a moment, then jammed it into the slot of his player, the mechanical clunk echoing throughout the room. Then he quickly lit up a smoke.

A few moments of tape hiss filled the air before the music started, distorted yet captivating: "*I ... am ... iron ... man,*" carried by a moan of electric guitars. The drums exploded, pounding like the footsteps of a lurking beast.

It was a revelation.

"You're gonna figure it out, island boy," said Blaze, his eyes closed, statue-still in the darkness, swaying to the hypnotic music like a shaman.

He began to speak softly. "Paperboy. Loverboy. Binocularboy. Outcast. Detective. Loser. Winner. *Vandal.*"

Half his face caught a colored light, and he opened his eyes quickly. "You contain multitudes now!" He pointed toward a collection of worn paperbacks near his stack of albums. "Walt Whitman wrote that. He was a poet. The Ozzy Osbourne of his day."

"Who's Ozzy Osbourne?"

He rolled his eyes, the hypnotic spell damaged but not quite broken. "Jesus, dude. Never mind."

He snatched the last four Mountain Dews off the table, ripped one free for himself, and flung the others my way. I stumbled back, barely managing to corral them with both arms. "Take 'em. You'll need the energy."

He came close and blew a stream of smoke directly in my face. This time, I didn't fan it away, instead letting it sting my wide-open eyes until they watered. A single tear escaped my eye and traced a path down my cheek, landing on the worn rubber toe of my left Ked.

I *was* Iron Man.

CHAPTER SEVENTEEN

Project Longshot

FIELD NOTE: Subject AM is on set for most of the day. Subject BJ has been off the island for 13 days. I am invisible.

For a few weeks in July, nobody knew I existed.

It was disorienting but valuable, allowing me to indulge my newfound enthusiasm for the case. After finishing my route each day, I'd float through Wildcliffe like a ghost, my undercover maneuvering undetected and my notebooks filling with fascinating new observations.

I was sitting at the kitchen table, drinking chocolate milk and rereading a section of the Blaze Field Manual called "The Value of Shoe Prints" when the phone rang. The humming and whirring from the sewing machine above me tapered off, and Mom's footsteps padded across the hardwood floor to the upstairs phone.

I sat perfectly still, straining to hear. It was muffled.

"Why hello, Cindy-doll!"

Cindy-doll?

I snatched my notebook from the table, raced to the downstairs phone, and gingerly lifted the handset. I'd removed the phone receiver with a screwdriver a few days earlier for just such situations. Nobody used it anyway.

An enthusiastic female voice. "Yes, Florida. I think it's Gainesville, where Burt is from, but I'm not sure. I'm still getting the details myself." *Burt? Who's Burt?*

"Interesting," Mom said.

"Yes, it's a good one. It's the sequel to *Smokey and the Bandit*. I just got off the phone with the line producer, and you were the first person I thought of!"

Sequel to *Smokey and the Bandit?* I muffled a scowl by biting on the index finger of my left fist. It was official. Calls had been made. Mom had been approved. The Cult was making its move.

"Listen, you're busy with your family, and I respect that, but you balance things well. It would be a two-month gig, the money is great, and the wardrobe budget is practically unlimited. Plus, you get to dress Burt Reynolds! *Hubba-hubba!* Honey, we'll have a blast!"

"I'm honored even to be considered." It was much worse than I'd imagined. Superman was bad enough, but now the Bandit?

"Listen, girl," Cynthia continued. "You got the stuff. I've never seen a local pick it up this quickly. I'm not blowing smoke. I don't need an answer on this call but think it over, and we can talk more when you're on set."

"Sounds great. Thank you again for the offer. Bye for now!" said Mom. Two clicks and the phone went dead. I stared at the receiver open-mouthed, then quietly placed it back into the cradle and flipped to a clean page in my notebook.

FIELD NOTE: Stakes raised. AM going to Florida to work on Smokey and the Bandit 2. Ask Blaze what "hubba-hubba" means.

I coasted down the long, sloping West Bluff road, hook-shotting newspapers with a Kareem Abdul-Jabbar like grace toward the Victorian homes that lined the bluff like a window display of wedding cakes. On this clear morning, seven miles away, the Mackinac Bridge looked close enough to grab. Despite my bone-deep panic, the sight of the big bridge was comforting. As the final newspaper bounced across the Chenevert's lawn, I adjusted my courier bag and glided past the Grand Hotel porch, where early risers sipped coffee and nibbled expensive pastries.

My mind drifted to Blaze. Who would have thought the chain-smoking metalhead with the astonishing array of insults and sharp knuckles would end up my only ally? He stood by me when everyone else treated me like I was hauling vials of ebola in my courier bag.

I had a new mission. *Project Longshot.* Over the previous week, I'd investigated every island residence that A) didn't have a newspaper subscription and B) had the same owners since 1959. These were the mysterious, sometimes abandoned homes, shacks, and bungalows, forgotten in the shadow of the island's tonier residences, tucked away at the ends of trails nobody knew existed. I had no idea what I was looking for, but at least the project was adequately named.

It was a longshot.

Just one more house remained on my list, which had been graciously provided by Patrice at the *Island Gazette*, my new Number One Fan. My run-in with the law hadn't gone public, and she was still under the delusion I was chasing extra credit for college.

At age eleven.

I rode behind the Grand Hotel golf course and past Fort Mackinac, then swerved left at Garrison Road, where a groggy gaggle of Girl Scouts raised an American flag. A distorted rendition of the *Star Spangled Banner* blasted from speakers mounted on the side of the scout barracks. I picked up momentum until my eyes filled with tears of island wind.

Past Skull Cave, shaking off that horrific night earlier in the summer. So much had happened since then. Seeking refuge in a cave for the night felt almost quaint. I yearned for the days when the only thing to fear was a cannibalistic Wendigo ripping off my shaggy blonde head. Before I'd lost my friends and family. Before I was thrust into the woodchipper of the legal system.

Before I was alone.

A bump jostled Sluggo, sending a few papers flying out of the front basket and onto the road, but I didn't stop to pick them up. Turning right onto Scott's Road, I heard waves crashing on the rocky shore. A cool breeze cut through the trees, and I vibrated like a rising kite in the wind.

———

The battered old cottage was barely visible as towering white pines shrouded it in shadows. Decades of neglect had left the hues of yellow and green faded, dull, and jaundiced.

Duct tape crisscrossed the two upper-floor windows,

creating the impression of a drunken comic book character with Xs for eyes. A tangle of shrubs engulfed the front porch, obscuring the weed-choked front walk like a gang of spiky porcupines defending against intruders. To the right of the porch was a fence, weathered with time, leaning at a precarious angle as if it would topple in the slightest breeze.

I took a few steps, careful not to crunch the dead leaves layered deep across the front lawn. Removing a rolled-up *Gazette* from my courier bag, I eyed the porch. A tentative toss. The paper landed on the steps with a thump. I slid a heftier *Wall Street Journal* from my bag and hurled it. A louder thump this time cut through the stillness. I held my breath and waited.

Feeling bolder, I kicked my left foot up like Mark "The Bird" Fidrych on the mound at Tiger Stadium, sending the next newspaper spiraling hard and fast. It hit the rusty screen door with a loud clang.

Nothing.

I glanced left and right as I crept up the front steps. A few battered wicker chairs, covered in dust, sat neglected. An ashtray with a few butts. Virginia Slims. *Women's cigarettes.* I'd seen Virginia Slims in magazine ads. Sexy tennis moms staring at the camera as if they'd just wrapped up a rigorous set of doubles and lit up a heater to unwind. *You've come a long way, baby.*

But how long had those smokes been there? Impossible to tell.

Peering through the smudged window, I made out the darkened shapes of wooden chairs and tables covered in thick dust and cobwebs. The cushions on the couch had long lost their color and shape, and the fabric was torn and frayed. I could've been looking through the window of Wildcliffe twenty years in the future, if it had been left to rot by the family that was supposed to nurture it. Can a cottage die?

There was nothing here. Time to hop on Sluggo and beat it.

A faint creaking sound caught my attention, and I turned and looked up. A rotting plank of wood dangled by a single hook above the porch steps. I recognized it as the remnants of a front porch sign. Many an island cottage had one hanging from their front porch valance, with names like *Anne Cottage*, *Casa Verano*, and *Brigadoon*.

Wildcliffe had a sign.

I inched closer. The porch floorboards were spongy, and I wondered if they might give way at any minute. I craned my neck, trying to get a better look at the faded letters on the old sign. They were barely legible against the chipped and peeling paint.

Captain's Cottage.

I had heard of Captain Russell. We all had. Long dead, the Captain was one of those island characters around whom legends grow like untended vines. It was said he was a World War I hero. Some said he rode with Teddy Roosevelt in Cuba. Still, others claimed he was a boot-legger who used the remote cottage as his base of operations. Whatever the truth, he was rarely seen, except when he and his aging comrades would ride into town on horse-back and hit the bars, leaving behind wild stories and massive, unpaid bar tabs.

After the Captain's death, his heirs inherited the cottage. Rumors of late-night revelry and scandal circu-lated, but the descendants eventually stopped visiting. The once-vibrant hub of the Captain's existence had crumbled and rotted.

The sign creaked at a higher, weirder pitch.

I stared at the worn-out letters, the words *Captain's*

Cottage etched into the weathered sign. It stirred something, a memory struggling to resurface. It was more than an old, rotting sign. My neck grew stiff from craning upward, and the creaking grew louder, accompanied by other sounds. Echoes. The creak of Milton's door when we first trespassed. The slowing hum of Mom's sewing machine. The squeak of bats at Skull Cave. The resounding slam of my parents' door, shutting me out.

And then, a more recent door slam. Chief Richter's door? Slamming shut in my face. His final words echoed: "Check Kaplan College." The sign swayed and creaked in the wind.

Kaplan College. Kaplan College.

I stared at the swinging sign hard enough to bore holes in it. But what did it mean?

Captain's Cottage.

It struck like lightning, and my jaw went slack.

The chief's parting words were not "Check Kaplan College."

They were *"Check Captain's Cottage."*

———

The gate leading to the unkempt yard groaned when I pushed it open. Giant, oddly shaped cedar trees obscured my line of sight as I moved across the shrouded lawn. The yellow siding of a barn, scarred with chipped paint, peeked through the trees. I was about to break my promise to the chief and cross the threshold, tempting an all-expenses paid trip to juvie, hosing down human feces, and taking gut punches from demonic delinquents.

I slipped through the rotted, half-open door and entered the barn.

A thousand cracks allowed narrow shafts of light to

filter in, transforming the space into a twinkling shadow-land. There was a faint whiff of something familiar, but I couldn't quite place it. Decaying boxes were stacked atop hay bales, and shelves were crowded with neglected summer memorabilia along the far wall. A jumble of wooden tennis rackets with missing strings, a warped ping pong table, a pile of rusted bikes, and a row of cloudy glass jars filled with screws and bolts, all shrouded in a dusty network of cobwebs.

I navigated a path of daylight, stepping cautiously over a large umbrella that emitted a foul odor of rotted polyurethane. Three decrepit horse carriages occupied stalls, and a tarp and more boxes covered something in the fourth stall.

For ten minutes, I rummaged through crates filled with mildewing documents and newspapers from the 1920s and 1930s, chipped porcelain figurines of cats, and a cracked set of Russian nesting dolls.

As I was flipping through old record albums featuring groups with names like *The Graystone Monarchs* and *The Hokum Boys*, I was interrupted by a thumping sound. Was it a trapped animal? I swung my flashlight and caught a reflection from the fourth stall. Metallic. Gleaming. Intrigued, I moved past heaps of junk toward the source of the reflection.

In a dark corner, nearly buried under a pile of rotting boxes, a green tarp covered something that resembled another carriage. The tarp was riddled with holes and taped together in sections. I carefully set down the flash-light, moving boxes off the tarp and placing them on the hay-strewn floor. With a firm yank, I unveiled a dusty expanse of powder blue steel, scarred by a winding river of rust, and a rearview mirror cracked and bent forward. And at that moment, the faint smell that had greeted me when I first entered the barn suddenly made sense.

Gasoline.

It was a car. I continued to yank the tarp off. Across the grille, raised retro metallic letters spelled out OLDSMO-BILE. I rushed to the back of the car, my breath coming in short gasps, my heart pounding. I approached the vehicle's rear; the emblem gleamed like an art deco rocket aimed toward the stars. Next to it, the number *88*. I ran my fingers slowly across it as if it was crafted from diamonds.

An Olds Super 88.

I remembered what the chief had said.

"Here's the kicker. They found fibers on Marjorie's body that matched a '54 Oldsmobile Super 88. It made no sense."

Was I looking at a murder scene?

BAM! An ear-splitting crash behind me and the slob-bering snarl of a dog echoed through the barn. I spun around. A willowy female figure in a flowing dress, her long gray hair cascading down her shoulders, stood in the door-way. She was backlit by the afternoon light and held a taut leash attached to a German Shepherd. The dog was not wearing a flowing dress. If this creature wore clothes, it would've been a biker vest, a studded collar, and an eyepatch.

"What are you doing here!?" she snapped.

The dog crouched low and growled, baring its teeth and tugging hard against the leash.

Multiple options clicked and rearranged like some hyper-speed match of Connect Four. I picked one, slowly extending my right arm across my body and cautiously sliding a tightly-rolled copy of the *Island Gazette* from my bag. I held it in front of me with both hands like a peace offering to the Gods.

I took a deep breath and slowly blew it out. Then I spoke. "Are you interested in a subscription to the *Island Gazette*? I deliver this fine publication to most of the island, including many of your neighbors. Every time I ride by, I have a moment of regret that I'm not leaving one for you."

Silence, as the woman seemed to process my spiel. The hellhound growled, then glanced up at her impatiently, awaiting the GO sign.

I resumed, voice cracking and quivering. "Our readers tell us they couldn't start the morning out right without the *Gazette*. And the paper costs less than fifteen cents a day, including the Sunday special edition." I swallowed hard and continued. "Can I begin delivering for free for one month, and once you've seen all the great features, you can decide if you'd like to sign up for a one, three, or five-year subscription?"

The throaty growl subsided, and the dog began scratching its balls. I held my breath as the woman slowly crouched beside the animal and freed its spiked collar from the chain leash with a metallic click. Rising to her feet, she pointed at me.

"Kill!" she yelled.

Kill? Gee, that's a little extreme, I thought.

The dog went from zero to sixty like a GTO in a street race. All muscle. All speed. I dropped my paper and ran, vaguely recalling another door on the far end of the barn. I dodged the rusty lawn umbrella, hopped over three bags of long-expired oats, and hightailed it toward a small wedge of light. The devil-dog gave chase, teeth snapping like a shark with legs. I knocked over a wagon wheel in its path to slow the advance, heading for the back door, bracing for contact. The termite-ridden door smashed open, and I exploded into the sunlight, stumbling over an ancient croquet mallet hidden by underbrush. I could hear the hound whining inside, enraged.

I sprinted toward Sluggo.

"You won't get away with this!" the woman shouted through a cracked window. "I'll call the police!"

I continued to sell as I ran. "But wait! There's more! You also get a month free if you send in the coupon." I hurdled a bramble. "You'll find daily recipes for planning the family meals, home decor, and other articles written primarily for women!" The dog was out of the barn, snarling as it picked up my scent.

I hopped on Sluggo and pushed off.

"Then there's the section of local news from the Straits area, the editorial page, and classified ads," I shouted back. "The *Gazette* has many outstanding writers!" Out of range and riding away from Captain's Cottage, I heard a disappointed, feral whine.

I was safe.

For the first time in longer than I could remember, I laughed and laughed and laughed.

CHAPTER EIGHTEEN

This is Our Thing

"**A** car! Jesus on a popsicle stick. That is insane." Blaze was practically levitating.

I'd never seen him like this. He moved in so close that if I wasn't holding my breath, I'd cop a nicotine buzz from his Camel-infused exhalations. I was sitting on his ratty couch in the War Pigs Room. It was after closing time at the Haunted Theater, and my courier bag was still around my shoulder.

"Tell me you got pictures."

Oof.

I knew I had forgotten something. Blaze froze and turned slowly to look at me, his face a pinched scowl.

"So, to be clear," he began. "You discovered an Oldsmobile Super 88—the very same make and model that match the fibers found on Marjorie's body—hidden in a barn on Mackinac Island, where cars have been banned for seventy-something years, and it didn't occur to you to—oh, I don't know—*take a photograph?*"

I stammered. "The dog was ... he had fangs and a leather collar, and ... you weren't there, man!"

"Wait, back up." He faced me like an attorney cross-examining a hostile witness. "Now you're changing the story you *just* told me. The first time you told it, I distinctly remember you pulled back the tarp and stood back as it *all* clicked into place. You remember that part?"

Reluctantly, I nodded.

"Then you told me you ran your finger *slowly* across the metal Olds Super 88 emblem. Like it was a diamond."

"Did I say that?"

"Yup. It was a nice detail. I could picture it."

"Fine. I said that." And I thought the chief was tough.

"But in this *new* version, the moment you realized you discovered the most mind-blowing breakthrough of this case, a lady in a sundress holding a chihuahua scared you off."

"It wasn't a chihuahua!"

"Did it occur to you that instead of caressing the car softly like a new girlfriend, a better idea would have been to use your limited time to, oh, I dunno, maybe *take a picture!*" He slammed his fist into the Wall of Death. A cut-out of a naked woman from *Gent* magazine knocked loose and fluttered gently to the floor. "The defective detective strikes again!"

Blaze was now a poet.

"I'll head back up there tonight. There's something inside that car. I can feel it."

Blaze leaned forward, his eyebrows raised. "What makes you say that?"

Now it was my turn. I was on fire, pacing. "Think about it. Chief Richter said they searched for cars in Mac City and St. Ignace and couldn't find anything. But nobody would've expected the car to be hidden on the island.

Marjorie must've been in the car that night, probably wearing Eddie's engraved pocket watch around her neck. Milton said she never took it off. But who was with her?"

A cloud passed across Blaze's eyes. His fingertips tapped his chin.

I stopped. "What's wrong?"

He crouched like a baseball catcher and jammed his cigarette out on a dented Pepsi can on the floor. "I'm not sure going back is such a hot idea." He walked to the Wall of Death and pinned a few hand-scrawled notes into the drywall. One note read: WHO OWNS THE 88?

"What? Why?"

"We're in deep manure now." I stopped short. Did Blaze actually, I don't know, *care* about me? This was a new twist.

He stared at the wall, but his mind was somewhere else. "I don't want to see you get your brains blown out by some crazy shrew in a sundress, or, even worse, torn to shreds by her toy poodle."

"It wasn't a poodle! I told you. It was a German Shepherd."

"Sure it was."

"We can't wait, Blaze. She could move the car or, I don't know, maybe she'll cut it up."

"She strike you as handy with an acetylene torch?"

"What's that?"

"Look it up." He broke away from the wall. "Walk with me. The Phantom's head is falling off. The boss said the tourists are complaining that it's unrealistic." He grabbed his toolbox, and I followed him out the door and down a darkened hallway. "You ask me, *unrealistic* would be an improvement."

He stopped at a fuse box on the wall and pushed up a row of switches with the top of his hand. The place lit up.

He continued down the hall, walking fast. "So. I also learned something today."

A drooping Phantom character, its decaying head slanting sideways as if it had fallen asleep on the job, awaited us at a mock pipe organ. Blaze set down the toolbox, extracted a wrench, and skillfully restored the figure back to a semblance of creepiness. His proficiency with the tool surprised me.

"I swung by the library yesterday after my shift for a bit of light reading," he grunted, torquing on the wrench.

I reflexively burst into laughter. My smile faded when I realized he wasn't joking.

"What's so damn funny about that?" he asked.

"You at the library. I mean, come on ... really? You're kidding, right?"

"Listen, shitbird. I've got an IQ of one sixty-two," he shot back.

"Is that good?"

"Good? It's *great*."

He eyed the bolts on the Phantom's decaying undercarriage and switched to a socket wrench. "Anyhow, I spent a few hours doing some research. You ever hear of the *Wendigo defense?*"

My blank stare answered his question.

"Didn't think so. To some Native American tribes in Michigan and Canada, the Wendigo is real. It's not just some creepy story to scare kids around the campfire. It also happens to be a legal defense. They have records of people claiming to have been possessed by this Wendigo who did all kinds of horrible stuff."

"Like what happened to Marjorie Kitmore?"

"Even worse. I'll spare you the gory details." He reached for a hammer and began clanging the side of the Phantom's head, loosening a frozen bolt. "If this Eddie guy, the one Marjorie was into, was really an expert on Indian lore, maybe he got jealous of Lance and flew into some sort of freaky Wendigo rage. They say it's a lot like possession."

"Or maybe just the FBI thought that."

"*Exactly.* Or maybe the FBI *pretended* to think that to break him down because they didn't have a better idea. Grab me that adjustable."

I handed it to him.

"But it's all just a myth, right?" I asked.

"Maybe. Maybe not." Blaze now worked on straightening the phantom's long waxy fingers. "Ever see *The Exorcist?*"

Instantly I shuttered. I had seen it. The summer before, Gordon, Smitty, and I watched a pirated Betamax copy at Gordon's house. I had nightmares about pea soup for a week.

I shrugged it off. "I saw it. Kinda scary, I guess."

"*Kinda scary, I guess?*" he said in a high, mocking voice. "It's *horrifying*. I bet you had nightmares about pea soup for a week. And guess what? That freakin' flick is based on a *true story*. Demons are real, kid. And it doesn't matter if you're a lapsed Catholic or a jealous Chippewa. Evil shit is out there. And sometimes, just believing it is enough." He gestured to the gnarled Phantom, now reset in a proper position, as if to say, *I give you exhibit A.*

"So, who do you think did it?" I asked him.

"Truthfully? No longer sure. Originally I thought it was that Lance guy. But I got my reasons for thinking that."

"Oh yeah? What are they?"

Blaze fumbled the screwdriver but recovered it quickly. "I dunno. Maybe it's because he was in a fraternity. I hate guys in fraternities." He leaned his body weight into the tool, careful not to strip the corroded screw.

"But then I read about this *Wendigo defense*. Makes me wonder if the ivory-carving garbageman might've gone *coo-coo*, killed her, and stuffed her body inside Skull Cave."

The screw wouldn't budge. "But Uncle Milty's gotta be leading the pack, what with all that hide-the-creepy-shrine routine. Barring some dark horse, that's our big three."

He drenched the bolt with a squirt of 3-in-1 oil from a small tin can, and began working it again. "But now you add your Olds Super 88 into the mix. Shit, dude. We may have a four-way race depending on what's inside that car. A photo finish!"

He had a glint in his eye. "Down to the wire, with the fate of my bank account and your screwed-up parents on the line!"

"Glad you're finding this whole thing so fun," I said.

"It *is* fun. It's a sick, twisted movie, just like life." He dropped the screwdriver into the toolbox, where it landed with a clatter. "And the quicker you get that through your soft little skull, the better. Life ain't a paper route, Gertrude. It's pain, betrayal, and darkness."

He snapped the box shut, picked it up, and strode down the winding hall. I trailed like a confused puppy. Blaze stopped and I bumped into him. He turned and looked down at me.

"I admire your guts. It makes me want to puke out my *own* pea soup to admit it, but it's true. I don't think you should go back up there. But if you do, come straight to me with whatever you find. Forget the chief." He crouched down to my level, as serious as I'd ever seen him. "This is *our* thing, got it?"

"But If I screw up again, he'll send me to juvie."

"*Juvie?*" Blaze's lips twisted into a smirk. "Where do you get this stuff?"

"Him."

"He's just trying to scare you. Cops love control. Trust me. We don't want to get the local bacon involved. If you find anything, we go to the FBI in Detroit."

The image of the chief's huge, angry face loomed. Squeaky leather utility belt. Old Spice. Guns. "Nope. I can't risk it."

"Where are you going to say you got the evidence?" He stood up, waving his arms. "A gift shop? *Bloodstained Trinkets on Main?* Think about it!"

"We're still partners," I said. "Fifty-fifty. If I find anything, I'll make sure they know you helped."

"No! I told you! I'm the invisible man," he said.

Massaging his temples, he mentally vanished for a moment, deep in thought. "Okay, fine. I'll allow this ill-advised deviation from the Master Plan. But listen to me: grab anything you can from the car. Use zip-lock baggies. Then take the long way home. Avoid the main road and take Leslie Trail past Arch Rock. Then head straight to bed. *Nobody can see you.* Got it?"

He stopped at the fuse box and hit the switches. The overhead lights flickered and went out, casting the room into an eerie darkness, the only illumination the pulsing red-and-yellow glow from the mounted stage lights.

He turned to me, gleaming: "*And when he finds you, you'll soon find out. The devil's fire just won't go out. He burns you up from head to toe. The devil's grip just won't let go.*"

We remained silent, the weight of the words heavy.

The devil's fire …

"Is that, like, what's his name? Walt Whitman?" I asked.

"Negative. Judas Priest. *Sin After Sin* album." He turned away and called over his shoulder. "Don't forget to take pictures this time, scrotum-breath."

CHAPTER NINETEEN

Old Luke

The weathered clapboard shack had seen better days, but a picture window with smudge marks at the bottom revealed a lively group sitting around a kitchen table. I took in the night air and knocked on the door, waiting while a dog barked from inside. The door swung open, revealing a woman with jet-black hair and dark eyes. She shooed away the large dog trying to squeeze its head into the opening.

I was there to meet Old Luke.

Old Luke was a permanent fixture on the island. Every day on my route, I'd pass him striding up the Grand Hill towards the Village, his dark skin weathered by time and the sun, and his full head of white hair shining in the light. Despite his arthritic knees, he moved steadily and always had a lollipop lodged in his mouth. According to Smitty, Old Luke was Eddie St. Germain's uncle, but the details of their relationship were unclear. Old Luke had been the island's blacksmith in his prime, but he was retired and winding down like a well-worn clock.

She regarded me curiously. "You lost?"

"No. I'm Jack. The paperboy."

She waited for more.

"Is, uh, Mister Luke around by any chance?"

"Do you mean Old Luke? He's around back, sitting by the fire. What do you want?"

"Nothing, ma'am. I have ..." I hadn't thought this part through and started to stammer. "... some questions for him. Blacksmith questions. I'm thinking about maybe being ... umm ..."

"A blacksmith?"

"Yes!" I wasn't even sure what a blacksmith was.

She didn't look too sold, but her kitchen crew called for her to rejoin the revelry. "Approach him slowly," she warned. "He's not so crazy about strangers."

She stepped out of my line of sight and then reemerged. "Here," she said, handing me a bottle. The label read Old Crow Whiskey. "He's probably low by now." She winked and closed the door as the laughter rose again from inside.

I considered the bottle and then wandered to the side of the house. Shadows of firelight danced against a cluster of tall pines. A man sat on a folding lawn chair before a small bonfire.

Why was I there? Perhaps I was seeking a sign—any sign—some psychic nod that I should continue down the dark island path that would lead back to the Super 88. And who better to provide it than the island's resident enigma?

I approached him slowly. "Excuse me, sir," I said. "Are you Old Luke?"

He turned to me slowly, bones creaking. "I'm Luke.

Old? That's a matter of opinion. That may be true. It may not be. I'm seventy-six. Sound old to you?"

"I guess it's pretty old."

"Then I'm Old Luke." He stopped and shouted toward an open window. "Chrissy! Who's the kid?" The dog resumed barking.

A few moments later, she called back through the window screen.

"Dunno, Luke. Said he wanted to learn something about being a blacksmith or something. Shit, Luke. He's standin' right there. Just ask'm yourself."

I walked a few steps closer, holding the bottle before me. His eyes reflected the flames from the fire. He reached up slowly and took the bottle from me as if he'd been expecting it all along. He looked the bottle over.

"You obviously read my file, boy." He unscrewed the top and took a nip. "This," he said, smacking his lips, "I recognize as a good old-fashioned bribe." He sucked in snot, spat into the fire, and looked me in the eye.

"Is that what you told her? You wanted to talk about blacksmithing?"

I nodded.

"One of the damndest things about getting old is that all sorta people wanna ask you all sorta things. Because you've been on the planet for a certain amount of years, you're supposed to be some kinda expert. I ain't no expert about nothin.' I know how to shank shoes off a horse and put them back on. I also know a thing or two about repairing ferry boat anchors. But you don't strike me as a kid interested in working with metal."

"So sit and tell me why you're here, boy." He pointed at an empty lawn chair near the edge of the fire. I sat down. He cocked an eyebrow and waited.

"I want to learn about the summer of 1959. About Eddie St. Germaine, and what happened with Marjorie Kitmore."

The bottle slipped from his hands and hit the ground upright; some of the whiskey geysered up, but he deftly grabbed the bottle and brushed the dirt off the bottom.

"I'm gonna be real honest, kid. That ain't what I was expectin'. Why in God's name you wanna talk about that?" He adjusted his position, leaning forward. "'Sides ... you gotta give something to get something here at Old Luke's."

I pointed to the bottle. "I gave you that."

He scoffed. "Chrissy keeps my stash next to the front door. Think I don't know that? You just delivered it, like a paperboy. Yeah. You're the paperboy. I saw you around. What else ya got?" His eyes narrowed. "You roll in here interrupting my Tuesday night quiet time askin' questions about the bad old days, and you think you ain't gotta pay?"

I hesitated before reaching into my courier bag and feeling around, then pulled out four Tootsie Pops, one brown, one red, one orange, and one purple. I displayed them for Luke like a magician displaying cards. He smiled, his eyes glittering like emeralds.

"See, now you're gettin' somewhere. You did your homework. Old Crow, that I got plenty of. Tootsie Pops are a scarcity." He leaned over, plucked the orange one out of my hands, carefully peeled off its wrapper, and studied it momentarily. "If you play your cards right, I might let you in on a little secret."

"About what?"

"I just toldja. It's a secret." He popped the sucker in his mouth. "Why you wanna know about the Marjorie Kitmore murder?"

"I want to solve it."

He nodded thoughtfully, seeming to approve of my honesty, if not my sanity.

"Couldn't do much worse than them cops did back then. It always made me sad thinking about that family losing their angel daughter. But I also never liked that someone would get rich on it. Ain't right. But ..." He stretched his arms upward and they popped. "I guess the world ain't right."

"If someone can solve it, wouldn't that be good? There's a word for it. It starts with a 'v'... vim ... vin ...?"

"Vindication? That ferry boat sailed a long time ago. Anyone tell you what happened to my nephew after that summer?"

"I heard some stuff. That he ... you know ... died."

"Yeah. He died." He took a long breath that hitched a few times. Then he continued. "They humiliated that boy. The FBI put him in cuffs and marched him down Main Street to the police office for questioning. They didn't put no handcuffs on that rich college boy, who was just as much a suspect. But 'ol Eddie had to do a damn perp walk in front of the entire town. Saw it with my own two eyes." He slowly rubbed his face. It sounded like sandpaper. "He was born on this island, for chrissakes!"

I didn't dare move.

He snuck a quick suck on the Tootsie Pop. "So Eddie moved to Marquette and started working as a garbageman. Keep in mind, this boy was special. Strong as an ox. But he also had brains. He knew more about Chippewa lore than most of them so-called Ph.Ds working at the fort museum. And was he talented? *My God.* He engraved all kinda stuff. Scrimshaw, metal, you name it. Now, I'm not sayin' he shoulda been carved on Mt. Rushmore. He had his flaws, like all of us. But he weren't meant to be hauling trash. Here or anywhere else."

He cleared his throat and spit. "They found Eddie face-down in a gutter outside a bar called Shady's Alibi Room on Christmas Eve. Twenty below outside. They say he'd been drinking a fifth a day for two months. You can call him just another Indian drunk—and lotta folks did— but I know the real story. The boy had a broken heart. He killed himself. He just didn't use the barrel or the rope.

It was time to ask. "Do you think he killed Marjorie?"

"Hell no." He picked up a small log and pointed it at me. "Truth is, Eddie was with me that night. I was suckin' down PBRs, and he was engraving something special for Marjorie. He was going to give it to her the next day. Hell, I'll just tell ya. It was a wedding ring. He was gonna propose. As for me, I was hell-bent on takin' back some of my smithin' tools from my old boss. Let's call him Dick-weed. Thing is, Dickweed still owed me some back pay, which he wasn't willing to give. I figured those tools of his had some worth, so I decided to take 'em. Eddie helped me, although, truth be told, I'm not sure I ever really filled him in on the big picture. Anyway, I spent the rest of the night drinkin' and watchin' him work on that ring.

"Did you tell anyone?"

"How do you think he got off? The poor kid was fighting for his life. It got me in a world a hurt too. That Dickweed pressed charges. Said I stole his tools. Which, you know, I did. Wiped me out for a spell." He spit again, eyes flickering with lingering resentment, even twenty years down the line.

"Did you ever meet her?"

"I did indeed." The memory soothed him. He gazed at the fire and smiled. "She was a laugher, that one. I remember that the most. Big, loud, what do ya call 'em?

Guffaws. She'd visit Eddie back when no college types would come near the Village. Hell, no summer people would. Not sure what they thought would happen. Get scalped, maybe?" He snorted derisively. "They were different times. But Margie? She didn't care. She was like one of them hippy types, but before there even was such a thing. Guess now you'd call her a *free spirit.* We'd all sit around a fire—not unlike this one we got goin' here—and Eddie would tell stories. Yeah, he told stories about the Wendigo. He told stories about all kinds of things. That's why she loved him. She was the same way. But come on! They was tryin' to say Eddie got possessed by some skinny beast with horns on its head? Dumbest thing I ever heard." He grinned, exposing his amazingly perfect teeth. "Eddie may have been horny, but it wasn't from no demon possession. It was *Marjorie.* She was a doll-baby!" He cackled mischievously. I didn't know what he meant by *horny,* but I suspected it had nothing to do with Wendigo antlers.

Old Luke stared straight into the fire. "We'd hang out right in this very spot. Sometimes she'd sing a song. Ella Fitzgerald. Patsy Cline. I'd tell a few dirty jokes. We'd pass around a bottle of Boone's Farm. They'd snuggle. I'd try not to act jealous, even though I was. Hell. Who wouldn't want what they had?"

It got quiet. The glow of the fire warmed my face.

He pulled his Tootsie Pop out of his mouth and examined it. "So, what will you do with the money if you solve the case? Tell me you won't buy yourself an overpriced ten-speed or an air hockey table because that'll piss me off." He crunched down hard on the Tootsie Pop.

I hesitated. "I don't want to say. It sounds stupid."

"You know what sounds stupid? Coming up to the Village in the middle of the night and asking questions you shouldn't be askin'. Brave, but stupid. Give it to me straight: what will you do with the money?"

"I wanna buy a cruise to Cairo for my parents."

"I won't lie. That wasn't the answer I was expectin'."

"They're having problems. Not talking anymore. They always wanted to go to Cairo, but it never happened. If I can buy this ticket for them … I don't know. Maybe it'll keep them together."

Old Luke just nodded. A log popped. We both flinched.

"You're right," he said. "That *is* stupid."

My face fell.

"I'm kidding, boy. I like it. *Family.*"

The word *family* came out as rough as granite, but it sounded good. Then, as if he'd reached a verdict, he continued. "No. Really. I like it. Now do me a favor."

"Of course, sir," I said.

"Beat feet. I'm fadin'."

I stood up without asking questions and handed him my third Tootsie Pop.

"You keep it. But check the wrapper," he said. "I'll tell ya that secret."

I unwrapped a grape Tootsie Pop and used the orange firelight to illuminate the wrapper.

"The fella with the bow and arrow, is he shooting at a star?" he asked.

I looked closer, squinting. "Yeah."

"That's good luck." Another log popped. "Or maybe it's bad luck. I never quite got that one straight." He settled back into his chair and resumed staring at the fire, alternating between sips, licks, and memories of Eddie.

I assumed it meant our meeting was officially over. "'Night," I said.

"Yup," he responded, but his tired eyes were somewhere else, absorbed by the flickering firelight. I gave a feeble wave that he didn't notice and walked toward my bike, folding the purple Tootsie Pop wrapper in thirds and slipping it into my bag.

I had my sign.

CHAPTER TWENTY

The Glove Box

On most nights, the tapestry of stars above would guide me on my late-night rides, their twinkling lights serving as a celestial roadmap between the tops of darkened trees on either side of the road. Simply by looking up, I could trace my route effortlessly. Tonight was different. The sky was pitch-black, devoid of any guiding constellations. The ride to the island's northern tip would be slow and uncertain.

I seriously considered turning around and heading back to Wildcliffe, tucking myself in and replowing the same four pages of *Dune*, a book I'd been reading for months and wouldn't finish until I was thirty-two. I'd blissfully drift off to dreams of sandworms, spice, and the House of Atreides, unburdened by murder, divorce, pissed-off pals, and cute, disappointed California girls. I shook it off and kept going. Back to Captain's Cottage. Back to the Olds Super 88 and whatever might be inside the dilapidated car.

I stashed Sluggo behind a freakishly large oak tree across the trail from Captain's Cottage and walked closer to the house. What looked sad and sagging in the light of day appeared more angular and severe at night. It leaned toward me, daring me to approach. The feeble glow of a single lamp flickered in an upstairs window while the rest of the old house remained shrouded in darkness.

Was the Flowered Dress Woman still on the island?

I pulled Big Jack's stopwatch from the courier bag and clicked it, setting a tight ten-minute time limit for the mission. I knew exactly where to find the Super 88. I also knew where to enter the barn: through the back door, the same way I left it earlier that day.

A cool wind rustled branches, fortuitously masking the sounds of my footsteps as I moved across the backyard. I turned the rusted barn doorknob, expecting it to be locked. It wasn't. Apparently, Flowered Dress Woman had fallen for my paperboy act and neglected to secure the perimeter after I'd sprinted away. Just another snoopy salesman. No reason to get paranoid and lock doors. The question of who she was and why she was squatting in an abandoned cottage on the lonely northern tip of the island was one for another day.

Entering the barn, I beamed my flashlight toward the side of the partially covered car, revealing its gleaming 1950s trim.

I attempted to open the driver's front door, but it was locked. Moving to the back door, I grasped the handle, and with a satisfying click, it yielded. The door swung open with a sickly grind as if it hadn't been open in decades. How many crimes was I currently committing? Was it two or three? Breaking into a car in a barn I had already broken into, behind a house I was trespassing on. Was that one crime or multiple crimes? Regardless, I knew that

Chief Richter's sympathy had expired. No turning back now.

I reached into my bag for the comforting touch of Big Jack's Bushnell binoculars. No need for them, but it felt good having them with me. Rummaging my hand through the bag, I brushed the cold metal of a frontier-style cap gun. I impulsively bought it earlier that day at Sally's Gifts. Even though it was a stupid, worthless toy, it gave me a strange sense of security.

I slid awkwardly into the back of the car, perhaps the last place Marjorie Kitmore had ever willingly gone. The floorboard was rotted, leaving only a few scraps of stained carpet. I shined the flashlight across the dashboard. The car reeked of mold, rotting sealant, gasoline, oil, and who knows what else. A musty, sickly smell that had me stifling puke.

For unknown reasons, I recalled a raccoon that had died in the chimney of the Wildcliffe living room years before. We'd gagged on the mystery stench for a week until Big Jack located the carcass of the poor scavenger, which he named Rocky Raccoon. Later, we buried the mummified critter in the backyard. *You never forget your first smell of death.*

I ran my fingers through the cracks in the seats, feeling the gritty dust puff up and catch the beam of my flashlight. The interior of the old hulk took on the eerie ambiance of a tiny attic straight out of a bad slasher movie. As I contemplated the possibilities, a chilling thought crossed my mind: What if the door suddenly slammed shut and locked from the outside? Could I kick my way out? How much time would it take?

Would I wind up like Rocky Raccoon?

I braced my courier bag in the doorjamb to prevent accidental entombment and renewed the inspection of the rotted seat cushions. The stagnant air inside the old car was getting worse. To calm myself, I started humming a Black Sabbath ditty but quickly realized the brooding melody wasn't helping to lower my anxiety. I switched to an unsteady *Build Me Up Buttercup*, one of Mom's favorites.

My fingers grazed a scrap of paper, and I pulled it toward the light. It was a timeworn menu from Clyde's Drive-In in St. Ignace, meaning the car had spent some time on the mainland. As I glanced at the menu, my stomach rumbled, craving the taste of a 'Big C' Colossus Burger accompanied by Clyde's famous fries. I tucked the menu into my courier bag and focused on the dashboard. On the passenger side, the window had spidered as if struck by a rock from the inside.

Quickly, I scribbled down the details in my journal and scrambled over the seat. For the next two minutes, I delved into the junk and dust, sifting through the remnants of what was once a front seat. The decay hung in the air like a haze, and as I moved, the dust swirled into a tiny tornado.

Why do you build me up, buttercup, baby, I sang in a soft, hysterical little voice.

I coughed. A few hitches at first, followed by a deeper hack. Not good. Any louder and Flowered Dress Woman's dog might wake up. Then, who knows? Maybe off to juvie, my dog-mangled extremities manacled like Steve McQueen in *The Great Escape.* I covered my mouth with my elbow to silence my gagging cough.

This unexpected attack of pneumonia-like hacking was not helping my Grand Plan. I shifted toward the driver's side door and opened it, leaning out and stifling another hack. The inspection had been a bust, and if I continued to cough like this, I'd wake up half the island.

Stepping out of the Oldsmobile, it suddenly hit me

with crystal clarity. I couldn't believe I had overlooked something so obvious: the glove box.

I slid back in and popped open the latch. The musty scent of old paper. Maps, registration papers, and busted, ink-crusted pens spilled out in a jumbled mess. I grabbed the pile and began flipping through the documents. My fingers trembled as I snatched the faded registration and pulled it close, the flashlight catching the faint name on the paperwork.

Ethan Rossellini.

"Rossellini?" I gasped, my voice escaping involuntarily. It was the same last name as Lance.

In the tomb-like silence of the car, I whispered the names to myself, each syllable carrying a weight of possibility: "Russell. Rossellini. Russell. Rossellini." Could the eccentric Islander Captain Russell, known to all as simply *The Captain*, be related to Lance somehow?

I hastily stuffed the papers into my courier bag and plunged my hand deeper into the glovebox, sifting through the grime and debris in search of anything else. My hand brushed against something cold and hard.

In the glow of my flashlight, silver glinted. Then a yellowed ivory engraving stood against the aged metallic surface. I pulled my hand back like I'd been scalded. It was a pocket watch with the ivory lid closed.

The same timepiece draped on Marjorie Kitmore's neck as she drew her last breath?

Milton's plaintive recollection. *She never took it off.*

I reached for it, gingerly plucking it by the broken chain from the glove box.

Broken ... in a struggle?

I suspended the pocket watch in front of the flashlight, watching it spin leisurely. Its ivory face held a captivating design—a finely etched turtle seemingly lost in slumber. As it slowly spun, the gleaming silver back revealed delicate engravings, filigree entangled the letters MK. The facets reflected the flashlight, cutting through the dusty interior, turning the inside of the car, for an instant, into a miniature disco.

I remembered dancing *the hustle* with my mom and dad.

Weird thing to think about right now, Jack.

I looked closer. Tiny brown specks of paint.

Could it be twenty-year-old blood?

The last known creation of garbageman, dray-driver, storyteller, and artisan, Eddie St. Germain, who died in a freezing parking lot in Marquette, Michigan, on Christmas Eve, spun before my eyes. Whoever snapped it off her neck had to have left a print. I plucked a Ziploc from my pocket, dropped the watch inside, and zipped it.

After burning all my film photographing the car with the Brownie, I carefully closed the glove box and scrambled out.

The only sound was the soft whirring of my tires as I picked up speed. I focused on the pitch-black trail ahead, my mind racing with the possibilities inside the bag that rested in my front basket. The Super88, the pictures, the pocket watch, and the registration paperwork all pointed directly to Lance.

"Go right to bed," Blaze had advised. But my heart pounded with the syncopated beat of a jazz drummer. There would be no sleep tonight.

The wind rushed as I zoomed past the opening at Arch Rock, and my eyes were drawn to a burst of vibrant firelight. By day, Arch Rock, a colossal limestone arch towering 150 feet above Lake Huron, was a popular tourist attraction. Its huge, doughnut-like structure created a picturesque backdrop for Kodak moments, allowing a perfect view of the crystal blue lake below.

But on this moonless night, the rugged arch flickered with an orange firelight, casting an otherworldly glow. Yellow smoke drifted across the clearing. I skidded to a halt. Then I did something I still can't explain: I dropped Sluggo onto the gravel, as if in a trance, and walked toward the light.

The smell was barely noticeable at first, but as I walked closer, it grew stronger. It was no dead animal this time. No Rocky Raccoon. I stifled a gag. An imaginary, unseen hand on my back nudged me forward. One foot after another, but knowing the smarter move was to turn, hop on the bike, and pedal as fast as possible to escape the stinking, smoky tableau.

Shadows cut weird paths across the arch, advancing in front of the firelight. At first, they were obscure, the boundaries blurry. As they crossed into position, I recognized the unmistakable shape of antlers emerging from a misshapen skull. It danced, with spindly limbs shooting out spastically in all directions. I scrutinized the show in silence. The fog, pungent now, like the yellow hue of rotting mustard.

My mouth dried up as I stumbled toward the cliff's edge, the smoke thicker now and sweeping across the viewing platform. I strained to make out the images on the rock. The source of the spiky shadowplay was behind me. I whirled around as cedar branches cracked, gravel and dirt kicked up in a frenzy like the sound of a bull preparing for its final charge. All limbs froze.

My neck, stiff as a board, felt nailed in place.

Was it a dream? Has it happened? Had the Wendigo—

stalking, toying with me all summer—finally decided to make its carnivorous strike?

Was it time to feast?

I felt drowsy, my eyelids drooping momentarily like a swoon. Fear shuts us down. I once fell asleep in the dentist's office before getting a wisdom tooth pulled. I wanted to lie down on the ground and just sleep.

A sound rose—between a wail and a growl. It wasn't a dog's snarl or a deer's panicked bleat. It was otherworldly. Panic surged. Woke me right up. I stumbled backward and fell over a rotted log. A new fire surged with a low-bass whoosh, sending sparks scattering. Glimpses of charred skin and matted fur. A giant rack twice the size I'd ever seen.

Not possible. Spiked. Drenched in fresh, red blood. Not brown, dried, twenty-year-old blood.

Fresh. Red.

I scrambled to my feet and ran.

Flashes of fur through the putrid smoke, sprinting toward Sluggo, whimpering. I righted the bike and hopped on, pedaling as hard as possible. Closing in, illuminated by the fiery glow and obscured by yellow smog.

But I was getting away. The glow was diminishing.

Did it even happen?

I risked a last peek behind me.

The blinding impact of the tree sent a searing pain through my skull as my front wheel crumpled. I hit the ground and felt a sickening crunch from my courier bag, which had flown out of my front basket on impact. A high-pitched, ear-piercing wail echoed. I scrambled to my feet, my head pounding. I scooped up the scattered contents of my bag in the pitch dark and strapped the bag across my shoulder.

No time!

My fingers closed around the frontier cap gun. I aimed it blindly, frantically into the yellow fog, left, then right, then left again. Twitching like a rookie cop in a low-budget movie.

I turned and ran, leaving Sluggo behind.

I sprawled across the bedspread, staring at the ceiling fan as it turned slowly above me. My head pounded from the impact of the tree. Sweat, mud, and dust clung to my body. *Dune* sat on the bedside table, still bookmarked on page 35.

The courier bag sat on my stomach, rising and falling with each breath as I mulled over Blaze's Wendigo defense theory for the tenth time. It wasn't the demon itself but the *belief* that it could possess you. Like in The *Exorcist*, the spirit penetrated you. Was the Arch Rock Wendigo sighting real, or was it all in my fevered, cracked little brain? And who would believe me if I told them? Certainly not Blaze. Maybe best to keep this latest episode between myself and my future psychologist.

I sat up and began rummaging through the contents of the dirt-covered courier bag.

Big Jack's Bushnell binoculars were cracked down the center, with one lens missing. There went a summer's wages. I withdrew three notebooks, two already filled and the third in progress. The cap gun. The red plastic flashlight. The Blaze Field Manual. A Swiss Army knife. Two boxes of spare innertubes. Two rolled copies of the *Island Gazette*.

Was that it?

My hands shook like an old man's, and I dug deeper. Relief washed over me when I felt the Brownie camera. I removed it from the bag and noticed that the case was cracked from the bike crash. As I pulled it closer, the latch to the film chamber popped open like a jack in the box, and strips of celluloid spilled out.

The film was now useless.

I set the camera aside and dug deeper into the bag, foraging like a desperately hungry bear.

Somehow I knew what was coming.

Using the light from my bedside lamp, I turned the bag upside-down and shook it furiously. Old coupons, pen caps, and crumpled Now and Later wrappers rained down in a storm of scrap.

"No, no, no, no, no, NO!" I heard myself whispering.

No car registration. No hand-carved scrimshaw pocket watch. It was all gone.

CHAPTER TWENTY-ONE

Evil Genius

Should I tell Blaze what I saw?

Tanned, off-duty summer workers sipped cold beers, sunbathed, and chased frisbees in Marquette Park without a care in the world. Oh, to be twenty-one and unburdened by the weight of failure, a mild head wound, and potential demonic possession.

Oblivious fools!

They had no idea how good they had it!

I looked up at the statue of Father Marquette. He also struck me as a bit self-satisfied today. The famous French explorer stumbled upon the island in 1671, founded a mission, and ended up with a park named after him. Not bad for a few days' work. Perched directly on the top of Marquette's head, a grouchy seagull generously added to a collection of droppings, gifting the stately Father with a white, goopy, poopy yarmulke.

My humiliation from the previous night was indescribable. In my sweaty hands, I'd held the crucial evidence that could prove Lance Rossellini's guilt, bring closure to the families of Marjorie Kitmore and Eddie St. Germaine, and help stitch back together the unraveling Christmas sweater known as the McGuinns.

Then I lost it.

I'd seen *Jaws*. Without the big shark tooth Hooper found in the hull of Ben Garder's boat, the mayor wasn't closing the beaches, and the shark attacks would continue.

The proof was all that mattered.

It wasn't just the admission of what I had done; it was *how*—spooked by a demon that probably resided only in my sleep-deprived, paranoid, fat little head, then riding my bike into a tree. It was all so stupid and heavy. My walk to the Haunted Theater felt like snowshoeing in peanut butter.

After calling in sick to the *Gazette*, I'd returned to Arch Rock early in the morning to recover Sluggo, praying there might just be a Ziploc with a pocket watch and a bunch of essential papers waiting for me in a neat little pile.

There wasn't.

I scoured the forest near the overlook, combing through the undergrowth, desperate for any trace of what had haunted me the previous night. There was no sign of the yellow residue that had filled the air, no charred remains of trees, not even a single hoofprint with three menacing claws. Yet, there was Sluggo, right where I had abandoned him, the front wheel bent and useless.

All signs indicated a full-blown, bars-on-the-window, padding-on-the-wall mental meltdown.

The scent of melted chocolate blasted into the street from the overhead fans of fudge shops, creating a sugary fog aroma Willie Wonka himself would kill for. But today, it was nauseating. A carriage tour passed, the horse bumping into me, striping the shoulder of my Rocky Balboa T-shirt with gross, horsey sweat. Staggering on, I rehearsed the conversation:

'Well, Blaze, there was this ... well, ha-ha, it was a Wendigo. And to avoid being devoured and transformed into one of those demonic freaks, I rode away on my bike. Then, I hit a tree, and my bag busted open. Musta fell out. What fell out?
The evidence, silly! Yeah, all of it. These things happen. Ha-ha.'
'It's okay, Jacky boy! I'm sure we'll find more critical evidence. Must be tons of it laying around! Hell, maybe even one with even clearer fingerprints! Don't sweat it. Have a Mountain Dew!'

Doubtful. My best guess was more like this:

You useless pussy! You blew the only chance we had to solve this case! I hope Superman flies away with your mom under his arm, and they knock boots at the Palace of Solitude, you loser!

BAM! My left knee slammed into a wheelbarrow full of horse manure, nearly knocking it over.

"Hey, watch it!" yelled Rick, the shit-sweeper. "By the way, Chiefie told me you owe me twenty hours of scooping."

"I'll be there," I said and kept walking.

He snarled. "You better be!" *Sweep-sweep-scoop.*

My knee throbbed.

The pocket watch and the Wendigo.

The Wendigo and the pocket watch.

Two sides of a coin flipping through the air in slow motion like that 1979 penny. One side, the pocket watch, was rationality. Proof. Evidence. Logic. It implicated Lance. How else could it end up in the car? He must have snatched it off her during a fight in his grandfather's secret Oldsmobile. He shattered the window with her head, blood splattered like paint, leaving specks on the ivory pocket watch.

But on the other side of the coin was the Wendigo. Complete insanity. Possession, fire, and insatiable, inhuman cravings. The putrid stench of a demonic presence. Maybe it got Eddie. Last night, it almost got me.

Rationality vs. the supernatural. Were they all in me? *I contained multitudes.* Who said that? Was it Ozzy Osbourne? Walt Whitman? All a blur now.

And just like that, the decision was made. Confide in Blaze. Tell him the entire story, with all the details – the stinking fire, the bloodied horns, the terrifying screams, the missing pocket watch. He would know what to do. He always did.

And if I was doomed, who better to guide me?

I trudged up the Haunted Theater's rickety, red-carpeted stairs and abruptly stopped. A young man with a blonde crewcut, and massive linebacker shoulders swept the rug. He barely looked up. "We're not open yet."

"Where's Blaze?" I asked.

He paused his sweeping and looked at me. "What's the blaze?" A real troglodyte, this guy

"Not *the* Blaze. Just … Blaze."

"Oh, you mean that burnout who didn't show up for work?"

I glared. "Just … where is he?"

"Hell if I know. Probably in there sleeping. Old man Stauffer called this morning and told me to sweep the porch before they opened. Why, you know him?"

I had no time to deal with amateurs. "Yes, we're ..." *What were we?* "Business associates."

The linebacker looked me over, puzzled, then smiled and resumed sweeping. *"Business associates.* Whatever you say, kid."

"He lives inside," I said. "I'm going in."

"Go ahead. And tell him to get his ass out here and do his job. I got better things to do with my time. Like sleep."

I walked in tentatively. "Blaze?"

The aluminum foil wallpaper and heavy metal black light posters were now stark, empty white walls. The bed sheets were stripped and neatly folded on the stained mattress. And the smell–that ever-present stench of cigarettes, socks, and conspiracy–was overpowered by bleach and cleanser. I scanned the room. The Wall of Death, our meticulously crafted collage of clues and evidence, was wiped clean. Not a thread, not a note, no crudely scribbled insights, not a scrap of newspaper, not a naked lady picture remained. In a daze, I wandered into the bathroom. It was spotless, with a faint smell of cleanser.

"Blaze?!" Nothing but reverb and echoes.

I walked to the storage room, opened the door, and flicked on the lights. Rusted shelves were loaded with dismembered figures, crates, severed wax heads, and broken machinery, all illuminated in a sterile blueish glare. I scanned the room one last time before turning away.

That's when I noticed a cluster of yellow plastic boxes.

Newer, contrasting with the rotting brown paper crates surrounding them.

I grabbed the topmost container, placed it on the floor beside me, then peeled off the lid. Inside were smaller boxes. Ten or fifteen. Neatly packed. An illustration of a man pinching his nose stared at me. The small print read, "Baker Novelty Farm, Eugene, Oregon." I turned the box over. Written on the package was "PROFESSIONAL-GRADE STINK BOMBS." I recognized the product from the cheesy ads on the back pages of my Archie comic books.

I dug deeper into the crate. Under the row of stink bomb boxes were more garishly labeled mail-order packages.

CLAY SMOKE BALLS! Color: *yellow*.

I discovered five tin canisters of Kingsford lighter fluid, various cheap Bic lighters in different colors, and books of matches from Horn's Bar. Metal clamps, clotheslines, fasteners, and wire coils.

From a mental drainpipe, humiliation gushed like a flood of sewage.

I reached for another plastic box, tearing it open, already sensing what I'd find. A tangled mess of plastic antlers coated in fresh red paint. I picked up one set, and three more tumbled out, their cheap, plastic points clattering noisily against the cement floor.

Tearing open another box, I found a huge, neatly folded faux fur cape stitched together from various animal hides. Neatly placed under the fur covering sat a long, narrow skull, teeth dripping with garish, red blood. The soul-dead face of the Wendigo. I looked closer. A cheap prop. Likely made out of paper mache, like one of those dopey Easter bunnies they forced us to make in 2nd-grade art class. Laughable in the harsh fluorescent light. *How did this ever scare me?*

On the shelf sat a row of hand-held spotlights, each adorned with yellow plastic gels attached with clothespins. In the corner, four wooden poles, standing about five feet tall—stilts, leaned against the wall. The ideal instruments for recreating the unnerving, elongated stride that had horrified me the night before.

It wasn't just a costume. It was the props and lighting for a full-blown spectacle, complete with flames, yellow lights, thick plumes of smoke, and the horrible smell that could only be attributed to the Wendigo, courtesy of the Baker Novelty Farm.

It was a heavy metal production, written, produced, and directed by a flaming friggin' liar named Blaze.

I scanned the room. My gaze landed on a small trash can in the corner. I picked it up, poured the contents onto the floor, then bent down and sorted through the scraps of paper: two Stroh's empties, cigarette butts, and some snotty Kleenex.

Amidst the sea of discarded debris, a single object caught my eye—a glimmering purple beacon, the Tootsie Pop wrapper. Carefully folded into thirds, it was the same wrapper I had tucked away in my courier bag the previous night during my meeting with Old Luke.

If Blaze had the wrapper, he probably had everything I dropped when I crashed into the tree, including a certain Ziploc bag with a pocket watch and the car registration paperwork. I now had the definitive answer to Big Luke's perplexing question regarding the Indian and the star on the wrapper:

Bad luck.

My butt hit the floor with a thud. Dazed, I reached for a pair of the plastic antlers resting on the floor beside me.

A scrap of paper was impaled on one of the antler's points. I pulled it off.

Written in Blaze's familiar handwriting:

Dear Encyclopedia Brown (underwear) –
You're a better detective than I thought if you found this note.
And I already think you're pretty adequate. All I can say is
sorry. Someday you'll get it.

Love and kisses,
Andy Stanton (aka Blaze)

PS: KISS still sucks my sweaty, hairy balls.

For what seemed like over two hours, though it was probably only twelve minutes, I sat on the storage room floor, experiencing that disorientating phenomenon known as *complete betrayal*. Eventually, it visits everyone. It just stopped by Jack's Place a little sooner than expected.

How much of what Blaze had told me was true? Did he even know anything about detective work, or was he just in it for the money? Was his father even a cop? The questions swirled around like a tornado, growing louder and more intense until they reached a shrieking pitch. The room started to spin, and I felt myself getting queasy. I reached into my filthy courier bag and pulled out the Blaze Field Manual, flipping through its dog-eared pages in search of some hidden clue.

My fingers raced across the pages until I found a section titled "Identification and Apprehension." Most of it was obscured, covered in redaction marks, but I could now see the very top of some legible words peaking out behind the thick black line. I looked closer.

Chet nudged Joe and whispered wonderingly.

Wait. *Chet and Joe?* I recognized this sentence instantly. It was from the *Hardy Boys Detective Handbook.*

I remembered devouring it in the Island library years ago. Blaze must have stumbled upon the same book on one of his trips to the library, Xeroxed the relevant pages, "redacted" all Hardy Boys references, and passed it off as a field manual from his detective father.

I'd spent the entire summer using a detective guidebook meant for ten-year-olds. No wonder I liked it so much. It was now clear to me that Blaze—while being a liar and a thief—was also a genius.

With a suddenness that shocked me, I pushed myself up to my feet, strode over to a phone mounted on the storage room wall, and dialed. A voice answered.

"Hello?"

It was Jill. Butterflies.

"Hi. It's Jack."

"Oh." Her voice dropped into neutral. "Hi, Jack. How are you?"

"Great," I lied.

"That's great," she said. Frosty at best.

"Will you meet me on the set tomorrow at noon? They're shooting at Windermere Pointe. I have some things I need to explain."

There was a long pause.

"Okay. I guess," she said. *Click.*

Then I made the same call to Gordon. Then Smitty.

CHAPTER TWENTY-TWO

Big Jack's Pot Pies

The aroma of Big Jack's aftershave mingled with a mystery odor that seeped from the oven and spread like a mist through the kitchen.

"Your mom's got a late shoot tonight, so I'll be your chef," Big Jack announced, his voice exuding an abnormal cheeriness. He arrived on the last boat the previous night after two weeks off the island, appearing thinner and somewhat bewildered. Now, seemingly determined to make up for lost time, he was preparing dinner for us. Beth sat opposite me at the kitchen table, silently engrossed in a crossword puzzle, wearing a navy blue T-shirt adorned with yellow, ironed-on letters that boldly stated, "You're All Nuts."

Big Jack stepped over to the table, set two pies before us, and took a deep breath as if awaiting judgment. We'd been spoiled by Mom's piping hot pot pies, steam rising out of tiny puncture holes, browned to crispy perfection. These looked more like worn-out doggie chew toys. Utterly formless, the crust devoid of structure, barely identifiable as human food.

Beth considered hers blankly, then poked it with her fork. "Cold pot pie. It's like you read my mind, Dad," she said, her sarcasm barely disguised.

My right shoe connected with her shin under the table.

"Ouch, you little jerk!" she snapped.

Big Jack glanced at us over his shoulder as he struggled with the electric can opener. He'd forgotten to wipe away a dollop of shaving cream on his neck. He also sported black dress socks and loafers with his cargo shorts, as if he'd forgotten how to dress for weekends.

Mom would never let that look fly, I thought.

"Reflexes, Dad. I crashed my bike a few days ago, and now my left knee keeps twitching." I turned to Beth. "Sorry."

Big Jack resumed his struggles with the stubborn can opener. I discreetly signaled Beth to remain calm, mouthing "Be cool" and gesturing toward Big Jack while twirling my finger around my temple to make a 'cuckoo' symbol. We had our unspoken sibling code, and the message was crystal clear: *Give him a break.*

Beth cautiously resumed examining the pot pie as if half-expecting a plasma-drenched alien baby to burst through the crust and unleash an eardrum-piercing screech.

Big Jack placed a bowl of canned peach wedges in the center of the table. He sat down and cleared his throat. "I call this dish Peach-a-la-Pot. Or is Pot-a-la-Peach? I always forget. Topped off with some sliced tomatoes with ranch dressing. We're putting Mom's pies to shame. Dig in!"

An uncomfortable lull hung before we finally took our first bites.

The deeper I burrowed into the pie with my fork, the

colder it got. It was like those cut-away diagrams of the earth's core, only in reverse. I bit into a chunk. It was the first time I could remember a brain freeze from a chicken pot pie. "It's delicious, Dad," I lied, attempting to thaw the poultry popsicle with my tongue. "Mom's pot pies sometimes burn. But this? This is *perfect*."

Beth rolled her eyes as she broke off a corner of her doughy, raw crust and put it into her mouth, chewing slowly and attempting not to gag. "Interesting texture. So dad. Question."

"So Beth. Answer," said Big Jack, now eyeing his own dinner as if suddenly comprehending what he was subjecting us to.

"Why did Mom move into the guest room?" Her T-SHIRT should have said: *BETH: QUEEN OF SUBTLE.*

Big Jack froze, then composed himself. "Fair question. Let's see. First—she's up early; you know how she scurries around, getting ready for her day. So in that way, she did it for me. Doesn't want to wake me."

"Right. But you're hardly ever here," said Beth.

His shoulders slumped slightly, but he forged ahead, attaching a fake smile like a clip-on tie. "And then they've got her stitching the wardrobe for the extras. There's this huge scene in the park coming up. She's also sewing shirts for the dinner scene, which is the scene tonight. I think."

He rambled on. "The sewing machine she's been using in the house is loud, so she figured she'd move it into the guest room, plus all the research she has to do. It's awe-inspiring. She has to read through old Sears catalogs from 1912 and … anyway. So, yes, she's sleeping in the guest room."

Beth reached for the peaches and mumbled, "*The lady doth protest too much, methinks.*"

"What's that?" he asked.

"Nothing. Shakespeare Quotes for 500." She plopped a gelatinous peach onto her plate.

Footsteps echoed in the hallway, accompanied by male humming. Big Jack craned his neck to see down the hall. "It's your grandfather. He's been shooting pool all afternoon. I guess everyone is shooting something today. Join us, Dad!" he called. "I made chicken pot pie!"

Gramps sauntered into the kitchen, his University of Michigan baseball cap pulled low over his forehead. His kelly green pants, once vibrant, had faded to a dreary olive drab from too many washes. The golf shirt he wore bore the name of a local course, Wawashkamo. He never golfed, but he loved their bar.

"What have we here? A little meeting of the mind-less?" Gramps eyed the food on the table, then looked toward the kitchen counter, littered with speckled pots and pans. "Jesus. It looks like a typhoon blew through the place."

"Pull up a chair, Big Jack said. "We got pies, peaches, salad, and wheat bread. Plus, Nutty Bars for dessert."

"A sumptuous feast," Gramps said, but without much conviction. He stood a moment, likely calculating his odds of escaping to the Mustang Lounge for a perfect cheeseburger and fries, rinsed down with an ice-cold Pabst Blue Ribbon. But accepting that he was trapped, he slid back a chair and sat.

"Whatcha been up to, Dad."

"Playing pool with Milton. Few other fellas."

Beth shot me a subtle smirk at the mention of Milton while Gramps fumbled an unruly leaf of lettuce and a few overripe tomatoes, then slid the last pie onto his plate. The "Milton episode," as it was now known around Wildcliffe, was like a black hole in our conversations; we tried to avoid it at all costs. The party line was to chalk it up to "youthful indiscretion," an overzealous extra credit school project gone very wrong.

Beth knew something much deeper was going on, but thankfully, she was too focused on thawing out her dinner to push any buttons.

"Are these peaches?" Gramps asked, pointing at the blob of orange in a bowl.

"They are," responded Big Jack. "Fresh from the can!"

"Hmmm," said Gramps. "Reminds me of the goop you scoop out of a pumpkin on Halloween."

Beth stifled a spit-take by covering her mouth with her napkin, and I stared intently at my left shoe as if the winning lottery number was scrawled on the sole, lest I also bust out in a giggle.

"What happened to the whitefish I had sent over from Bell's Fishery?" asked Gramps.

"It's in the freezer," said Big Jack. He studied his own pot pie, then went for a peach quarter.

Gramps shook his head. "That fish was fresh, Jack. What are you waiting for?" He eyed his plate warily. "Not to say this lavish spread isn't mouthwatering."

"Whitefish is Ana's department. I do bacon and pot pies."

"And apparently canned peaches," said Gramps. He set his fork, still loaded with pie, back on his plate and made a show of stretching his arms over his head. "Yep. That bride of yours knows her whitefish." He looked around the table as if he had just noticed her missing. "Where is she, anyway?"

"On set. Another late night tonight."

"Why'd she move into the guest bedroom?"

"What is this place? Knotts Landing? I just explained this to the kids!"

Gramps reared back. "It was a harmless question!"

Big Jack let out an irritated sigh and rebooted his story. "They've got her stitching up the wardrobe for the extras. There's this big scene in the park coming up. They're on a deadline, so she's also sewing shirts for the dinner scene, and it gets loud and—"

"—Dad," interrupted Beth. "We already heard this."

"Gramps didn't!" said Big Jack, pointing with his fork.

"I'm gonna come right out and say it," blurted Gramps. "Since Ana took that job, you've been sulking around like you got diagnosed with—sorry, kids, but I gotta say it—pecker flu."

"Sulking? That's crazy. I'm fully supportive of her and her new job. It seems to make her very happy, and while I don't love that she puts in such long hours, I think it's exciting work, and I know it makes her very …" his voice trailed off.

"Lemme guess … *happy?*" asked Beth.

"Yes. *Happy*. I am fully supportive of the job because I know—"

Beth was chuckling now.

"What's so funny?" asked Big Jack.

"You sound like one of those hostage videos," she said. She broke into a parody of a hostage robotically speaking to a camera. *"I am being treated very well. My captors are lovely people. I am unharmed. The food here is delicious. My wife is very happy."*

"That's ridiculous," said Big Jack. "And, frankly, insulting."

Big Jack chewed furiously on a chunk of the pie, which sounded like crushing an ice cube. I concentrated on a slice of peach. To me, it was less pumpkin goop and more giant orange slug. That's when I decided to break the uneasy silence with a good old-fashioned non-sequitur. I stabbed a blob of peach with my fork and looked up with the contrived empathy of an experienced psychologist.

"So. Dad. How did you and Mom meet?"

Big Jack suddenly beamed. It was the first genuine smile I'd seen from him in months.

"1960. I was at a party for John F. Kennedy's election in Ann Arbor, and your mom was there, wearing these wayfarer sunglasses. At night. *Sleep Walk* by Santo and Johnny was on some record player. And when she first saw me, she kinda lifted them up." He demonstrated the move. "I saw those eyes, and let me tell you, it was over. I knew that night she was the one. It felt like the dawn of a new era." He smiled. "In a lotta ways."

He took a sip of wine, lost in thought. "But her past was a mystery to me. She grew up poor in Boring, Oregon, outside of Portland."

"Boring? You're making that up," said Beth.

"Nope. The town was actually called *Boring*."

"What was her life like?" I asked. It occurred to me that I knew nothing about Mom's past.

"Well, it was … not good. Her dad left when she was a kid, and her mom drank. A lot. It was a lousy childhood. That's all she'd tell me. But she worked hard in school and got a scholarship to college in Michigan. As far away as she could get from Oregon. Your mom made me promise never to pry into her life before we met, so I never did. Not her family, not her life in Boring. Nothing. She locked everything in a chest and tossed it overboard. The town, her family, everything. Fresh start. Full steam ahead." He nodded. "And I went along with it. Truthfully, I was happy to be a big, dumb knight in shining armor."

He shot a look at Gramps, who nodded back. Supportive. He knew damn well his son was cracked wide open.

"Your Gramps passed me the dealership, we had you two brats, and all was hunky ... something."

"Hunky-*dory*," Beth said. "Also a great David Bowie album," she added.

"Right. *Hunky-dory.* But in the back of my mind, I always wondered. Did she settle? We used to joke that she went from Boring with a big 'B' to boring with a small 'b.'" He rubbed his eyes wearily. "But now, with this movie thing, I don't know. Something's changed, and that joke isn't funny anymore. Maybe she sees a more interesting life."

Nobody dared speak. He sipped his wine and leaned back in his chair until it groaned. "Maybe she sees what she settled for." He looked up, staring at the ceiling as if the answers might be carved in the bead board.

"... boring with a small 'b.'" It was agonizing. But like a rotten tooth, at least it was out.

Beth spoke. "Can I be honest with you, Dad?

"Of course you can."

"I know you're feeling low, and I'm not trying to make it worse. But I feel this needs to be said."

Big Jack's eyes were tired, but he smiled gamely, ready for another psychic body blow. "Lemme have it."

She pointed at her plate. "This is the worst pot pie I've ever had in my life."

Gramps, giddy, dropped his fork on his plate with a clatter and pumped his fists. "Thank *Christ*, someone said it!" His cap flew off his head and landed in the peach bowl. "What about you, Jacky? You like that pie?"

I giggled, grateful for the new vibes in the room and Beth's big fat mouth. "Sorry, Dad. I can't lie. It's disgusting!"

Big Jack banged the table in mock outrage, rattling the silverware. "*Ingrates!* You're all a bunch of *ingrates!*"

Beth took a napkin off her lap and walked a few steps to Big Jack's chair. She wiped the stray shaving cream off his neck, then kissed him on the top of his head, lingering long enough to make it count. He hugged her close with one arm and wiped away a few stray tears with the other. It was impossible to know if they were tears of laughter or sadness, but I concluded it was a mix. One of the many lessons I learned during the summer of 1979 was that laughter and sadness produced nearly identical tears.

Big Jack got up and straightened his shoulders. "Whad-daya say we get outta this place, head downtown, and grab dinner and a cream puff at the Iroquois Hotel?"

In unison, all four of us were on our feet, practically knocking over our chairs and stampeding out of the smelly kitchen to head downtown. The Iroquois had the finest food on the island.

Tonight, we'd earned it.

CHAPTER TWENTY-THREE

Reassembling the Team

I spent the previous night on the Wildcliffe porch, rehearsing my speech to the gang. I envisioned a windswept scene at Windermere Pointe with Gordon, Smitty, and Jill, where I would vividly recount my recent experiences in all their twisted, sad, exhilarating glory. This time, I was determined to leave no detail out—from my parents' troubles, the cruise to Cairo, the Wendigo, the pocket watch, the Chief, Blaze's shocking betrayal, and the true motive behind the break-in at Milton's. I would pace along the rocky shoreline, gesturing. Think JFK during the Cuban Missile Crisis. Troubled, but noble.

Then, with a lump in my throat, I would seek their forgiveness. I imagined the scene unfolding before me—the three of them embracing me in an awkward, yet heartfelt group hug. Jill's eyes would glisten with a newfound spark, a hint of admiration, maybe even infatuation. Gordon and Smitty would pat me on the back, declaring me their leader for life. After all, it takes a confident young man to humbly admit his mistakes to his friends.

It didn't quite go that way.

"Stop squirming, Jack!" Mom tugged at the fabric near my ass crack and began hand-stitching my baggy knickers to prevent them from slipping down to my feet as I walked. It was the final adjustment to an outrageously humiliating outfit that included a poofy light blue shirt, suspenders, and a red tie. *A tie!*

"I'm not here to be an extra, Mom."

She carefully stitched while I winced as if she were sewing together patches of my own flesh.

"I only came here to talk to those guys for a few minutes," I gestured. Just twenty feet away, Jill, Smitty, and Gordon waited in the extras holding tent, arms crossed and aloof, also dressed in 1912 attire, but much more stylish than my silly get-up.

Mom kneeled, fitting my pants. She had pins clenched in her teeth. All business. "Stop squirming and let me ... *hem ... your ... knickers!*"

I heard a distant cackle and looked over. Smitty grinned. "Yeah, Jack! Let your mom *hem ... your ... knickers.* Otherwise, you ain't gettin' near us!"

Jill and Gordon remained stone-faced, but at least one of the crew was warming up.

"You look very handsome," said Mom. "Here, put on this hat." She slapped a wool, newsies-style slouch cap on my head.

"No, ma! I look like one of the Little Rascals!"

"Shush, and let me finish." She stepped back and

inspected my outfit, hands on her hips. "Approved! Now go!" It turns out I'd be in *Somewhere in Time* after all.

The four of us strolled around Windermere Pointe, tracing leisurely figure eights, while Reeve and Seymour performed their "falling in love" routine. The constant camera cuts and the booming instructions of the Very Important Brit through his Very Loud Megaphone significantly hindered my heartfelt confession. As the director fine-tuned the actors' performances, we were repeatedly instructed to "go back to one" to restart our casual stroll.

A female production assistant in a T-shirt approached us several times, gesturing animatedly and urging us to appear "less serious."

"Imagine you're kids," she suggested.

"We are kids," Gordon retorted.

"Okay, fine. Then imagine you're kids from 1912."

We traded baffled looks, but I did as I was told, and finished up my story like a kid from 1912.

"And cut!" the Very Important Brit yelled. "Resetting for pick-up shots!" Oddly the moment lined up perfectly with the climax of my story. The actors relaxed, and the three turned to look at me. I awaited a verdict.

Gordon spoke first. "So you lied to us because you didn't think we could handle the true story? *Nobody's* parents are more messed up than mine."

"Yeah. At least you *have* two parents," said Jill.

"That's not it," I said. "I guess I was embarrassed. And the more I screwed things up, the more embarrassed I got."

"By the way, guys, Jack also lied to me," said Jill. "*Repeatedly.*"

Smitty looked over. "Sweet. What did he lie to *you* about?"

"It's *not* sweet," Jill snapped. "First off, he said he would help save the narwhals. Total lie. He just wanted to sound noble. Or something like that."

"What's a narwhal?" asked Smitty, turning to me.

I looked down, avoiding Jill's probing gaze. "Truthfully, I'm not sure," I said. "But I know they're endangered."

Jill rolled her eyes. "They're whales. With a horn. And *then* he promised not to break into Milton's apartment. Went and did it anyway."

Smitty shrugged. "That lie we already knew about."

"How?"

"We were with him," said Smitty.

"*What?*"

"But let's keep it between us. We were …" He turned to Gordon. "What's the word for it again?"

"Accomplices," Gordon answered.

"I think it's *accessories,*" I added.

Three grizzled grips planted dolly track and cranked up lights for the next shot.

"How did you meet this Blaze creep again?" asked Gordon.

"You guys told me his dad was a detective. I figured he might know about crime, so I went to the Haunted Theater and asked him to help me investigate the Marjorie Kitmore murder."

"Guess he helped, alright," Gordon exclaimed, a wide grin stretching across his face. "He helped himself to your evidence!"

Gordon's infectious grin gave us all permission to chuckle, which soon escalated into an uproar. The more we laughed, the harder it was to stop. It was the most ludicrous tale I had ever heard, and it was about me. A blast of feedback from the bullhorn jolted a squawking flock of seagulls into flight.

"Kids! Stop laughing!" announced the Very Important Brit.

Smitty called back, "But the production assistant lady told us to be less serious."

We continued our lazy figure eight.

"So, what's the plan now?" Gordon asked.

"I have no idea," I replied.

Smitty shook his head like a doctor delivering bad news. "Well, Jack. Looks to me like your parents are getting divorced." He resumed snickering.

"It's not so bad," Gordon said. "You get *tons* of gifts. Trust me. Guilt pays!"

"You guys are the worst!" Jill said, but a smile crept across her face, unable to resist the absurdity of the moment. Because it wasn't the worst. It was the best. To be with friends, chattering about the weirdness of life, contemplating things we couldn't control, and celebrating the simplicity of utter failure.

Listening to God laugh.

"Wait!" Smitty blurted out. "I got an idea!" His gaze shifted toward Mom on the far side of the set, brushing dust off Reeve's bowler hat as she chatted amiably with him. "Because you're right, Jack. We see your mom every day. She's, like, the most popular person on the set now. How do you go back to real life after all of this? She's not going to be able to do it." Smitty took in his surroundings, then his stylish outfit. "Truth is, I don't think *I* can do it either. I've had skirt steak and shrimp for three weeks straight."

He gestured toward the set. "See all that stuff on the table over there? The cereal, Snickers bars, Cokes, little ham sandwiches, gum, jello containers?"

We nodded.

"It's all free!" He shook his head in astonishment. "How do you walk away from that? You can't!"

"I get it! But what's your idea?" I pressed.

"Oh right. The idea. Ready? *Get your mom fired.* Problem solved!"

"*Fired?* What are you talking about?"

He looked at Jill. "Your dad is a, what was it—a production designer guy, right?"

"You remembered," said Jill. "How sweet."

"I don't know what a *production designer guy* does, but what would happen if he, like, lost the designs?"

She cocked an eyebrow. "Well, he's got me as his assistant, so that wouldn't happen. But hypothetically, I think you're asking what would happen if he forgot all the plans and designs, and the entire crew and equipment arrived on set with nothing to shoot?"

Smitty looked at her blankly for a moment. "Sure."

"My dad would be in a lot of trouble."

"Do you think he'd get hired again?" asked Smitty.

"Probably not. Everybody in this business talks. It's like a small town, or, like a, I don't know, a—"

"—cult?" I blurted out.

Jill punched my shoulder a little too hard. "Not funny," she said.

Gordon was nodding, catching on. "I'm getting it. What if the wardrobe from a scene just sort of, you know, *vanished?* Same thing, right?"

"On a period movie like this? With tons of costumes?" said Jill. "It would be a disaster. The wardrobe is essential. It would be Pink-slip City."

"What's a pink-slip?" I asked

"It's what they give you when you're fired," said Gordon.

"And that's your mom's main thing, right?" asked Smitty. "Clothes and stuff?"

"Yup," I replied with a nod. "One of her responsibilities is to make sure the right clothes racks are set up for each scene. She's always talking about how hard it is to keep everything organized."

Gordon continued. "You tell Big Jack to swing by the set. He'll witness the whole freak-out when they find out the costumes are gone. And just when everyone starts losing their minds, he steps in to protect her. She'll see what Superman *really* looks like. *No cape required.* She'll fall in love with your dad all over again."

"Shit man, she'll probably be *glad* she got fired!" Smitty piped in.

"You can't do that!" said Jill.

"Why not?" Smitty shot back.

"Well, first of all, it's bad for the movie. They need that wardrobe. It's a really important scene."

"Wait a minute." Gordon stopped, and we all stopped with him.

"Really important scene? *Really important scene?* We're talking about my boy's family unit here. They'll figure out the costumes. They got tons of sewing machines. I saw them," continued Gordon. "But Jack's mom needs to get fired. End of discussion. So either get on board or—"

"—fine. You're right. I'm on board," Jill said.

But Gordon continued. "Or you'll have to find some new friends because—"

"—I said I'm on board!"

Smitty picked up the rant. "Because this is some serious family stuff, and—"

"—for the third time: I'm. On. Board!"

"Oh. Sorry," said Smitty. "Sweet!"

Jill turned to me. "It's your mom we're talking about, Jack. What do you think?"

Despite the ethics of it all, I couldn't think of a better idea. "How would we do it?" I asked Jill.

"Well. Let me think. They're filming a really important scene on the beach the day after tomorrow. It's the moment when Richard and Elise first meet. They're calling it the *Is it you* scene. If the wardrobe disappeared? Let's just say your mom won't be invited to the wrap party."

"So it would be bad?" I said.

"Worse than bad," Jill said.

"Good," I said.

"Kids!" the Very Important Brit called from his megaphone, irritated. "Saunter *slower!*" He was right. We were almost race-walking, energized by this twisted new scheme.

I looked toward Mom. She was standing with Cynthia, inspecting an extra's dress folds. Guilt shot through me like an electrical current. It passed. Mom's Hollywood career was almost over.

"Let's do it," I said.

"And … *action!*"

Operation Pink-Slip had been approved.

CHAPTER TWENTY-FOUR

Stealing Scene 242

The next day, I embarked on my fourth break-in of the summer. We treaded up the narrow stairway to the wardrobe department at the Mackinac Hotel studio offices. The last time I'd been there was for Mom's interview in June, and it felt like I'd lived at least three lifetimes since.

I'd pulled the wardrobe master key from Mom's ring earlier and copied it at the hardware store. I smiled as they ground it for me, fake sweet, careful to replace the original before Mom noticed. The freshly cut copy fought me at first but eventually slid into the lock with a thunk. The door swung open, and we walked in, closing it behind us.

Jill removed a piece of paper from her pocket, unfolded it, and examined it with her flashlight. "Scene 242," she said. "The *Is it you* scene, it says here on the call sheet."

Smitty leaned over her shoulder. "Wonder why they call it that," he asked.

"Because Jane Seymour says that in the movie."

Smitty thought about it for a second. "I like it. It's like 'Yo, Adrian,' from *Rocky*, except for chicks."

"We're looking for three costumes and their backups, plus all the extras' stuff and accessories," Jill said. "One for Jane, one for Chris, and one for Christopher Plummer. Usually, they're hanging on the racks and labeled by scene number."

She looked up from the call sheet, and we followed her gaze. There were rows and rows of clothing racks, separated by large yellow cards labeled with scene numbers. I noticed Mom's handwriting on the cards.

The greater good of society.

The greater good of ...

The greater good ...

"Huddle up!" I called out. The team gathered. "We don't want to be here more than thirty minutes." I looked at Jill. "When's call time tomorrow?"

She scanned the sheet. "Noon. That means the camera, grip, props, and wardrobe will be prepped by eight a.m. They'll load it all up and transport the stuff to the location with a horse-drawn dray."

"Got it. You two check that row over there," I directed Jill and Smitty. "Gordo, you and I will search the other row. Once we find the costumes, we pack 'em up ... and we lose 'em."

We split up. I beamed my light onto vintage outfits, immaculate tuxedos, and patterned dresses. "This is bonkers," I said in a low voice, inspecting the scene numbers on the racks. "I'm a criminal. There's no other way to say it."

"Well, at least you're doing something," said Gordon. "Me? I'm sittin' around on my ass as my family goes down the terr-let." Gordon often pronounced *toilet* as *terr-let*. It was the first time I'd heard him bring up his home life without being asked. It felt good.

"Cool hat," he added absently as he scanned his flashlight across a rack.

"I guess we all have our coping mechanisms," I said. "Yours is to ignore stuff."

"That's me." Gordon aimed his light toward a collection of button-downs. "Yours? Go rogue, ditch your pals for a dirtbag, break into an old man's house, get busted, find a car in a barn, and screw up a murder case."

"Yup," I nodded, smiling in the dark. "Sums it up."

Smitty called over. "Don't forget crapping in your cutoffs over a fake Wendigo! And by the way, what's a *coping mechanism?*"

I called back. "I'm not sure. I heard it in a movie."

Jill piped in. "I know. A *coping mechanism* is a—"

She was interrupted by a prolonged, multi-octave fart that echoed through the storage room. "Ew!" she cried. "Excuse me, but there is a *lady* present!"

"Sorry," snickered Smitty. "I downed a can of Chef Boy-Ar-Dee spaghetti and two bottles of Pepsi for dinner. Been blowing wet ones ever since."

After an eternity of searching, we still hadn't located the wardrobe for scene 242. The four of us moved up and down the racks, double-checking each other's work and scouring the room with flashlights while time rapidly ticked away.

"Jackpot!" I heard Smitty call out from the other side of the room.

He motioned to us. We followed him through an open door to a small room filled with a stack of neatly arranged crates, each sealed shut with tape and labeled with Mom's perfect handwriting.

SCENE 242.

We descended upon the crates, pulling off the lids to reveal five dresses, five pairs of oversized brown pants, and five black tuxedos. The crates also held additional clothing for the extras, bolts of fabric, hangers, and accessories, like belts, jewelry, scarves, and cufflinks. Another crate contained measuring tape, scissors, needles, boxes of thread, two irons, and three portable sewing machines.

We stared at the load in stunned silence. "There's no way we can haul all this out of here," said Gordon. "We brought one idiotic little red wagon."

I surveyed the mountain.

"We're gonna need a dockporter."

"Is this Foster Dupree?" I said into the phone.

The voice on the other end of the line was raspy and rattled. A woman's voice giggled in the background.

"Why do I get the sense I'm talking to an eleven-year-old? It's freaking me out. Who is this?"

"Uh, Jack McGuinn. The paper boy. And I'm … almost twelve."

For an instant, he sounded concerned. "It's three in the morning. You okay?"

"I'm fine. You gave me your business card on the dock one morning. Said if I hooked you up with some redcaps, you'd give me a cut." *Redcaps* were luggage runs outside the normal hotel loads, and dockporters were always prowling for extra cash.

"Little dude, the first ferry doesn't even get in until seven thirty."

"This is a different kind of load. Are you interested or not?"

"Call me in three hours. Or better yet, *never.*"

"I've got thirty bucks."

Foster breathed through his mouth, mumbled something, then coughed. Bed springs creaked. "You caught me at the right moment. The fellas left me high and dry with the tab at the French Outpost, and now I'm flat-busted."

"Bummer, man," I said, pretending to understand what he had just mumbled.

"It happens. What can you do?" he snorted. "Money's like the tide. It comes in. It goes out. Besides, the night wasn't a total bust. I met a nice new friend. Sara."

The woman in the background laughed. "It's *Sandy,* ya lug!" More laughing and sheets rustling. "And what's *my* name, Sandy?"

"Don't know, don't care," I heard her say.

The two of them either started kissing or eating a peach. Either way, it was gross. I held the phone away from my ear and waited. Foster eventually returned. "Sorry, you had to hear that, kid. Just one of those nights. So. Where's the pick-up?"

"We'll meet you on the side of the *Somewhere in Time* offices at the Mackinac Hotel. My mom works as a seamstress on the movie, and we have to–"

"—hurray for Hollywood, but I don't care," he cut me off. "How many pieces?"

"Five suitcases and one … I don't know what it's called. Like a box from the olden days with travel stickers all over it."

"It's called a steamer trunk," Jill piped in.

"A steamer trunk?" Foster scoffed. "It's 1979, man. Who uses a steamer trunk? Doesn't matter. It's probably a bitch to ride. I want forty."

"I got thirty."

"Okay, fine." More creaky bed springs. "See you in half an hour. I need to freshen up. *Come here, you ...*" A giggle, a click, and a dial tone.

I stared at the phone receiver blankly, hung up, and regarded the stack of suitcases. We'd transferred the wardrobe from scene 242 into five suitcases from the props department, replacing what was in the crates with modern-day costumes. Then we carefully resealed them. The next day, when Mom opened the crates, she'd find no trace of the approved wardrobe—or any supplies to quickly whip something up. Panic would ensue, along with a large helping of mayhem. If all went according to plan, a pink-slip would follow shortly after.

Greater good greater good greater good ...

Smitty glanced at the suitcases. "I got an idea."

"This is your second idea in three days, Smitty," I said, honestly impressed.

"I know, man. It's a personal record." He gestured toward the suitcases. "We have time to kill until the dock-porter gets here. Let's reenact scene 242 with you and Jill. Me and Gordon'll be the camera crew. It'll be fun!"

Jill didn't hesitate. She popped open a suitcase, revealing Jane Seymour's elegant white dress. "Be right back!" she exclaimed, vanishing from sight. Moments later, she reemerged, adorned in the dress from scene 242.

Our collective jaws dropped. The dress, though slightly oversized for her petite frame, draped around Jill with an unexpected elegance. She'd undergone a stunning metamorphosis. The funky, sunburned, New Wave California girl dissolved into a miniature incarnation of Jane Seymour herself.

She spun around with arms outstretched like royalty on display. She regarded her hands. "Wait! I'm missing the finishing touch," she said, skipping off to a section of shelves. She yanked on a pair of white silk gloves and returned, grinning. "Now we're cookin'. *A lady needs her gloves,*" she said in a faux upper-crust accent.

"I don't think gloves are part of the costume," I said. "Those are tagged for a different scene."

"Well," she shrugged. "They are now."

"You're up, Jack," said Gordon.

"What do you mean 'I'm up'?"

Smitty pointed toward a suitcase with a brown suit. "*Change.*"

"No way I'm putting that stuff on!"

"You owe it to your mom," said Smitty. "Think about it." He gestured to the costumes. "She did all this work, and if our evil scheme goes according to plan, it'll never see the light of day."

I considered the pile of brown wool and the bowler hat. He had a point.

"Show some respect, McGuinn," said Gordon.

A few minutes later, I returned in the full Richard Collier getup, swimming in Reeve's clothes. The fabric hung off my scrawny body like a coat on a hanger, and the bowler hat practically sat on my shoulders. The guys howled, but Jill smiled.

"All right, everyone! Places!" said Gordon. "Jill, you look amazing. Jack, you look like a demented scarecrow. Let's do this thing!"

Gordon struck a director's pose, one foot on a suitcase. "Positions, everybody!" He'd obviously been paying attention to the Hollywood lingo during his stint as an extra.

Smitty scanned the script pages he had found pinned to a corkboard. "Jack. It says here you walk behind Jill. She turns to you and says ... *Is it you?* And you kind of fumble around and say …" He looked back at the script again, confused. "Where is Jack's line?"

Gordon looked over Smitty's shoulder and pointed to the script page. "It's right there!"

"Oh yeah. Okay. You say, um … *'Yes.'*"

Gordon snatched away the script. "Smitty, you be the cameraman. I'll handle directing." Wordlessly, Smitty began cranking his right hand forward as if operating a camera.

"This one's for a picture!" yelled Gordon. "Positions, everybody."

"Scene 242, take one!" said Smitty.

"And … action!" called out Gordon.

Jill walked slowly, occasionally peering back over her shoulder. I trailed behind her, attempting not to trip over my pant legs, grasping the waistband with one hand.

Gordon read from the script. "Close-up on Richard, smitten by the woman whose photograph he fell in love with at another time. The camera moves in on her face." Smitty's imaginary camera obediently moved from me to Jill as if capturing every detail of the scene.

Gordon hissed, "And … *line!*"

Jill looked at me and smiled shyly. My knees weakened as her forehead furrowed with concentration. She opened her mouth to speak, but closed it a moment later, unable to find the right words.

"Is it you?" she finally asked, her voice laced with vulnerability.

I was speechless, pushing my giant bowler hat back to see her more clearly.

"Line, Jack!" hissed Gordon, as Smitty moved in for an imaginary close-up of my face. I could see him grinning, his hand still cranking the invisible camera. It was ridiculous, embarrassing. And, yes, *romantic*.

Jill reached out for my hand. I struggled, the words lodged inside me. I took her satin-gloved hand in mine and gazed intently into her eyes. She asked again, this time more emphatic. "Is it you?"

Finally, I was able to speak. "Um, yup." *Yup?*

Her eyes held mine, then she looked away, only to gaze back again. The moment went on far too long. It was a dance of fleeting glances, a silent conversation. Then something happened I would never have imagined. A glimpse of truth no screenwriter could create, forever etched in my memory to this day.

My pants fell down.

"Cut!" Gordon's voice echoed, a mix of annoyance and amusement. "Come on, Jack, no clowning around! Stick to the script." Smitty, unable to contain himself, let out a burst of uncontrollable laughter, while Jill joined in, her girlish giggles filling the room.

"Reset! Back to one!"

From across the room, keys jingled and footsteps echoed. I instantly froze, Reeve's massive pants pulled halfway up. Smitty was still doubled over, his hands on his knees, but now silent. Gordon was a statue, frozen hands gesturing in the air. Jill's eyes darted sideways. I glanced at the blazing lightbulb, then around the cramped storage room—no hiding place. Smitty reached to the wall and clicked off the light.

"Act like mannequins!" Jill whispered.

We crept out of the storage room like a platoon on night patrol and positioned ourselves among the mannequins, striking poses. The distant footsteps merged with the off-key whistling of "YMCA."

A beam passed. A security guard in a brown rent-a-cop uniform, strolled down the aisle, still whistling. He stopped short. His head snapped to his right. He looked directly into my terrified eyes and extended his arm toward me. His hand moved inches past my cheek, and he plucked a slouchy newsies-style cap from a shelf, not unlike the one I'd worn in the scene the day before. He popped it on his head.

"Cheerio, guv'nor," he said in a terrible English accent. "Fancy a cuppa tea? Very well. Tip-tip!" He glanced around the room, making sure he was utterly alone, grabbed a long black overcoat, and slid it on."Bloody poppycock. Care for a biscuit? Why you're a dodgy … umm … geezer."

He didn't seem so sure about *geezer* but he rambled on.

I clamped my molars down on the inside of my cheek to keep from giggling. I was more worried about Smitty. His lack of self-control was mythical. He'd crack up at a funeral, and the performance three feet away was legitimately weird. Plus, he had gas. I thought I heard a tight, squeak from under the mountain of carefully constructed costumes, and I silently mumbled a prayer to Flautus, the God of flatulence, to protect us in our time of need. Thankfully, the rent-a-cop returned the jacket and the hat to the shelf and resumed strolling. I breathed a silent sigh of relief as we heard the door shut and lock.

Suddenly, a thunderous gastronomic eruption reverberated through the room, fueled by Pepsi and Chef Boy-R-Dee. The sound seemed to defy the laws of acoustics, echoing with astonishing resonance.

It was time to go.

Foster arrived at 3:30 am on the dot, his bike tires crunching gravel as he rolled to a stop. He straddled his gold Schwinn Heavi-Duty, his ropey, muscled forearms resting on the longhorn handlebars. His sun-bleached hair was twisted in wild corkscrews as if rousted from some R-rated romp. He regarded us all curiously, a bemused grin on his face.

"Here it is. Five suitcases and a steamer trunk," I said.

Foster surveyed the antique load. "Where'd you get this luggage? I thought the Titanic sunk."

"We borrowed them from the props department. They're from the movie."

Foster fell oddly silent. "Four kids with luggage at three-thirty in the morning. Why do I have the odd feeling I'm getting roped into a dubious venture?"

"Everything is on the up and up," I assured him.

"It's for the greater good of society," Smitty added somberly.

Foster looked at Smitty, pondering whether this mysterious gibberish was worth unraveling. He rolled his bike closer to the suitcases and began to load them into the large wire basket, one by one. He made a V shape with the two biggest bags and then stacked the others inside.

"Lift the steamer trunk on top. I'll strap it down and be on my way."

Smitty and Gordon grabbed either side of the trunk and placed it on top of the load. Foster reached the front of his basket and grabbed a long bungee cord, stretching it over the load and attaching it to the stem of his handlebars.

"Where am I taking it?" Foster asked.

"That's an interesting question," I answered, rubbing my chin thoughtfully. "Let's imagine a situation where the people who own these bags aren't so generous. Let's imagine they don't tip."

I shot a look at him, gauging his response. "In a situation like that, what would you do?"

Foster pondered the options. "In a situation like the one you described, there's a slight chance their bags may never end up on the boat with them. There's even a tiny chance that if they were *ungrateful* for my assistance, their bags could end up all over the place. Orphaned."

"Meaning?" I asked.

"Meaning one might end up on the three o'clock Arnold Line to St. Ignace. Another on the two o'clock Shepler's to Mac City. Hell, another might not go anywhere. It might stay in the luggage storage room on the Straits Transit dock."

He scratched his head. "Shit, kid. I can even imagine a situation where a suitcase ended up in the break room of Sally's Gifts. You just never know. All kinds of crazy things can happen during a day on the docks. Especially when it's busy."

"Well, this," I said, "… is one of those situations."

I took out a twenty-dollar bill, a ten, and an extra five from my pocket. I carefully creased the bills in thirds, tucked the loot in my palm, and presented them with an earnest handshake, mimicking the wealthy tourists I'd watched execute the same maneuver. He accepted the tip, smiled sideways, and slid the cash into his pocket.

He pushed off with the luggage, slid his butt onto his bike seat for counterbalance, and rode away with all the wardrobe from scene 242.

CHAPTER TWENTY-FIVE

The Blue Butterfly

I hesitated outside the master bedroom, unsure if I wanted to look in. I held my breath and slowly pushed open the door. The room was dark and still, the curtains drawn tightly.

Big Jack slept fully clothed on top of the covers, snoring lightly. For him, it was another lost weekend where he showed up on the last boat without fanfare. He was still a ghost, even after the night of the pot pies, when he shared family secrets and confided his fears. But nothing really had changed, despite the healing power of Iroquois Hotel ice cream puffs. Big Jack was still a mess, and we were still left to wonder if whatever Mom had tossed overboard decades earlier, had drifted back to shore. Much like the Marjorie Kitmore murder, the Great Mom Mystery remained unsolved.

I pulled the old door shut and stood in the dimly lit hall, feeling a sense of guilty and giddy anticipation. Operation Pink-Slip had begun. I could only wait for the fireworks that were sure to follow.

Across the hall was the guest room. I headed in.

Despite the room's slightly musty scent, the old furniture was cozy and inviting. This was now Mom's room. I made my way to a small table where a sewing machine and an array of supplies lay across the surface. Bolts of colorful fabric were neatly stacked on a nearby shelf, and a half-finished garment hung off the back of an old wooden chair.

I touched the sewing machine. Still warm. I jotted down the observation in my notebook and inspected the room for clues about her plans. Maps of Florida? A script for "Smokey and the Bandit 2"? A contract?

Anything.

The closet door was slightly ajar, and I reached inside for the pull chain. I froze as my eyes settled on an unfamiliar stack of photo albums on the floor. Randomly plopped down, most likely during Mom's haphazard relocation. One binder caught my eye, tucked between the others. It had a wider spine and looked less store-bought. I bent down and slowly slid it out, careful not to let the others topple.

The frayed red felt cover, wrapped with a faded gold ribbon, felt oddly off-limits. So, of course, I untied it. A round inset in the center contained a wrinkled black and white photograph of a little girl, maybe six or seven. Written in large cursive handwriting:

Property of Ana Tetreault.

I took the scrapbook to the bed, planted myself on the old, springy mattress, and opened it to the first page.

Childlike drawings decorated the initial pages, mostly in crayons but some in pencil.

An assortment of paper dolls adorned in unique outfits with fold-over tabs. A few had taped notes attached, bearing encouraging comments ranging from "Exceptional" to "You have an excellent eye, Ana!"

Carefully, I flipped the page of the thick scrapbook. My eyes landed on three black-and-white photographs of a young girl standing with hands on hips with a proud grin. Each shot showcased a different wardrobe sample for what appeared to be a school performance of *Peter Pan*. Notes accompanied the detailed sketches in her fanciful script. Bolder lines revealed more confident ideas.

Was she an artist? And if so, how did I not know it?

But a voice answered the question: *Because you never asked, you selfish little ingrate.* Mom often included a sketch in my lunchbox, carefully paperclipped to my zip-lock baggie full of veggies. Maybe a dinosaur in a stylish tux, warning me, "T-Rex says DEVOUR those carrots!" Beth's Thirteenth birthday featured hand-drawn invitations with paper-thin fashion models holding up number 13s in various poses.

Turning another page, I discovered a collage of magazine cut-outs featuring film stars in glamorous gowns, skirts, and bathing suits. It was clear she knew exactly what she was looking at and why. The following pages were illustrations devoted to famous fashion and costume designers from the 50s and 60s, hand labeled with Edith Head, Givenchy, and Walter Plunkett. Although their names meant nothing to me, I assumed they were fashion legends.

I flipped the page to a series of sketches in charcoal, colored pencil, and watercolor, all exquisitely detailed. Her talent was developing.

Light-headed now. This was no mere scrapbook. It was

a portal to another dimension, pulling me into the kaleido-
scopic imagination of a person we labeled "Mom." A
responsible human being who scrambled my eggs, took my
temperature when I felt ill, mended my socks, and tightened my scarf in winter. And yet, she made art? It
answered so many questions. How she managed to make
every room in our McGuinn universe instantly cozy, even
her blindfolded rendition of "To Sir With Love." That
particular stunt was undoubtedly not the by-product of an
ordinary mind. And there was her personal style: understated, casual, not fussed-over, but somehow perfect.

I turned the page.

Marlon Brando, in the film *On the Waterfront*, she'd
scribbled *How could I make him look better, more relaxed?*

Beneath a photograph of Jimmy Stewart and Grace
Kelly in the movie *Rear Window*, she'd scratched the question in ink. *How can I top this?*

On the next page, an award certificate, aged but
screaming with consequence. "Congratulations," it read.
"First Place Junior Costume Design Competition." She
was getting noticed. A letter surrounded by hearts and
stars, highlighted by a neatly worded annotation that said,
GOOD GOD!

Dear Ana,
I was blown away by the sketches and designs you sent. Your
talent and creativity are impressive, and you have a bright
future ahead of you in the fashion world. We will be keeping
an eye on you. Please send me more when you're ready!
- Edith Head

Unbelievable. She was getting personal letters from her
heroes. Some woman named Edith Head. I was witnessing
the blooming of a career right before my eyes.

As I continued to flip, I discovered she was offered a chance to study abroad in Paris. A brochure: *American Airlines makes the world smaller!*

Illustrations and designs surrounding another brochure were all Egyptian-themed: *Visit the land of the pharaohs!* A hand-scrawled list of movies in the margins: *The Ten Commandments. Land of the Pharaohs? Serpent of the Nile.* The genesis of the Cairo dream?

I turned the page to reveal a series of designs occupying four pages of the book. A wedding dress made of soft white lace, a flowing skirt, and a delicate train accented with pearls and crystals. The sketches outlined every detail, from the sleeves to the intricate bodice, with detailed notes in her now familiar designer's hand.

Was it for a movie? Had she reconnected with Edith Head and was taking a shot at the Big Time? I imagined her burning the midnight oil to add the final touches to the design that might launch her career, meticulously packaging up the drawings, and tenderly planting a kiss for luck on the envelope before dropping it in a blue metal mailbox. Praying this was her way out of Boring (with a big 'B').

I turned the page—one large black-and-white photo.

Mom and Big Jack on their wedding day danced gracefully, as if possessed by an unseen force. Dad's smile was sheepish and open, like the proverbial cat that got the canary. Mom looked radiantly happy, her eyes flashing as she looked into his eyes.

But my eyes were drawn to her dress. It was the one she'd designed.

It wasn't for Edith Head.

It wasn't for the movies.

It wasn't for recognition.

It was for her wedding day.

I ran my fingertips across the black-and-white image.

Spirits from another era. Not frazzled, disconnected co-CEOs of McGuinn Family & Co. Not two strangers on different cars of the midlife Ferris wheel. Just newlyweds dancing.

After the photographs of her wedding, there were no more clothing designs. Baby pictures. Highchairs and birthday parties. Photos of the four of us on adventures, at the zoo, at the beach. Class pictures and report card highlights. Mementos stuck in the book with Elmer's Glue-All and loving care. Life on Mackinac Island. Wildcliffe. Sledding in Brighton. Big Jack and Mom hosting parties. Gramps and his crew mugging to the camera. Me and Beth. Sheepish. Growing. But still, the funky annotations, quips, jokes, arrows, hearts, and doodles.

Her art had become her family. And by all objective measures, she had created a masterpiece.

—for a time.

A few pesky tears splashed down on the album page with deep, hot *thwoks*. An unsteady breath, and I regained my composure.

A few pages later, I was looking at something she called a "vision board." A newer entry. Not yesterday new, but not twenty years old either. They were sketches for a dress shop. The exterior had a simple sign in the window with arched words reading, *The Blue Butterfly.* The shop was small, but as she put it in her doodle, "adorbs," a phrase she loved and used whenever possible. I always assumed it was short for "adorable."

Her artist's pencil conjured an inviting space with comfortable seating and warm lighting. I could feel the breezy vibe of the place, and even if I couldn't give two craps about "fashion" and never would, I wanted to hang out there. Touches of whimsy and personality, like a chandelier made of colorful glass beads and a wall covered in vintage hat boxes.

As I shifted, something fluttered to the floor. I picked it up. A hand-painted butterfly, its body yellow, its wings a vibrant—now faded—blue. It was the sign in her drawings. I returned the butterfly to the book and tucked it behind another picture securely taped on the page.

That was the end of the scrapbook.

I closed it, set it aside, and went to her work table, searching her papers for … for what?

For more.

I noticed an unsealed envelope sticking out from an old cigar box on the sewing table. I snatched it up and hesitated for a brief moment. I had already invaded Mom's privacy to such an extent that any possibility of redemption was laughable. I sighed with resignation and began reading:

Dear Cynthia,

Girl, I am so flattered you thought of me for Smokey and the Bandit 2! Who wouldn't want to work on a movie with Burt Reynolds? Swoon! But after some serious soul-searching (and a few glasses of wine), I must decline the offer. The timing isn't right. The demands of the job have been tough on my family. I've been working long hours and missing important moments with my kids and husband. Working on "Somewhere in Time" has been one of the most rewarding experiences of my life. A lifelong dream somehow tracked me down on Mackinac Island, proving the universe works in magic ways. I have you to thank for that.
Your biggest fan,
-Ana

She was never planning to leave us.

The Great Mom Mystery was solved. It wasn't some dark, mysterious trauma. Nor was it regret over playing it safe with Dad. It wasn't the Hollywood Cult and wasn't Superman's inseam.

She had tossed her former life overboard, not because she was forced to, but because she *chose* to. She met a great man. They started a family. She didn't tell him about her former dream because … *who knows why*. Maybe it was too intertwined with a life she wanted to forget. Or maybe she simply lost interest in designing clothes. Decades later, by an act of complete providence, coincidence, and fate, she was given a chance to work on a movie and see what it was like.

And she seized it.

The drama existed only in our fevered, immature minds. Dad began to worry that he was the *safe choice*, as if Mom had lost interest in him. Old insecurities swam to the surface.

Men are such idiots.

I refolded the letter with shaking hands and slid it back into the envelope. I felt feverish. Enlightened. Stupid. And most of all, ashamed. I checked my watch—10:27 a.m.

Terminate Operation Pink-Slip!

There was still time if I could track down the bags. Scene 242 was scheduled for noon.

I fled the room, scrapbook clutched tightly in my hands. I carefully placed it on the floor before my parent's bedroom door.

It would be impossible to miss.

CHAPTER TWENTY-SIX

Unclaimed Luggage

With the velocity of a musket ball, I catapulted out of Wildcliffe and leaped onto a battered Sluggo. Earlier that morning, I'd pounded the bike back into shape with a croquet mallet, and now I tested the machine with a hard left turn, I raced down Mission Hill toward the shore. Maneuvering recklessly, I executed a hard left, leaning turn with a hint of reckless abandon, my right pedal scraping against the pavement, igniting a shower of sparks that exploded like fireworks.

At least, that's the way I remember it.

It was already 11:15 AM. Scene 242 was supposed to roll at noon, and Mom would discover that the costumes in her boxes were about sixty-five years out of date, with no backups anywhere in sight. I had forty-five minutes to track them down. The island may have been small, but it might have been Manhattan if you were trying to locate lost luggage. *It contained multitudes.*

I strained to remember the conversation with Foster the

night before. He mentioned his ideas of where he "might" stash six suitcases if he had to lose them. At the time, it was coded hypothetical banter. But now, it was my only lead.

I remember he said something about Sally's Gifts— something about the break room and the steamer trunk.

I skidded to a halt in front of the store. My eyes adjusted as I stepped inside and quickly scanned the place, searching for any sign of a break room. Sally's Gifts bloomed with oddly shaped balsa wood boxes and racks of moccasins. The aroma of chemically treated leather mixed with lacquered wood made my head spin instantly. An arsenal of slingshots adorned a glass display case along with ninja throwing stars, sharpened to a razor point. T-shirts, keychains, and shot glasses. Cap guns and rubber spears. Naked lady playing cards and racks of Official Mackinac Island Fudgie T-shirts in every color. If a souvenir shop could visually represent the fevered mind of a typical kid in 1979, it would look a lot like Sally's Gifts. I saw a door in the back and made a beeline.

The break room was a claustrophobic labyrinth of half-empty boxes and mothballed knick-knacks. My eyes darted around, scanning for a steamer trunk. Foster said he *might* hide it here, but he wasn't entirely sober when he said it.

I lifted a mismeasured curtain that divided the room, and my eyes fell on a plump man with his arms folded and his head resting on a card table. His guttural snores echoed, punctuated by soft intermittent puffs of breath. Despite all my instincts telling me to turn away, I couldn't resist looking closer. An ample posterior punctuated by a Grand Canyon-sized ass crack was exposed below a hitched-up T-shirt.

Below his ass was the steamer trunk.

I stifled a gag. How could I extract the trunk beneath

the sleeping behemoth's cheeks without waking him and risking another visit to Richter's office?

Boy thief strikes again.

Smitty once told me a story about how you could make a person pee their pants while they slept simply by placing their hand in warm water. He'd never personally tested it, but it was time. I had to eliminate this lug, and the clock was ticking. Scanning the room, I noticed two rusted metal cat bowls sitting on the floor, coated in years of grime and neglect. The food bowl was caked with green mold, while the water bowl was a swampy brown. I held my breath and silently raised the putrid water to the table. Carefully, I maneuvered his fingertips into the bowl. He remained perfectly still. I hid under a souvenir bear skin rug, my breathing heavy. Sweat pooled in my ears, and time ticked slowly as I waited for something to happen.

Without warning, the dam broke. The cashier's eyes shot open, and he leaped up, looking down in sudden, dumb confusion as a lake of urine expanded across the front of his cargo shorts, forming pee-soaked tributaries and deltas. He bolted from the room, stumbling over a crate of Davy Crockett-style beaver pelt hats and leaving me with a clear path to the trunk. I grabbed the handles and dragged it through the store, leaving a long meandering scratch on the old wooden floor as I struggled towards the door.

Sluggo's basket was too small to haul the trunk. With a grunt, I lifted it to my waist and headed toward the Arnold Line dock, the closest place I could think of to set up a command post.

"Hey, kid! Got a light?" a thin, shaggy-haired tourist blurted. As he walked with his blonde girlfriend, a camera swung from his sunburned neck like a pendulum. *Such wit.*

"Very original, Agnes," I said. His amiable grin dropped, and his girlfriend burst out laughing.

"Little smartass!" he shouted back.

He was right. Why did I call him Agnes? *That was so Blaze.*

A horse-drawn carriage clopped past in the opposite direction. "How about a ride to the Arnold dock?" I called up, already drenched in sweat.

"Only paying customers, ya little freeloader!" Taxi Chad shot back. He must've recognized me from my unpaid rides on his luggage rack with the boys.

"I'll pay you extra, man!" I pleaded, but he shook his head and kept going. My feet tangled, and I tripped, losing my grip on the trunk. It skidded through a moist pile of horse manure.

Taxi Chad glanced back, face twisting into a triumphant smirk. I heaved the trunk back up, dirty but determined.

I gritted my teeth and pushed the steamer trunk until it was hidden inside the Arnold Line freight shack. *One down, five to go.* What else had Foster said last night? Something about an 11:30 ferry to St. Ignace? Three boat lines were operating in 1979. Three 11:30 ferries to St. Ignace. A lightning-quick round of *rock, paper, scissors,* and I was off to the Shepler's dock. I'd be hoofing it without Sluggo, which was still parked back at Sally's Gifts.

The Shepler dock extended into the harbor, yards from the Turtle Wizard Arcade. It took everything I had to resist ducking in for a healing pinball game with *Captain Fantastic.* Instead, I sprinted toward an overloaded luggage cart pushed down the dock by a lanky deckhand in navy blue shorts and a white polo shirt.

"Stop!" I yelled, waving at him.

The deckhand peeked dubiously over his shoulder.

"My suitcase is on that cart!"

He didn't slow down, his sunburned arms outstretched. "Captain Bob is on a schedule. If this cart's not on this boat by 11:30, I'll swim with the fishes like Luca Brasi, understand?"

"Um. Not really. Who's Luca—"

"—If your suitcase is on this cart, grab it. But make it quick."

I studied the Rubik's cube of luggage—large, hard-sided suitcases with colorful tags, soft duffel bags, wheeled carry-on satchels, golf clubs, grocery bags for the thrifty traveler, and even a pet carrier, thankfully devoid of a yapping chihuahua. As the ferry engines roared, I frantically yanked on bags, searching for a glimpse of a 1912-era suitcase plastered with vintage travel stickers we had stolen from the props department the night before.

"Careful! You're gonna start a landslide!" the deckhand said.

The cart hit a dip in the dock. A stray plastic cooler slid down and cracked me hard in the head. A quick Northern Lights show illuminated the inside of my skull, staggering me for a moment.

And there it was. It stood out among the pile of modern luggage like a silent movie star. Perfectly aged by Hollywood's best. The prop suitcase, stuffed with at least some of the wardrobe from scene 242.

I pulled on the handle with all my might, setting off a chain reaction that unleashed a thunderous cascade of suitcases, tumbling and colliding onto the dock.

"Goddammit! I told you! Now you're gonna help me

reload this crap because I won't be the reason the eleven-thirty leaves at eleven thirty-two! This ferry pulls out in sixty seconds, and now this crap is all over the dock! Now grab that suitcase and ..."

But I was already gone, stealing away like a thief in the night with my suitcase stuffed with Superman-sized wool pants, shoes, and accessories. The intensity of his profane tirade blended with the aural mosaic of Main Street—the clacking of horse hooves, the whirring of bike chains, and the laughter of fudge-high kids—until I could no longer hear him yelling.

I tucked the suitcase under my arm and ran to the Arnold Line dock, fingers cramping.

As I sprinted past the Murray Hotel, the dulcimer-playing hippie kicked into the 1812 Overture.

Bling, bada-bling, bada-bling-bling-bling-bling-bling!

In an instant, Main Street vibrated with a renewed sense of energy. Families rode their rental bikes with heightened confidence, horses smiled, and tourists window-shopped with a newfound sense of purpose. The suitcase felt lighter, and I picked up the pace. The dulcimer mallets danced across the strings faster, plucking each note with precision, building to a climax. As the last note was struck, the cannon from Fort Mackinac ignited, punctuating the finale with a thunderous blast.

At least, that's the way I remember it.

Two bags down, four to go, and I was fresh out of ideas.

It was between boats on the Arnold Line dock, and aside from a few early birds waiting for the next ferry, I was alone. *What else had Foster said?* I was two-for-two on my guesses, but now my fatigued melon felt wiped clean. Two measly bags were not going to cut it for Mom.

I scrutinized the distant break wall and strained with spoon-bending concentration to remember Foster's banter from the night before. Almost as if drifting across the marina, I could hear it. Vivid and real.

"One bag's tagged for the noon Straits Transit to Mac City, and another is at the end of the dock down there." It was almost as if the voice was right behind me.

"A third is tucked under my bed." *Under my bed?*

"The fourth you can forget about, though. That bag is airborne."

I was losing my mind. Again. I spun around.

Foster, straddling his porter bike, casually unloaded a few suitcases from his basket onto a luggage cart. He was wearing Ray-Ban aviators and looked like a worn-out fighter pilot.

"Tony Boom, the Chippewa dockporter, saw you stumbling down Main Street earlier with that big steamer trunk, so I figured you might have a little buyer's remorse," he said. "And before you ask, I'm not refunding your tip."

"Foster! You're just the guy I'm looking for!" I practically hopped in his basket. "Listen, everything's different now."

"You don't say," said Foster. I couldn't tell if he actually cared, but I began babbling like a guilty man on sodium pentothal. "I found my mom's old scrapbook, and it turns out she's a real artist. Like, she knows all about wardrobe stuff and isn't working on the movie for some deep, dark reason like my dad thinks and truthfully, like I thought too, and so this whole Operation Pink-Slip idea has been called off and …"

I stopped, waited for his reaction, got nothing, and plowed on. "I can't prove anything without the pocket

watch and the paperwork. I'll never get the reward for the
Marjorie Kitmore murder, but it's okay because ultimately
I was wrong about mom, and solving the murder was
always just a means to an end because it's … I … I mean
….." I stopped again.

Foster's fingers stroked his chin. "Jack. It's Jack, right?"

"Yes."

He pulled off his sunglasses slowly and fixed me with
concerned blue eyes. "What the *hell* are you even talking
about?"

"Nevermind. Did you say one suitcase is on the Straits
dock, one is under your bed, and another is down the
dock?"

"Yup."

"Okay, good. I wasn't sure if I was hearing voices in
my head. Ghost voices or something."

Foster just looked at me blankly.

"Anyway. That's five suitcases. Where's the sixth?"

"Ah, you can forget number six," Foster said. "It's a
goner. I took it to the airport and put it on a Cessna
heading to Milwaukee." He chuckled and casually reat-
tached a bungee to his wire basket.

"Why?" I asked, genuinely curious.

"I dunno. I like the airport."

Five out of six would have to do. Time to resume the
mission. "Where do you live?"

"There's a shack behind the Windy." "The Windy" was
short for the Windermere. "Door's open." He pointed
down the dock. "Another suitcase is down there behind
that stack of kegs."

"Question," I said. "Once I get the bags together, can
you ride them to the set for me? I'll pay you." I paused.
"Someday."

He shook his head. "No can do. Nine check-outs,

fifteen check-ins. You're on your own this time, son." He nodded toward the freight shack.

"Check in there. Who knows, you just might find what you need."

Did I sense a hint of a smile?

CHAPTER TWENTY-SEVEN

The Face in the Porthole

Soon, the word spread across the island like a ferry's wake: the paperboy had been spotted wrestling a set of ancient-looking suitcases on Main Street. The Bat Signal flicked on. And there I stood, on the dock, with the crew staring blankly at four huge suitcases and a steamer trunk. I had just completed two more mad dashes, one to Foster's place and the other to the Straits Transit dock.

Jill spoke up. "Well. I have to say. This is a surprising turn of events."

"Yup," agreed Smitty. "I definitely did not see this coming."

"I found a scrapbook. It turns out Mom's got a dream."

Gordon looked at me cross-eyed. "Huh?"

I shook my head. "Nevermind. It's complicated. Listen, I gotta get this stuff to the set." I checked my watch. "Like *now*."

"Call that dockporter," Smitty said. "Dude is solid."

"He's busy." I glanced over to the doorway of the freight shack, remembering Foster's cryptic suggestion. *Who knows? You just might find what you need.*

"I'll be right back."

Sunlight peeked through the cracks in the wooden planks, casting slanted rays across the space. The air was filled with the musty scent of old hay and decaying paper. In one corner, a precarious tower of old dray wheels threatened to topple at any moment. Stored by a clean-up crew against the wall, four industrial-grade brooms, three shovels, and a rusty push lawn mower waited patiently. A large anchor chain painted in Arnold Line green lay coiled near a window, while stacks of cardboard boxes filled with outdated boat schedules cluttered the floor.

In a bike rack, a snarl of rusted bicycles gathered dust. I inspected the metallic jumble: a handlebar-less Sears model, a worn-out Western Flyer missing its front tire, a few rusted Roadmasters, and a gold three-speed bike covered in ancient dust.

But no cart. Just as I was about to head out, a sparrow darted in through an open window, its flight path guiding my gaze downward.

Parked away from the tangle of bikes in the rack sat a battered old dockporter bike. It was faded yellow, a classic Schwinn Heavy-Duti. Its oversized Wald utility basket, corroded but intact, had a wooden plank on the bottom for reinforcement. Frayed rubber inner tubing encircled the basket's edge, protecting luggage it hadn't carried in years against scratches. The seat was positioned just right, allowing the dockporter—probably now a father of four living in Grand Rapids and selling auto parts—to see over the bags. The basket was adorned with corroded fobs and tags from old island hotel keys, held in place with rusted wire, adding a touch of mystique to the rig. I squeezed the tires. Low on air but ridable.

I grabbed the bike by the handlebars and wheeled it out into the sunlight.

"I'm gonna ride it," I said, straddling the worn-out Schwinn and staring at the luggage. Jill tested the weight of the steamer trunk while Smitty unwrapped a cube of grape Bazooka gum.

"Are you out of your mind?" Gordon said, inspecting the old bike. "It's massive. The seat is way too high. You probably can't even reach the pedals."

"Just load me up."

A familiar voice echoed from above. "When you said you wanted to be a dockporter, I didn't think you meant this summer!" Cap Riley looked down, leaning against the ferry railing in his standard pose, shaking his head. "I smell trouble, my boy, and it's emanating from your general direction."

I squinted up, shielding my eyes from the noonday sun.

"Don't tell me. You told God your plans. And now he's laughin' his ass off at you." Riley turned away. "Best if I don't witness this," he called over his shoulder. "They call it *plausible deniability.*" The door of the pilot house slammed shut.

I glanced toward the loading ramp, weighted down with passengers shuffling onto the ferry. Something caught my eye. A flash of a T-shirt. Black. Worn jeans. Black. A shock of long stringy hair.

Red.

Was that …? Not possible.

I shook it off and turned back to the luggage.

"Alright," I said. "The best dockporters start by forming a V shape with the suitcases. They put one in the back of the basket, then another across the handlebars. Then you have a natural platform to stack the rest of the bags."

"How'd you know that," asked Gordon, hefting up a suitcase.

"Jack's been watching porters for years. It's some kinda obsession for him," said Smitty.

"It's not an obsession," I said. "It's a career path. Do you think I'm going to toss newspapers my whole life? Put the blue one on top, but leave a space for the steamer trunk." I pointed toward the row of vending machines against the freight shack. A list of names was carved crudely into the dock's wood under the word *BLACKJACK.*

"If you wanna ride blackjack—that's twenty-one bags in the basket—you gotta start training early."

Jill glanced at the blackjack list, mildly curious, then at the steamer trunk. "How do you keep the stuff from sliding out of the basket?"

"Bungee cord," I said, indicating the frayed cord attached to the basket. "Luckily, this old rig came fully equipped."

Gordon reached out and grabbed the handlebars, giving them a skeptical shake. "Kind of a hunka junk, if you ask me," he said, glancing dubiously at the bike.

"But see, I *didn't* ask you," I shot back. "Just stack the bags." I was snappy and felt oddly protective over the old machine.

"The streets are a madhouse today," Jill said, her eyes darting toward Main Street before returning to me. "It's going to be like threading a needle. Drunk. Seriously, are you sure you're up for this?"

Smitty snapped a Bazooka bubble and patted the load. "Never mind the traffic, Jill. Jack here's used to it. No different than the paper route. Just a lot heavier."

He gave the load a test lift, his forehead creasing with concern. "Whoa. A lot heavier." He scanned the bike. "And Gordon does have a point. You'll need a damn ladder to see over those bags with the seat set that high. But that's not even the worst part." His attempt at a pep-talk was quickly unraveling. "The tires are practically flat, the chain is rusted beyond belief, and the front wheel is bent. And check this out ..." He gestured. "A bunch of spokes are missing. Also, this —"

Jill kicked him lightly in the ass. Smitty abruptly halted and flashed me a double thumbs-up. "All minor stuff! You got this, buddy!"

The boys grabbed either side of the steamer trunk and plopped it on the load, obscuring the view in front of me.

Smitty hooked one end of a bungee cord on the front of the basket and handed me the other end. I stretched it over the load and attached the hook to the stem of the handlebars, mimicking what I'd seen dockporters do hundreds of times. I looked toward the ferry's upper deck to see if Riley was watching, secretly hoping he'd witness my first load ever.

And that's when I saw him. He was leaning on the railing, grinning at me with a smoldering ciggie poking from his mouth.

Not Riley.

Blaze.

It wasn't possible. He'd left the island, I assumed. *Never assume.* The sudden blast of a ferry horn shocked me. My initial impulse was to abandon the bike, and luggage, dash onto the boat, rush up the steel stairs, and pummel Blaze's face like I was Tommy "Hitman" Hearns.

"What are you waiting for? You gotta go!" said Gordon.

"It's Blaze!" I hissed. "Look!"

They followed my finger toward the upper deck. All they saw was a six-year-old kid in a souvenir captain's hat holding a box of fudge in one hand and shoving a Red Vine in his mouth with the other. All three stared at me with caution and concern, as one might look at some sad soul who'd lost his mind but didn't know it.

I looked again. There he was. Now he wore blue surgical gloves and swung the pocket watch like a hypnotist, rotating his other hand in a mocking "queen of the parade" wave.

"See?" I yelled.

Again they looked, following my jutting finger.

Again, he'd vanished. The ferry's engines revved, and the boat pulled slowly away from the dock. There was nothing I could do. I was strapped behind the heavy load like a fighter pilot on an aircraft carrier, wedged between two impossible choices.

I also wasn't entirely sure the whole thing wasn't a hallucination. It had been that sort of summer.

I frantically scanned the ferry. *Where was he now?* Blaze's face poked up through one of the round portholes on the lower deck. *How did he move so quickly?* His nose pressed against the glass, face twisted in a demonic, soundless laugh. He vanished from the porthole and popped up two portals over, like some burnout whack-a-mole.

The ferry steamed from the dock; we locked eyes.

Mine were on fire. Agonized.

His were mocking. Delighted.

But then something extraordinary happened. His grin

faded, and his face dropped. And for an instant, I saw something else. *Regret? Sadness?* It lasted only an instant, and the twisted grin returned, spreading across his face, his lips curling back to a sneer. He disappeared from the porthole.

The ferry revved and glided toward the open straits. He reemerged on the upper deck. Seething, I shook my fist at the disappearing ship like Snoopy, cursing the Red Baron. I screamed. "Thief! Liar! Coward! Dirtbag!"

He waved back, but his friendly gesture swiftly morphed into an extended middle finger. Not content with that, he spun around to deliver a sneaky behind-the-back middle finger, and as if that wasn't enough, he audaciously went for a double middle finger.

I felt eleven. Not *almost twelve*. Eleven. A dumb little child who got betrayed. A dim, shaggy knucklehead standing on a dock who was not even clever enough to summon the proper insult when it mattered. A failure on every conceivable level. I gazed with trembling rage at the face in the porthole, and a word popped into my head, the one word that summed up everything I now despised about the dark, spindly figure on the ferry.

The word reverberated across the harbor, escaping my lips with an intensity fueled by pain.

"You're the Wendigo!" I screamed, the echoes carrying across the bay. "A soul-sucking cannibal! Can you hear me? YOU'RE THE WENDIGO!"

It may not have brought the satisfaction of reclaiming the pocket watch or solving the Marjorie Kitmore case. It couldn't secure a ticket to Cairo to save my family. But at that moment, it felt perfect.

"YOU ... ARE ... THE ... WENDIGO!" I took another breath. "And KISS rules!" My voice carried over the water as the ferry grew smaller, its wake stretching into the straits.

And then it was over. Gasping for air, my surroundings came back into focus. A gaggle of tourists quietly backed away from me as if they'd accidentally happened upon an enraged baboon in the wild. Jill, Smitty, and Gordon exchanged glances from a distance. Finally, my breathing returned to normal.

Jill spoke. Tentative. "Guys. I have an idea."

"What?" I croaked, my throat raw.

"I say we all pretend that whatever that was … " she gestured toward the ferry and back to me. "... never happened."

I stifled a smile and nodded.

"Works for me," added Gordon, giving a thumbs up.

Smitty spoke. "Dude. Your mom needs her stuff. *Go!*"

One last look at the bike. The rusted longhorn handle-bars were designed to support big loads like this one. The cracked and worn rubber grips felt rough against my sweaty palms. The frame's top tube was plastered with decades worth of bike license stickers. The ancient, frayed bungee cord strained against the vintage luggage, locking it in place. I tested the weight of the load one last time, rocking the bars left, then right. Side to side. It was solid. *Enough.* I nodded to the crew and kicked off.

CHAPTER TWENTY-EIGHT

The Dockporter

My sharp left turn onto Main Street was perilous—a swooping weave that nearly wiped me out. The load shifted to the left, and the sharp edge of the steamer trunk's steel trim sliced into the ancient bungee cord that held everything in place. If the cord snapped, it was game over. I added this to my ever-expanding list of Things That Could Go Horribly Wrong.

A voice called out from behind me, breaking through the dull panic that had set in. "Hold the trunk with your left hand and lean right. Coast for five seconds, then straighten."

I wiped the sweat off my face with my shoulder and did as I was told, shooting out my arm to shove the trunk back and easing off the pedals for five seconds. It worked perfectly. The load shifted back into place, and I regained my balance.

A yellow blur whizzed past—the voice was Foster's,

wheeling his own massive load of luggage, shooting gaps through the masses like a waterbug. As he disappeared, he called back, "Eyes on the road, not on the load!"

I refocused, letting the words from a master reverberate in my mind.

Main Street was pandemonium. I was a salmon swimming upstream against a relentless current of tourists scrambling for their last summer fix before temperatures dropped. I could see the road in front of me only half the time. For the other half, I was on the bottom of the pedal stroke, blinded by vintage suitcases stacked in a vintage basket rigged to a vintage dockporter bike.

I recalled reading in Nat Geo Kids that the average human had their eyes closed ten percent of the time due to blinking. I did the math. Ten percent of the time, I was blinking. Half of the time, I was on the downstroke. According to my calculations, I was riding utterly blind for a whopping sixty percent of the ride. My calculations went further. If the ride took, let's say, ten minutes, six minutes of it would be total blindness. You can scoff, but I double-dog dare you to ride a bike down any busy street in America for six minutes.

With your eyes closed.

My peripheral vision was a sweat-induced kaleidoscope of distorted images, colors, and chaos: fudge signs, red and yellow carriages, and gift shops. I bobbed up and down on the pedals like a buoy in rough waters.

A heavyset couple on a rented tandem bicycle zigzagged toward me, perhaps victims of a few too many Rumrunners at the Chippewa Hotel pool. The man wore a T-shirt imprinted with *Stupid* in big, bold letters.

Noted, I thought grimly.

On the down-pedal, my vantage point vanished again. I braked hard and felt the rear wheel lift off the ground for a sickening second. The rotting vinyl point of the bike seat dug into my tailbone as I leaned back and pulled up on the bars. The tandem wobbled across the centerline of the road, the riders giggling. I braced for impact. They swerved with inches to spare, colliding with the curb and slowly toppling to the sidewalk like a pair of felled, fudge-gorged sequoias. As I passed, I saw the woman's T-shirt read *I'm With Stupid.*

Confirmed.

The rattle of bike chains and fenders scraping enveloped me in surround sound. Gordon, Jill, and Smitty held formation like a squadron of fighter planes escorting a B-17 bomber into enemy territory.

"Comin' through! Clear out! Watch the bike!" they yelled.

While I appreciated their support, it added a new level of apprehension. We were now a legitimate spectacle: a kid riding an unsafe—not to mention stolen—load of luggage on an oversized, dilapidated bike, surrounded by the Lollipop Guild. Cameras snapped. I wondered how I must look—open-mouthed, tongue out, gasping, arms quivering like jello on a trampoline.

Even years later, I'm still puzzled by how I could hear the individual rubber fibers of the single bungee cord snapping under strain, singing their final, off-key notes. The sound started as a faint *twang,* then a *tweeng,* followed by a series of discordant *pings,* a symphony performing a nightmarish requiem. The cord steadily disintegrated before my very sweat-drenched eyes. And then—

—*SNAP! A COWBOY'S WHIP.*

Luckily, it barely grazed my left cheek as it slingshotted

into the air like a tasered python. The load shifted hard, this time to the right, and I reached out and shoved it all back into its axis, but there was no way it would last. The next bump would be Dumpsville.

I rolled to a stop in front of the Windermere Hotel, barely able to keep my bike upright. My wingmen surrounded me, eyeing the bungee-less load.

"That's gonna be an issue, boss," Smitty said, adjusting his shorts and re-tucking his shirt. I caught a quick glimpse of his beaded belt.

"Gimme that." I pointed at his belt.

Smitty frowned. "Wait, what? I love my belt. It's all broken in."

"If you don't gimme that thing, your face will be all broken in!"

"Easy, Jack!" said Gordon as Smitty pulled his belt through the loops and handed it over.

"Sorry, guys. I'm just—I dunno ..."

"Freakin' out?" finished Smitty.

"Something like that."

Gordon slid his belt out and handed it to me wordlessly.

"Aw," said Smitty. "How sweet. Would you give him your tighty-whities with the brown racing stripe down the middle too?"

"Only if he asked nicely."

Gordon and Smitty broke into an impromptu *Three Stooges* routine, with slaps and pokes capped with a *nyuk-nyuk-nyuk*.

I ran the first of the belts through a suitcase handle and buckled it, then ran another belt through the loop, then ran it through another handle the same way. It wouldn't hold. "Too short," I said, shaking my head.

"I got this," Jill declared, stepping forward to take

charge. With a swift motion, she reached down and pulled out her own Mackinac Island bead belt with a *whoosh*. She sensed all of us staring at the belt in her hand. She met our gaze, her expression unyielding.

"What? They're rad."

"We never even voted you in," Smitty said.

"She's in," I declared. "Help!"

Jill unraveled the snarl of belts with skilled hands and deftly intertwined them around the luggage's suitcase handles. Then she added her own to complete the makeshift bungee system. It was an impressive feat of engineering, concluded in under a minute. We were slack-jawed.

"My dad showed me a few knot tricks between takes on *Gumball Rally* in Arizona."

"Great movie," said Smitty absently, stunned by her knotting exhibition.

"Jack!"

A voice called from my left. Beth was jogging up, breathless, and holding a plastic bag that said Wild Style T-shirt Shoppe. She eyed the luggage and the bike suspiciously. "What are you up to?"

"Not now, Beth! I promise to explain everything later."

"Fine," she said, reaching into the plastic bag. "But put this on." She held up a starched red T-shirt. "I printed it for myself, but it makes more sense for you."

"No time." I turned my wrist and checked my watch. "Gotta go!"

"I'm your older sister, and I'm pulling rank. Wear it. You're getting a lot of attention, and it'll be good for my business." She jammed a stack of business cards into my rear pocket.

"Hold the bars, guys," I sighed, resigned. I grabbed the

shirt and yanked it over my polo without reading the iron-on letters. All four broke out in laughter.

"Damn. That's perfect," smiled Beth.

I looked down. It said: IN MY DEFENSE, I WAS LEFT UNSUPERVISED.

The blaring of the noon siren interrupted my impromptu fashion show, the harsh noise revving up slowly like an air raid warning. "It's noon. They're supposed to start shooting now! I gotta go!"

The gang geared up for the last leg of the ride, strad-dling their bikes and readying to push off.

"Wait," I said, holding up my hand. "It's my family. I need to ride the load. Alone."

Smitty sighed. "I was hoping you'd say that."

"Ride it," said Jill, patting the steamer trunk.

"Go save your family, Jackass," said Gordon.

"Don't die," said Beth. "And sell some shirts, will ya?" She winked. "Hotshot."

Once I escaped downtown, the traffic thinned. The ride would be a cakewalk on a typical day. But today was not typical. Different bike, different load. Legs fried, arms piano wire, mind mush.

"James," I gasped, picking up speed. "That's going to be your name from now on."

A gust of wind blew me off balance, and I swerved into the left lane. I took a deep breath and continued the one-way conversation I had started with the bike for some reason.

"I decided on James because the last dock porter to ride twenty-one suitcases, 'High-Rise' Jimmy Oliver, is on the Blackjack wall of fame. Jimmy means James."

James the bike was also struggling. Its tires were as soft as old party balloons, and the spokes made odd, pinging sounds with each rotation. My voice rose above the short gusts of lake wind.

"It's a long story, but I got involved in this cold case. It was a murder, and ... well, the real reason was to make money to buy a trip for my parents because my dad was worried my mom was losing interest in ..."

Another strong gust of wind pushed us. I had to strain to keep us on course.

"That part's complicated. Nevermind. Doesn't matter. But I misread the whole thing. I thought she was bored with us, but it turns out she just loves making clothes. And she's really good at it. Like, way better than I even knew. Designing, sewing, fabrics, all that stuff. So I set her up to get fired today."

James responded with the screeching of worn-out pedals and the bending of fatigued spokes.

"I know, I know. It's bad. But that's why we gotta get to the set as quickly as possible." I was having a heart-to-heart with a Schwinn Heavy-Duti.

"Passing on your left!" I turned. A sleek, low-slung ten-speed bike rider, dressed head-to-toe in spandex, flew past and shot me a concerned look. How long had he been listening as I conversed with my bike?

As I bobbed up and down, I could see the set ahead. A row of cedars lined the beach with twisted, oddly shaped trunks. The bright movie lights cast a soft, almost ethereal glow across the rocky shore. As I drew nearer, I could see the crew members scurrying about like busy ants, their heads disappearing in and out of the flaps of tents like Bedouins. But today, nobody was shooting anything.

Not without the wardrobe.

I pumped harder, driving James toward the lights of

the set. My muscles screamed, and my breath came in ragged gasps, but I was almost there.

    Scene 242. The *Is it you* scene.

It was my first dump as a dockporter. And it was spectacular.

I weaved off the pavement. The front tire of my bike lodged in loose stones. The grinding halt catapulted me over the handlebars. The elaborate bead belt bungee network snapped, and bead specks burst across my line of sight in slow motion like sprinkles on a frosted cupcake.

With a sickening crunch, the bike landed, sending the suitcases flying. The steamer trunk tumbled, end over end, disgorging its contents in a chaotic jumble. I landed in a hard heap, my face smacking a smooth chunk of driftwood.

But the oddest aspect of my dump was that no one noticed. Lying with my head pressed sideways, I dislodged an orange bead from my eyelid. Behind a gnarled cedar, Mom stood with Cynthia and the Very Important Brit.

"Talk to me slowly, like I'm a wee lad. How did we *lose* the wardrobe?" asked the Very Important Brit.

Mom stepped up."I packed everything yesterday before we wrapped up for the day. It was organized in boxes and labeled for scene 242."

Cynthia joined in. "I saw it with my own eyes. We went through the same process we go through every day. We have the wardrobe sent over on the dray in the morning with the camera, grip, and electric gear. It makes no sense."

The Brit shook his head and pointed to the shoreline where Seymour, Reve, and Plummer tossed rocks into the water. "I've got three movie stars over there skipping stones. They are skipping stones! One of them is a Bond Girl. One is Captain Von Trappe, and the third is Superman. They get paid no matter what they do. So unless you can fire up those sewing machines and recreate this film's three most iconic costumes, we're paying actors ... *to skip stones!*"

"This is all my fault. I take full responsibility," said Mom.

The Very Important Brit smiled indulgingly. "Your willingness to fall on the sword has been duly noted. But it won't help us ... *make ... our ... day!*" He stormed off in a high state of piss-off, kicking stones out of his way.

Trapped beneath the bike, I emitted a feeble groan. Nothing. I gathered my strength and mustered another attempt.

"I've got the wardrobe from scene 242!" I yelled. Lowering my voice, I added, "Well, most of it."

A few shocked crew members untangled me and hauled me to my feet. I felt like a battered boxer, bruised but standing.

"This is ... the wardrobe." The repetition was unstoppable. "This is the wardrobe." Then, I bellowed in a burst of urgency, "Mom!"

Her startled voice cut across the beach. "Jack!" She rushed over, put her arms on my shoulders, and checked me over. "Oh my God! Your nose is bleeding!" She did a doubletake. "And where did you get that T-shirt?"

"I'm fine, Mom." I pulled her a few steps away from the crew on a throbbing knee. "It's a long, weird story, and I don't want you to ask me about it right now. Just gather this stuff up and dress your actors."

"But how—"

I raised a finger to my lips to quiet her as the Very

Important Brit materialized, disbelief etched on his face. He glanced at the wardrobe, which was hastily scooped up, and then back at me.

"Wait. Aren't you the young lad who magically appeared with the penny at the Grand Hotel? The penny boy?"

I offered a sheepish smile and an aw-shucks shrug. "Yes, sir. I guess I am … *the penny boy.*"

"Someday—not today, mind you—I'd love to hear how you came into possession of our wardrobe." He raised his megaphone. "First team actors, please report to the wardrobe tent! Ladies and gentlemen, we are back!"

Mom shook her head, looked at me, and returned to work.

The Very Important Brit stopped to inspect my shirt, reading it aloud. "In my defense, I was left unsupervised. I quite like that. Where might I find one? Or perhaps many?"

I reached into my back pocket, fished out one of Beth's business cards, and handed it to him.

"Talk to my sister."

What happened next was a blur. A set medic hurriedly stuffed cotton balls up my right nostril to stem the bleeding. At the same time, another production assistant handed me a delicious lemonade, an icepack, and a Snickers. Before I knew it, a director's chair with a yellow cloth backing that read *Somewhere in Time* in black iron-on letters magically appeared. I found myself seated a few feet away from the director and the Very Important Brit as scene 242 unfolded before my eyes.

I was a VIP. *If they only knew.*

Mom put the final touches on the costumes. A pearl necklace adjusted here, a small brush dusted Reeve's bowler there, Plummer's tuxedo tie straightened to perfection. She was the eye of the hurricane, the calm center amidst the storm of activity. After living briefly inside her vivid scrapbook, I understood why. Mom was a pro.

As the actors hustled into position, the camera rolled into place. The crew adjusted lights and checked sound levels as the actors ran through final rehearsals. Despite the chaos that preceded this moment—the problem I created, then solved—the stage was finally set for scene 242.

The Very Important Brit lifted his megaphone. "Alright, everybody, this is for picture! Quiet, please! And … *action!*"

To this day, the two most beautiful humans I've ever seen closed the space between them. Reeve as Richard Collier approached, moving through the cedars slowly. As we watched, time seemed to stand still. The air crackled as if the very universe held its breath. Seymour, as Elise, poised on the precipice of a swoon, eyes sparkling with emotion and recognition. Both confused and certain. And then, with a delicate pause, she began to deliver the line: "Is it—"

"*Shit!* I need to cut!" yelled the cameraman. The entire crew exhaled, the spell broken.

The Very Important Brit let out a groan. "What's the issue now!?"

"There's a ferry in the shot. Can't have a modern boat full of tourists in 1912."

"Fair enough! Good eye. Okay, everyone, relax until the ferry clears the frame. Actors, kindly hold your positions and keep your motors running."

The crew hustled with tweaks before the camera rolled again.

My gaze fixed upon the ferry as it sliced through the waves, forging its path towards Mackinaw City. I recognized the distinctive bow of the Straits of Mackinac II. Despite everything, I had to laugh.

Blaze was on that ferry.

Even from a half-mile away, he managed to ruin the moment. Was he peering back at us from the upper deck? Off to the mainland, to the Detroit FBI, to claim the big fat reward. *Our reward.* Was he still wearing those ridiculous surgical gloves and swinging the pocket watch back and forth like—wait! *Gloves!*

"Mom! Wait!" I yelled. "Have Jane wear white gloves!"

She looked over at me. "But she's not wearing white gloves in the scene."

"She should. Trust me on this one. *A lady needs her gloves,*" I said. Jill had delivered the line with far more style the previous night, but it was the best I could muster.

Mom looked at Cynthia, who nodded gamely. "Not a bad idea. Let's give it a try."

"Oh, wait. I don't think we have any gloves on set," Mom said.

I called back to her. "We grabbed a few pairs and tossed them in the blue suitcase over there." I pointed. She shot me another withering look. "You have a lot of explaining to do, Jack."

"Just check the case."

She returned with white silk gloves moments later and slid them onto Seymour's graceful hands. "Ana, I love these," said Seymour. "What a great idea!"

Mom shook her head incredulously, a smile barely concealed, and glanced in my direction.

"What do you think?" Mom asked the director. Seymour displayed her shimmering white gloves, making a playful, mesmerizing pattern with her fingers. The director nodded.

"Love it! Let's shoot!"

"Okay, everyone!" said the Very Important Brit. "The ferry has cleared the frame. Jane's now apparently wearing *gloves*. Positions! Let's do this thing. Scene 242, take two! And ... *action!*"

"Looks like you're moving up in the world, kid."

I looked up from my chair to see Big Jack standing above me. He flashed a sly grin and motioned toward my director's chair. Dressed in fresh khakis and a crisp white shirt, he looked years younger as the lake breeze ruffled his hair.

"They said I could watch."

"Nice of them. However, you are the offspring of the talented, unrecognized wardrobe designer Ana McGuinn. They better give you a chair, or I'll have to rough them up." He pointed at my face. "What the hell happened to your nose?"

I absently touched the bloody cotton ball that protruded from my right nostril. "Long story."

He considered me. "You've got a lot of *long stories* this summer."

I waited for more.

"Lucky for you, today I'm not interested."

"Did you see the scrapbook?" I asked.

"See it? I practically broke my toe on it."

"Pretty crazy, huh."

"Yeah." He shook his head. "Pretty crazy."

"I was thinking. Maybe we—I dunno—maybe we *over-reacted* a little?" I looked up and studied his face.

He watched Mom working across the set, never making eye contact with me, and said, "Despite what your friends say about you behind your back, you're not as dumb as you look."

"Take ten for camera reload!" someone called out.

He hit me with a sideways smile. "As much as I'd love to stay and chat, I'm going to talk to your mother. Just some, you know …"

"… grownup shit?"

"Yeah," he said, letting the profanity slide. "Grownup shit."

He gave me a quick shoulder squeeze and walked off. I watched closely as he approached and gently touched her arm. She turned, surprised, and he moved closer. He whispered a few words, then guided her away from the bustle. I unconsciously pulled my notebook from the courier bag hanging on the back of the chair, my eyes never leaving their private exchange.

Big Jack removed something from his pants pocket. Then they were blocked by a hulking Panavision camera rolling into position on a dolly track. They re-emerged into my line of sight, with Big Jack clutching the butterfly design that had fallen from the scrapbook. Mom took it gently from his hand, stared at it, and then back to him. He was gesturing as he spoke, nodding. Comfortable. I was curious, but the details of their secret conversation were irrelevant. It was the look in their eyes.

I recognized it.

Sweet. Mischievous. *New.*

I'd seen it that morning in the scrapbook. As they danced. On their wedding day.

A deal was going down. I knew it because I was a trained investigator. If Blaze and the *Hardy Boys Detective Handbook* had taught me anything, it was how to follow leads. Analyze evidence. Surveil suspects. Yup. They were likely discussing a dress shop. It would be called *The Blue Butterfly.* I jotted down the intel, circling key phrases and connecting lines. The case was closed.

I shut the notebook and slid it back into my courier bag.

CHAPTER TWENTY-NINE

Read All About It!

Long morning shadows stretched across the Arnold Line dock. I sat on a luggage cart, legs crossed with Smitty and Gordon and folded the last newspapers for my final summer route. Two freight boats loitered nearby, poised to ferry lights, props, cameras, and wardrobe from the rock to Mackinac City, where the film gear would be loaded onto CB radio-equipped semi trucks bound for Universal City, California.

Somewhere in Time had wrapped.

Summer was over.

Technically, summer wasn't over until the family loaded up a U-Haul full of McGuinn family crap and hit the road for the depressing drive down I-75 back to Brighton. Back to low ceilings and school shopping. Starched Toughskins from JC Penney's and squeaky, new tennis shoes. Pencil cases, a gleaming green Trapper Keeper organizer with plastic dividers, and a rainbow set of highlighters I'd never touch.

I'd played many roles that summer. In addition to paperboy, son, brother, grandson, and friend, I added detective, thief, photographer, background extra, liar, ghosthunter, vandal, lockpicker, and most importantly, dockporter to my resume.

Life at Wildcliffe was better. Mom moved back to the master bedroom, and Big Jack rolled in that Friday night with an artery-clogging slab of bacon. He cooked it up the following morning, and we ate breakfast together on the porch. The 730-foot *SS Edward Ryerson* rolled through the Straits, and Big Jack stopped mid-chomp to admire its angular lines. The McGuinn Men's fascination for big ships was legendary.

"If a '59 Eldorado could float," Dad murmured as the sleek boat powered past the island.

Gramps nodded in agreement. "On it goes," he said.

Later that afternoon, Mom and Dad met with a real estate agent to discuss "street-facing options." I could only assume it had something to do with *The Blue Butterfly* dress shop, and my spirits secretly soared.

A cart of lights and camera gear was rolled onto the freight boat with a low roar of hard rubber wheels on corrugated metal. Gordon and Smitty tossed more folded newspapers into Sluggo's basket. Generally, they'd never show up to help me with this menial task, but today was different. After weeks of working as extras in the movie, they felt part of the *Somewhere in Time* family. And the family was leaving. We were mostly quiet, focusing on the work, except for Smitty, who absently butchered the theme from *Grease* with off-key whistling.

A gust of wind stirred dust, and a few pages of the

Detroit Free Press flew off the cart. I snatched a loose sheet before it blew into the lake and pulled it down, casually scanning it before refolding it.

I froze.

At the bottom half of the Michigan News section was a large picture of Marjorie Kitmore, the same Mona Lisa photo that had hooked me in June when it appeared in the *Island Gazette*.

But this wasn't the *Island Gazette*.

It was the *Detroit Free Press*. Below her photo was another, smaller picture. I pulled the page closer. A teenage boy wore a black dress shirt with a white tie. I couldn't tell whether it was a mugshot or a bad high school class picture, but it was definitely Blaze, his red hair pulled back in a tight ponytail, sneering at the camera.

ARREST IN A 20-YEAR-OLD MURDER

MACKINAC ISLAND MICHIGAN – A murder that occurred 20 years ago on Mackinac Island, Michigan, may finally be solved. New evidence in the cold case led to the arrest of Lance Rossellini, 48, of Grosse Pointe. After an hours-long interrogation by the FBI, Rossellini confessed to murdering Marjorie Kitmore in a jealous rage in 1959.

Rossellini allegedly murdered Ms. Kitmore in a car his grandfather had hidden in a barn on the island's remote northern point. He then drove her body to a well-known island landmark, Skull Cave. Once there, he desecrated the body to make it appear that it was a ritual murder connected with the Wendigo, a mythological creature associated with Native American tribes of the area, to cast suspicion on a romantic rival. The vehicle was a family secret, as motorized vehicles have been banned on Mackinac Island since 1922. Eccentric cottage owner "Captain" Anthony Russell brought the car to the island in 1955.

Sonofabitch. He'd gone and done it. Blaze had somehow taken our evidence to the FBI, laid it all out, and cracked the case. It was hard not to admire his follow-through, if not his complete lack of morals. I continued to read.

In a bizarre twist, the pocket watch that contained the finger-print evidence linking Rossellini to the crime was handed over to the FBI by Rossellini's estranged son, Andrew "Blaze" Stanton, 18.

I squinted, then reread the sentence a few times to make sure I wasn't suffering the lingering effects of having an orange bead lodged in my eyelid a week earlier.

Blaze was Lance Rossellini's son?

A blast of wind ripped the page out of my hands, and I watched as a shred of the peacock fluttered away over the harbor. I grabbed a fresh paper from the pile, madly rifled through it to find the story, and continued reading.

Stanton had been put up for adoption by Rossellini. Seventeen years later, he discovered evidence that was overlooked in 1959. This led the FBI to arrest and charge Rossellini.

The evidence included a fingerprint on the pocket watch, fiber matches from the car, and other vital documents. When asked how he obtained the evidence, Stanton stated, "Some kid helped me."

"Some kid helped me?" I snorted. The guys looked over. Smitty started to speak, but I waved him off without lifting my gaze from the page. The guys sensed I was reading something juicy, grabbed newspapers from the stack, and started reading.

The Kitmore death is the only recorded murder in Mackinac Island history and has stymied authorities for decades. At the time, there were two suspects. Edward St. Germain was a local who was also romantically linked to Kitmore. Detroit FBI questioned him in the summer of 1959, and he was released. Still, there were resentments within the island's small Native American community that St. Germain was never adequately absolved. St. Germain died in Marquette, Michigan, two years after the murder.

Rossellini left the island immediately after the body was discovered. He communicated only through his attorney. Rossellini was also absolved of any guilt. Many believed he benefited from top-flight legal representation and an understaffed police department.

Smitty shouted, "What the ffffu—*udge?*" having landed on the explosive revelation.

Gordon was next. "Wait! So your burnout buddy from the Haunted Theater was the murderer's *son?* Why would he go around telling people his dad was a detective?"

"Why not?" Smitty said. "Sounds a lot cooler than 'my dad's a murderer'? Besides. It worked."

"Worked?" said Gordon.

"Like a charm." Smitty gestured to me. "Think about it. He ended up pulling in Jack. Got himself a partner to do all the work."

Gordon pondered this for a second or two, then nodded slowly in approval. "Okay, then explain why he stole the evidence and cut Jack out. *Major* dick move, you ask me."

"I know the answer to that one," I said without looking up. "It was his family. He needed to ride the load. Alone."

Stanton praised the assistance of the local police, particularly the chief of police Roland Richter. When reached for comment, Richter, a rookie in 1959, was thrilled to hear about the arrest but surprised he had been mentioned. "I don't remember doing anything, at least not this summer. Although in 1959, we did all we could. I'll sleep better tonight than in the 20 years since that awful summer."

Blaze was now tipping his hat to a man wracked by guilt as time passed and the case got colder. Anger toward Blaze melted away like a Double-size Tastee Freeze on a hot day.

Put up for adoption by Rossellini in 1962, Stanton spent years trying to connect with his birth father. Rossellini was a failed businessman who owned several car washes in Metro Detroit but mainly lived off a trust fund left by his wealthy grandfather.

Stanton began to suspect that his father may have had a role in the murder after discovering a trove of letters from Rossellini's sister, Sandra Morehouse, 60, of Naples, Florida, pleading with him to confess.

And I'd bet a signed Gordie Howe puck that she owns a snarling hellhound and shacks up at Captain's Cottage smoking Virginia Slims, I thought. The mystery of Blaze's prolonged stay on the island was solved. Before heading to Detroit, he must have visited his aunt at Captain's Cottage to compare notes.

Morehouse, who still visits the now dilapidated family cottage, pleaded in the letters for Rossellini to confess, said Stanton. "When I found those letters," he said, "I headed to the island and discovered the truth."

A representative from the Kitmore family had little comment other than to say they had every intention of paying the $25,000 reward. When asked what he planned to do with the money, Stanton said he would likely "keep enough to buy a keg of Lowenbrau and a Stratocaster guitar and donate the rest to some island *thing. Maybe the library. The legal section sucks. Although I did find a solid selection of Hardy Boys books and a Xerox machine that came in handy."*

I swallowed hard. Even through the printed pages of the *Detroit Free Press,* Blaze managed to deck me in the sternum with a final "Hertz Doughnut."

Stanton has no immediate plans to return to the island, saying he "couldn't stand the smell." He plans to apply for a stagehand position with the heavy metal band Black Sabbath. "I've got experience with lights and smoke, so I think I could help." Black Sabbath's management team was unaware of the story but expressed interest in having someone with Mr. Stanton's apparent moral character on the road with the band.

It has been a hectic summer for the small island. Not only was a cold case murder solved, but Hollywood has been on location with Christopher Reeve, Jane Seymour, and Christopher Plummer. The filming of Somewhere in Time is wrapping up this week.

"All three of you knuckleheads reading at the same time? That alone could be a headline." I looked up, startled. Jill had a Jansport pack strapped on her back and a Dodgers cap pulled down low. No New Wave band T-shirt. Today she sported a bright green shirt that said *I Love Mackinac Island,* with a turtle design, a compass, and a sailboat.

Smitty began to recount what we had just read. I raised my hand, signaling him to wait. I retrieved a newspaper and offered it to her.

"Take a look at section C, front page. Michigan news section. But save it for the boat ride. You won't believe it."

She accepted the paper and scanned the page briefly. Then she turned back, motioning for me to join her. We strolled toward the ramp, the buzz of the film crew surrounding us.

"So, we're out of here," she stated, punctuating her words with a thumb pointed toward the crew. "You probably noticed."

"Back to California?"

"Yup. Back to California."

"Going to California with an aching … in your heart?" I cocked my head, feeling like one of the world's great wits for integrating a song lyric into the conversation.

She looked at me blankly.

"Never mind," I said. "It's a Zeppelin song. Blaze turned me on to it."

Zeppelin? Please. Dinosaurs. Now, if you said "Can't Stand Losing You" by the Police, maybe.

I stood for a few seconds, whistling the theme from *Grease* so off-key that it made Smitty's earlier attempts sound like Frankie Valli. I'd never said goodbye to a girl before. Thankfully, she took charge.

"Listen, Jack. I want to thank you for a great summer. I've been to some cool places, but this one was the best. Mostly thanks to you and your delusional little mission." She tucked a stray strand of hair behind her ear. "You really know how to show a girl a good time."

Two years later, I'd hear the same line in *Raiders of the Lost Ark* and wonder if she had something to do with it. But at the moment, it just sounded nice. "You're a little dumb and shallow but sort of deep too. It's weird."

"Thanks … I think."

I glanced toward the freight boat as dockporters pushed a cart full of camera gear up the ramp and onto the SS Huron.

"Do you still think we're a cult?" she said.

"Sorry about that. I was kinda confused."

"Don't apologize. You were worried about your family, and you did something. You were wrong about almost everything, but you weren't wrong for caring."

She glanced over her shoulder to ensure her dad wasn't watching us and kissed me on the cheek. It lingered. Then, she backed away and looked at me directly. "It was very sweet."

I stared back with a ridiculous smile clamped on my face. "Um. Thanks."

Thanks?

That's it?

You're a complete amateur, I thought.

"You're welcome," she said, nodding with determination as if she'd just made a decision. "Bye, Jack. Someday you're going to be a great dockporter." She pointed toward the soda machine and the Blackjack list carved in the dock. "Who knows, maybe you'll be one of the greats."

She turned and headed toward her father, taking his hand and pulling him up the ramp, disappearing inside the SS Huron.

Ten minutes later, the ferry, flanked by three other barges carrying the equipment, rounded the break wall, disrupting the calm waters of the morning, shattering a polished mirror reflecting the summer sky above. The churning water momentarily caught my attention, and I watched the foamy surface dissolve into nothingness.

I never saw her again.

———

"I know it was you."

I spun around. Milton hovered near the ramp with a

blank look, puffing on a large cigar. He wore his signature gray suit and a green bowtie and held a copy of the *Detroit Free Press*. "Just read a fascinating article. They finally solved the Marjorie Kitmore case. Said 'some kid' helped."

Fake shock and a gulp. "Wow. Really?"

He shook his head, his gravelly voice dropping even lower. "Don't take up poker. You're the world's worst liar." He took a step closer.

"I know it was you. You're 'the kid.'"

I backed away, one step from the edge of the dock.

But he didn't move any closer, and his face softened. "She was the love of my life." He seemed to be talking to himself as much as me.

I stared at him, unblinking and afraid to move.

"That's what you're wondering, right? You saw those pictures of Corrine on my wall that night you broke in and smashed up the wine. And I also know you went back there with the chief for a closer look."

"But she looked exactly like Marjorie Kitmore," I said.

"I know she did. Her name was Corrine. We were together for about five years in the 30s. Then she died. I guess I've never moved on." Again, he was somewhere else. "But why would I *move on?* Should I *move on* from Charlie Chaplin and Billie Holliday? Jack Benny? You kids can watch Star Wars nine times in the theater, and from what I hear, it's nothing but Flash Gordon in color. And I should *move on* from love?" I waited for him to continue.

"Walk with me," he said.

We moved slowly down the dock toward Main Street. "When I first met Marjorie in the summer of 1959, I was shocked. She'd come to one of the matinee shows and approached me in between sets to say hello. I couldn't believe my eyes. I even reached out to see if my hand would pass through her like a ghost. When it didn't, I asked her if she could sing. She said she could. And that was pretty much it. You may think it's weird, and you'd be right. But it made me happy. And at the risk of sounding immodest, I think it made her happy too."

We walked past a waiting dray. The team of horses clomped impatiently.

"Milton," I asked. "Are you mad at me?"

"For what?

"For everything I did."

He stopped and put a gentle hand on my shoulder. "Not at all. I might've been a little salty for a day or so. And Christ knows I'll miss those wine glasses."

An obvious question lingered. "So why did you take the pictures of Corrine down?" I asked.

"Truth is, I knew it made me a suspect. My entire life has been about making people happy. Even a hint of something like this would ruin me. So yeah, of course, I cleaned up the apartment. Not because I was guilty, but because I was shitting bricks." He managed a grin. "Call it a testament to your impressive detective skills. I may be a sentimental old fool, but I'm no idiot."

We resumed walking. "Also. I know all about your folks. Your gramps told me about it."

My face flushed.

"It's okay," he said. "Old men gossip. Contrary to popular belief, we're much worse than old women. I'm just happy to hear things are better." He noticed Sluggo leaning up against the freight shack, loaded with newspapers. "Now go deliver the papers, boy. The island needs to hear the good news." He turned away, hobbling off on ancient knees in a cloud of stogie smoke.

"I'll see you around town," he called back over his shoulder.

I straddled my bike, pulled out my stopwatch from the courier bag, and slid it into the mini bungee I had mounted on the basket as a holder.

Last ride of the summer.

Last chance to break my delivery record.

Forty-three minutes and fifty-two seconds.

I reached down to push the start button but paused. I took in the island's view from this angle. Wildcliffe on the bluff. Lush green trees. White walls of Fort Mackinac. Father Marquette in the park. In the distance, Milton, head up and shoulders back, walked to the Waterview for his morning nap. I pulled the watch from the bungee cord and returned it to my courier bag.

What's the rush?

EPILOGUE

2009

"The end."

Just past the boardwalk's edge, Jack, Sara, and John settled on a thick, low-lying branch of a cedar tree. The late afternoon sun painted long shadows, forming peculiar forms on the smooth white rocks. Hours had passed since Jack's story began, and now they were embraced by the cooler lake breeze of the fading day.

"See that rock over there?" Jack pointed to the back of a granite marker by the side of the road, nestled in the shade. "Go check it out."

The kids ran over, cautiously peering around the small monument to examine what was carved in the stone. Their eyes widened in unison.

John looked up at his dad, utterly baffled. "Wait. They're *buried* here?!"

"No, you morbid little maniac!" Jack laughed. "That's just a monument to scene 242. It's famous now. And that's the exact spot where they filmed it."

"The '*izzit you*' scene," said Sara.

"Well remembered," said Jack.

"Is there a monument to where you crashed your dock-porter bike and dumped the luggage?" John asked with a sly grin.

"No, they didn't make one for that."

"They totally should. It's way cooler."

The kids sprung into action. "Alright, let's get ready for the big bike crash scene," John shouted, acting the director. "Places. And … *action!*"

Sara acted out a crude rendition of Jack's crash, pretending to ride a bike, holding imaginary handlebars, and jogging down the shore road. "Mommy! Wait! I got the costumes!"

She executed a fairly convincing pratfall on a grassy stretch near the monument and then hopped up and put her hand over her nose. "My nose is broken." Then she launched into a loud fake cry. "Wah!"

"You guys *suck!!*" called Jack. "I never said I cried!"

"And … cut!" yelled John. "That was perfect! Let's move on to the next scene, where Dad gets cotton shoved up his nose, and Blaze leaves on the ferry with the pocket watch." The kids, out of breath, wandered back to their dad.

"So, what happened to the butterfly dress store?" Sara asked.

"The Blue Butterfly? They opened it up the next summer," Jack smiled. "Your grandma Ana ran it for eight years until she passed away."

"Was it just like in the scrapbook?" Sara asked.

"Almost exactly," Jack replied.

"Did they ever go to Egypt?" John asked.

"That very winter. Your grandfather isn't that stupid. He knew how to take a hint. Eventually."

"Did Gramma like Ee-git?" Sara asked.

"It's E-*gypt*. Not really. They got mugged at the pyramids."

"What?!" said Sara.

"Kidding," Jack smiled. "They had a great time. They picked up a ton of fabrics for the Blue Butterfly too. That's how she started her first dress line. She called it *Nile Style*."

"Cool name," said John.

"Right? The next summer, she did a line of dresses inspired by *Somewhere in Time*. She called it *Pieces from Elise*. They always rhymed."

The metal-on-metal sound of a bicycle kickstand drew their attention toward the shore road. Erin held a wicker picnic basket under her arm as she positioned the old green Schwinn. "There you guys are!"

She moved to Jack, set the basket on the stones, and hugged him tightly.

"I'm guessing you're no longer mad?" he whispered.

"I wasn't mad, ya big baby. Just in need of a bike ride." She gave a mischievous wink, "I grabbed a forty-ounce Mickey's Malt Liquor from Doud's and rode up to St. Anne's cemetery. I had a sneaky sip with Gramps. Poured a little beer on his headstone for you. *On it goes.*" She mimicked poring a bottle.

"How gangster of you," Jack said.

"He sends his love from the great beyond," she smiled.

"No doubt the old scoundrel was happy to see you again. He was a big Erin fan." He placed his arms on her shoulders and looked into her eyes. They shared a kiss.

"Mom, you won't believe the story Dad told us!" Sara's words rushed out like water from a broken dam. "He was eleven years old and solving a murder case. But that's not all. He met this strange guy named Blaze. But that wasn't all. Gramma started working on a movie called *Blue Butterfly*, I think—"

"*Somewhere in Time*," said John.

"Whatever, and Dad and *his* dad worried that she would run away and be on *another* movie called *Smoking a Bandit* ... I think."

"*Smokey*, not Smoking," said John.

"Whatever. Anyway, he stole some costumes—but it was for the greater good of ... *siriaty*? Was that it? And then he saw this stinky ... wendukie was it? Demon thing, but it was really that Blaze guy on stilts and—I can't remember the rest, but it was a long story, and it all ended up right here on this very spot where we're standing!"

"Yup, and Dad even crashed his bike right over there," added John.

"Lord. That yarn's class. Got it all. Mystery. Ghosts. Murder. Movies. Family drama. Even Superman," said Erin.

"And a kiss from another girl!" said John, playing the troublemaker.

"On the cheek!" piped in Jack. "And for the record, I never saw it coming! It was like a swarm of bats! She just swooped in!"

Erin smiled. "Don't you two believe that! Your father was incorrigible, probably even as a wee lad, even if he played the innocent." She kissed her husband on the cheek. "But we worked that all out."

After a picnic of sandwiches, chips, and a few oranges, they relaxed on a worn plaid blanket and watched the early evening ferries passing through the straits.

Erin's thoughts drifted to the bike ride she had taken

up to the heart of the island. It was always a revelation to realize how much better life felt while in motion; how the simple act of pedaling brought a sense of liberation. *The ride.* Jack had opened her eyes to this during that crazy summer of 1989. Twenty years ago.

On the other end of the blanket, Jack thought about Blaze. Where would he be now? He envisioned him, crouched like a panther backstage at a Black Sabbath concert, his fiery red hair cascading down his back, waiting to trigger a pyro as 20,000 rabid fans blissfully sang along to "Iron Man" in unison. The idea that Blaze might be some typical dad with graying hair, a spare tire around his middle, and a mortgage would not do anyone's memories any good.

"How did you and Mommy meet?" Sara asked, breaking them both from their reveries.

Erin crunched a carrot and looked at Sara. "Summer of 1989. Your father was a dockporter. Young, dumb, and wild." She flashed a wicked smile at Jack. "I cured him. The end."

"Time for my version," said Jack. "Your mother was talented, sexy, and had the wrong boyfriend," Jack replied with a wink. "I saved her. The end."

"I heard it took ya a long time to pop the question, Dad," said John.

"Zip it, germ," said Jack. "I'm going to wind up back in the doghouse. I just got out."

"What's the doghouse?" asked Sara.

"It's where idiot husbands go when their wives are mad. Smells like rotted Alpo and dog poo."

"Ga-*ross*," said Sara.

"Ka-rect," said Jack.

"C'mon. Can we hear the real story?" asked John.

"Yeah. Like the long version?" Sara chimed in.

Erin and Jack moved closer, smooshing the kids between them. Jack was utterly storied-out for the day. He shook his head and reclined on the blanket, closing his eyes. Then he spoke.

"Guys, that's a whole other book."

THE END

If you want to read the "other book" and find out how Jack and Erin met, order *The Dockporter*.

AFTERWARD

On *Somewhere in Time*

For those fortunate enough to be there, the summer of 1979 remains etched in our memories as a time of pure magic. The communal giddiness expressed in *Somewhere in Crime* mirrors the genuine excitement that engulfed Mackinac Island during that remarkable season. It left an indelible mark on many of us, altering the course of our lives in unexpected ways. My brother Scott and I—a decade apart in age but both captivated by the process of filmmaking we saw unfolding in front of our eyes—caught the fever and embarked on careers in Hollywood that spanned decades collectively.

Years after its premiere, the film has ascended to a revered status among its fans. This enduring love is commemorated yearly during the *Somewhere in Time* Weekend at Grand Hotel. This celebration includes screenings, appearances by the cast and crew, costumed balls, and a host of special events.

In today's fast-moving world, where cynicism often

prevails, the film's enduring charm and romance are more essential than ever. As one who was privileged to be there during the filming, I can affirm that the same unwavering positivity accompanied the making of Somewhere in Crime.

Christopher Reeve, Jane Seymore, Christopher Plummer, the wonderful director Jeannot Szwarc, and the entire cast and crew were not invaders (despite what our misguided hero Jack may have thought); they were respectful, joyful guests. And many of them keep coming back all these years later, including the still-stunning Jane Seymour.

So on behalf of myself and Jim, we extend a heartfelt thanks to the real filmmakers behind *Somewhere in Time*. We collectively tip our 1912-era bowler hats to everyone involved in creating this cinematic gem. You not only enriched our favorite island but touched our lives.

Somewhere in Time lives on, reminding us of the power of love, the enchantment of a bygone era, and the profound impact that movies can have on our souls.

—Dave and Jim
   July 2023

ACKNOWLEDGMENTS

From Dave: To my beautiful wife Mardy and daughter Kelly, who supported writing a prequel to *The Dockporter* every step of the way. To Jim Bolone, Mackinac legend and ever-tolerant partner in crime. To Dan Riney, our eagle-eyed copy editor, who not only can spell but knows who <u>wasn't</u> the host of "Jeopardy" in 1979. To designer Stephanie Tam, who was invaluable as a cover designer and creative partner. To our beta reader, your insights and ideas were spot-on! To all the fans of *The Dockporter*, particularly our Facebook group and newsletter subscribers, who post, comment, vote, and love. We are building something special. To our amazing ARC readers, thank you for caring. To my mom and dad, who created the legend of Brigadoon and allowed us the freedom to be whatever we wanted. To my siblings, Amy, Scott, and Greg, who are just about the best people on Earth. To the people of Mackinac Island, who embraced *The Dockporter* and made us both feel like we never left. And finally, to the late Christopher Reeve, who stood up in the Mackinac Theater in 1979 when the projector's sound went out on *Superman* and narrated the movie for us. What a Legend. *On it goes.*

From Jim: Always for my three: Anna and Charlie and Grace. Dave McVeigh — thank you for stirring up this man's life and plunging with him into the always uncertain —albeit exciting—sea of creativity. Thank you to my six brothers and sisters who played a colossal role in shaping my life and their spouses (my second set of brothers and sisters) Rose, John, Larry, Diane, Danny, and Sandy! Thank you to all of our Beta readers, and ARC readers! Special thanks to Jessica Klimesh and Dan Riney, whose writing and editing prowess made the whole thing better. And for the car and Tootsie Roll Pops ... thank you, Max and Tasha! For Samuel Joseph Oliver. Wingtips and third grade, forever. I dedicate this work to Ken Burcar, a dockporter, and a warrior — and above all else, a very loving and good man whose friendship I cherish.

AUTHORS

Dave McVeigh is a creative director, filmmaker, and business owner living in Cebu, Philippines, with his wife, Mardy, and daughter Kelly. He's worked on film and television campaigns for Disney Channel, HBO, Warner Bros, Nike, and more. A University of Michigan graduate, he is Michigan-born and raised and spent 23 summers on Mackinac Island, where he specialized in stone-skipping, dish-shlepping, bike-riding, and fudge consumption. He also hauled luggage in his bike basket, where he formed friendships that grow stronger every year.

Jim Bolone grew up in Detroit, Michigan, attended public school, and graduated from Wayne State University with a B.A. in English. He has been a bartender, waiter, historical interpreter, and drummer. His work has appeared in Big Pond Rumors (Toronto), Scarlet Leaf Review, Typishly, Adelaide Literary, Of Rust and Glass, The Walloon Writers Review, The Ohio Journal of English and Language Arts, and Learning for Justice Magazine. Jim lives in Northern Ohio, where he teaches secondary-level writing. He enjoys spending time with his three very cool adult kids and also riding his bicycle and his motorcycle.

Somewhere in Crime is the second novel in the **Mackinac Island Novel Series.**

ALSO READ

This is the second book in the

Mackinac Island Novel Series.

If you enjoyed *Somewhere in Crime* please leave a review on Amazon. It makes a big impact. Join the mailing list at: TheDockporter.com.

Our Facebook Group is also a blast.

facebook.com/groups/mackinacdockporter

Made in the USA
Monee, IL
03 August 2023

40445034R00204